The Mammoth Book of

NEW JULES VERNE
ADVENTURES

Also available

The Mammoth Book of

NEW JULES VERNE ADVENTURES

Edited by Mike Ashley
and Eric Brown

CARROLL & GRAF PUBLISHERS
New York

Carroll & Graf Publishers
An imprint of Avalon Publishing Group, Inc.
245 W. 17 th Street
New York
NY 10011–5300
www.carrollandgraf.com

First published in the UK by Robinson,
an imprint of Constable & Robinson Ltd 2005

First Carroll & Graf edition 2005

ISBN 0-7867-1495-6

Printed and bound in the EU

CONTENTS

COPYRIGHT AND ACKNOWLEDGMENTS

INTRODUCTION
Return to the Centre of the Earth

Jules Verne was a phenomenon.

In a writing life spanning over forty years, he produced
more than sixty novels of adventure and exploration, creating
a sub-genre of fiction that exploded on to the world at a
time when both the advances of science and technology,
and the physical exploration of the world, were proceeding
at an exponential rate.

Jules Verne was born in Nantes in 1828, to a prosperous
middle-class family. His father was a successful lawyer who
hoped that his eldest son might follow him into the profession. But Verne dreamed of adventure. As a boy, living in
the port of Nantes, he day-dreamed of sailing around the
world. Family legend has it that he even stowed away aboard
a ship, only to be dragged home by his irate father when
the ship docked further down the French coast. In 1848
Verne did escape – though only as far as Paris, where he
combined working on the stock exchange with penning much
bad poetry and short comedy plays which were staged at
the Théâtre Lyrique and the Théâtre Historique, without
success or critical acclaim.

He sold a few short stories around this time, the first
being "Les Premiers Navires de la marine mexicaine"
(usually translated as "The Mutineers" or "A Drama in
Mexico") which appeared in the monthly magazine *Musée
des familles* in July 1851.

It was not until 1863, with the publication of his first
book, *Five Weeks in a Balloon*, that success and acclaim eventually came to Verne. This is the story of Dr Fergusson, his

friend Dick Kennedy and loyal man-servant Joe Smith, and
their intrepid balloon journey across the continent of Africa
from Zanzibar to Senegal. Headlong adventure alternates
with much (often, it must be said, *too* much) scientific detail
– but the story caught the imagination of readers in France,
Britain and America. The novel was a best-seller, its docu-
mentary narrative convincing some readers that it was a true
account.

Verne was fortunate that his publisher, Jules Hetzel, was
one of the most enterprising in France, and he saw the
potential in Verne's work. He gave Verne a contract for three
books a year and also used Verne as the final catalyst to
launch his new magazine for younger readers, the *Magasin
d'Education et de Récréation*. The first issue appeared on 20
March 1864 featuring the opening instalment of Verne's new
novel, *Les Anglais au Pôle Nord* (*The English at the North
Pole*).

With a publisher keen to bring out his books, many seri-
alized during the year and published in volume form in time
for Christmas, Jules Verne's writing career was under way.
Over the course of the next ten years he wrote the novels
for which he is famous today: *Journey to the Centre of the
Earth* (1864), *From the Earth to the Moon* (1865), *Round the
Moon* (1870), *Twenty Thousand Leagues Under the Sea* (1873),
Around the World in Eighty Days (1873), and *The Mysterious
Island* (1874). These novels sold in their tens of thousands
and Verne became a wealthy man, often turning out two
novels a year in a non-stop writing routine that was to last
until his death in 1905.

His later books abandoned much of the scientific detail
of his early novels, and he concentrated on portraying adventures set in the four corners of the globe. While these were
not as popular as his scientific romances, and sales declined
towards the end of his life, his work was still in sufficient
demand after his death for his publisher to bring out several
volumes co-authored with (and some wholly written by) his
son Michel.

Verne is often cited today as one of the founding fathers

of science fiction, along with H.G.Wells. The fact is that Verne rarely extrapolated from scientific advances to create visions of the future – his novels were firmly grounded in the here and now of the late Victorian period. The genre Verne created had no name – though it's as much the fore-runner of the modern techno-thriller as it was science fiction – and there were precious few other exponents: he was a craftsman who chiselled out his own niche to create stories wholly Vernian. In his better known and most highly regarded novels, he tapped into the burgeoning scientific curiosity of the age and brought a clear-minded technological under-standing to stirring stories of derring-do and adventure in various parts of the world – as well as under the sea and in space.

Looking back, it is easy to credit Verne with greater orig-inality than in fact he possessed. His first novel, *Five Weeks in a Balloon* (1863), was suggested by Edgar Allan Poe's "The Balloon Hoax" (1844). Another Poe story, *The Narrative of Arthur Gordon Pym of Nantucket* (1837), inspired Verne to write a direct sequel, *The Sphinx of the Ice-Fields* (1897). His two-part novel *From the Earth to the Moon* (1865) and *Round the Moon* (1870), were preceded by Irish author Murtagh McDermot's *Trip to the Moon* (1728), whose hero's return from the moon is assisted by 7,000 barrels of gunpowder and a cylindrical hole dug one mile deep into the moon's surface – a foreshadowing of Verne's means of firing his own characters moon-ward from the barrel of a giant gun. Verne's *Clipper of the Clouds* (1886), and the sequel *The Master of the World* (1904), featuring a massive propeller-driven airship *The Albatross*, lifted ideas from the works of the US writer Luis Senarens (*Frank Reade Jnr and his Air Ship*, *Frank Reade Jnr in the Clouds*, etc) with whom Verne corresponded. *Journey to the Centre of the Earth* (1864), was not the first story of subterranean adventure: the German physicist Athanasius Kircher (1601–1680) was the author of *Mundus Subterraneus*, and in 1741 Ludvig Baron von Holberg published *Nicolai Klimii iter Subterraneum*, the story of moun-taineer Klim and his adventures after falling down a hole in the Alps and discovering a miniature subterranean solar system. *Mathias Sandorf* (1885) is Verne's take on Dumas' *The Count of Monte Cristo* (1844), while his fascination with shipwrecked heroes can be traced back to Defoe's *Robinson Crusoe* (1719) and J.R. Weiss' *Swiss Family Robinson* (1812): Verne even referred to his own 'castaway' books as Robinsonades.

However, to accuse Verne of lack of originality would be to miss the point. He was original in his genius of marrying the latest technological breakthroughs with geographical adventure, written with a keen eye for scientific detail which convinced the reader that, no matter how far-fetched the adventure, the events portrayed were indeed *possible*. The first submarine had been built and tested by Cornelius Drebble in 1620 and a submarine, the *Henley*, was used in the American Civil War in 1864, so Verne was hardly predicting the vessel. But his vision of a super-powered submarine capable of travelling around the world was the inspiration that led to the first nuclear-powered submarine eventually launched in 1955 and named the *USS Nautilus* in deference to Verne's creation. It was Verne's vision in pushing the barriers of technology and exploring the world that emerged which was a major factor in encouraging the technological revolution that occurred in the second half of the nineteenth century.

Verne also created some of the most memorable characters in fiction. Once encountered who can forget Phileas Fogg, Captain Nemo, Impey Barbicane or the mysterious Robur, forerunners in some ways of the later "mad scientist". If he were alive today Verne would have been an ideal candidate for continuing the James Bond novels!

Jules Verne's writing life encompassed much of the second half of the nineteenth century, a time of great upheaval, scientific enlightenment, and social change. His work, reflecting the ideas and ideals of his time, has the enduring appeal of all literature written with passion and commitment. That it is still being read over a hundred years after it was written is a testament to Verne's ability to communicate to generation after generation of readers the wonder of adventure and exploration.

This volume, published on the centenary of Verne's death, presents twenty-three stories in homage to the French master of adventure. Using as a starting point the works of Jules Verne, his ideas, stories and characters and the life of the man himself, the gathered writers have produced a range of entertaining, adventurous, and thought-provoking stories. Ian Watson, for instance, reveals the true adventures that inspired *Journey to the Centre of the Earth*. Mike Mallory unveils the mystery of the later life of Captain Nemo, whilst Molly Brown recounts the final endeavour of the Baltimore Gun Club. There are further sequels to Verne's best known books, as well as stories based on some of his lesser known novels and stories.

We'd like to think that Jules Verne would have approved.

A DRAMA ON THE RAILWAY

Stephen Baxter

We are all the products of our childhood and one may wonder just what events the young Jules-Gabriel Verne witnessed that later fired his imagination for his great adventure stories. Here, as a prelude to those later adventures, Stephen Baxter takes a flight of fancy to Verne's infancy and the dawn of the railways.

"He came to Liverpool," the old man said to me. "The French fellow. He came here! Or at least he rode by on the embankment. He came with his father to see the industrial wonder of the age. And not only that, though he was only a child, he saved the life of a very important man. You won't read it in any of the history books. It was all a bit of a scandal. But it's true nonetheless. I've got proof . . ." And he produced a tin box, which he began to prise open with long, trembling fingers.

It was 1980. I was in my twenties. I had come back to my childhood home to visit family and friends.

And on a whim I had called in on old Albert Rastrick, who lived in a pretty old house called the Toll Gate Lodge, on the Liverpool road about half a mile from my parents' home. I'd got to know Albert ten years before when I had come knocking on his door asking questions about local history for a school project. He was a nice old guy, long widowed, and his house was full of mementoes of family, and of the deeper history of the house itself.

But he had been born with the century, so he was eighty years old. His living room with its single window was a dark, cluttered, dusty cavern. Sitting there with a cup of luke-warm tea, watching Albert struggle with that tin box, I was guiltily impatient to be gone.

He got the box open and produced a heap of papers, tied up with a purple ribbon. It was a manuscript, written out in a slightly wild copperplate. "A Drama on the Railway," it was titled, "An Autobiographical Memoir, by Lily Rastrick (Mrs.) *née* Ord . . ."

"Lily was my great-great-grandmother," Albert said. "Born 1810, I believe. Produced my great-grandfather in 1832, who produced my granddad in 1851, who produced my father in 1876, who produced *me*. All those generations born and raised in this old house. And all that time that tin box has stayed in the family. Go on, read it," he snapped.

I gently loosened the knot in the purple ribbon. Dust scattered from the folds, but the material, perhaps silk, was still supple. The paper was thick, creamy, obviously high quality. I lifted the first page to see better in the light of the small window: "It was on the 15th Sept. in the year 18— that I defied the wishes of my Father and attended the opening of the new railway. But I could scarce have ima-gined the adventure that would unfold for me that day!"

Albert levered himself out of his chair. "More tea?"

Lily wrote:

"I stayed the night before in Liverpool, which was never so full of strangers. All the inns in the town were crowded to overflowing, and carriages stood in the streets, for there was no room in the stableyards.

"Thankful was I to stay in a tiny garret in the Adelphi hotel thanks to the generosity of my friend, Miss— the renowned actress, of whom I was a guest that day, and of whose company of course my poor Father quite disapproved. It didn't help that Father had been one of the most fervent opponents of the new railway in the first place, for he saw it as a threat to his own livelihood – and mine, for in the future, as I was an only child, I would inherit the Toll Gate Lodge which was our home, and my Father's source of income. How right he was! – though, aged but twenty, I scarce saw it at the time.

"In the morning we all made to the railway yard. The engineers had assembled eight strings of carriages, with special colours to match the passengers' tickets, and eight locomotives to pull 'em, all steaming and panting like mighty horses. I peered at the engines, trying to pick out the bright blue flag that I knew would be borne by the famous *Rocket* itself.

"Of course no carriage was allowed to upstage the Prime Minister's! It had Grecian scrolls and balustrades, and gilded pillars that maintained a canopy of rich crimson cloth. The interior had an ottoman seat. It was like a perfect little sitting room, except that it was a peculiar oblong shape, four times as long as it was wide, and it ran on eight large iron wheels!

"At precisely ten o'clock the Prime Minister himself drove up to the yard in the Marquis of Salisbury's carriage, drawn by four horses. He was greeted by clapping and cheering, and a military band struck up *See the Conquering Hero Comes*. His train was to be pulled along by a locomotive called the Northumbrian, which was adorned by a bright lilac flag, and would be piloted by George Stephenson himself. The train consisted of just three carriages, in the first of which would ride the military band, the second the Prime Minister himself and his guests, and the third the railway directors and their guests – one of whom was me!

"I cannot describe my excitement as I clambered into the carriage, which was decked with silken streamers, a deep imperial purple. I admit I was callow enough to use my nail scissors to snip off a few inches of a pretty streamer which I tied up in my hair . . ."

I fingered the bit of ribbon that had bound up Lily's manuscript, and wondered.

I grew up in a quiet cul-de-sac in a little outer-suburb village a few miles from Liverpool city centre, on the road to Manchester. The cul-de-sac emptied out southwards into the main road.

Behind the houses ran a railway embankment. It cut straight past the northern end of the road, running dead straight west to east, paralleling the main road in its path from Liverpool to Manchester. We kids were strictly banned from ever trying to find a way to the railway embankment, or to climb its grassy slopes. But we did know there was a disused tunnel under the embankment behind one of the back gardens, from which, our legends had it, robbers would periodically emerge.

When I was small, steam trains still ran along the line. Great white clouds would climb into the air, and my mother would rush out to save her washing from the soot. The trains were always a part of our lives, sweeping across the sky like low-flying planes. Their noise didn't bother us; it was too grand to be irritating, like the weather.

As a kid you are dropped at random into time. That embankment, covered by grass and weeds, was there all my life, a great earthwork vast and unnoticed. I didn't know we were living in the shadow of a bit of history.

For the railway line at the bottom of my road was George Stephenson's Liverpool & Manchester Railway, the first passenger railway in all the world. And, seven years before Queen Victoria took the throne, Miss Lily Ord, great-great-grandmother of my old friend Albert, attended the railway's opening – and so, maybe, did a much more famous figure.

"Soon all was ready. The Prime Minister's train was to run on the southerly of the two parallel railroad lines, so that he might be seen from the other trains, which would all run on the northerly line.

"At twenty minutes to eleven a cannon was fired, and off we went! Enormous masses of people lined the railroad, cheering as we went past and staring agog at such a sight as they never saw before in their lives.

"As we left Liverpool we passed between two great rocky cliffs. Bridges had been thrown between the tops of these cliffs, and people gazed down at us, so distant they were like dolls in the sky. I marvelled that all this was the work of man. But the hewn walls were already cloaked by mosses and ferns.

"Inside our carriage, crammed shoulder to shoulder, we talked nine to the dozen as we glided along!

"My friend Miss — the actress was a guest of Mr —, one of the railway directors, though what their relationship was I was never absolutely clear. But as the panting iron horses gathered speed, Miss — became distressed. I was forced to exchange seats with her, so she could sit well inside the carriage.

"I found myself sitting next to a charming gentleman who introduced himself as M. Pierre Venn (or perhaps *Vairn*). To my surprise he was French! – he was a lawyer from the city of Nantes. It seemed M. Venn had advised one of the railway directors regarding investment from wealthy individuals in France, many of whom have an eye on the railway for a replication in France itself, depending of course on its success. I admit I was surprised to learn that Frenchie money had been used to build an English railway, even so many years after the downfall of Napoleon! But Money has always been ignorant of national rivalries.

"M. Venn was with another Frenchman, a dark, rather sullen man whom M. Venn introduced as a M. Gyger, but this gentleman had not a word to say to me, or anybody else – quite unlike the voluble Frenchie one expects. He did little but glare about rather resentfully and I quickly forgot him. (Of course I remember him well now! – but I run ahead of myself.)

"M. Venn was also accompanied by his pretty wife, and their child, their first-born, a little boy of two or three they called Julie, and they were much more fun. That scamp of a boy was decked out in a pretty sailor's costume, for Nantes is evidently near the coast, and the child was already obsessed by the sea and all things nautical. But he had also discovered a new passion for Mr Stephenson's railway; I am not sure how he managed it, but even before we set off he was already a bundle of soot, which got all over our clothes and hands! The little boy laughed so much, his joy at the experience of the journey almost hysterical, that I think all forgave him.

"M. Venn offered me some profound thoughts on the meaning of the marvellous experience we were sharing. 'Never has the dominion of mind more fully exhibited its sovereignty over the world of matter than today,' he said, 'and in a manner which will surely beneficially influence the future destinies of mankind throughout the civilized worlds.' And so forth!

"However as well as his interest in the Future of Man M. Venn also seemed intrigued by the Presence of Woman. He complimented me on my accent, which he said sounded Scotch, and the rosewater scent I wore, and the purple ribbon in my hair, before moving on to the colour of my cheeks and the suppleness of my neck. That is the way of the Frenchie, I suppose. Or it may be that Mme. Venn did not understand English.

"It wasn't long before we emerged from deep beneath the ground to fly far above it. Over a high embankment we bowled along, looking down at the tree tops and drinking in the fresh autumn air . . ."

Somewhere among those trees was the site of my future home. And perhaps Lily was able to make out the line of the toll road from which her father made his living.

The history of my home village has been determined by the fact that it lies on a straight line drawn between the centre of Manchester and the Liverpool docks. As the Manchester cotton trade grew and the port of Liverpool began to expand, it was an obvious place through which to build a road.

A hundred years before George Stephenson, a consortium of Liverpool merchants petitioned for an act to set up a turnpike road, the first in Lancashire or Yorkshire save for the London trunk routes. They installed one of their gate-keepers at the Toll Gate Lodge, where my old friend Albert was born, and indeed died. The turnpikes were a smart social invention; by making those with the strongest vested interest in the roads, the users, pay for their upkeep, the British road system was massively and rapidly improved.

The new road was a huge success, and it galvanised the local economy. But by the early 1800s the thirty miles sepa-rating Liverpool and Manchester, by now two engines of the Industrial Revolution, were traversed daily by hundreds of jostling horses, wagons and stagecoaches. So the local land agents and merchants began to conceive of schemes for a railway. They were fortunate enough, or wise, to choose George Stephenson as their chief engineer. The success of the railway was a calamity for the toll road, though, and the gatekeepers who made a living from it; Lily's father had been right.

The geographical logic endured. In my lifetime yet another transport link, a motorway, was built through the same area. So within fifty yards or so of my front door there were marvels of transport engineering from the eighteenth, nine-teenth and twentieth centuries.

The trains stopped repeatedly, so that the notables could admire views of cuttings and viaducts and countryside, and lesser people could admire the notables. At one stop, twenty-year-old Lily managed to talk her way into a ride on the foot-plate of the Northumbrian with George Stephenson himself.

"I was introduced to the little engine which carried us all along the rails. She (for they call all their curious fire-horses mares) goes on two wheels, alike to her feet, which are driven by bright steel legs called pistons, which are propelled by steam. All this apparatus is controlled by a small steel handle, which applies or withdraws the steam from the pistons. It is so simple an affair a child could manage it.

"The engine was able to fly at more than thirty miles an hour. But the motion was as smooth as you can imagine, and I took my bonnet off, and let the air take my hair. Behind the belching little she-dragon which Mr Stephenson controlled with a touch, I felt not the slightest fear."

I envied Lily; it must have been the ride of a lifetime.

"Mr Stephenson himself is a master of marvels with whom I fell awfully in love. He is a tall man, more powerfully built than one of his engines, with a shock of white hair. He is perhaps fifty-five." (Actually Stephenson was forty-nine.) "His face is fine, but careworn. He expresses himself with clarity and forcefulness, and although he bears the accent of his north-east birthplace there is no coarseness or vulgarity about him at all. He told me he is the son of a colliery fireman. He learned his mechanicking working on fire engines down the mines. He was nineteen before he could read or write, and his quest to build his railway was frustrated by the linguistic contortions of the 'Parliament Men' who had opposed him. But this was the day of his triumph."

Stephenson built his railway, all thirty miles of it, in just four years. It was a mighty undertaking, with cuttings and viaducts engineered by armies of navvies. Stephenson had to build over sixty bridges, including the one behind my neighbour's back garden. My embankment was three miles long, forty-five feet high and amounted to half a million cubic yards of spoil removed from cuttings miles away.

"The train passed over a very fine viaduct, and we looked down to see the graceful legs of his mighty bridge striding across a beautiful little valley. I heard a gruff voice which could only have been the Prime Minister's, emanating from the carriages behind, as he called the spectacle, 'Stupendous!' and 'Magnificent!' – for so it was.

"But, it is a strange thing for a man who had proven himself so brave, I thought the Prime Minister didn't much enjoy the ride. He said that he could not believe sensible people would ever allow themselves to be hurled along at such speeds! And later I heard him say that if Mr Stephenson's railway caught on, it would 'only encourage the lower classes to travel about.' A good thing too I say! . . ."

twisted and neatly caught the boy in his great hands, thus saving the child from a painful fall: the Prime Minister had the reactions of a soldier, despite his age, and an instinct for the safety of others. With the boy in his arms he stumbled backwards into his ottoman – but he remained safely in the carriage.

"And then the Rocket reached our train. I distinctly heard the Prime Minister call out, 'Huskisson, for God's sake get to your place!' But it was too late.

"Everybody else had scrambled out of the way, off the track or behind the coaches – everybody but poor Huskisson, who, hampered by a bad leg and general portliness, fell back on to the track. The Rocket ran over Huskisson's leg. I heard a dreadful crunch of bone.

"When the train had passed others rushed to help him. George Stephenson quickly took command. One man began to tie his belt around the damaged leg, which pumped blood. Soon the patient would be loaded aboard a single carriage behind the Northumbrian, and hurried off to Manchester. Mr Huskisson, to his credit, did not cry out once, though I heard him say, 'I have met my death. God forgive me!'

"As for the Prime Minister, he clambered down from the carriage at last, but to the right hand side. The Venns and I still stood where we had been, I trembling with fear and emotion.

"The Prime Minister handed the little French boy back to his father. Then he bowed stiffly to M. Venn. 'Sir, your quick thinking preserved my life.'

"M. Venn was quite modest. He ruffled little Julie's hair. 'Perhaps you should thank this small fellow.'

"'But I scarce thought the day would ever come when *I* of all people owed my life to one French gentleman, let alone two!'

"M. Venn said, 'We are no longer enemies, sir. And I for one would not see a countryman of mine commit such a craven act as an assassination of this kind.'

"At that the Prime Minister's formidable eyebrows rose, and I could see that he was thinking through the events of the hour in quite a different light – as was I. But of M. Gyger, who had tried to call the Prime Minister into the path of the advancing Rocket, there was no sign.

"And little Julie Venn, who had that day ridden faster than any small child in history, *and* saved the life of a Prime Minister, laughed and laughed and laughed."

I checked out some of the details later. The Rocket, perhaps the most famous steam locomotive ever built, really was running that day, alongside seven of her sister engines, including the Northumbrian. And there really was a fatal accident, when William Huskisson MP managed to step out in front of the speeding Rocket.

I've come across no account of a Monsieur Gyger.

Albert couldn't tell me why anybody would have wanted to try to kill the Prime Minister that day, French or otherwise. France and Britain were not, at that time, at war. It made no sense – until it occurred to me to check who the Prime Minister actually was.

Grand, aloof, distrustful of new technology and the working people alike, it was Arthur Wellesley, first Duke of Wellington, victor over Napoleon at Waterloo just fifteen years earlier – a man who many French people would surely have loved to see in his grave.

The eye-witness accounts of the day say nothing about the Prime Minister holding a small boy at the time. On the other hand, they don't say he wasn't. Maybe the incident was hushed up for the sake of international relations – or simply to save Wellington embarrassment.

The rest of the day rather fizzled out for Lily Ord. The mood was subdued after the accident. She rode on with her companions to Manchester, but the Prime Minister was greeted by boos and thrown stones; his government wasn't popular with everybody, and nor was the new railway, a "triumph of machinery". Wellington wouldn't travel by rail again for thirteen years, and then only because Queen Victoria persuaded him.

At Manchester Lily said her goodbyes to the "Venns".

"Little Julie lifted our spirits. In his mother's arms he fairly bubbled with excitement, and he rattled on with a high-speed gabbling, as if bursting to tell the story of his day, but he was quite incomprehensible!

"M. Venn took my hand. 'A memorable day, Miss Ord,' he said.

"'Quite so. Sir, you showed remarkable composure –'

"'For a Frenchman?' He smiled. 'My dear, you must not allow the foolishness at Parkside to colour your memories of the day. The railway is the thing – the railway! You British with your relentless desire for trade, trade, trade, will take Mr Stephenson's marvellous invention and fling it around the world. When the whole of the globe is wrapped up like a fly in an iron spider-web, Mr Stephenson's locomotive will carry us around the world in a hundred days, or less – ninety, eighty days!'

"Little Julie was laughing and kicking; he would not be without imagination, I saw. But this was one flight of fancy too much for me.

"And besides, M. Venn was holding my hand a little too tightly, his gaze a little too warm. As I looked into his eyes – just for a second, I confess it! – I saw another world opening up, a world of possibility every bit as remarkable as a planet girdled by railway tracks. But I knew it could not come to pass. I gently extricated my hand.

"I said my '*Au revoir*' to Mme. Venn and Julie, and looked for Miss —, who was arranging our passage back to Liverpool . . ."

Albert only had that one fragment of memoir. I'd like to know what became of Lily Ord, if she was happy as she raised a family of her own in the Toll Gate Lodge.

And I'd love to know if her tall tale held even a fragment of truth.

"Isn't it at least possible?" Albert said to me, earnest, wheezing slightly. "*Venn, Vairn* – she wasn't used to French accents – could she have misheard the name? Lily wrote all this down long before he became famous, of course. And isn't it possible all this affected *him*, young as he was? The mighty steam engines – the great metal road, the sense of speed, of plummeting into a new future – I'm only telling you because you've started to write your own science fiction, Stephen. No wonder he made up all those stories of his! And it all started here."

Albert died a few years later. His family, always remote, took away his effects, and the old Toll Gate Lodge was sold, passing out of the family's hands after two centuries. I don't know what became of Lily's manuscript.

　　Albert did leave a few tokens to friends. I was sent a small envelope that contained a length of silken streamer, imperial purple. One end was neatly hemmed, but the other had been cut crudely, as if by a small set of scissors. And when I lifted the ribbon to my face I could detect faint scents, almost vanished, of soot, and rosewater.

JEHAN THUN'S QUEST

Brian Stableford

Verne's early stories are not immediately identifiable with the advancement of science. Indeed his very first story, "The Mutineers" (1851) and his third, "Martin Paz" (1852), were more inspired by the revolutionary zeal that was flooding Europe. Only "Un voyage en ballon", also known as "Drama in the Air", and probably inspired by Edgar Allan Poe's "The Balloon Hoax", gave thought to new technology. His fourth story, "Maître Zacharius" (1854), also known as "The Watch's Soul", saw a change in direction. Whilst Verne was exploring technology – the desire to make the perfect watch – though in a historical context, this story is more fantastic than technological, drawing more upon the works of Hoffman than on Poe. It concerned a master clockmaker who, in creating a new mechanism for his watches, believed that he had imbued the watch with something of himself – his soul. The locals, though, were suspicious of Zacharius and Verne used the opportunity to consider mankind's fear of progress and how we need to embrace new technology not destroy it, a view that Verne would modify in later years. Here, Brian Stableford revisits the story and considers its aftermath.

The day had been clear when Jehan Thun set off from the inn on the outskirts of the city of Geneva, but the weather in the lake's environs was far more capricious than the weather in Paris. He had hoped that the sky might remain blue all day, but it was not long after noon when grey cloud began spilling through the gaps in the mountains, swallowing up the peaks and promising a downpour that would soak him to the skin and render his path treacherous.

There were villages scattered along the shore of the lake but he had no thought of asking for shelter there. The time seemed to be long past when one could be confident of receiving hospitality from any neighbour, and the people in Geneva who had recognized his surname had looked at him strangely and suspiciously, although none had actually challenged him. It would have been better, in retrospect, to avoid Geneva altogether, since the Château of Andernatt was on the French side of the lake and he could have followed the course of Rhone, but he had hoped to find the city of his ancestors more welcoming by far than any other he had passed through on his flight from Paris. At least the many repetitions of his grandmother's story had drummed the stages of the route that she and Aubert had followed into Jehan's mind: Bessange, Ermance, ford the Dranse; Chesset, Colombay, Monthey, the hermitage of Notre-Dame-du-Sex.

When Jehan's grandparents had made that journey the churches of Geneva had still been affiliated to Rome; now, fifty years after Calvin's advent, they preached a very different faith. Notre-Dame-du-Sex was on the French shore, but Jehan was not at all certain that the hermitage would still be occupied. The apparatus of charity that had supported the hermit who gave temporary refuge to Aubert Thun and the daughter of Master Zacharius had been transformed for several leagues around the city, just as the environs of Paris had been transformed before St Bartholomew's Day.

The rain began before Jehan had reached the Dranse, but it was no deluge at first and the torrent had not become impassable. The downfall became steadier as he left the shore, though, and the further he went up the slopes the greater its volume became. He dared not stop now, or even relent in his pace. It had taken his grandparents more than twenty hours to reach the base of the Dent-du-Midi, but they had been slowed down by Old Scholastique; he reckoned on covering the same ground in fourteen hours at the most – as he would have to do if he were to avoid spending the night on the bare mountain.

He had hoped that fifty years of footfalls might have smoothed the paths a little since his grandparents' day, but it seemed that hardly anyone came this way any more; parts of the path had all but disappeared. On a better day, the Dent-du-Midi would have served as a fine beacon, but with its top lost in the clouds he was unable to sight it.

Jehan Thun was a man well used to walking, but the gradients in and around Paris were gentle, and he was glad now that he had had to cross the forbidding slopes of the Jura in order to reach Geneva, for his legs had been hardened in the last few weeks. His cape and broad-brimmed hat protected him from the worst effects of the driving rain, but that would not have been enough to sustain him had he not been capable of such a metronomic stride. He had walked like an automaton since St Bartholomew's Day, but even an automaton needs strength in its limbs and power in its spring.

It was a close-run thing, in the end; had he been a quarter of an hour later, he would not have been able to catch a glimpse of the hermitage before darkness fell. Had he not seen it in the fast-fading twilight he could not have found it, for no light burned in its window, and it had obviously been abandoned for decades, but the roof had not yet caved in. It leaked in a dozen places, but there was enough dry space within to set down his pack. He lit a candle—not without difficulty, for all that he had kept his tinder dry.

There was no point in trying to gather wood to build a fire that would burn all night, so Jehan made a rapid meal of what little bread he had left before wrapping himself more tightly in his cloak and lying down in a corner to sleep. Even as he reached out to snuff out his candle, though, he was interrupted. A voice cried in the distance, in German-accented French, asking what light it was that was showing in the darkness. For a moment he was tempted to extinguish the candle anyway, in the hope that the other traveller would not be able to find him once the guide was gone – but that would have been a terrible thing to do, even if the other turned out to be a bandit or a heresy-hunter. Instead, he shouted out that he was a traveller who had lost his way, and had taken refuge in an abandoned hermitage.

A few minutes later, a man staggered through the doorway, mingling curses against the weather with profuse thanks for guidance to the meagre shelter. He took off a vast colporteur's pack, letting it fall to the floor with a grateful sigh. He was approximately the same age and build as Jehan Thun; even by candlelight Jehan could see the anxiety in the way the newcomer measured him, and knew that it must be reflected in his own eyes. He imagined that the other must be just as glad as he was to see that they were so evenly matched, not merely in size and apparent health but in the manner of their dress.

"I did not see you on the path ahead of me," the newcomer said, "so I presume that you must be coming away from Geneva while I am going towards it. I don't know which of us is the wiser, for they say that Geneva is like a city under siege nowadays. My name is Nicholas Alther. I was born in Bern, although my course takes me far and wide in the Confederation, France and Savoy."

Jehan knew that the complications of Geneva's political situation extended far beyond matters of religious controversy; although the city was allied with Bern it was not a member of the Swiss confederation, and its position as a three-way juncture between Switzerland, Savoy and France created tensions over and above the residue of Calvin's reforms.

"My name is Jehan Thun," he admitted, a trifle warily. "I'm stateless now, although I've recently been in France." Jehan watched Nicholas Alther carefully as he spoke his name; there was a manifest reaction, but it was not the same one that the name had usually evoked in Geneva, and Nicholas Alther did not make the same attempt to conceal it. "Thun?" the colporteur echoed. "There was once a clock-maker in these parts named Thun."

"That was a long time ago," Jehan said, very carefully.

"Yes," Alther agreed. "He was a fine mechanician, though, and his work has lasted. I have one of his watches in my pack – my own, not for trading." So saying, the colporteur rummaged in one of the side-pockets of his capacious luggage and brought out a forty-year-old timepiece. Jehan Thun observed that its single hand was making slow progress between the numbers ten and eleven. "You doubtless have a better one," Alther prompted, as he put the device away again and brought out a cheese instead.

"No," Jehan confessed. "I have no watch at all."

"No watch!" Alther seemed genuinely astonished. He offered Jehan Thun the first slice of cheese he cut off, but Jehan shook his head and the other continued, punctuating his speech with the motions of his meal. "Perhaps you are not related to the old clockmaker – but your French has a hint of Geneva in it, and I doubt there was another family hereabouts with that name. Aubert Thun must have been one of the first men ever to use a spring to drive a clock, or at least a fusée regulator in place of a stackfreed – and the escapements he made for weight-driven clocks will preserve his reputation for at least a century more, for they're still in use in half the churches between here and Bern. He was a greater man than many whose names will be better preserved by history, although I don't recall hearing of anything he did after he quit Geneva."

Jehan Thun looked at the colporteur sharply when he said that, wondering whether Alther might have the name of Calvin in mind, but all he said, reluctantly, was: "Aubert Thun was my grandfather."

"Did he abandon his trade when he went away?" the colporteur asked.

"No," Jehan admitted, "but there are locksmiths and clockmakers by the hundred in Paris, which means that there are escapements by the thousand and far more watch-springs than anyone could count. He had the reputation there of a skilled man, but there was no reason why rumour of his skill should carry far. It has surprised me that his name is still remembered here; he told me that he was only an apprentice to the man who first used springs in Genevan watches and first put verge escapements into the region's church clocks."

"Is that true?" Alther replied, his features expressing surprise. He had wine as well as cheese, and offered the flask to Jehan Thun, but Jehan shook his head again. Alther took a deep draught before continuing: "I heard the same, but always thought Master Zacharius a legend. Even before Calvin, Genevans were reluctant to think that anything new could be produced by the imagination of a man; everything had to be a gift from god or an instrument of the Devil. The tale they tell of Thun's supposed master is a dark and fanciful one, but nothing a reasonable man could believe."

Jehan knew that the conversation had strayed on to unsafe ground, but he felt compelled to say: "I agree, and I'm sorry to have found people in Geneva who still look sideways at the mention of my grandfather's name. Master Zacharius did go mad, I fear, but the stories they tell of him are wildly exaggerated."

"And yet," Alther observed, "you're coming away from Geneva. Are you, by any chance, heading in the direction of Évionnaz . . . and the Château of Andernatt?"

Jehan suppressed a shiver when Alther said that. Colporteurs were notorious as collectors and tellers of tales, for it oiled the wheels of their trade; Alther's stock was obviously broad and deep. He said nothing.

"I've seen the château on the horizon," the colporteur went on, eventually, "and that's more than most can say. No one goes there, and it seems to have fallen into ruins. Whatever you're looking for, I doubt that you'll find it."

"My destination might lie further in the same direction," Jehan pointed out.

"There is nothing further in that direction," Alther

retorted. "Évionnaz is the road's end. I've travelled it often enough to know."

"The world is a sphere," Jehan said, knowing as he said it that it was not an uncontroversial opinion, and hence not entirely safe. "There is always further to go, in every direction, no matter how hard the road might be – and the Dents-du-Midi are not impassable at this time of year."

"That's what I thought before the rain set in," Alther grumbled, following his cheese with some kind of sweet-meat – which, this time, he did not bother to offer to his companion, "but the people of Évionnaz think the world has an edge, no more than a league from the bounds of their fields. They never go to Andernatt."

"I have not said that I am going that way," Jehan said, rudely. "But if I were, it would be no one's business but my own." He felt that he had said too much, even though he had said very little, and he indicated by the way in which he gathered his cloak about himself that he did not want to waste any more time before going to sleep, now that the colporteur had finished his meal.

"That's true," Alther agreed, shrugging his shoulders to indicate that it was of scant importance to him whether or not the conversation was cut short. "I'll venture to say, though, that you'd be unlikely to meet the Devil if you did go that way, whether or not there's anything more than a ruin at Andernatt. There are half a hundred peaks on this side of the lake alone where Satan's reported to have squatted at one time or another – and that's not counting dwellings like this one, whose former inhabitant was reckoned his minion by the Calvinists down in Geneva."

"I'll be glad of that, too," Jehan assured him, and said no more.

Jehan Thun and Nicholas Alther parted the next morning on good terms, as two honest men thrown briefly together by chance ought to do. They wished one another well as they set off in near-opposite directions. Whether Alther gave another thought to him thereafter, Jehan did not know or care, but he certainly gave a good deal of thought to what Alther had said as he made his way towards Évionnaz. It was a difficult journey, but when he finally reached the village, huddled in a narrow vale between two crags, he was able to buy food and fill his flask. He passed through with minimal delay into territory where the paths that once had been were now hardly discernible. No one in the village asked him where he was bound, but a dozen pairs of eyes watched him as he went, and he felt those eyes boring into his back until he had put the first of many ridges between himself and the village.

Jehan no longer had precise directions as to the path he must take; he had not dared to mention the château in Geneva. All he had to guide him now was vague advice handed on by his grandmother, which told him no more than to steer to the left. Inevitably, Jehan soon became desperately unsure of his way. While the sun descended into the west he wandered, searching the narrow horizons for a glimpse of the ruins that Nicholas Alther claimed to have seen. At least the sun was visible, so he was able to conserve a good notion of the direction in which Évionnaz lay, but by the time he decided that he would have to turn back he knew that it would be difficult to reach the village before nightfall.

Then, finally, he caught sight of a strange hump outlined on a slanting ridge. He was not certain at first, given the distance and the fact that he was looking at it from below, that it really was the remnant of an edifice, and it seemed in a far worse state than he had hoped, even after hearing Alther's judgement.

Because it lay in a direction diametrically opposite to the route that would take him towards Évionnaz, Jehan Thun knew that he would be in difficulty if there were nothing on the site but broken stones, but he had to make the choice and he was not at all confident that he could find his way back to his present location if he did not press on now. He decided that he must trust to luck and do his utmost to carry his quest forward to its destination.

Again he reached his objective just as night was falling, and again he saw no light as he toiled uphill towards the crumbled stonework, until he lit his own candle – but this time, there seemed at first glance to be no roof at all to offer him shelter, merely a tangle of tumbled walls, cracked arches and heaps of debris.

He did not realize for some little while that he had only found an outer part of the ancient edifice. He might easily have laid himself down to sleep without making any such discovery, but as chance would have it he was fortunate enough to see a flock of bats emerging from a crevice behind a pile of rubble. When he climbed up to see if he could insinuate himself into the gap he did not expect to find anything more than a corner of a room, but he was able to make a descent into a much broader and deeper space that had two doorways. These gave access to further corridors, each of which contained a stairway leading into what had seemed from beneath to be the solid rock of the ridge. He quickly came to the conclusion that the château must have been much larger than it now seemed, built into a groove in the ridge rather than perched atop level ground. The lower parts of its walls had been so completely overgrown that the casual eye could not distinguish them from the native rock that jutted up to either side.

One stairway turned out to be useless, the wooden-beamed storage-cellar to which it led having caved in, but the other led to further rooms and further portals, some with ceilings and doors still intact. The route was awkward, not least because of the stink – the bats had been depositing their excreta for generations – but he managed to open three of the closed doors to expose further spaces beyond, two no bigger than closets but one of a more appreciable size. This one had a slit-like window, through which the stars were clearly visible, although no such aperture had been discernible from the side of the hill he had climbed on his first approach.

That first room was uninhabitable, but when he went on again he found one that the bats had not yet turned into a dormitory; the shutter on its window was still intact. The bare wooden floorboards seemed more hospitable than stone, and they seemed remarkably free of dirt, so Jehan set his pack down. He was so exhausted that he stretched himself out and blew out his candle without making a meal.

His thoughts immediately returned to what Nicholas Alther had said about Master Zacharius, and he began to regret not asking exactly what story it was that Alther had heard. According to his grandmother – who believed far more of the tale than her husband – her father had put his soul into the spring of a clock commissioned by the Devil, thus conceding the Adversary power to transmogrify and finally obliterate his work. Aubert Thun's son, Jehan's father, had been as sceptical as the old man, and Jehan had the same attitude; he would never have come here had it not become impossible for him to stay in Paris – but once the capital of France had become as unsafe for Protestants as Geneva had once been for Catholics, the only choice remaining to him was the direction in which to flee. Since he had had to go somewhere, and had no other destination in mind, it had seemed to Jehan that he might as well do what his grandmother – who had died of natural causes thank God, long before the massacre – had always wanted his father to do. Now that he was here, though, he could not help reflecting lugubriously on the fact that he had come in order to have a destination at which to point his automaton limbs, not because he believed that there would be any treasure to find or any curse to lift.

He decided before he fell asleep he would explore the ruins as thoroughly as was humanly possible on the following day, and then make further plans. The food he had bought in Évionnaz would be enough to sustain him for more than a day, although it should not be difficult to find pools of rainwater to drink. He would have to decide soon enough whether to retrace his steps in the direction of inhospitable Geneva, or to make his way back to the Rhone and follow the path that Nicholas Alther had presumably been walking, or make his way eastwards along the north shore of the lake

– or go on into the Dents-du-Midi, into a bleak and empty region which the people of Évionnaz took to be the limit of the world.

In the morning, Jehan Thun was woken up by a hand placed on his shoulder. The room was still gloomy but the shutter had been partially opened; the beam of sunlight streaming through the narrow window brightened the plastered walls, reflecting enough light to show him that the person who had woken him was very short and stout: a dwarf.

That was a terrible shock – not because it was unexpected, but for precisely the opposite reason. His grandmother had told him that the Devil had come to her father, Master Zacharius, in the form of a dwarf named Pittonaccio.

"Who are you?" Jehan stammered, quite ready to believe that he was face to face with the Devil. The moment of awakening is a vulnerable one, in which deep impressions can be made that are sometimes difficult of amendment.

The little man paused momentarily, as if he had not expected to be addressed in French, but he answered fluently enough in the same language. "I am the Master of Andernatt," he said, proudly. "The question should rather be: Who are you? You are the invader here – are you a bandit come to rob me of my heritage?" His Germanic accent was not as pronounced as Nicholas Alther's, but was evident nevertheless.

"I'm no bandit," Jehan said.

"Are you not? Are you a guest, then? Did you knock on any of the doors you passed through last night? Did you call out to ask for shelter?"

"I saw no light," Jehan protested.

"You would have seen a light had you taken more care to look around," the dwarf replied. "My chamber has a broader window than this one, and I lit my lamp before sunset. I suppose you did not see my goats on the ledges either, or my garden in the vale."

"No," said Jehan, becoming increasingly desperate as the challenges kept coming. "I saw no goats – but if I had, I'd have taken them for wild creatures. Nor did I see a garden, but it was dusk when I approached and I was fearful that I might not reach the shelter of the ruins before night plunged me into darkness."

"The stars were shining," the dwarf observed, "and there's near half a moon. Your eyes must be poor – but I suppose you came from the direction of Évionnaz, from which my window would have been hidden. You still have not told me who you are, or what business you have here."

Jehan Thun hesitated fearfully; he felt a strong temptation to declare that his name was Nicholas Alther, and that he was a colporteur who had lost his way – but he had no pack of goods and trinkets, and no good reason to lie. In the end, he plucked up his courage and said: "My name is Jehan Thun. My grandfather was Aubert Thun, apprentice to Master Zacharius of Geneva."

The dwarf recognized the names, but he did not look sideways in suspicion, let alone recoil in horror. Instead, he smiled beatifically, and the expression caused his unhandsome face to become quite pleasant. "Ah!" he said. "The answer to my prayer! There have been others here before you, searching for the clock, but none named Thun. Zacharius must have been your great-grandfather, Master Jehan, for Aubert Thun married the clockmaker's daughter, Gérande."

Jehan was terrified already, so the fact that the dwarf knew all this gave him little further distress. "And you?" he said, in a quavering voice. "Are you . . . ?" He could not say the word. His grandmother had been twice devout, once as a Catholic and once as a Protestant, and had prayed incessantly for her father in either mode, but Jehan had never been able to put quite as much trust as that in the attentiveness of Heaven or the menace of Hell. Even so, for the moment, he could not say either "the Devil" or "Pittonaccio."

"Not even his great-grandson, Master Jehan," the dwarf said. "My name is Friedrich – very ordinary, as I'm sure you'll agree; but I'm Master of Andernatt nevertheless, at least for now, and I do have the clock. I have nearly completed its reconstruction, but have faltered lately for lack of proper tools and a skilful hand. Have you brought your own tools?"

"I've brought my grandfather's," Jehan confessed.

"Then you're a wiser man than those who came before you. Did you also bring his skill?"

The truth seemed to have taken firm hold of Jehan Thun's tongue; he could not seem to twist it. "I'm not a watch-maker," he confessed. "I'm a printer – or was. The mob was as anxious to smash up my press as to break my neighbours' heads. I can cast and trim type, and work in wood, and I have some skill as an engraver, but I haven't curled a spring or wrought a fusée since I helped my father in his shop as a boy. Times have changed, and it's the printing press that has changed them. There are hundreds of clockmakers in Paris, but only a dozen printers as yet – at least one less, now."

The dwarf looked at him long and hard then, as if he were following some train of thought to an unexpected terminus. "I have a printed book," he admitted, finally. "It's a Bible."

"I printed a great many of those myself," Jehan told him. "Too many, perhaps."

"Well," said the dwarf, "whether you called out or not, Master Jehan, you're a guest now, and the most welcome one I've ever had. Come to breakfast – and then I'll show you the clock."

The corridors that Jehan Thun had thought rather labyrinthine the previous evening were even more extensive and complex than he had imagined. They were, however, far better ventilated than the initial barrier of bat droppings had suggested and many of them were dimly illuminated by daylight creeping through window-slits and cracks in the masonry. One such slit overlooked the "garden" to which the master of the ruins had referred – which was actually a vegetable-plot and orchard. Jehan Thun saw immediately why he had not caught sight of it before; the dell in which it was situated was itself a covert, hidden by a massive buttress of rock. There was evidently another way into the cavernous part of the edifice from that side, which allowed the dwarf to avoid the difficulties of the way by which Jehan had gained entry.

The dwarf took him to a room more brightly lit than the rest, which also looked out over the garden. It had a fire burning in the grate, but the chimney let out into the same covert, so its smoke would not have been easily visible as Jehan Thun had approached on the previous evening. There was a cookpot simmering beside the fire, and various items of game hung from a rack on the chimney-breast. The furniture was sparse but there was a sturdy table and two good chairs. Jehan sat down gladly, and ate a good meal.

The printed Bible that the dwarf had mentioned was laid flat on a shelf; the dust on its binding implied that it had not been opened for some while. Jehan lifted the cover to inspect the quality of the printing, but the type was florid Gothic and the text was not in Latin.

"Come, Master Jehan, my godsend," said the dwarf. "I will show you what you came to see."

According to Jehan's grandmother, the iron clock of Andernatt had been fastened to the wall of a great hall. It had been shaped by Master Zacharius to resemble the facade of a church, with wrought-iron buttresses and a bell-tower, with a rose-window over the door in which the clock's two hands were mounted. The same witness had testified that the clock had exploded and its internal spring had burst out like a striking snake to secure the damnation of its maker.

The clock was not in a great hall now but in a small room that had no window. The buttresses and the bell-tower must have been transported in several pieces, but they had been reassembled so carefully that they seemed whole again. The window had been pieced together, and all of its glass replaced, although the cobwebbing cracks made it obvious that the stained-glass had once been shattered. The doors of the church had been replaced, with newer wood, and they stood open to display the inner works of the clock – but the giant spring that Master Zacharius had set in place was not there now, nor was the verge-escapement that had regulated it. There was, instead, a more complex mechanism. Its most prominent feature was a mysterious brass rod, mounted vertically on a spindle, pivoted so that it might swing from side to side, whose lower extremity was shielded by a polished silver disc.

This remarkable object caught and held Jehan's gaze for several seconds, delaying his search for the clock's most unusual feature: the copper plate between the door and the dial, in which words appeared as each hour struck.

His grandmother had described this plate as a magic mirror, on which words appeared and disappeared by diabolical command, but his grandfather had assured him that there was nothing magical about it. There was actually a series of twelve plaques mounted on the rim of a hidden wheel, which rotated as the clock's spring unwound and the hands made their own rotation. Each plaque was itself held back by a tiny spring, which would release as the hour struck, displaying the motto inscribed on the plaque with startling suddenness in a space that had been occupied only a second before by a blank face of copper.

The original set of plaques furnished by Master Zacharius, Aubert Thun had assured his grandson, had been inscribed with conventional pieties, many of them taken from the Sermon on the Mount – but once the clock had been installed at Andernatt, its owner had replaced the plaques with a new set offering different maxims.

"Your grandmother is convinced that the replacement was the work of the Devil," Aubert Thun had told him, "but it was not even a task that would have required a locksmith's metal-working skills, once the wheel's casing had been removed. Her father was already mad, but the discovery that his work of art had been altered was the ultimate insult. That is why he tried to stop the clock – but the spring broke because its iron was too poor to sustain its stress. No spring could power a clock like that for very long, for the alloy is not yet discovered that can bear the strain of continual winding in a strip so vast. Now that the necessity is obvious, better materials will doubtless be devised, but Zacharius could only work with what he had, and it was not adequate to his ambition.

"It was Zacharius's vanity, not his soul, that was embodied in the mechanism – and it was his vanity, not some diabolical bargain, that struck him dead. My wife would never believe it, though, and she will swear to her dying day that she saw the dwarf Pittonaccio disappear into the bowels of the earth with the spring in his grasp, bound for the Inferno. She believes that she and I were cursed on the day he died, and that all the force of her constant prayers – and mine – has only served to keep the curse at bay. Your father is an exceedingly devout man, and I do not criticize him for that, but you must make up your own mind what to believe, and there are better fates than to live in fear."

Jehan had taken his grandfather's word over his grandmother's, far more determinedly than his father had, and had tried very hard not to live in fear. Aubert Thun had not lived to see the death of his son on St Bartholomew's Day in 1572, and Jehan driven into exile – but Jehan knew that Aubert would have been adamant that it was the way of the world that had brought that evil day about, and that Jehan's printing-press was no more to blame for his father's death than the residue of any curse that had once attached to the Clock of Andernatt. Jehan Thun's grandmother had, however, carried the conviction to her grave that she and her son were cursed – and now that Jehan had seen the cellars and inner rooms of the Château of Andernatt, he understood far better how she might have witnessed the broken spring being borne into the hollows of the mountain, whether or not it was bound for Hell.

Jehan asked the dwarf about Zacharius's broken spring, but the present Master of Andernatt told him that it was long discarded, replaced by a far better mechanism.

As the dwarf had said, the clock was not quite finished, but very nearly so. The parts scattered on the floor of the room were all tiny, and they all required to be fitted into the narrow space above the rose-window, behind the part of the facade that resembled a bell-tower – an awkward task, hampered by the casing of the wheel bearing and concealing the motto-engraved plaques.

"The face of the tower can still be removed," the dwarf told Jehan, "and I can compensate for my lack of stature by standing on a stool, but I don't have your slender fingers or your delicate touch. Even if you have not dabbled in clockwork since you were a child, your own work must have maintained your dexterity; my escapement is not as delicate as a fusée. You could complete the work in a matter of days."

"I don't understand the mechanism," Jehan Thun objected. "I've never seen its like."

"It's simple enough, once explained," the dwarf assured him.

Jehan Thun's gaze redirected itself then to the blank copper plate that would presumably be eclipsed by a plaque if the mechanism were actually to prove capable of moving the hands and activating the chimes.

"You need have no fear on that score," the dwarf said. "I've replaced the maxims that caused your grandmother such distress."

"With the original set?" Jehan Thun asked.

"Those were discarded long ago. I made my own replacements. They're all in place, but now that the casing is sealed they can't be seen until the clock is completed and started. I trust that you didn't come here with no bolder hope than to melt down the remains of the mechanism and separate out the precious metals therefrom. You did say, did you not, that you are no bandit?"

"I expected to find the clock in ruins, like the château," Jehan Thun said, hesitantly. "My grandmother told me that the place was considered accursed, and that no one would be living here."

"Calvin redoubled the fear of the Devil that the good people of Geneva already had," the dwarf told him, "but there are always men who are careless of curses. Had I not been here to hide and stand guard over the pieces of the clock they'd have been looted long ago. Even I could not resist a whole robber band – but it's a clock, after all, not a gold mine. You wouldn't have come so far just for a little metal, I'm sure – but I'm equally sure that you haven't come in the hope of reclaiming the spring that might or might not have been the soul of Master Zacharius."

Jehan considered the possibility of telling the dwarf about his grandmother's sorrows and delusions, and how she had begged his father to make the journey in order to destroy the last remnants of the clock and lift the family curse with prayer, but he did not want to do that. "I came to examine the fusée," he said, eventually, although he was not entirely certain that it was true. "One of the few things on which my grandparents agreed, save for the fact that they loved one another very dearly, was that it was a new type, better than any previously used in a spring-driven clock. Aubert thought that he could reproduce it, but he never contrived to do it, and came to believe in the end that he had misremembered some small but essential detail. Alas, he was in Paris by then."

"You came to study the fusée?" the dwarf repeated, in a tone that had a strange satisfaction in it as well as a certain scepticism. "But you say that you're not a watchmaker, Master Thun – merely a printer."

"There's nothing mere about printing," Jehan retorted. "Had printers not put the word of God directly into the hands of every man who can read there would have been no Lutheran armies, no Calvinist legions. Printing is changing the way that men think, believe and act – but I'm a printer without a press, and there are hundreds of clockmakers in every city in Europe eager to discover a better escapement for watches. Is that escapement the one my great-grandfather built to regulate the missing spring?"

"No – but your grandparents were mistaken about the originality of the first escapement. There was only one thing new about the fusée I discarded, and that was its material. It was brass, not iron; it did not rust, but if it worked any better as a regulator than any other it was by virtue of the quality of its workmanship, not the detail of its design. The one I have made is better adapted to its own mechanism; it could not regulate a watchspring any more than a pendulum could drive the hand of a watch. On the other hand, what you say is perfectly true: there are a hundred clockmakers in every city in Europe who would be eager to know what might be done with my mechanism, and you shall share in the profits that will accrue from the dissemination of the secret if you will help me finish my work. Once we have completed the clock, you will be better equipped than you could have hoped to spread new knowledge throughout the continent – and beyond, if you care to. The world is, as you doubtless know, a sphere, and there is always further to go in every direction than the cities we already know. There's a new world now, beyond the Atlantic Ocean, and a vast number of undiscovered islands in the far Pacific."

It did not seem remarkable to Jehan that the dwarf's comment about the world being a sphere was echoing a statement he had made the day before, in another place. "Very well, then," he said. "I shall fetch my grandfather's tools. If you will explain what needs to be done, I shall do my very best to carry out your instructions."

Jehan Thun was as good as his word, and so was the dwarf. Working to instruction, Jehan's nimble hands pieced together the last parts of the mechanism, although it was no mere matter of assembly. There was a good deal of drilling to be done, a great many threads to be worked, and an abundance of accurate filing, as well as a certain amount of casting. Fortunately, the dwarf possessed a crucible and a vice, and a good stock of charcoal with which to charge his furnace. The dwarf's own fingers were thick and gnarled, and he could never have done the delicate work that Jehan did, but he was a clever man with plans and his strong arms could certainly work a bellows hard.

Once Jehan had set to work the hours seemed to melt away. Because there was no natural light in the room where the clock was kept, Jehan did the greater part of his work in a different one much higher in the château's hidden structure, but he soon became used to shuttling back and forth between the two. He worked long into the evening, conserving that fraction of his labour that did not need good light, but the dwarf was conscientious about interrupting him, not only to make meals but also to explain the new mechanism he had built for the clock.

"It's a secret that no one else has discovered," the little man bragged, "although it's obvious enough. How long have there been slingshots and other devices in which solid objects swing freely at the ends of cords? At least since David slew Goliath. Children play with such devices – and yet no one has observed, as I have, the isochronism of the freely-swinging weight – or if anyone has, he could not go on to the naturally consequent thought, which is that a pendulum might do as well as a system of weights or a mere spring to regulate the motions of a clock. Just as the descent of weights requires refinement by escapements, so does the swing of a pendulum, so I devised one appropriate to it.

"I have tried out my pendulum in humbler boxes with elementary faces, but never in a clock with two hands, let alone a masterpiece like the Zacharius Machine. I could have got it working, after a fashion, but a masterpiece is a masterpiece, and it sets its own standard of perfection. I might have gone to Geneva in search of a skilled clock-maker, but how could I dare, given my appearance? Even before Calvin came, Master Zacharius was remembered by many as a sorcerer, and those who hold such opinions are always among the first converts to any new fad – including Calvin's philosophy. Of all the cities in the world, why did Andernatt have to be placed so close to Geneva? No one actually casts stones at me in Évionnaz, or any other village within hiking range, but the way they look at me informs me that it would not do to linger too long in any such a place, let alone make any attempt to settle there. I was a wanderer before I came here, although I did not want to be. I am a recluse now, although that would not have been my choice before I realized how fearful people are of anything out of the ordinary. Dwarfs are not rare, you know, and they cannot all be the Devil in disguise, but men who do not travel far do not realize how many kinds of men there are."

"Noblemen employ dwarfs as clowns and jesters in France, Italy and the Germanic states," Jehan observed. "They like automata too, to strike the hours on church clocks or merely to perform mechanical acrobatics for credulous eyes."

"I am not a clown, Master Jehan," the dwarf said. "Nor am I a jester. I am the man who discovered the isochronicity of the pendulum, although I would wager that history will give the credit to a taller man – perhaps to you."

"History often makes mistakes," Jehan assured him. "Master Zacharius never received credit for the fusée, because there was a man named Jacob the Czech who worked in Prague, and Prague is a far better source of fame than poor Geneva. I do not charge this Jacob with theft, mind, for the device is obvious enough once a man's mind turns in that direction, just as your pendulum-clock might be. There may well be another man who has already made the discovery – in Florence, say, or Vienna – whose discovery has not yet been communicated to the other great cities of Europe. I think that luck has more to do with matters of reputation than height."

"Yet Pittonaccio was reckoned an imp," the dwarf reminded him. "Had he been as handsome as you, he might have been reckoned an artificer himself, and your great-grandfather might never have gone mad. But Pittonaccio's long dead, for men of my kind rarely live as long as men of yours."

"My father might have lived a while longer," Jehan said, sombrely, "had he not been a Protestant in Paris at an unfortunate hour. Hatred is not reserved for those of strange appearance; it thrives like a weed wherever faith puts forth new flowers."

The dwarf allowed Jehan to have the last word on that occasion, perhaps because he did not want to offend his guest in advance of the clock becoming workable. On that score, he did not have much longer to wait, for Jehan still felt that he was more automaton than man, and the work that he did allowed him to conserve that placid state of mind, absorbing him completely into matters of technical detail. The hours sped by, and the days too – six in all – until he arrived at the time when the last piece of the puzzle was correctly shaped, and ready to be fitted.

When he had set it in place, Jehan Thun stepped back, and looked at what he had done.

It did not seem, now that he had finished, that it was his work. He was a printer, after all, not a locksmith or a clockmaker. He had played at being a locksmith and a clockmaker when he was a child, using the very same tools that had served him so well now, but it had always been play rather than work. Clockmaking had never been his vocation, even though circumstance seemed to have turned him into something more like clockwork than flesh, at least for a while.

He watched the dwarf set the hands of the clock.

He watched the pendulum swing back and forth, with a regularity that was quite astonishing, in spite of its utter obviousness.

"If only the world were like that," he murmured.

"It shall be," the dwarf assured him. "We have the example now, far better than any commandments from on high."

As he spoke, the clock's faster moving hand reached the vertical, and the clock began to chime.

Even though he had watched the dwarf set the clock's hands, Jehan had not bothered to wonder whether the time that was being set was correct, or take any particular notice of what it was.

The clock chimed seven times, and with a barely-perceptible click the blank face of the copper plate was replaced by a plaque bearing words. They were not inscribed in red but in black, the letters having been engraved with loving care by a patient short-fingered hand.

TIME, said the legend, IS THE GREAT HEALER.

Jehan let out his breath, having been unaware of the fact that he was holding it. His grandmother could hardly have objected to such an innocent adage. There was little enough piety about it, but there was certainly no diabolism.

Jehan became aware then that the clock was ticking as the pendulum swung back and forth, almost as if the machine had a beating heart. He was not afraid, however, that he had surrendered his soul to the mechanism while he worked to complete it. If he had lost that, he had left it somewhere in Paris, smeared on the bloodstained cobbles.

"It's a masterpiece all right," the dwarf stated, his tone indicating that he was only half-satisfied, as yet. "All that remains is to see how well it keeps time. I can compare it against my watch, for now, but in order to prove that it can do far better I'll need to calibrate it against the movements of the zodiac stars."

"A pity, then, that you rebuilt the façade in a room that has no window," Jehan observed.

"I can measure brief intervals accurately enough," the dwarf assured him. "The question is how well the clock will measure days and weeks. Even so, the more rapidly information can be conveyed between the clock and the observation-window, the better my estimates will be. You may help me with this too, if you wish. I hope you will – but if you would like to leave, to carry the secret of the pendulum to the cities of the world, you may go with my blessing."

"I'm in no hurry," Jehan assured him, "and I'm as interested as you are to see how accurately your clock keeps time."

What he had said was true; Jehan Thun was momentarily glad to have the prospect of further work to do – even work that could not possibly absorb his mind as the intricate labour of delicate construction. Any hope that it might permit him to extend the quasi-mechanical phase of his own existence was quickly dashed, however. Indeed, the work of attempting to calibrate the clock against the movements of the stars was worse than having nothing to do at all, for it involved a great deal of patient waiting, which made the time weigh heavily upon his mind. Waiting called forth daydreams, memories and questions, as well as the horrors of St Bartholomew's Eve and its hideous aftermath.

For weeks before his arrival in Andernatt Jehan had been walking, not with any rhythmic regularity but at least with grim determination, never laying himself down to sleep until exhaustion had robbed him of any prospect of remembering his nightmares. For days after his arrival at the château he had been able to focus his attention on demanding tasks, which had likewise been devoid of any kind of rhythmic regularity, but had nevertheless supplied him more than adequately with opportunities for grim determination. Now that the clock was finished, though, he could not use the time it mapped in any such vampiric fashion. Its demands were different now, not suppressing thought but nourishing and demanding it, forcing him to fill the darkness of his own consciousness with something more than blind effort.

At first, there was a certain fascination in scurrying back and forth between the dwarf's observatory and the room where the clock was entombed, to check the position of the hands against the position of the stars. Perhaps – just perhaps – there might have been enough activity in that to keep dark meditation at bay, if only the sky had remained clear. But this was a mountainous region where the air was turbulent, and the sky was often full of cloud. It was not always possible for the dwarf to make the observations he needed to make, and although the dwarf was philosophical about such difficulties, they preyed on Jehan Thun's mind, teasing and taunting him.

There was also a certain interest, for a while, in discovering what was inscribed on the other plaques, which had been hidden from Jehan while he worked on the completion of the clock by their housing. He did not see them all within the first twelve hours of the clock's operation, nor even the second, but it only required two days for him to see each of them at least once, and thus to reconstruct their

order in his mind. One o'clock brought forth the legend
CARPE DIEM. Two o'clock supplied TIME TEACHES
ALL THINGS. Three o'clock suggested that TIME OVER-
TAKES ALL THINGS. Four o'clock claimed that THERE
IS TIME ENOUGH FOR EVERYTHING. Five o'clock
observed that TEMPUS FUGIT. Six o'clock warned that
OUR COSTLIEST EXPENDITURE IS TIME. Eight
o'clock advised that THERE IS A TIME FOR EVERY
PURPOSE. Nine o'clock pointed out that FUTURE TIME
IS ALL THERE IS. Ten o'clock stated that EVERYTHING
CHANGES WITH TIME. Eleven o'clock was marked by
TIME MUST BE SPENT. Midnight and noon alike,
perhaps reflecting increasing desperation in the expansion
of the homiletic theme insisted that TIME NEVER WAITS.

All in all, Jehan Thun concluded, while there was nothing
among the legends to which a good man could object, there
was also nothing as adventurous or imaginative as the blas-
phemies that his grandmother had seen . . . or imagined
that she had seen.

He had not thought to question the dwarf as to what he
had read before discarding the allegedly blasphemous ones,
but now he did. "Was there really one that said: *Whoever
shall try to make himself the equal of God shall be damned for
all eternity?*" Jehan asked his host, while they were gathering
apples in the orchard one day.

"I can't remember the exact wording," the dwarf told
him, "but I think not. The sayings were pithier than that,
and more enigmatic. Do you not approve of mine? I'm a
clockmaker after all – or would be, if I had not been cursed
with the body and hands of a clumsy clown. A clock ought
to symbolize time, do you not agree? Common time, that
is, not the grand and immeasurable reach of eternity."

"Even common time reflects the time of the heavens,"
Jehan observed. "The movements of Creation spell out the
day and the year, with all their strange eccentricities."

"The stars are mere backcloth," the dwarf informed him,
as he moved off up the slope with his basket half-full. "The
Earth's rotation on its own axis specifies the day, and its

rotation about the sun defines the year. The eccentricity of the seasons is a matter of the inclination of its axis."

"So says Copernicus," Jehan agreed, "but how shall we ever be sure?"

"We shall be sure," the dwarf told him, "When we have better clocks, more cleverly employed. Calculation will tell us which of the two systems makes better sense of all that we see. Better mechanisms will give us more accurate calculations, and more accurate calculations will enable us to make even better mechanisms."

"And so *ad infinitum*?" Jehan suggested.

"I doubt that perfection is quite so far away," said the dwarf, smiling as he set his basket down by the door. "And I doubt that mere humans will ever attain to perfection, even in calculation – but there's scope yet for further improvement. The milking-goat is tethered on the far side, where the grazing is better. Will you come with me to soothe her?"

Jehan agreed readily enough, and they went around the ruins together, to the side that looked out towards Évionnaz. They saw the platoon of soldiers as soon as they turned the corner, for the approaching men were no more than a thousand paces away. The men – a dozen in all – were heading directly for the château.

"That's Genevan livery," the dwarf said bleakly. "Not that a party of men carrying half-pikes would be a more reassuring sight if their colours were Savoyard or Bernese."

"Their presence may have nothing at all to do with the château, let alone the clock," Jehan said, although he could not believe it. He knew, as he watched the armed men coming on, that he had spoken his name too often during his brief sojourn in the city. He had stirred up old rumours and old memories that had been too shallowly buried, even after all this time. Someone had begun asking questions, and exercising an overheated imagination. The dwarf's presence here might not be widely known, but the little man had been to Évionnaz and other villages in the vicinity; the suspicion that he had been joined at Andernatt by Aubert

Thun's grandson had been the kind of seed that could grow into strange anxieties.

"They're soldiers," the dwarf said, "not churchmen. They have lived with clocks all their lives. They cannot be so very fearful." But he too sounded like a man who could not believe what he was saying. He had been a wanderer before settling here; he knew what fears were abroad in a world torn apart by wars of religion. He knew, probably better than any man of common stature ever could, how often people spoke of witchcraft and the devil's work, and what fear there was in their voices when they did so. He knew that Geneva was a city under permanent siege, where all kinds of anxiety seethed and bubbled, ever ready to overflow.

"We should run and hide," Jehan said. "They will not stay long, whatever they do while they are here."

"No," said the dwarf. "I shall receive them as a polite host, and speak to them calmly. I shall persuade them, if I can, that there is nothing here to be feared. What manner of man, do you think, is the one who bears no arms and who seems to be guiding them?"

Jehan shaded his eyes against the sunlight and squinted. The dwarf was presumably afraid that the man walking with the captain at the head of the column might be a churchman, but he was not. "I know him," Jehan said. "He's a colporteur by the name of Nicholas Alther. Our paths crossed on the far side of Évionnaz, and he guessed where I was bound. He told me he'd seen the ruins of the château on the horizon. That may be why they brought him as a guide – but he didn't seem to me to be a fearful or a hateful man."

This judgment proved not unsound, for as the party came closer Jehan was able to read in Nicholas Alther's face that he was certainly not the leader of the expedition, and that he would far rather be somewhere else, about his own business.

"I know him too," murmured the dwarf. "I've seen him in Évionnaz, and bargained with him for needles and thread – and metal-working tools, alas." Raising his voice, the little man added: "Ho, Master Alther! Welcome to my home. Where's your pack?"

Alther did not reply, but thumped his chest to imply that he was out of breath in order to excuse his rudeness. It was the captain who spoke, saying: "This is not your home; the land belongs to the city of Geneva, and the ruins too. You have no right here."

"I am doing no harm, captain," the dwarf replied. "I make no claim upon the land or the house; I merely took shelter here when I was in need."

"Is your name Pittonaccio?" the captain demanded.

"No," said the dwarf. "It's Friedrich Spurzheim – and Spurzheim is a good Swiss family name, worn by many a man in Geneva and even more in Bern. I'm a Christian, as you are, and I have my own Bible."

It was the first time that Jehan had ever heard the dwarf's surname – and he realized, as he heard the little man's fore-name spoken for the second time, that he had never addressed him by it, or even thought of doing so, since he had first heard it pronounced. He had always thought of his host as "the dwarf."

The captain did not repeat the name either. "Where is the Devil's clock?" he demanded.

"I doubt that the Devil possesses a clock, or needs one," Friedrich retorted, boldly. "If he does, he certainly does not keep it here. The only clock here is mine."

Jehan was not in the least displeased to be offered no credit for the restored Clock of Andernatt. He had seen the expression on the captain's face before. There had been soldiers abroad on St Bartholomew's Eve and the day that followed; there were always soldiers abroad when there was killing to be done, for that was their trade.

Jehan felt fingers plucking at his sleeve, and allowed himself to be drawn aside by Nicholas Alther.

"It was not I who betrayed you," the colporteur whispered, fearfully. "They do not know that I met you on the road. For the love of God, don't tell them. I could not refuse to lead them here, for they knew that I knew the way, but

I mean you no harm. Say nothing, and they'll let you alone
– but you must say nothing, else we'll both be damned."
He stopped when he saw that the captain was looking at
him, and raised his voice to say: "This man only took shelter
in the château – he has nothing to do with the clock."

The captain immediately fixed his stare on Jehan's face.
"Are you Jehan Thun?" he demanded.

"I am," Jehan replied, knowing that it would do no good
to lie.

"What business have you here?"

"I was a Protestant in Paris, until it became impossible
to be a Protestant in Paris," Jehan said, flatly. "My father
was born in Geneva, which is a Protestant city, so that was
where I came – but everywhere I went in the city, people
who heard my name looked strangely at me, and I was afraid
all over again. My grandmother had spoken of a village
named Évionnaz as a remote and peaceful place, so I decided
to go there, but when I arrived I found the same dark stares,
so I continued on my way. Friedrich Spurzheim is the first
man I have met hereabouts who did not look at me that
way, and he made me welcome as a guest."

"Are you a clockmaker?" the captain asked.

"No," Jehan said. "I'm a printer. I made Bibles in Paris.
My father was murdered, my press smashed and my home
burned."

"Have you seen the Devil's clock?"

For the first time, Jehan hesitated. Then he said: "There
is only one clock in the château. It is shaped to resemble a
church. There is nothing devilish about it."

"Lead us to it," the captain instructed.

Jehan exchanged a glance with Friedrich; the little man
risked a brief nod of consent. Jehan led the way around the
château, through the garden and in through the door on
whose step the basket of apples still lay. Then he led the
captain and his men to the Clock of Andernatt.

It was an hour after noon; while the soldier was studying
the clock, the hour struck and the words CARPE DIEM
appeared, as if by magic, in the space beneath the rose window.

"What does that say?" demanded the captain of Nicholas Alther, his voice screeching horribly.

"I don't know!" the colporteur replied.

"It says *Carpe Diem*," Friedrich told them. "It's Latin. It means *Seize the Day*. The other mottoes . . . ."

But it did not matter what the other mottoes were, any more than it mattered what *carpe diem* actually signified. It would have made no difference had the motto been in French or German rather than Latin, or whether it had been a quotation from the Sermon on the Mount.

Much later, Jehan guessed, the captain and all of his men would be willing to swear, and perhaps also to believe, that the mysterious legend that had appeared as if by magic had said HAIL TO THEE, LORD SATAN or DAMNATION TO ALL CALVINISTS or CURSED BE THE NAME OF GENEVA, or anything else that their fearful brains might conjure up. They would also be willing to swear, and perhaps also to believe, that when they attacked the clock with half-pikes and maces, sulphurous fumes belched out of its myste-rious bowels, and that the screams of the damned could be heard, echoing all the way from the inferno. They would probably remember, too, that the château itself had been buried underground, extending its corridors deep into the rock like shafts of some strange mine, connected to the very centre of the spherical Earth.

When they had finished smashing the clock the soldiers smashed everything else Friedrich Spurzheim had owned, and cast everything combustible – including his printed Bible – into the flames of his fire. They killed his milking-goat, and as many of the others as they could catch. They ripped up all the vegetables in his garden and stripped the remaining apples from his trees. Then they smashed the shutters that remained on some few of the chateau's windows, and the doors that remained in some few of its rooms. But they did not kill the dwarf, nor did they kill Jehan Thun. They worked out all their ire and fear on inan-imate objects, and contented themselves with issuing dire warnings as to what would happen if Friedrich Spurzheim or Jehan Thun were ever seen again within twenty leagues of Geneva.

Afterwards, when the captain and his men were preoccupied with the items they had kept as plunder – which included, of course, the silver disc that had served as a pendulum bob – Nicholas Alther took Jehan aside again, and offered him something wrapped in silk. Jehan did not need to unwrap it to guess that it was the colporteur's watch.

"Your grandfather made it," the colporteur said. "You should have it, since you do not have one of your own. It keeps good time."

"Thank you," Jehan said, "but it isn't necessary. You owe me no debt."

"I didn't betray you," Nicholas Alther insisted. "I didn't want this to happen."

"I know that," Jehan assured him, although there was no way that he could.

"I won't repeat the tale," the colporteur went on, in the same bitter tone. "If this becomes the stuff of legend, it shall not be my doing. There will come a day when all this is forgotten – when time will pass unmolested, measured out with patience by machines that no man will have cause to fear."

"I know that, too," Jehan assured him, although there was no way that he could.

When the soldiers had gone, Jehan went back to the clock's tomb. Friedrich was waiting for him there.

"One day," Jehan said, "you will build another. In another city, far from here, we shall start again, you and I. You will build another clock, and I shall be your apprentice. We shall spread the secret throughout the world – all the world. If they will not entertain us in Europe, we'll go to the New World, and if they are madly fearful of the devil there, we'll go to the undiscovered islands of the Pacific. The world is a spinning sphere, and time is everywhere. Wherever men go, clocks are the key to the measurement of longitude, and hence to accurate navigation. What a greeting we'll have in the far-flung islands of the ocean vast!"

The little man had been picking through the wreckage for some time, and his clumsy hands had been busy with such work as they could do. He had detached half a dozen of the plaques from the wheel that was no longer sealed in its housing. Now he laid them out, and separated them into two groups of three. TIME OVERTAKES ALL THINGS, TEMPUS FUGIT and TIME NEVER WAITS he kept for himself; THERE IS TIME ENOUGH FOR EVERY-THING, THERE IS A TIME FOR EVERY PURPOSE and FUTURE TIME IS ALL THERE IS he offered to Jehan. "I'd give you the pendulum itself," Friedrich said, "but they stole it for the metal, and the escapement too. It doesn't matter. You know how it works. You can build another."

"So can you," Jehan pointed out.

"I could," Friedrich agreed, "if I could find another home, another workplace. The world is vast, but there's no such place in any city I know, and wherever there are men there's fear of the extraordinary. It's yours now; you're heir to Master Zacharius, and to me. You have the stature and the strength, as well as the delicate hands. The secret is yours, to do with as you will. The world will change regardless, so you might as well play your part."

"Wherever we go, we'll go together, Friedrich," Jehan told him. "Whatever we do, we'll do together, even if we're damned to Hell or oblivion."

And he was as good as his word – but whether they were damned to Hell or oblivion we cannot tell, for theirs is a different world than ours, unimprisoned by our history; all things are possible there that were possible here, and many more.

AUTHOR'S NOTE.

Jules Verne is rather vague about the exact time-period in which the events of "Master Zacharius" take place and exactly what kind of escapement mechanism the Genevan clockmaker is supposed to have invented. So far as history is concerned, though, small spring-driven clocks and watches were reputedly invented by Peter Henlein *circa* 1500; given

that "Master Zacharius" takes place before Calvin's refor-
mation of Geneva, that implies a date somewhere in the
first two decades of the sixteenth century. Verge escapements,
consisting of crossbars with regulating weights mounted on
vertical spindles, had been in use in weight-driven clocks for
some time by then, so the escapement credited by Verne to
Zacharius must have been either a stackfreed (a kind of
auxiliary spring) or a fusée – a conical grooved pulley
connected to a barrel round the mainspring.

The latter invention is usually credited to Jacob the Czech
circa 1515; I have assumed that to be the device Verne might
have had in mind, but I have also credited Zacharius with
manufacturing a fusée in brass, although history has no
record of that being done before 1580. The discovery of the
isochronicity of the pendulum is, of course, credited by our
records to Galileo in the early seventeenth century; pendulum
clocks first appeared in our world *circa* 1650 and were first
equipped with recoil escapements ten years thereafter, some
87 years later than the device credited to Friedrich Spurzheim
in the story.

"Master Zacharius" was one of the earliest stories Verne
wrote, and embodies ideas that he subsequently set firmly
aside; this sequel is, I think, far more Vernian in the best
sense of the word.

SIX WEEKS IN A BALLOON

Eric Brown

Verne's first novel, Cinq Semaines en ballon, *was a huge success, not simply because of the book itself, but because of several associated publicity stunts. One in particular was by Verne's friend Félix Tournachon (usually called Nadar) who planned to emulate the adventure in the story and fly a balloon from Paris across Europe to Africa. He never made it, getting only as far as Hanover, but it captured the imagination of the French who blurred fiction and reality and treated Verne's work as a real story, which forms the basis for the following tale. Over the years there have been many who have taken Verne's tales as true, because he was able to blend scientific achievement so faultlessly into a story that it was wholly believable. Well, usually. We'll come to* Hector Servadac *later. It was this success that established Verne's reputation, and assured the confidence of his publisher, Jules Hetzel, cementing a relationship that would last for thirty years.*

I arrived in Glasgow from the west coast on the 8th of February, 1930, and made my way to the British Dirigible Company depot on Sauchiehall Street, intending to catch the noon flight for London.

It was a short walk from the bus station, but I witnessed much poverty and degradation on the way. Entire families made their homes on the pavement, and my progress was impeded by the incessant importuning of child-beggars. I gave them what little change I had in the pocket of my threadbare overcoat, and in doing so experienced a curious, double-edged guilt. I felt guilty for being unable to give more and, paradoxically, for being in the situation where I could give at all.

I arrived at the dirigible depot, which was guarded by both black-shirted militia and a division of the local constabulary, with seconds to spare. The last of the passengers were crossing the swaying drawbridge on to the gondola, and I just had time to buy an early edition of the *Herald.*

The purser gave me a resentful look as I proffered my ticket and hurried across the drawbridge to the *Spirit of London.* I wondered whether it was my tardiness or the state of my overcoat that had roused his ire.

The gondola was only half-full and I found a window seat with ease. Ever since German planes had downed the *Pride of Benares* last year, the public had shied away from air travel.

A klaxon sounded. Hawsers whipped away from capstans on the platform. With a sudden lurch we were in the air, floating silently over the bomb-sites and the few remaining tenements standing after the recent blitz.

Already I longed for the solitude of my island retreat. The crass advertisements which decorated the interior of the carriage sickened me with their creators' assumptions that the populace might be so easily tempted. Outside, the eye was offered no respite. The ruin of the city gave way to the slag heaps of the country, with pathetic stick-figures scratching for coal and whatever growing thing might be stewed in the pot. Even the air of this benighted land sat heavily upon my chest.

I opened my notebook and reread the first lines of the poem I was working on: *As I stood at the blackened gate/With warring worlds on either hand* . . .

For the next hour I reworked the line and then, tired,

tried to absorb myself in the *Herald*. War coverage predomi-
nated – the usual exaggerated claims of success, with little
actual analytical reportage of the politics behind the conflict.
But what did I expect, with the newspapers of Great Britain
in the strangle-hold of the capitalists?

I tossed aside the rag and pulled from the inside pocket
of my coat the letter which was one of the reasons for my
journey south.

*Dear Sir, Ever since reading your piece on the war and its
evil in the* New Statesman, *I have considered writing you this
letter. A very long while ago now I was involved in a series of
events which became famous after being published in a book by
my master, Dr Samuel Fergusson. You will know this book as* Six
Weeks in a Balloon, *published in 1863. It is these events about
which I wish to speak to you. Such is the nature of things at the
moment – and I am sure I need not spell out my meaning – that
I feel constrained from revealing my thoughts herein, but if you
were able to make the trip to London I would most gratefully
receive you and apprise you of my story.*

Signed, Joe Smith.

The letter was intriguing in itself. Why might Joe Smith
wish to tell me, a lowly journalist, about his balloon adventures in Africa? I had read the book – who had not? – and
was aware of it as another piece of Imperialist propaganda,
all the more obnoxious for its xenophobia.

I was also aware of its influence on events at the time,
and the significance it had played in exaggerating Anglo-
German enmity ever since.

I was more than intrigued by the line in his letter, *Such
is the nature of things at the moment – and I am sure I need
not spell out my meaning – that I feel constrained from revealing
my thoughts herein.* What heretical inside story might the
loyal manservant have to tell me of that famous balloon
journey taken nearly seventy years ago?

I witnessed an ugly incident as I stepped from the London
depot. Night had fallen and with it the temperature, and I

was one among hundreds of citizens who, bundled up in their winter wear, departed the station and hurried into Baker Street. Most were so intent on thoughts of home that they failed to notice the fracas across the street, either that or they effected not to notice.

Six militiamen had arrested a pamphleteer and were giving him a beating for his troubles. At one point the man fell to the ground, and a militiaman stamped upon his face, again and again. I made to cross the road, if not to intervene physically, then to register my vocal protest, when I felt a hand grip my upper arm like a tourniquet.

"Caution, Comrade. There's nothing you can do but get yourself arrested, and we need men with conscience for the coming fight." And before I could catch a glance at my interlocutor, he thrust a pamphlet into my hand and became one with the flowing commuters.

The militiamen were carrying their victim, dripping blood now, to a waiting black Mariah. I stood, buffeted by the crowd, and glanced at the pamphlet. *Revolution!* It proclaimed: *Workers must Unite* . . .

The pamphlet was the crude propaganda of the British Communist Party, and I dropped the paper and hurried south through the darkened London streets.

As I walked, I despaired at the plight of my country, gripped as it was between rapacious capitalists on one hand and on the other the heedless lackeys of Stalinist Russia.

I had given no thought to Smith's Kensington address when I received his letter. Now, as I turned into the wide, affluent street and paused outside the three-storey Georgian town house, I wondered for the first time how Fergusson's manservant had found himself elevated to such palatial accommodation. He would be well past retirement age now, and so presumably was not still 'in service'. My curiosity was piqued.

The bell was answered by a middle-aged housekeeper who, when I introduced myself, said that Mr Smith was expecting me.

I was escorted up a flight of wide stairs to a mahogany

door on the first floor. I must have looked out of place, in my stained overcoat and farm boots, amid such bourgeois decadence.

The housekeeper opened the door, announced me, and invited me to enter.

After the February chill of London, the heat of a blazing log fire hit me in a wave. The second thing that struck me was what filled the room. Maps and navigational charts covered all four walls, between bookshelves stocked with bound journals and atlases. Occasional tables and bureaux held globes and scale models of balloons and dirigibles.

Last of all I noticed my host, who rose from an armchair beside the fire and advanced with a smile and an outstretched hand.

Joe Smith, the trustworthy servant of Dr Samuel Fergusson, who more than once risked his life for that of his master – and how I had scoffed at that upon reading the book in my youth! – was a short, square, thickset man of ninety-five, but with the vigour of someone thirty years his junior.

"Glad you could make it, sir!" he beamed. "Can I get you a drink?"

"A whisky – and please, call me George," I said, a request he later ignored.

He poured me a whisky. Joe Smith's speech, I noted, was true to his working class roots. I had feared from the tone of his letter that I might find someone affecting the manner-isms of the class he had spent so much of his life serving.

Glass in hand, I admired the room, or rather the models of balloons, dirigibles, and all manner of airships that filled it.

Joe stood beside me, hardly reaching my shoulder. "Quite a collection," I murmured.

He smiled. "Dr Fergusson's," he said, "like everything else in the house. I didn't have the heart to get rid of anything when he passed on."

I recalled the extended news coverage of Dr Samuel Fergusson's death, of heart failure at the age of eighty, some twenty years ago. I had not mourned his passing.

"I still find it hard to think that he won't walk though the door at dinner-time and demand his first whisky of the evening."

"Dr Fergusson left the house to you?" I asked.

"The house and everything in it, as well as almost half his fortune."

"And you couldn't bring yourself to move out?"

He smiled, and murmured something about this being his home.

I was overcome by the urge to tell the feisty retainer that his loyalty was no more than a Pavlovian response to his extended slavery. I managed to hold my tongue.

Joe Smith talked me through the collection of flying machines, each replica lovingly reproduced in the tiniest detail.

The journalist in me, recalling my summons here, took over. "Have you any doubt at all that the technological progress in the seventies and eighties, the development of airships from balloons to navigable dirigibles, was largely down to the popularity of Fergusson's book?"

"No doubt about it at all!" Joe Smith said. "You should have seen all the hullabaloo after the book was published! Of course, you're too young to have been around then. My word, the commotion! The house was besieged by pressmen and well-wishers and all! What a sight! And the lectures! Dr Fergusson was booked up two years solid with appointments at this institute and that, all the way from Brighton to Aberdeen."

We took our seats before the roaring fire, and Joe Smith went on, "And scientists and inventors – they beat a path to Dr Fergusson's door. Later he even sank some of his own money into a company manufacturing the early steerable balloons."

I shook my head. "All from the publication of a single book," I said, hoping to direct Joe back to the reason for his summons.

My words seemed to have the desired effect. He reached out to a bookshelf beside his armchair and withdrew a calf-bound volume of *Six Weeks in a Balloon*.

I said, "Do you agree that what Fergusson wrote also contributed to the deterioration in relations between Germany and Britain at the time . . . ?" And in consequence, though I did not add this, to the present chaotic state of world affairs?

Joe had been leafing through the volume, a reminiscent smile playing on his lips, and he looked up at me almost sadly.

"That is true, sir. Little did I realize at the time that the adventure of crossing Africa might have such far-reaching consequences." He paused. "Of course, if the telling of our momentous journey had concentrated *only* on our crossing, then the world might not now be at war."

I took the book from him and leafed through the pages, stopping at Chapter Seventeen: *The Germans Attack – Kennedy Injured – Treachery! – A Close Shave – We Escape the Hun!*

A colour plate showed the *Victoria*, and its intrepid crew of Dr Samuel Fergusson, his friend Dick Kennedy, and loyal manservant Joe, under attack from German guns.

I wondered if chapter seventeen, and a later account of German bellicosity in chapter twenty-five, might have been the most incendiary words ever written on the subject of Anglo-German relations.

"You should have been around to witness the scenes, sir! The cabinet was recalled, if I remember rightly. The German ambassador to London was summoned to Downing Street."

"But the Germans denied all responsibility," I said. "They even claimed that they didn't have troops in that part of Africa."

Joe looked at me, his gaze steady. At last he nodded. "And they were right, sir."

I lay my whisky aside. "What?"

Joe cleared his throat. "That, sir, is what I wanted to see you about. I have had it on my conscience for a long time now." He laughed to himself, but without humour. "Can you imagine what it has been like, to live with the knowledge of the terrible lie for almost seventy years?"

"The terrible lie . . ." I repeated.

"We crossed Africa, sir, from Zanzibar to Senegal, and in all that time we came upon but one serious attack, and that by the Arabs in the southern Sahara."

"But chapter seventeen, all the detail . . ."

"All lies, sir. The Germans did not have an expeditionary force on the banks of the Nile, still less did they attack us."

"And chapter twenty-five? Where Fergusson reported watching a platoon of German infantry attack a Berber encampment, and then turn their attack upon the *Victoria* . . ."

"Again, sir, a fabrication, inserted into the book with the express intention of inflaming nationalistic passions and creating enmity against the German state."

"It certainly worked," I murmured. As a direct result of the passion provoked by German hostility reported in *Six Weeks in a Balloon*, and subsequent press reports of German atrocities in the continent, British positions in Western Africa were strengthened. This precipitated the strained relations between the two nations for the rest of the 1800s, which in turn brought about the eventual war, which began in 1908 and had been going on ever since.

Joe Smith rose and crossed the room to a small Sheraton bureau, from which he withdrew a sheath of documents. He carried them back to the fire and laid his cargo upon the table.

"The original manuscript of *Six Weeks in a Balloon*, sir, the first typescript, and the second script which included the inserted fictional chapters. I discovered these among my master's papers shortly after his death."

I picked up the hand-written manuscript and turned a couple of pages. I looked up at Joe. "But they're in French."

Joe nodded. "Dr Fergusson was acquainted with a French writer at the time, one Jules Verne, who he employed to write up a rough account of our adventures."

I shook my head. "I'm not aware of the name."

"Verne wrote three or four science-based adventure stories for boys, before his death from typhoid in 1870."

I turned my attention to the typescripts. The first, I took

it, was a direct translation from the French. I leafed through the pages until I found Chapter Seventeen, which recounted the balloonists' flight over that region of Africa known as the Mountains of the Moon.

I picked up the second, bulkier script. Chapter seventeen was headed with the familiar: *The Germans Attack*, etc.

Joe Smith said, "When Verne handed in the first draft, Dr Fergusson consulted General Gordon, and several ministers in the cabinet. Only then did he rewrite chapters seventeen and twenty-five." Joe Smith looked up at me, almost shamefacedly. "He swore me to secrecy. He said he was changing the story for the good of the Empire . . . And who was I, an uneducated manservant, to object?"

"I wouldn't blame yourself, Joe. You were a dupe in the power of evil forces."

"Lately, sir, I've been thinking, and looking at the state of the world, and I came to realize that what Dr Fergusson did was wrong." He shook his head. "It's too late to make reparations, sir, but the least I could do was ensure that the truth was known before I passed on."

"The promulgation of truth is always honourable."

"I've read your journalism. It strikes a chord. You write with integrity. I knew you were the man to approach."

"I'm flattered —"

Joe Smith smiled. "I'm an old man, sir. I want you to publish the truth, and damn those in power. They wouldn't harm a citizen nearing ninety-six, would they?"

I felt my throat constrict. His faith in the honour of the ruling regime was at once terribly innocent and dangerously optimistic.

"I wouldn't publish anything while you might suffer the consequences," I said.

Joe poured me another whisky and we talked for a further hour.

"The other evening," he said, "I was attempting to list the benefits that might have come from the war. I could think only of the improved transportation system!"

I smiled. "There have been medical advances, too. The

cure of tuberculosis has saved many a civilian life, as well as those of soldiers returning from the war."

I turned my attention to his bookshelves, stocked with the leather-bound volumes of Dickens and Trollope.

He noticed my interest. "I like a good novel, sir. Have you by any chance written a . . . ?"

I interrupted. "I have many a good idea," I said, "but hardly time to commit them to paper. Perhaps one day, when the war is over . . ."

I noticed Palgrave's Golden Treasury on his shelf, among other volumes. "You enjoy poetry too?"

"It is one of the consolations of old age," Joe said. "My favourites are the War Poets, Owen, Graves, Sassoon, all dead now, alas." He indicated a dozen back numbers of the *Adelphi*. "I enjoyed your poems, too, until the government closed down the magazine."

"The dabbling of an amateur," I said, "though I rather think I will be writing more verse at the front."

Joe Smith looked shocked. "You've been called up?"

"I volunteered. I join my regiment in the morning." I paused, and felt an explanation was due. "People often mistake patriotism for nationalism, Joe. I love England, but hate what she is becoming. I believe that we are facing a terrible evil in the new Germany that's emerging from the old order, even if the war was originally based upon a lie. Mussolini is making pro-German noises, and the German minister of Foreign Affairs is an evil schemer called Hitler who'll soon be in power. As reluctant as I am to pitch in my lot with the blimps in charge of this benighted land, Joe, I feel I must do my little bit."

I finished my drink, consulted my watch, and made my excuses. "I have an early start . . ."

We stood and Joe showed me to the door. "It has been an honour talking to you, Mr Orwell," he said.

"The honour has been mine, Joe."

As I stepped out into the freezing night, Joe Smith quoted, "'There may not always be scientists, but there will always be poets' . . ."

I paused. "I don't recognize the line."

"From *Six Weeks in a Balloon*, sir."

"Dr Fergusson wrote that?" I asked, surprised.

Joe Smith laughed. "The line is Jules Verne's," he said.

We shook hands, and I took my leave of the worthy Joe.

It was only a mile to the cheap hotel I used when in London, and I elected to walk. Turning my collar up against the wind, and murmuring to myself, "*There will always be poets . . .*" I squared my shoulders and set off into the dark and freezing night.

LONDRES AU XXIᴱ SIÈCLE

James Lovegrove

*One of the great discoveries in recent years was of a lost novel
by Jules Verne. Not a latter-day, unpublished one, but an early
one.* Paris au XXᵉ Siècle *had been completed in 1863, so must
have been his second novel, but was rejected by Hetzel partly
because he believed the predictions would not be believed. Verne
buried the manuscript in a safe and there it remained until discovered by his great-grandson in 1989. Here Verne really had let his
imagination take free rein and his vision of the future is remarkably prescient. Perhaps it was because the work was rejected that
Verne subsequently kept his stories within the close parameter of
the plausible and as a consequence whilst we had more believable adventures we lost the true technological predictions. The
book is as much a travelogue of the future as Verne's later books
became travelogues of the Earth in the present. As such it leaves
itself open for satire, as the following story shows.*

[Editor's Note: With the discovery of Verne's early "lost"
novel of 1863, *Paris au XXᵉ siècle*, came the simultaneous
discovery of a hitherto unknown sequel, judged to have been
written in 1904, toward the end of the writer's life and

career. The event aroused little excitement in Vernian circles simply because, whereas *Paris* . . . was an intact manuscript of some 200 pages (complete with margin notes by Verne's regular editor Hetzel), the manuscript of the belated sequel was burned – in all likelihood by Verne's son Michel – and survives only as a set of charred fragments. The title page itself has been lost but we may reasonably infer from the content that the novel is called *Londres au XXIᵉ siècle* (*London in the Twenty-First Century*). Reinforcing this supposition is the fact that the story features the same protagonist as *Paris* . . . , Michel Jérôme Dufrénoy, still a poet but now an older and much sadder and wiser man than the self-martyring young firebrand of the previous novel. We present here the full extant text of *Londres* . . . , commending it to readers not only for its many startlingly accurate prognostications, so typical of Verne, but for its brevity, so untypical of Verne.]

pp. 3–5
/"M Dufrénoy," said Mr Smith the publisher, "I have run a thorough analysis of your verse collection on my totalizer and have been served with a statistical conclusion that backs to the hilt my professional instincts. The book has been subjected to every form of critical and linguistic computation available. Every word, every phrase, every rhyme, has been scrutinized by the machine and checked against the preferred standards. It is as if your poetry has been looked over by a thousand of the most median public minds, appraised by a thousand pairs of eyes that recognize what is 'popular', what will sell."

"And the result?" said Dufrénoy, although the publisher's tone of voice and down-turned lips had already given him his answer.

"Alas, the sales projections for the book are minimal. Indeed, the totalizer predicts that not only will we sell less than a dozen copies but those dozen copies will almost instantly find their way into second-hand bookshops, from where half of them will be sold again and half thrown away after sitting untouched on the shelves for a year. In effect, we will sell a negative number of copies, as it is predicted that the half-dozen volumes purchased from the second-hand shops will be bought by the very people who passed them on to the second-hand shops in the first place, forgetting they used to own this selfsame book a short while earlier. You see, the totalizer's assessment of your poetry is that it neither captures the imagination nor lodges in the memory. Therefore, with regret, monsieur, I must tell you that Smith and Daughters respectfully decline to be your publisher."

"But," expostulated Dufrénoy, "you are saying that because your machine informs you my poetry will not sell, you are not prepared to attempt to sell it!?"

"Why does this come as a surprise to you?" replied Smith with a calm gesture. "You know that we in publishing are in a business, much as everyone is in a business these days. Who, in 2005, can *not* afford to be in a business? Thus we employ statistical projection methods to enable us to judge what books we should and shouldn't put out. Our margins for error are fine. We cannot financially afford the least slip-up."

"So you will publish only something which you know beforehand people will buy?"

"Is this so strange?"

"But you base your judgements on a mechanized distillation of public taste."

"Exactly!" said Smith, rubbing his hands with satisfaction. "The totalizer is programmed to reflect nothing but the essence of the average man's and woman's literary likes, that which the busy person will choose to flick through while speeding to the office by pneumotube or the holidaymaker will idly read while lazing beneath the sun-like arc lights at an indoor vacation lido. Which is not to say, M Dufrénoy, that your poetry is bad. On the contrary, in my opinion it is excellent. Beautiful, limpid, elegant, exquisitely expressed, and above all original. 'Original', however, is what we cannot afford. 'Original' is the last thing anyone needs. 'Original', to put it finely, is not a marketable commodity."

Dufrénoy was stunned, although in truth he had not

expected any other response. It was, after all, his one hundred and fifteenth rejection by a publisher, and by now he was becoming/

pp. 17–18
/his twelve-year-old grandson Michael had come to visit, transported for the weekend from his home on the Kent marshes where he lived in one of the towns magnetically suspended above the floodplain, the "hovervilles" as they were known. Michael was a reluctant guest at his grandfather's since the apartment was mean and dingy and situated near the base of a seventy-storey dwelling complex in run-down Muswell Hill. Little sunlight penetrated down through the urban canyons to the lower-level abodes, hence illumination down there had to be provided by sulphur-gas streetlamps which burned throughout the day as well as the night, shedding an unsteady bronze glow and a Hadean odour. Michael was accustomed to skies that reached from horizon to horizon and air that was constantly freshened by sea-borne breezes. The city, and especially his grandfather's part of it, was to him a fusty, almost subterranean place, and his infrequent visits were conducted out of a sense of duty and with a greater than usual pre-adolescent surliness which even Dufrénoy's most strenuous efforts at inculcating jollity could never dispel.

For the most part the boy sat and watched entertainments on Dufrénoy's videophote set, a particular favourite of his being a song-competition presentation in which contestants with little or no musical talent vied to deliver the blandest possible rendition of some popular standard, their goal being to cause the least trouble to the ear of the listener and thus gain greater approbation than their rivals. Another of Michael's preferred pastimes was a battery-powered toy, the Game Wallet, manufactured by the Worthington Novelty Company of Newcastle. This bauble consisted of a steel box with an inset window in which, by means of an ingenious development of Brownian motion, tens of thousands of phosphorescent vapour particles were manipulated electrostatically to form images. The images, controlled by magnetic cards purchased separately, presented the player with various games and puzzles to be solved, from relatively straightforward old standbys such as Hangman and Noughts and Crosses to more abstruse fare such as Moon Cannon Target Practice and Transglobal Travel Time Challenge.

Dufrénoy would look on with something close to despair as his grandson played with his Game Wallet often for hours at a stretch, mesmerised by the fizzing luminous patterns, thumbs manipulating the box's brass control keys with blurring dextrous speed. How alien the boy seemed to him, a creature not merely from a different generation but from a different planet as it were! What did Michael know of books? Of literature, of culture? Very little, it appeared. Such things were not required learning at school any more, where the subjects of science and economics were pushed to the fore, to the detriment of all others. It pained Dufrénoy to think that all the/

pp. 49–50

/and from there the protest march wound southward along Whitehall toward the gates of Downing Street, where it halted and the protestors set up a chant, brandishing placards and stamping their feet. They called for the Prime Minister to emerge from his residence, which eventually he did, capitulating to their demands with a bleary, sheepish grin on his face. Dufrénoy could scarcely believe it. He didn't know which was more astounding: that the Prime Minister had the nerve to face members of the electorate after the heinous crimes he had committed, or that the protestors were not baying for the man's blood but rather *objecting* to his decision, announced earlier in the day, that he intended to resign. He had said that morning at a press conference that he considered his position untenable in the light of the revelation that he had slaughtered his wife and children in cold blood (as proved by the fact that several eyewitnesses had come forward to testify that they had personally seen him standing over the bodies, knife in hand, bathed in gore). Moreover, the Prime Minister had said, it did not behoove the nation's representative on the world stage to be a convicted rapist and the recipient of several sizeable bribes from corporations involved in shady dealings, as revealed in an exposé in one of the newspapers yesterday. Indeed, anyone who, like him, appeared in covertly-taken photographs, some of which showed him cavorting with prostitutes of both sexes and others of which depicted him belabouring a member of His Majesty's Opposition with a crowbar in a backroom at the House of Commons, was not the slightest bit deserving of high office.

The people, however, ardently felt otherwise. For the Prime Minister was nothing if not a man of immense charm and charisma, whose face, not least when viewed via videophone transmission, had a convincingly handsome and self-assured demeanour to it, indeed a kind of saintliness which endeared it to any who set eyes on it; not to mention his voice, which exuded a desire to be trusted and which worked on the machinery of the soul in much the same way that a mechanic could work on the engine of an antigravity aircraft, finding its faults and fine-tuning them out of existence.

And so there was great joy among the crowd of protestors when he came out from Number 10 to address them, and even greater joy when the content of his speech was a solemn statement to the effect that he had, after consultation with his Cabinet and much soul-searching, decided to recant on his previous decision and not resign after all. The joy turned to delirium when he added that he was going to postpone the General Election which was due next year, pushing it back to the year 2011, in order to allow greater time for his policies to take effect.

Dufrénoy strode away in disgust, remembering the time back in 1968 when he was still a resident of Paris and there had been unrest among Parisian students for a similar reason, namely that both the President and the Prime Minister had tried to resign after an adultery scandal that saw them having an extramarital affair, not in itself unusual among French politicians, but *with each other?* While the old-guard establishment was demanding the two men's heads on a plate, the radical youth of Paris urged the exact opposite, and thus was sparked off the practice, now widespread across the world, of politicians attempting to outdo one another in the egregiousness of their misbehaviour while still maintaining the goodwill of the electorate. It was for that reason that Dufrénoy had emigrated from France, thinking that surely among the sober, staid British such temptations to flout the public trust would be at the very least resisted, if not/

pp. 84–85
/and hard as he tried, Dufrénoy could not halt them from entering his apartment. There were ten of them pressing against the door, and he was but one elderly man.

"Good morning, sir," said the leader of the advertising troupe, proffering his card, which read Albion Home Improvement Supplies Ltd. "We shan't take up much of your precious time, I promise." As he spoke, the other members of the troupe were rapidly setting up scenery, unfurling backdrops from suitcases and pinning them to screw-together steel frames, and pumping air into inflatable rubber props such as furniture and plants. In very short order they had created a kind of impromptu stage in Dufrénoy's living room, and divesting themselves of their overalls, to reveal costumes underneath, they began to act.

Dufrénoy had little alternative but to sit and watch as the advertising troupe ran through a series of playlets, each outlining a domestic scenario which might require the remedial application of some product or other available from Albion Home Improvement Supplies Ltd., for instance the installation of an extra layer of glazing in bedroom windows to prevent infants dying of hypothermia during a savage cold snap akin to the one that gripped France for three years in the 1960s, or the introduction of new kitchen apparatus to appease an irked wife who was struggling to cook meals on outmoded and antiquated oven equipment. That the

widower Dufrénoy obviously lived by himself and was
patently too old to have infant children was of no consequence to the troupe, who had a job to do and did it regardless of the status or circumstances of the person into whose
home they had barged their way. It must be added that their
performance was somewhat perfunctory and listless as a
result of their having to deliver it, on average, twenty times
a day, five days a week. It had gathered, one might say, rust
and a certain unevenness of function, as will any device used
repetitively, constantly, and without thought. Dufrénoy
himself remained unmoved by the actors' efforts, apart from
a small tear of bored frustration that crept from his eye
toward the end. He would rather the gigantic billboards that
covered the side of many a tower block and dwelling complex,
the videophone commercials with their endless jabbering
singsong refrains, the troubadours on the pneumotube who
strummed their guitars to commuters and extolled the virtues
of a particular brand of dentifrice or "gentleman's invigor-
ation pill" – anything to this thespian intrusion into his
apartment, this invasion of his living space and his psychic
space as well, that invaluable free area of the mind into
which daily the wormy efforts of the advertisers were making
deeper inroads/

pp. 120–121

/lamenting that he barely had time to compose poetry any
more. He was of pensionable age but, having worked sporad-
ically and to little profit during his lifetime, he found himself
with scant funds to retire on, and so was obliged to eke a
living by whatever means he could. Currently this entailed
a kind of literary piecework, Dufrénoy employing his skills
with pen and paper to furnish the less verbally gifted with
articulacy. In other words he was a ghost-writer, not of
fiction nor even of non-fiction but of letters, *curricula vitae*,
job applications and other such mundane communications.
The working man and woman had little need of or love for
literacy and the written word, but in some areas of life a
better-than-basic grasp of language was still desirable, and

that was where Dufrénoy came in. The irony of him, an expatriate Frenchman, being more fluent and accomplished in the tongue of Shakespeare than most Englishmen, was not lost on him.

It was not lucrative work, since there were many others like him who offered the same service. Payment was low and grudgingly given because people understood that this was something they *ought* to be able to do for themselves, and hence furtively resented having to hire someone else to do it on their behalf. Dufrénoy earned pennies at a time and yet counted himself grateful. But each hour that he spent drafting a note of complaint or a bank loan request for some unlettered stranger was an hour he did not spend marshalling words into sonnet-form or iambic pentameter, *rime riche* or blank verse, painting emotion with the colours of the alphabet, expressing the agony and loneliness of his life with all the syntactical precision and sensory honesty he could muster, searching for new and different modes of/

pp. 137–138
/came to him, like the shock of being doused with ice water, that instead of the father regarding the son as a disappointment, as was commonly the case, here the roles were reversed and the son was of the view that everything his father had ever been or done was a source of shame.

For Jerome was now as unlike Dufrénoy as it was possible to be. It wasn't merely that his name was accentlessly anglicised, for that was expectable and acceptable; the lack of acute and circumflex, though, was symptomatic of much else. Jerome was without distinguishing mark, nothing stood out on him, he had been planed and smoothed to fit in with twenty-first century British life, he was reduced, whittled, ordinary. He worked at a bank in the City, as Dufrénoy himself had once been a bank clerk (before that terrible, embarrassing incident when he spilled ink on The Big Book). But where Dufrénoy *père* had found bank work hard and dispiriting, Dufrénoy *fils* adored it. He boarded the gun-fired Bullet Train at Romney station each morning with the eager, carefree air of a man going on a jaunt to the seaside, and chortled as the explosive detonation set the train hurtling along its track on frictionless runners with near-concussing force. The ten-minute journey to Liverpool Street was, for Jerome, an opportunity to prepare for the tasks of the day ahead. He would get his brain churning with some mental arithmetic, adding five-figure numbers together and making compound-interest calculations, so that, like an athlete arriving at the starting blocks, he would be warmed up and ready for the nine-till-five race that awaited him when he reached his workplace.

Jerome, nearly forty, was prospering and well on course for a junior partnership by forty-five and a senior partnership by fifty. His life was following a perfect arc of development, almost as if it had been designed that way by a totalizer. He had a pretty wife and two lively children, and all of them loved him unquestioningly. Given his upbringing, and especially the temperamental instability of his father, it was nothing short of a miracle that he had turned out so totemically normal.

"Then again," Dufrénoy mused with some chagrin, "it is always the case that we turn and become that which our parents are not." Jerome's rebellion against his paternal exemplar had seen him throwing himself wholeheartedly into the embrace of conformity, and in/

pp. 169–171

/heatwave held sway for the next five years. The streets sweltered and piles of urban dust silted up in the gutters like grey-black snowdrifts. The Thames dried up and its cracked-mud bed became a venue for sunbathers and intrepid promenaders. After a while a new sport developed, whereby the winds that sometimes howled inland along the dead river's course were put to use propelling wheeled yachts. Landlubber seamen would hoist sail and hurtle at speeds of anything up to fifty knots along the desert-like channel, veering between the pilings of the many bridges. Meanwhile the sun glared down on London like an eye that would not close. Even at night-time there was a memory of its blaze in the still-parched air and the perturbingly bright moon. Some people said the world was coming to an end, which would have seemed feasible but for the fact that elsewhere on the planet weather patterns remained normal. It was Britain alone that was affected by the heatwave.

There was, naturally and inevitably, a slow exodus to other countries that in time became a stampede. Once a few rats were seen to abandon the sinking ship, all the rats wanted to leave. The crops were failing, year after year, and the price of imported food rose steeply as other nations took advantage of Britain's desperate straits and imposed swingeing tariffs. In the dwelling complexes like the one Dufrénoy lived in, people started dying. Starvation was the principal cause of death but the heat took many victims as well – the very young, the very old, the already sick, those in general too weak to cope. The sight of corpses piled on street corners, rotting in the heat, became so commonplace that even from the faintest-hearted it failed to elicit so much as a wince. Rats proliferated, bringing disease and, worse, the threat of attack, for in their hordes the rodents became bold and would band together and pick off those solitary individuals, usually tramps and children, who seemed most defenceless and least threatening. London's famous pigeons likewise turned feral, until soon Trafalgar Square and various other landmarks were no-go zones for the capital's citizenry. The verminous grey birds would swoop without warning, whole flocks of them pouncing on human prey and pecking and scratching their victims to death, whereupon the pigeons would feast lustily and greedily on their kill. It was a time when the natural order of things was well and truly out of kilter. The balance of existence was wrong.

Dufrénoy survived largely by virtue of the fact that he was inured to deprivation and suffering, indeed this had been a characteristic of his life almost since birth, and even in old age he was hardy and phlegmatic, a veteran of countless campaigns against vicissitude. Jerome had taken off to France with his family, neglecting to invite his father to join them in exile, but Dufrénoy did not hold this against him. All too clearly, all too painfully, he understood his son's choice, and he respected it.

There was no let-up during those years of Britain's tribulation, until finally, like a ghost from forgotten times, the rain came. The sound of its pattering was so unfamiliar that for a while people did not comprehend what this noise portended, this gentle hissing from the sky, the soft wet plashing of droplet after droplet upon baked stone surfaces and dust-velveted roads. Nor did they truly fathom why the sunlight had faded. They had forgotten what clouds were. They thought this dimming of the day an unnaturally premature twilight. Some fancied that it was, at last, The End.

It was certainly the end of the drought. Down came the rain, and thunder grumbled distantly in low/

pp. 203–205

/and I shall be a living poem," said Dufrénoy to himself, "a testament to all that London is and has been."

Who is to say that his insanity was not, in truth, the clearest-eyed sanity conceivable? Certainly, as he clambered up the face of the billboard, Dufrénoy had never experienced such a sense of pure, exhilarating omniscience. The higher he rose, the more apparent the patterns of existence became to him. The city was lines, London a vast page upon which forty million individuals wrote their life-poems, in their hearts, inside their heads, almost without being conscious of it. Bombarded from all sides by noise and demands on their time and their pockets, by advertisements perpetually clamouring for their attention and the relentless pressure to spend and buy and possess, by the panoply of capitalism arrayed in all its chrome and gilt splendour, by messages of want that undermined their self-confidence and made them feel incomplete, *still* they resisted, fighting a rearguard action in the depths of their souls as they struggled to cling on to that last vital, intact part of themselves that the moneymen and the corrupt bureaucrats and the avaricious plutocrats so badly wished to reach and conquer. You would not know it unless you looked deep and hard into their eyes. Even in the dullest of gazes, the deadest of expressions, you might find it. The Great Heat had tempered people, tested their mettle and forced them to rediscover an inner flame which had almost, almost gone out. In Dufrénoy the flame had continued to burn more or less constantly, although it had many a time guttered and nearly failed, for example back at Père-Lachaise cemetery, beside de Musset's tomb. But it flared nonetheless, unquenchably, and now he understood that he was not alone; and he was not a poet. He was poetry. Everyone was poetry.

On he climbed, using the cigarette-smoking bas-relief figures on the billboard as his rockface, ascending by means of handholds and toeholds found in their pitted steel surfaces, the ridges of their fingers, the contours of their faces and hair, till at last he gained the summit and the whole of London seemed spread out at his feet, man's fantastic creation, an epic of brick and metal and glass.

He wanted to shout his ecstasy across the rooftops but he was out of breath and dizzy with vertigo. He hung on to the billboard's top edge while the shadows of whirring airships passed over him and the wind whipped at his clothes. He could let go, he could fall, he could die, and perhaps he would, but not now, not yet, not till this moment of triumphal revelation had passed, and maybe it would not, maybe it would never pass, maybe it would last for ever.

For London was different now, new life crackled in its electric nervous system, new blood pulsed along its roadway arteries. One could tell. One could smell it. The citizens who had deserted the city were back in their droves, and more besides, foreigners who had ridden in with the returning wave, scenting a wiped-clean slate and fresh opportunities. Of the forty million and more who lived in the capital these days, a quarter at least were immigrants from other lands who brought with them their own mores and traditions. Now there were Turkish markets on the streets of Islington, Mongolian restaurants in the borough of Richmond, Latvian vendors hawking their wares on the paths

of Hyde Park, Nigerians and Congolese playing music down
at the Wapping docks and the Isle of Dogs, Polynesians
setting up cafés on every bridge from Tower Bridge to
Teddington, Argentines touting their services as rugby
coaches to the children of the well-heeled, artists from
Montmartre erecting their easels on the South Bank (coming
to be known as the *Rive Sud*), and London was welcoming
and subsuming them all, happy again to be a place where
people wanted to be, glad to have a plenum of inhabitants
once more.

Possibly no one saw this – truly saw this – but Dufrénoy.
He alone of all Londoners, a one-time immigrant himself
but now more of a native than most, understood his home
city's renaissance. This New Jerusalem! And the old man
atop the billboard need never write another line of verse
again, because all around him/

[Editor's Note: There is no more. This last passage occu-
pies the anteprepenultimate, prepenultimate and penulti-
mate pages of the ruined manuscript. The final page is
unreadably singed, with just a single word legible at the foot:
"*Fin*". It can only be speculated whether Dufrénoy throws
himself from the billboard after all or else remains there in
perpetual suspense at the novel's close. The reader may
choose Dufrénoy's fate according to his/her own inclination.

Londres au XXIᵉ siècle is barely even a footnote in the
Verne canon. There are Vernian scholars who reckon it is
not actually the master's work at all but rather his son's, for
in Verne's declining years Michel assisted with the writing
of the novels and may well have authored some of them
wholly by himself. In the light of this, the section which
details the father's being a disappointment to the son can
be seen, perhaps, as a riposte by Michel to Verne's anguish
over the waywardness and lack of achievement of Michel's
early years – Verne junior getting his own back in literary
form. In which case, one might go so far as to venture that
it was out of guilt that Michel set fire to the manuscript, if
indeed he was the culprit – guilt brought on by the death

of his father in 1905, not long after *Londres . . .* was completed. Could Michel have come to regret creating that closing image of an elderly writer who has all but abandoned his craft, hanging on to a vast billboard by his fingertips while a post-apocalyptic vision of a "New Jerusalem" feverishly fills his head?

Were there more of *Londres . . .* in existence, one might be able to form a cogent opinion. As it is, an unmistakable whiff of mortality and remorse permeates the few crisp-edged clusters of pages we have. As with every burned work of art, it is as if the creator has been immolated along with the creation. This much, in the end, is all we can assume – that Michel Verne, grief-stricken, consigned the manuscript to the pyre and then had a last-minute change of heart and rescued what he could before the artefact was fully destroyed. He thereafter kept hold of the remnants as though they were relics of his own father. Even the loved ones whom we haven't loved as much as we should, should be remembered as if we loved them completely.]

GIANT DWARFS

Ian Watson

After his failure to sell Paris au XXe Siècle, *Verne returned first*
to the war novel, with Les Forceurs de blocus *(not published*
until 1865), better known as The Blockade Runners, *and to*
the adventure novel with Les Anglais au Pole Nord *(1864),*
the first of the Captain Hatteras stories featuring a highly atmos-
pheric journey into the far North. While writing this novel Verne
became intrigued by the theory propounded many years earlier
by Captain John Symmes of Ohio that the Earth was hollow
and that there were entrances into the Earth at both the North
and South Poles. The idea had led to a satirical science-fiction
novel, Symzonia *(1820) by the pseudonymous Adam Seaborn*
and, more importantly, had inspired Edgar Allan Poe, who used
the idea in The Narrative of Arthur Gordon Pym *(1838),*
which Verne had recently read and would later continue with the
sequel Le Sphinx des glaces *(1897). Verne approached the*
concept of a hollow Earth with his usual scientific thoroughness
and produced one of his best novels, Voyage au centre de la
terre *(1864). Here Professor Lidenbrock and his nephew Axel*
follow clues left by the explorer Arne Saknussemm and descend
into the bowels of the Earth via a volcano in Iceland. Far below
the surface they discover a vast subterranean sea and witness sea
monsters and a giant humanoid. For the first time Verne had

allowed himself to go beyond the facts into the fanciful and produced his first great novel of science fiction. It launched what became known as Verne's "Voyages Extraordinaires".

The next two stories reconsider the novel from two entirely different perspectives.

Twenty-five leagues beneath the surface of the Earth, I certainly never expected to be rescued from troglodytes by *Germans*. My amazement would grow the greater as I became acquainted with those same Germans! Ah but whatever my reservations about Monsieur Verne's character I should take a leaf out of his book and begin at the beginning of the tale . . .

In the Dordogne, some thirty-five leagues inland from Bordeaux, Pierre and I were cantering across grassy upland near the village of Montignac-sur-Vézères when all of a sudden his chestnut stallion Pompey collapsed and Pierre was thrown right over the horse's head. Immediately I reined Diana in, jumped down and ran to Pierre, crying, "My love!" Pompey was squealing horribly. I could see that his front legs had disappeared into the ground, into a crevice that had opened up. Pierre was already scrambling to his feet.

"Be damned!"

He seemed winded, for he paused to collect himself – by stroking his moustaches. What an elegant figure of a man. I loved his wavy brown hair and piercing blue eyes. Captain Pierre Marc-Antoine Dumont d'Urville, soldier, explorer, adventurer.

"Are you all right, my love? Your ribs, your everything?"

"My pride is injured, that's all, Hortense. Mark you, this was not Pompey's fault."

We'd had some spirited discussion about the respective merits, or demerits, of Pompey and Diana. Poor Pompey, he was suffering such pain.

So far as Pierre could tell by peering then reaching into

the hole, both of the horse's trapped legs seemed badly broken. Pierre stood up decisively.

"He's ruined – and in misery." He unholstered his bulky revolver.

Monsieur Verne was later to study that revolver with some interest, and it plays a subsequent role in this narrative too (all be it only as a cosh), so maybe I should say something concerning it. Our genius of an author loves to describe in detail technical and scientific matters. I should match my humble story-telling skills to his redoubtable ones. Seriously, I mean it. I'm always willing to learn.

A thousand of the unusual revolvers had recently been manufactured in Paris, where Pierre had managed to procure one. Although I wasn't previously much interested in guns, Pierre had been keen to show off his acquisition to me, like a child with a new toy – and I have a very retentive memory for facts. The invention of a French-born doctor named le Mat – in support of the Confederate army in the civil war currently raging in America – the revolver in question sported two barrels. The larger central barrel would fire grapeshot. A slimmer barrel would fire bullets coming from a nine-chamber cylinder revolving around the central barrel. The nose of the hammer was movable to accommodate this double action. Should you happen to be faced by a mob, Pierre had explained, the spread of shot would cause multiple damage and cool ardour. Such a revolver would be valuable in penal colonies, not to mention should you suddenly come upon several partridges feeding together and wish to bag them all.

"Look away, Hortense!"

"Certainly not," I replied. "Do you think I will faint or have hysterics, like your wife?"

Pierre shrugged and fired a single bullet. Some blood and tissue sprayed from Pompey's head, which promptly slumped.

Just as well I did not look away, for it was as if the deto-nation was a trigger. Or the reason may have been that Pompey's now dead weight shifted. The ground gave way more so. Pierre and I both needed to jump back. Pompey's entire body slid into the widening hole, disappearing from sight. Moments later, a muted thump sounded from underground.

What I now know to be called a *doline* had opened up, a "swallow-hole" through which rainfall would in future drain into a subterranean cave. That is the geological explanation for what had happened: we had been riding the horses on top of a system of caves and part of a cave roof had given way.

Since no further collapse seemed imminent, Pierre lay down and inched forward cautiously to inspect. Of course I joined him in this.

"Go back, Hortense. Our combined weights may –"

"I wish to see."

In fact there was little to be seen. The sun shone brightly from a sky containing only a few white woolly clouds, but below was darkness. Soon we both withdrew, stood up, and brushed our clothes. By now the dark brown mare had ambled over and was staring at the hole from a safe distance. Diana pawed with one hoof. Her nostrils flared. What might she be thinking or feeling? At its best the Tarbenian breed is very intelligent as well as brave, with graceful action, elegance and endurance – quite like myself, perhaps? The trouble is that the breed requires constant infusions of English thoroughbred blood alternating with Arab blood, or else it tends to degenerate, retaining of its ancestral magnificence little but a thick heavy Andalusian neck. My grandfather bred horses, so I know more than a little about the matter, not to mention being acquainted with the saddle – *and* with bare-back riding – from an early age when most girls would play with dolls.

"Alas," said Pierre, "it seems that Pompey now has a grave, a natural one. However, I'm not some primitive chieftain who buries an expensive saddle along with his steed! We need a long rope and a strapping farmboy to assist me." He eyed my mount.

Promptly I said, "Diana'll carry us both, if I take it easy

– she isn't slack-backed. We'll leave her saddle here, and you can hold on to me."

"My dear, surely I shall take the reins!"

"Have you ever ridden bare-back before? Besides, *I* did not lose my mount!"

"Oh Hortense, you mettlesome filly!" Pierre burst out laughing – quite lasciviously. Doubtless he was remembering the previous night when he had ridden me, and vice versa. Of course Pompey's death was shocking and sad but we must retain our spirits and good humour. Pierre and I were well suited in this regard. Oh was I to remain forever merely a mistress? Of course there was the matter of his wife's large inheritance to which he would lose access – that inheritance had paid for his various adventures in exotic places.

I'm spending a little too long upon the start of this unparalleled adventure which we were about to share. Suffice it to say that we returned in company with a hulking, beefy-faced, and amiable lad called Antoine, me still riding Diana, Pierre maintaining his dignity upon a carthorse laden with rope, Antoine trotting beside us at no great speed, carrying an oil lantern.

Antoine obviously assumed that he should descend into the abyss on behalf of the posh gentleman. Without further ado he began roping himself to the sturdy carthorse. But I intervened. I was lighter and slimmer – surely it was more sensible for me to go down? Pierre wouldn't countenance this. He himself would make the descent while the lad controlled the carthorse, *if*, that is, I didn't feel reluctant to be left alone with the lad.

So it was that presently Antoine and I heard Pierre shouting from below that, in the light from the lantern, he could see big pictures upon one wall of the cave, of bison and other beasts – vivid pictures in red and black and violet. Other pictures were visible along a passage which led from the cave in a downward direction.

"I must see where that passage leads!" he called up to us.

It was a full hour before my Pierre returned, amazed, to the cave, and thence to us who had awaited him – Antoine phlegmatically so, I with increasing concern. Had there been a second lantern, I swear I would have gone in search of my lover.

Numerous weeks were to pass. Professors of Prehistory were to visit our discovery, the hole now rendered safe by timbers, and a simple stairway constructed. One professor declared the cave paintings to be tens of thousands of years old because the animals depicted were extinct. Another denounced the pictures as a hoax – though of course *not* perpetrated by Captain Dumont d'Urville, who was well-known as an adventurer but also as a man of honour.

Pierre was much less excited about those pictures, vigorous but primitive, than about where that tunnel led to. On his first sortie he had reached an underground river, alongside which a wide ledge provided ample safe footage. Wisely he had returned before the oil in the lamp was half-consumed.

On a second sortie, with obliging Antoine as porter, Pierre reached an underground lake. What he was soon calling "the route" took a sideways twist into a passage running through geological formations differing from the limestone hitherto. A route indeed! – for if a passage forked, presenting an ambiguous choice, a small stick-like figure scrawled in ochre often pointed faintly. Presently that route began to descend through rocks more impervious to water. Ever to descend!

How could it be that our primitive ancestors – or one ancestor such, of genius and courage – had penetrated so far? Obviously the cave artists used something to light their work. Perhaps a small bonfire? They would be fairly close to the light of day, to some entrance which later collapsed, and it was difficult to imagine them carrying burning brands deeper and deeper into the bowels of the Earth. Phosphorescent lichen existed here and there in the depths but its light was very feeble.

Greatly enthused, Pierre contacted an acquaintance of his, the geologist Charles Sainte-Claire Deville, who was likewise an adventurer – he had explored active volcanoes such as Vesuvius and Stromboli. Monsieur Deville was already a member of the Academy of Sciences in Paris, and influential.

And lo, it transpired that Monsieur Deville himself was in correspondence with that young writer Jules Verne who had just recently caused quite a stir with his novel *Five Weeks in a Balloon*. Monsieur Verne was quizzing Monsieur Deville concerning questions of geology and volcanoes, because he was planning a new novel – about none other than a journey to the centre of the Earth!

Presently Messieurs Deville and Verne hastened to the Dordogne, to accompany us underground with suffiicent food, water, lamps and so forth (carried by Antoine) to allow for a return journey of four days in total. Yes, to accompany Pierre and Antoine *and me too*. I had insisted, and I had prevailed. I think Pierre was proud of me, even though he raised trivial objections such as regarding the privacy that a woman requires for matters of personal hygiene. What, in *darkness*? Actually, Verne was the one who most demurred about the participation of a woman in a scientific enterprise. I understood that Verne was married, yet at the same time I sensed, as women can sense in a way inexplicable to men, that in the past the author had experienced disillusionments which made him bitter towards my sex in general. Disillusionments, yes, though also excitements – a woman has instincts. However, Verne was a junior participant in this enterprise, under the wing of Deville. Deville and my Pierre were the men of experience; and for a fairly generous sum Pierre had bought the land which gave access to the cave. Verne was lucky to be invited to participate in our initial foray – and he was eager to do so.

"How," he exclaimed, "can I possibly contemplate writing about a journey into the Earth – when what I write may be contradicted by reality? But oh what a novel I shall now be able to write!"

Interestingly, according to Deville, half a century ago a bizarre American by the name of Symmes had sent a proclamation to the Academy of Sciences in Paris to the effect

that the Earth is hollow and habitable within, accessible –
so the American declared – by way of a big hole at the
North Pole. The Academy had responded scornfully and
declined to sponsor him.

Imagine us in the simple though adequate inn of Montignac-
sur-Vézères after we returned safely from those four days
underground.

Ah, I have not mentioned our small but powerful
Ruhmkorff chemical lamps, which were far superior to the
simple oil lamp with which Pierre originally descended, and
which wouldn't cause an explosion should we encounter
fire-damp – these, courtesy of a mine owner, at whose
mansion Deville sometimes dined. Visualize us: bearded
Deville, moustachioed Pierre, the clean-shaven Verne with
his curly dark hair, stalwart laconic Antoine – and me, tall
and slim, my dark hair gathered in a tight bun.

Those two days of outbound subterranean travel had taken
us some eight leagues in a generally north-easterly direction
into the roots of the Massif Central, and some three leagues
downward from our original height above sea level. Latterly,
our downward progress was increasing – and whenever we
encountered an ambiguous branching of routes, we would
find a stick figure as guide.

Jules enthused, "It seems as if we're being invited to travel
deeper – to the very centre of the Earth, just as in the novel
I'm planning! I chose Iceland as an entry point because of
volcanoes and empty lava tubes, but here there's an opening
in France itself."

Pierre nodded. "Certainly this merits a serious expedition, with supplies sufficient for several weeks or months."

"Might it be," I ventured, "that the stick figures aren't
the work of our primitive ancestors – but that the truth is
the reverse? Those guide-marks were made by explorers from
within the Earth, venturing up to the surface?"

A tic afflicted Jules' left eye. His voice became clipped.
"I suppose next you'll suggest that these venturesome
troglodytes painted the bison and other beasts in the cave,

from sheer astonishment, or as a warning of what lives on the surface!" He was a man who could veer quickly from witty bonhomie to irritability.

"Perhaps it's wise," I said, mildly yet stubbornly, "to entertain all possibilities."

"Only within the bounds of scientific possibility, my dear lady! What would these denizens of the underworld feed upon? Sheep abducted from the surface?"

"What of the legends of fairy folk abducting people and taking them underground?"

"So you believe in fairies!"

"I only wish to keep an open mind."

"One that a wind blows through because it is mostly empty."

"That's damn'd unfair," said Pierre. "Hortense has a very full mind, uniquely her own."

"Full of fancies perhaps. Reason plays no part in feminine lives."

Diplomatically Deville asked Jules, "Have you read the work of Darwin, *On the Origin of Species*?"

"I only just bought the translation – I'm reading it at the moment."

"A sub-species of *Homo* adapted to life underground seems unlikely . . ." Deville commenced lighting a pipe.

"Still," said Pierre, "we'll be well advised to take revolvers and a good supply of gun-cotton too. Personally I'm glad of your suggestion, Hortense."

I smiled. "Let's hope we don't need to use the revolvers."

Pierre gaped at me. "*We?*"

Pierre led me aside.

"Taking you underground initially was an *indulgence*. Now we're planning in terms of weeks or months. Stern stuff, men's stuff."

I whispered, "If I don't go with you, I shall tell your wife everything! Including your opinion of her performance in bed. Then you'll have no money for gun-cotton or anything else."

He groaned. The noise was very similar to what I could evoke from him by other means. "My peach, this expedition of ours will be the talk of France – maybe the world! Journalists will seize upon your participation. Mathilde would be very stupid not to put two and two together."

"Maybe the expedition will make us all rich, then you'll have no further need of her!"

"Hmm," he said and played with his moustache.

"I shall go underground," I said, "a day before your official departure; so that no one will see me, and I'll await the four of you. I want an adventure such as no woman has experienced before! If my adventure must remain a secret afterwards, so be it. At least *I* will know what I have achieved."

"Verne won't like this. If the temperature increases progressively the deeper we descend, a man can strip to the waist . . ."

Men could be so illogical. "If heat increases progressively, then you won't be able to descend far or you'll melt. Verne must grin and bear me, or there won't be any expedition, so there! Fortunately Deville has a less nervous attitude towards women."

"You can be very stubborn." Nevertheless, Pierre's eyes twinkled.

Not all of our time since Pompey's demise had been spent at that village in the Dordogne. Pierre had affairs to attend to in Bordeaux, and he was obliged to spend some time with his wife even if Mathilde was accustomed to frequent adventurous absences on Pierre's part. I refer to Pierre's business affairs – our private affair could be conducted with perfect ease in Bordeaux where Pierre maintained me in a pretty apartment. Our jaunt to Montignac-sur-Vézères had been a special holiday outing because I love riding, and Pierre could hardly ride with me publicly in the city, or else tongues would wag. Anyway, by the tenth of September our expedition was fully provisioned and ready – and I made myself scarce, to spend a night underground all on my own half a league along our destined route, so that I shouldn't feature in the official photographs of departure. I wasn't in the least bit worried about the isolation nor the darkness. Next day I even conserved my chemicals until I saw the lamps of my fellow explorers approaching

Now I really must leap forward in time – back to where I began this narrative – skipping over many undoubtedly fascinating details of rocks and tunnels and shafts and galleries and caverns.

Six weeks had passed and we had journeyed in a mainly east-northeasterly direction for some 200 leagues, which put us almost directly underneath the Bavarian city of Munich – at a depth, by our manometer of compressed air, of an incredible 25 leagues. We imagined the bustle of Germans up on the surface, so remote from us (as we thought!) that they might as well have been on the Moon.

All of us were still fully dressed. As we descended, contrary to scientific wisdom the temperature had risen only moderately, then stabilised. Personally I would have preferred Antoine to shed some garments – not, of course, so as to admire his musculature, but because his clothes had become smelly with sweat, he being of all of us the most burdened . . . by a silk rope-ladder a hundred metres long, mattocks, pickaxes, iron wedges and spikes, long knotted cords, meat extract and biscuits. To a greater or lesser degree all of us were burdened – myself included; I insisted on this! – but Antoine was more weighed down than the rest of us. At the end of every Saturday's march he received payment for his labour. To his phlegmatic mind the money seemed the entire rationale for a journey which continued to amaze the rest of us, not least when we came . . .

. . . *to an underground sea of vast expanse!*
From the strand on which we stood the walls of an immense cavern stretched away to right and to left, into invisibility. Far ahead was a horizon of water – and we could see a long way because the very air seemed phosphorescently alive with light. Masses of cloud hid any view of a roof, those clouds stained kaleidoscopically (maybe I mean prismatically) by what must have been auroras at even higher

altitude. Widening out to half a league, the shore of this ocean was richly vegetated by ferns the size of trees and by umbrella-crowned trees which I saw to be enormous fungi. No wonder the air was invigorating compared with the tunnels that had led here! Perhaps for this reason – coupled with the release from two months' confinement in stygian natural corridors – I became headstrong, spurred by delight at the *aerial* denizens of this subterranean realm, namely butterflies rather than birds, butterflies of all sizes and hues, and dragonflies with huge wingspans such as must have flown in the forests of the Carboniferous Era and which still survived here hidden away beneath the earth.

Shedding my pack, I ran impulsively towards an enchanting yellow and purple lepidopterous creature half my own size that had alighted nearby upon the gritty loam, studded with pointy orange flowers such as I had never seen before, to suck at their sweetness. For a fanciful moment I almost took it for a fairy, and thought myself in fairyland.

"Come back, you stupid girl!" I heard Verne shout imperiously. "That may be poisonous! This isn't a dress shop!"

The papillon fluttered away, more as if swimming than flying – the air felt denser here than on the surface of the world. If it had been Pierre who called to me to observe caution, events might have transpired differently. However, it amused Pierre to give me my head. I was quite fed up with Verne's little volcanic explosions, so I followed the object of my admiration somewhat farther. Oh Verne was such a bundle of contraries! He could be perfectly charming one moment then the next moment so facetious and curt, fairly snapping at any dissent from his own viewpoint. Maybe his impatience and nervous tension was a sign of genius, but his bilious attacks and facial twitches made him less than the perfect travel companion. Though his insomnia would have made him a good sentry, had there been anything to guard against in the dark tunnels hitherto!

As I came closer to the enchanting papillon amidst the floral undergrowth, of a sudden I heard Deville call out, "Look, look!" He was pointing to the sea, offshore.

Peering between some giant tree-ferns I espied two monstrous heads rearing up from the water, one with a long toothy snout like a crocodile's –

"An ichthyosaurus!" I heard Deville shout –

— the other like a serpent –

"A plesiosaurus!"

The two monsters joined combat ferociously while the water foamed and sprayed, thrashed by oar-like flappers and tail-fins. Thank God that I hadn't rushed to bathe but had been distracted by beauty – and now I was doubly distracted by the battle offshore. Thus it was that I paid no attention to my vicinity.

Abruptly I was seized from behind by the thighs and by the waist and dragged backwards, losing my balance, too surprised to cry out. As I sprawled, *little men* swarmed over me – muscular naked little men, four, five of them, all as pasty white as could be! In those first moments I feared an animalistic rape of me, for the exposed male genitals of the dwarfs all seemed disproportionately large compared with the bodies. The eyes, too, bulged – such big eyes! Breath panted from barrel chests. You might have expected that sweat reeked too, but actually the smell was floral. These persons must bathe regularly in streams that fed the underground ocean and brush themselves afterwards with squeezed flowers – only a madman would venture into water where monsters dwelt such as were battling. A hand clamped over my mouth. Hands gripped my clothing, and I was lifted. The dwarfs were beginning to bear me away – for what purpose? Sexual? Cannabilistic? Sacrificial? All the while my companions evidently noticed nothing, so locked must their attention have been upon the prehistoric sea monsters.

I struggled and I writhed, but those dwarfs were strong and persistent. Giant fungi and tree-ferns shifted above me as I was borne backward through undergrowth. My captors uttered guttural words to one another. The idea came to me that they might regard me as a goddess and were carrying me away to be worshipped, confined in some primitive cave-temple. They would bring me offerings of fish, and of course there would be a priest whom I would come to understand and to cultivate till he would be quite in my thrall and who would co-operate in my escape. After returning to the surface I would exhibit the dwarf priest in Paris and I would become rich and famous, not least because of the memoir I would write, maybe with some assistance from Verne – if he could bring himself to offer this and if I could bear to accept it and to work with him to our mutual advantage. *Twenty-Five Leagues Under the Earth* might be a good title.

Maybe the priest would try to copulate ceremonially with me in that temple, to promote the fertility of his tribe! My vivid imagination summoned up the scene of degradation to which I might be subjected, perhaps many times – then an image, too, of myself giving birth in primitive circumstances to a dwarf who would be a vile caricature of me. By now we were crossing some open ground, perhaps quarter of a league distant from the place of my abduction. I bit the hand clamped upon my mouth, and as it jerked away from my teeth I screamed.

Did I hear a distant echo of my cry, from the lips of my dearest Pierre, distraught at my mysterious disappearance? I think that was an echo of my own cry bouncing from the mighty wall of the vast cavern. A new hand gripped my mouth even more firmly than before – new, I reasoned, since I did not taste any blood upon the palm. My bite had been quite savage. I could be *wild*, as Pierre knew well. In actuality the dwarfs had not behaved savagely towards me, not as yet – no blow had struck me. It was *I* who had been the savage, perhaps with due reason, but nevertheless. And, truth to tell, it was myself who smelled animalistic rather than my naked abductors. I had of course brought an adequate supply of good perfume for the journey, reasoning that I would need to mask bodily odours, but those big squat noses of the dwarfs probably detected the imposture. Carried away by the dwarfs like some princess in a fairy tale, I was such a mixture of fear and fancy and reason and rage.

Then I heard a sharp bang – and abruptly my right leg dropped, my boot striking the ground. Jerked sideways, I glimpsed one of my captors sprawling, blood gushing from his stout neck. As the echo of that first bang rebounded, I heard another such – and my left leg became free. Another dwarf was collapsing, blood running from his back. I assumed that my Pierre had found me already and had used one of the Purdley More rifles to deadly effect and with great accuracy.

In panic the other dwarfs let go of me. With a spine-jarring jolt all of me was upon the ground. Three dwarfs were running for the cover of vegetation. A gun chattered unbelievably quickly and yet another dwarf fell before the remaining two reached cover and disappeared. What sort of weapon could fire so quickly? Surely not any rifle, nor even the Colt revolvers. Circumspectly I lay still, as though in a swoon, squinting.

Three men, *who were not my companions*, ran towards me from out the undergrowth beyond. Two wore black uniforms, black boots, smooth steel helmets on their heads – and carried guns such as I never saw before. Imagine a black pistol stretched out almost to arm's length. The third man, who was shorter and stocky, wore black leather trousers and a jacket with many pockets flying open to reveal a holstered pistol at his hip – he clutched a rifle equipped on top with what looked like a miniature telescope. A roughly trimmed dark beard jutted from his chin at the same angle as his nose. Abundant short hair curled rebelliously.

Since it seemed these strangers were intent on rescuing me, I sat up.

The strangers – six in total – proved to be Germans. Thanks to visits during my adolescence to an aunt of mine in Alsace-Lorraine I was fairly conversant with the German language. So as not to keep the reader in suspense I shall state right away that these six constituted an expedition similar to our own, into the hollow Earth. Their starting point had been from deep labyrinthine salt mines in Poland just outside of Cracow, rock salt resting upon the compact sandstone which breaks surface elsewhere as the peaks of the Carpathian Mountains. But here ends all similarity between our own and *Ernst Schäfer's* expedition, as well as any anxiety that we had been preceded in our discoveries by Germans!

THEY HAD SET OUT IN THE YEAR 1943. Excuse me if I sound shrill: yes, *eighty years* after ourselves. Of course they were as astonished as I was by this incongruity, and disbelieved me at first.

"No," said Schäfer, their bearded leader, whose crack shots had killed two of the dwarfs without even risking grazing me. "It must be that you are from a subterranean colony of French people who have been here for a very long time, and who have lost track of the years." He surveyed my smart if rather soiled clothing, puzzled. "You were born down here, yes?" We were at their improvised camp, a recess in the cavern wall.

"Certainly not," I said.

I was much more easily persuaded of the futurity of Schäfer and his men on account of the equipment and the guns they had with them, and the way they introduced themselves – with such titles!

The leader was SS Hauptsturmführer Ernst Schäfer, zoologist, geologist, and veteran of Tibetan exploration, who wore on his finger a death's-head ring. Then there was Untersturmführer Karl Wienert, geographer and geophysicist. And Ernst Krause, cameraman. And Dr Josef Rimmer, geologist and diviner. Plus two tall blond soldiers – and porters – Schwabe and Hahn, who belonged to something called the Leibstandarte Adolf Hitler.

"The *what*?"

Schwabe clicked his heels. "We are the élite of the Waffen-SS who have the sacred duty to protect the Führer."

"Would that be the leader . . . of Prussia?"

"Of Greater Germany, which rules all Europe!"

I bridled. "Including France?"

"*Jawohl.*"

And evidently including Poland . . .

"And he's called Adolf Hitler?"

Of a sudden becoming an automaton, Schwabe angled his right arm high into the air, hand like a blade.

Schäfer finally conceded that I was telling the truth about my origin, and soon he became hectically enthusiastic in discussion with Wienert and Krause and Rimmer, the general drift of which I could follow . . .

Apparently the previous year (which I took to mean 1942) had seen an official expedition to some island in the Baltic led by a scientist called Fisher. Fisher believed that the world is hollow – but Fisher was sure that we all live on the *inside* concave surface of the Earth. So by projecting mysterious rays upwards, at the angle of Schwabe's salute, it should be possible to spy on the activities of the British Navy hundreds of leagues distant. The experiment failed, as Schäfer had foreseen it would. Yes, the world is hollow, but obviously we live on the outside surface, and deep beneath our feet, as was now proven, was even more *Lebensraum* than in the conquered lands of the East, or alternatively vast spaces suitable for slave workers – Jews and Slavs could be deported here. But, Gentlemen, kindly imagine the *military* implications of being able to travel back to an earlier year! Something that lay underground between Poland and France evidently intermixed or linked the present with the past. Powerful localised magnetic fields perhaps. The contours of our respective journeys may have traced out some potent pattern akin to a Tibetan mandala. I had noticed a pennant resting against the rock, a jagged hooked cross in a circle its emblem. Maybe the symbol was Tibetan. Tibet seemed important to these Germans.

The two "SS" soldiers soon went out on patrol, but it wasn't long before the two uniformed men hastened back, and Schwabe reported, "Hauptsturmführer, the body of the Untermensch has gone!"

As I quickly learned, Schäfer – who was very vain about his prowess with his Mauser rifle – had shot a dwarf a few hours prior to my rescue. He had shot it directly through the heart, so that Krause could photograph its unblemished head from several angles (using a wonderful future device known as an Arriflex hand camera) and so that Schäfer himself could make detailed measurements using callipers, to record in a notebook. Not wishing to share habitation with the corpse, the Germans had concealed it a short distance away for possible further study. Evidently other dwarfs had quietly sneaked close and carried the body away.

I now began to entertain a suspicion as to the true reason for my recent abduction by the dwarfs. The motive might not be that I should become the object of their carnal appetites (whether rape or cannibalism), nor yet that I should be kept as a goddess. They may have been taking me hostage in an attempt to protect themselves from further murders! Why should they have distinguished between French intruders and the German invaders of their cavern? A hostage would make sense.

"Excuse me," I said to Schäfer, "if you wanted pictures and measurements, why did you not ask? If only by mime! And you could have offered a gift – some food, or a mirror. A mirror might have been ideal."

I unleashed a veritable torrent. The dwarfs were degraded parodies of humanity far worse even than Jews! All that the dwarfs merited was extermination. Preceded by study – study was a scientific duty. These degenerates might well be descendants of the same dwarfs that once populated the Earth three hundred thousand years ago when there were three suns in the sky. They might be descended from a sub-race such as the Hottentots, but had lost pigmentation underground.

Scarcely could I believe that these were the countrymen of Goethe. Could reason have so departed from that world only eighty years in my future, at the same time as science had apparently advanced so much, as witness that wonderful camera? During our journey Deville and Verne had often discussed that book about the "evolution" of species by the Englishman, Darwin, which I mentioned earlier. By now I had some understanding of the ideas, since I'm quick on the uptake – not that Verne generally seemed to think so. It seemed to me that these future Germans had interpreted the ideas of Darwin strangely indeed, or maybe the German translation was wildly inaccurate! Purity of race was a veritable obsession with these new masters of Europe. I heard words from them such as superhuman, and subhuman. Schwabe and Hahn were certainly fine physical specimens, both of them tall strapping blonds (Hahn looked less fanatical). I think Schäfer compensated for his own lesser stature by throwing his weight around – he seemed driven and tormented by inner demons.

"The dwarfs have the lustfully sensual lips of Jews," Schäfer was saying. "If we had not rescued the Frenchwoman, they would undoubtedly have ravished her." He paused and stared at me. "Mademoiselle Hortense," he addressed me, "you are not by any chance Jewish yourself?"

"Would it matter if I am?"

"Answer me, damn it!" What a flash of temper. Not unlike Verne, come to think of it.

"My parents never mentioned such a thing to me." These Germans might aspire to the stature of giants bestriding future Europe, but in other regards, dear me.

"Hauptsturmführer," I said sweetly, "I think the little people kidnapped me as a way of protecting themselves from *you*."

The Little People: fairy folk, diminutive ogres . . . in tales of old that my Grandma told me such beings *did* kidnap people and take them under the Earth – and in the subterranean domain time behaved strangely so that a century might elapse during what to the abductee seemed only a weekend. Could it be that the dwarfs could exploit the temporal distortions underground, and choose to visit the surface during different epochs which to us were far apart? If so, I'd been right that long ago from our point of view they painted those pictures of animals in the cave we first ventured upon. Maybe from their point of view that was only a thousand years ago.

That the dwarfs went naked wasn't necessarily a sign of degenerate barbarity. Living among the giant fungi and treeferns and beautiful papillons was akin to dwelling in the

Garden of Eden in innocence. True, fierce toothy monsters swam in the sea . . .

But then, in the biblical Paradise there was at least one serpent.

And *Nazis* in this one. Such, I gathered, was the name of the political party which these Germans revered.

"Those dwarfs' lives are not worth living," snarled Schäfer.

"Everyone's life is worth living," I suggested, "to the person who is living it."

"Oh no it is *not!*" he shouted. Snatching up his rifle, he stormed out.

Dr Rimmer – the diviner and geologist – drew me aside, and appealed to me softly. "Please do not provoke Schäfer. He suffered a terrible tragedy. He took his young bride with him on a lake to shoot ducks. In the boat he stumbled and the shotgun went off by accident, killing her. This has made him bitter and unpredictable. Oh I would so much rather I was seeking gold in the River Isar."

"So it's *gold* you divine for, not water?"

The geophysicist Wienert overheard this.

"Listen to me, Rimmer: you and Himmler" (whoever *he* was) "would have caused every geologist in Germany to retrain as a diviner! That's the main reason you're here, to keep you out of harm's way. Stop entertaining the lady with fantasies."

"I was explaining . . . never mind. Do you suppose the dwarfs have a fixed abode, or are nomads?"

"An abode where they might keep golden treasure?"

"I was thinking about the Nibelung miners of legend. Those are dwarfs."

"Who, if I recall, wear aprons and don't go naked."

"Ugly creatures, by all accounts, yet very clever. Part of our collective Teutonic race-mind, eh? Why should that be so?"

When Schäfer returned, now sulking – he mustn't have shot a dwarf – I said to him, "Hauptsturmführer," for how absurdly pompous that title sounded, "the dwarfs that live here may be the clever Nibelungs of your German legends.

Don't they deserve some respect, or at least merit some caution in your dealings with them, rather than your simply shooting them?" I almost added *like ducks*, but this would have been to go too far.

Schäfer glared at me. "Did you *wish* to be ravished by them, then? You are no German woman, that's perfectly plain. France is a nation of utter immorality."

Oh-la-la, I thought.

"In fact," he went on, "I would expel you from our protection forthwith . . . !"

If it were not for the fact that . . . ?

Ah, if set free I might elude the dwarfs and tell my companions all about their German rivals, not to mention the mysterious twist in time which had brought our two parties together. Consequently I must remain a prisoner of the Nazi Reich.

Presently we ate – oily-tasting steaks from some amphibious creature which Schäfer had hunted, accompanied by boiled vegetation which Krause had spied a dwarf eating raw. Then Schäfer declared he was tired, consulted a steely bracelet-watch, and decreed night-time. The electric air of the vast cavern knew no darkness, but the Germans were methodical about observing day and night – as indeed we also had been during the everlasting darkness preceding our arrival here. Their day happened to end hours earlier than a French subterranean day. Hahn sat guard.

As I lay under the blanket upon the loam, waiting for the other Germans to fall asleep, I thought about the large eyes of the dwarfs. If eternal daylight – cavernlight – was usual for them, why did they have big eyes? Was it because the cavernlight was dimmer than sunlight, although after weeks of darkness it seemed bright enough to me? Or was it because the dwarfs spent a lot of their time elsewhere than in the cavern? What did they use to light their way, however dimly, in the tunnels? Lanterns of some sort? How little we knew of the lives of the dwarfs.

What had become of my companions? Wouldn't they have heard the gunfire earlier on, even if the battle between the monsters was preoccupying them? There had been no halloos. They must be searching in the wrong direction.

Finally I judged that all were asleep except Hahn. That vigorous young man may have spent a couple of months underground with no female company. I did hope he wasn't too pure in mind and body. Sliding closer to him, I whispered, "Manfred, I can't sleep."

Modesty forbids detailing my further enticing whispers, but presently he and I were some way from that recess in the cavern wall, half hidden by the fronds of small ferns.

"Your helmet . . . I can't kiss you properly."

So his steel helmet joined the gun lying close to us. I began to unbutton his uniform while his hands did things which I did my best to blank from my awareness. He was certainly muscular and eager, yet a man is at a certain disadvantage when his trousers descend below his knees, whereas when a woman's skirts are lifted she is not similarly impeded. Which of the two objects would hit Hahn's head harder: the discarded helmet, or the gun? Would the blow be hard enough? How exactly would I reach either of those while he was grasping and groping? If I gripped his jewels and squeezed hard, would he scream and wake the others? Perhaps persuade him to let me ride him? Would an SS man be ridden by a woman? Maybe this excursion of mine into acting was a big miscalculation.

As I struggled to decide, whilst seeming to struggle amorously, something descended violently nevertheless upon Hahn's head.

A hiss in my ear: "It's Pierre. What the devil are you up to?"

"Trying to escape, what do you think?"

"Hmm!"

Beside Hahn's concussed head lay Pierre's double-barrel revolver, of which he had let go. Pierre and I whispered, me urging the need to relieve the Germans of their weapons. Pierre saw the sense of this. I arranged the German helmet upon Pierre's head the correct way then I lifted Hahn's "submachine" gun while Pierre readied his pistol. Softly we trod toward the recess.

Schäfer promptly sat up "*So, Schwabe, have you emptied yourself* – ?" The helmet confused Schäfer only momentarily, and his hand darted towards his holstered pistol. I shouted, "Don't move or I shit," mixing up *scheisse* with *schiesse*, but Schäfer understood me well enough and desisted.

The others stirred awake.

Well, we did succeed in impounding the hunting rifle and Schwabe's sub-machine gun and the pistols of the three other scientists, but the Hauptsturmführer stubbornly refused to yield his own pistol.

"You will have to kill me first," he said.

Arrogance, pride – then I remembered about his dead bride and his anguish. I thrust this knowledge aside. Here was a man who believed in exterminating mortals he deemed lesser than himself.

"Leave us one gun," pleaded Rimmer. "The dwarfs . . ."

"You're superhuman, aren't you?"

We left the pistol, even though this obliged us to run off in some haste. Don't forget, Schäfer was a crack marksman.

Pierre led me to a grove of ferns, where Deville and Verne proved to be waiting, armed with our own Purdley More rifles and Colt revolvers. Hasty explanations on my part followed, astonishing everyone. They hadn't even seen any dwarfs – and they were flabbergasted by my brief account of the German expedition and its origin. Pierre at least had seen the Germans close up, and those guns of the future were persuasive evidence.

"We must return to our baggage," urged Verne. "Those dwarfs – Antoine might not cope. Time, time!" he exclaimed.

"It's several hours since we left Antoine," agreed Deville.

"Not that sort of time, man! I refer to the link with the future!"

The novelist was busy thinking.

As we made to leave, redistributing the weapons amongst us, a rustle in the undergrowth disclosed a dwarf. The naked being rose to stare at us intently, apparently unafraid, taking close account not merely of ourselves but of what we carried, and maybe counting the guns.

"Hallo!" cried Verne, but the dwarf turned and swiftly disappeared. Soon we heard a guttural voice answered by many other voices. When we returned to Antoine, for once he was deeply perturbed and crossing himself. He too had seen "little people." They in turn had watched him.

We decided that we should set off back to the surface as soon as we replenished our water supplies. Of meat extract and biscuits, ample remained. Dried fish would have made for welcome variety, but time spent in catching and drying was out of the question. A thorough wash would have been a delightful idea, but the Hauptsturmführer still retained his pistol.

Would he retain it for much longer? Much about the dwarfs was surmise on my part, but I think Schäfer had greatly underestimated them. I imagined a wave of dwarfs overwhelming the German camp. Somehow I did not think that the Germans would be killed. I imagined the Germans becoming chattels of the dwarfs, forced to labour for them. No, perhaps the dwarfs would march the Nazis to some point distant in time and release them on an Earth before human beings existed.

Within an hour we were lighting our way through darkness once again. Verne began to discourse about time and the future.

"If only some machine could be made to take advantage – a time machine . . . Hmm, we have a duty to warn France about the future ruled so evilly by Germans. Will people believe us when we only have a woman's word for it? We have the sub-machine guns. Our industrialists can copy those. Just imagine a larger, more powerful version mounted on a tripod. France will have an advantage in arms."

"An advantage," I pointed out, "*only* until other nations steal and copy – and that'll be soon enough. War will become an even more horrible slaughter. I say we should hide the German guns before we ever reach the surface."

"How typical of a woman to hide evidence!"

"And who *obtained* the guns?" I enquired ironically.

"And by what means?" Pierre murmured softly to me. "Hmm."

"Don't be silly. Was I supposed to wait feebly for rescue?"

"Future wars might indeed be terrible," conceded Verne. "When I think of the ten thousand workers killed in Paris in 1948 . . . It's enough to make one thoroughly misanthropic rather than hopeful – when there's so much to be hoped for from science! Ach, dominion by Germans who have twisted science to serve some racial madness . . . that cannot be. Without the weapons, what proof have we? Yet the weapons will produce evil."

Ah, my opinion was now his opinion. "Plainly we must warn the world. Nevertheless, the tangling of time seems almost incredible."

As we steadily made our way back to the surface, as dark day followed dark day Verne continued to muse. Was it possible to harness time? To step out of its flow and back in again elsewhen? Yet by employing what possible technology? He quizzed me. "Did you mention powerful magnetic fields . . . ?"

A practical method eluded him. And how could our countrymen best be apprized of the future menace of the Nazis?

"I wonder, I wonder if a novel might be the most effective way. A tale about hostilities between France now, and Germany of the next century . . . Different worlds at war. Hmm, a war of the worlds, employing a time machine based on a plausible scientific rationale . . ."

CLIFF RHODES AND THE MOST IMPORTANT JOURNEY

A Land at the End of the Working Day Story

Peter Crowther

You can always be sure you'll get your money's worth with Peter Crowther. Whilst the following story is inspired by Journey to the Centre of the Earth *it's much more than that. Peter gets to the heart of our fascination with all of Verne's* Voyages Extraordinaires *and takes us on not just one adventure, but many.*

"That which is far off and exceeding deep, who can find it out?"

Ecclesiastes

1 The two strangers

"I DIDN'T EVEN KNOW this place existed!" is the second thing the taller of the two strangers says, hands (one brandishing a piece of creased paper) on his hips as he looks around Jack Fedogan's bar, his having blown in with his companion, a shorter man with beer-bottle-bottom glasses, blown in off of the nighttime street on a cold and blustery late autumn evening.

And who could blame him.

The curiously named The Land at the End of the Working Day walk-down bar, situated on the corner of 23rd and Fifth, just a stone's throw from the tired regality of the Chelsea Hotel, is not your average watering hole, not even given the myriad strangenesses that make up twenty-first century Manhattan. And, in truth, there are a lot of folks who don't know the bar is there, finding it only when their need is great – and that's not always simply the need for beverages . . . such as one of Jack Fedogan's generous cocktails or a bottle of imported beer from his well-stocked cellar or a bottle of his crisp Chardonnay or chewy claret, always grown on the right slope and its vines always facing the afternoon sun; nor is it just the need to hear some of the best jazz piped over a bar PA this side of New Orleans. There are needs and then there are needs – and you can take *that* one to the bank.

So the stranger's opening gambit isn't too unusual.

As he walks down the stairs, the glorious harmonies of Stan Getz's tenor and Lou Levy's piano from Getz's *West Coast Jazz* album from 1955 are wafting through a soft fog of cigarette smoke ("smoking ban, shmoking ban," is Jack's attitude) and occasional glass-chinking, and mingling with muted laughter from the table along from the counter and in front of the booths. But once he's spoken, only the music remains . . . while the patrons size him up. And the little guy, too – the little guy who looks like a cross between Peter Lorre and that mad scientist fella used to be constantly getting on the wrong side of good ol' Captain Marvel.

Tonight, though, it's quiet in the Working Day.

Sitting in a booth at the back of the room is a tall, black man – he's tall even when he's sitting down . . . even slumped over a little, like he is right now – who's nursing his fourth Manhattan and repeatedly turning over a pack of Camels on the table in front of him, working slowly but with admirable determination on emptying the pack into the ashtray. So far he's managed to cram seven butts in there and, as the strangers descend the stairs, he's considering starting on number eight. But it won't help the figure on the bottom of his bank statement, the one he received only this morning and which he's been worrying about all day . . . particularly the accompanying letter asking him to come in for a meeting.

Two booths away from him, a woman wearing a little too much pan-stick is checking her face in a tiny mirror she's taken from her purse. She's sitting with her back to the proceedings and is using the mirror to check the new arrivals. It's a process she's worked in bars all around Manhattan – and, before that, in similar establishments in Philly, Miami and Des Moines. Over time she'll do other bars in other cities, finally winding up several years hence spending the final few minutes of her life at a table in a sleazy dive out in Queens where the PA spurts Hip-Hop when she really wants to hear The Carpenters or Bread, and where the barkeep calls her "Lady", spitting it out at her like bad meat. She doesn't know that she's checking the mirror to try figure out the road that lies behind her, the one she's travelled to get where she is today . . . with all the bad decisions and failed relationships hovering over the blacktop like heat haze. But there's no answers in a mirror, just like there's no answers anyplace. Only more questions. She doesn't spend too much time in one place, this "lady", for that very reason. The more time you spend the more questions you get asked. It's for this reason that she is about to leave the Working Day and, in so doing, provide a springboard for the adventure ahead – for, after all, as all children know, life is just one big series of adventures.

At the table over by the counter – the noisy table – there are other questions being asked and answers given. But these questions are not as difficult, nor the answers as potentially distressing. Minutes earlier, as the strangers are crossing 23rd, big Edgar Nornhoevan is addressing the slender Jim Leafman – Laurel to Edgar's Hardy . . . Norton to Edgar's Ralph Kramden. Listen:

"Okay, this one," Edgar drawls, wiping beer froth from his top lip, "who said this one? *He has never been known to use a word that might send a reader to the dictionary.*"

Jim Leafman, unsung star of Manhattan's Refuse Department, shakes his head. He's been doing a lot of head-shaking this past half-hour. He doesn't like this game – doesn't know diddly about writers and their creations, or about statesmen (and women, of course) or politicians or Captains of Industry. Jim prefers it when they just tell a few jokes but, with McCoy late – McCoy Brewer, now gainfully employed by the Collars and Cuffs shirt and necktie emporium down on 21st Street – he's left to handle Edgar by himself, and he isn't making too good a job of it.

"No idea," Jim says with a shrug as the woman with the make-up weaves her slow and reluctant way past them, then up the stairs and out into the night . . . which, if she had poetry and not bile in her soul, she might say is calling to her on this particular evening. But she just does what she does, this casualty of life, and doesn't ask questions.

Outside, the two strangers dodge a Yellow and, glancing at the dog-eared parchment held by the taller of the two, they look up through the gloom . . . their eyes scanning the landscape of concrete towers, rain-slicked streets and store-windows.

"There's nothing here," says one of them, the smaller one.

"There must be," comes the reply, though it has more of hope in it than of conviction.

Then, a door opens at the base of one of the buildings and a solitary figure emerges, pulling its coat collar up against the breeze. For a second, the figure seems to see the two men and they think that she – for it is clearly a woman, they now see – is about to come over. But no, the figure turns and heads off in the direction of downtown.

They watch her go and then return their gaze to the now darkened area from which she emerged. And they see a dimly-lit sign.

"The Land at the End of the Working Day," the taller of the two men reads, squinting into the gloom, saying it almost reverentially. "It's here," he says softly, and they smile at each other and continue across the street.

2 Ernest Hemingway was a bullfighter?!

Meanwhile, back in the Working Day, "Well *guess*, for crissakes," is what Edgar snaps at Jim.

"I don't know," Jim protests. "How can I guess if I don't know?"

Edgar sighs, takes a deep sup of his beer and blusters, "Okay, then who did he say it *about*?"

"Edgar, I have no idea."

"I'll give you a clue," says Edgar, and he gets to his feet and mimes a matador waving his cape groundwards at an approaching bull.

Jim looks around, smiling apologetically, feeling a little like Walter Matthau's Oscar sitting alongside Jack Lemmon's Felix, the latter noisily busy unblocking his sinuses.

"Oh, Jesus!" Edgar says, thudding back into his seat. "It was William Faulkner talking about Ernest Hemingway."

"Ernest Hemingway was a *bullfighter*?"

Edgar glares at his friend and pulls another card out of the box.

"Okay, how about this –"

"Why don't I get a go yet?"

"Because you haven't answered one *correctly* yet."

Jim studies his bottle of Michelob, turns it around in his hands a couple times. "That doesn't seem fair to me."

"Okay," Edgar says, his face lighting up as he removes another card from the small box in front of him on the table. "Who said this –" He glances up at the sound of shoes on the stairs leading down into the bar, sees two sets of feet descending, and continues. "– and about whom? *His ears made him look like a taxicab with both doors open*."

"That would be Howard Hughes about Clark Gable," one of the men – the tall one – says in a loud voice with just a trace of an accent to it: English? French? German? Edgar can't pinpoint it. And then he turns to face a frowning Jack Fedogan and says: "I didn't even know this place existed."

"We feel much the same about you," Jack grunts, placing a freshly polished glass upside down on the shelf along the mirrored back wall.

"Wonderful place," the man says.

Jack Fedogan nods. "What'll it be?"

"Tell me," the man says, lowering his voice to a slightly conspiratorial level. "Do you have a back room?"

"A back room?" Jack repeats, placing a second glass on the shelf. "You mean a restroom?"

The stranger shakes his head and looks around for some kind of acknowledgment that he's using a standard language. "Ah, such a quaint euphemism – you may be assured that if I had wanted to urinate or defecate then I would have asked for a room in which to do just that and not one which I desired to use simply for a rest. I would have asked for a toilet or a lavatory, perhaps even a loo or a bog, or a john or a head –" He stops and considers for a few seconds before adding, "or even a Crapper, named after the gentleman who devised the modern toilet pedestal. But no, barkeeper, I mean simply a back room – or, perhaps, a room in the back?"

"You bein' funny?" Jack says.

"Are you laughing?"

Jack shakes his head and, flipping the towel over his left shoulder, leans both hands on the counter rail in front of him.

"Then I think it's safe to say I am not being funny."

Jack nods a few seconds, sizing up the stranger, taking in his clothes, the unfashionable winged collar and foppish folded necktie.

"You some kind of inspector?"

The man shakes his head.

"So –" Jack stands straight again. "– who exactly *might* you be?"

"Ah," the man begins, waving an arm theatrically, "I *might* be Monsieur Aronnax, professor in the Museum of Paris, or Ned Land, the Canadian whaler, about to board the *Abraham Lincoln* on an expedition to find the fabled narwhal that later turns out to be the *Nautilus* . . . which, of course –" He turns to the smaller man beside him. "– would make my diminutive friend here Conseil, the professor's devoted Flemish servant boy."

The small man nods, his eyes closing for the briefest of seconds.

"Or," the tall man continues, turning back to Jack, "perhaps I might be Dr Samuel Fergusson or Dick Kennedy – 'a Scotsman in the full significance of the word . . . open, resolute and dogged' – fresh from five whole weeks travelling the skies in a balloon."

Jack nods at the little man. "And him?"

"Ah, a good point, barkeeper," the tall man says, with a nod and a wink, and he turns to his companion once again and adds, "which would make him Joe, Dr Fergusson's manservant."

The small man nods again, this time adding a small bow to the repertoire.

"But you're neither of those?" Jack Fedogan says.

"Indeed not," the man says. "Mayhap I'm–"

"*Mayhap?*"

"Yes, mayhap then I am Phileas Fogg, a phlegmatic – even Sphinx-like – Byron with moustache and whiskers –"

"Which would make the little guy Jean Passepartout, yes?" says Jack.

And for a few seconds, silence floods into the Working Day. Edgar Nornhoevan and Jim Leafman watch, enraptured.

The tall (even while he's sitting down) black man in the end booth lets out a smile – his first for the day – as he reaches for the pack of Camels.

3 In the presence of a literary man

"My, oh my," the tall man exclaims, "I do believe, my dear Meredith, that we are in the presence of a literary man."

Jack Fedogan shakes his head. "Uh uh, I just remember all my classic literature – particularly Jules Verne and Thomas

Hardy – from school." And then he says, "You could also be Michael Ardan – 'an enthusiastic Parisian, as witty as he was bold' – which, moo-hepp mee-hype, could conceivably make Doberman here Ardan's worthy friend J. T. Maston, fretting over his telescope as Ardan, President Barbicane of Baltimore-based Gun Club, and the industrious Captain Nicholl undertake their journey around the moon."

For a few seconds the silence in the bar – the *West Coast Jazz* CD being between tracks – is absolute until the tall man slaps the counter and lets out a throaty roar of a laugh. "Capital!" he exclaims loudly, "absolutely capital."

"So, whyn't we start right from the top," Jack says.

The tall man's smile is warmer now as he holds out a hand. "In reality," he says, "I am Horatio Fortesque, a literary scholar of some repute – particularly within those circles whose members appreciate the great works of Monsieur Jules Verne – while my companion here is Meredith Lidenbrook Greenblat."

"Lidenbrook?" Jack says, his voice quizzical against the surety of Lou Levy's piano on "Serenade In Blue" as he shakes the two men's hands.

"Jack, I didn't know you knew so much about books," is what Edgar Nornhoevan says as he sidles up to the bar, empty glass held in his bear-like hand.

The bartender shrugs, polishes a piece of counter and pushes a couple of shot glasses first one way and then the other. "Verne was always a favourite of mine," he says, making a so-what with his mouth before he adds, "along with Dick Prather's Shell Scott books, John D. MacDonald's Travis McGee and Ed McBain's 87th Precinct yarns. I guess some things you don't forget."

Edgar is shaking his head, looking at Jack head-on but keeping a weathered eye trained on the two strangers right alongside him.

"You need that filling?" Jack asks.

"Oh," Edgar says, looking down in surprise at the glass – *now where did* that *come from!* – and then, nodding, "sure, one more."

"And Jim?"

Jim Leafman gets up from the table and shuffles up to Edgar, planting his own glass on the counter. "Guess I'll squeeze another one in," he says, turning to the tall stranger and giving him a sly wink. The stranger chuckles.

"So, you strangers in town?" Edgar asks, immediately feeling like a putz: after all, he silently reasons to himself, this is no two-muddy-cross-streets shanty town circa 1850, it's twenty-first century New-goddam-York.

But the tall man doesn't seem perturbed by the question, and he shakes his head. "I've lived in Manhattan most of my life," he says, his voice softening out a little and losing some of the clipped precision he'd sported earlier against Jack. "Come from south american stock," says Horatio Fortesque, "Bolivia to be exact, and my name was originally Bill," he says. "Martinez – William Martinez," he says. "Horatio Fortesque seemed altogether a wholly more appropriate name for someone so immersed in the literary world," he says, aiming the words to nobody in particular and up into the air above the counter.

"Edgar Nornhoevan, Horatio," says Edgar, holding out his hand. "And this here's my good friend Jim Leafman," he says as the stranger shakes first Edgar's hand and then Jim's. "We drink here pretty much all the time."

"I'm delighted to make your acquaintance," Fortesque gushes . . . with just a little too much butter on the bread as far as Edgar is concerned.

"So, how about your friend?" Edgar says, nodding to the Peter Lorre lookalike standing just in Horatio Fortesque's shadow.

"I made Mister Meredith Lidenbrook Greenblat's acquaintance through the internet," Fortesque says, imbuing the word 'internet' with almost W. C. Fields-like pomposity. "In a chat room," he adds.

Jack Fedogan places two beers on the counter in front of Edgar and looks over at the two strangers. Picking up the slack, Edgar says, "Buy you a beer?"

"Certainly, that's most kind of you," Fortesque trills.

Then, to Jack, "Do you have imported beers?"

Jack nods as he presses the eject button on the CD player behind him. As he consigns the *West Coast Jazz* CD into its case and removes one of the disks from *Time Signatures*, the four-CD Dave Brubeck retrospective, he says over his shoulder, "What did you have in mind?"

"Something English," Peter Lorre chirps up, the phrase hissed out rather than actually spoken, and then, correcting himself, "Something British, I mean."

"I spent some time in England," Jim Leafman says, reaching for his beer.

"I got Tetley's on tap," Jack says, "plus in bottles I got Old Peculier, Black Sheep, Marston Moor, Landlord, Cropton's Two –"

"Landlord," says Lorre, drooling.

"Tetleys is fine for me," Fortesque says and then, turning to face Jim, "Whereabouts?"

"Pardon me?"

"In England. Whereabouts did you stay?"

"Oh," Jim says, taking a deep sup of his beer as he casts his mind back to the days before he worked at the Refuse Department ("Sanitation", he tells most folks) . . . the time he now regards as BC – Before Clarice – before he parked up his '74 Olds that, at the time, was two parts yellow and eight parts rust (the rust is now winning the battle), parked it up outside the travelling salesman's apartment building with the .38 sitting in his lap . . . and then seeing the guy walking along the street, the guy who was sticking it to Clarice behind Jim's back, seeing him in his fancy shoes and his fancy pants, fancy shirt and fancy sports jacket, knowing that he smelled of expensive cologne and not sewage the way Jim smelled . . . maybe even, down behind the zipper, smelled a little of Clar –

"It was a long time ago," Jim says, emerging from the beer and the memories, licking his top lip at the residue of the former and blinking his eyes hard three times at the latter.

"I said *where*," Fortesque says, with just a hint of irritation in his tone.

"York shire," Jim says, splitting the word into two, the second part sounding like the areas where the little folks lived in those *Lord of the Rings* movies. "Leeds," he adds.

"How long were you there?" asks Fortesque.

In your eyes, sings Carmen McRae, Brubeck tickling the ivories, Eugene Wright on bass and the indefatigable Joe Morello handling the drums. They sound so close they could be right here in the bar and, just for a second, both Jack Fedogan – who knows the song well, and the original album it comes from (*Tonight Only!*) – and Fortesque turn around momentarily before settling back to what appears to be a genesis of conversation.

"Oh, around six maybe eight months I guess." Jim looks down at his beer and, without looking back up, he says softly, "I was twenty years old."

"Quite a journey for a young man to make," Horatio Fortesque says, reaching for his pint glass of Tetleys and nodding first to Jack, then to Edgar, and finally to Jim Leafman, unsure as to whom he owes the gratitude.

"Yeah, I guess," says Jim.

The Lorre-lookalike snakes out a hand and grasps the bottle of Landlord, pours it into the glass alongside it.

"You want to sit down?" Edgar asks.

Fortesque and Lorre nod and the quartet move over to where Edgar and Jim were sitting just a few minutes earlier.

"But it was nothing like a journey I saw a man take night after night," Jim says, sliding his beer around on one of Jack's Working Day coasters. "Every night," he says, "right up until –" And his voice trails off.

4 What the hell's 'tipsey'?

"I'd been up in Leeds maybe around a week, maybe a little less," Jim Leafman says, glancing around just in time to see Jack move his counter polishing a little closer to their table.

Edgar settles back on his chair and glances at the two

strangers, who seem relaxed about Jim's story. He looks across at the tall black man, smoking – always seems to have a cigarette on the go – and back at Jim.

"Got a little job at a newsagent store – little more than a newsstand – in the city and rented a small apartment. They call them flats," Jim explains to his audience and receives nods and blinks to let him know they all understand.

"The place I lived was called Headingley – maybe three miles from the town centre – a big student area: the Leeds University campus is enormous. Anyway, because it was – still is, I guess – such a big student dormitory, Headingley was a really fun place: cheap supermarkets, charity stores filled with used books and record albums – this was before CDs," he says.

More nods, more blinks.

"But best of all were the pubs. There were stacks of them – the Original Oak and the Skyrack, right across from each other next to St Michael's Chur–"

"Just keep to the point, Jim," Edgar says. He's listened to Jim Leafman's stories before, of course.

Nodding and contrite, Jim carries on. "Anyway, this one night I'm in the pub with this English guy –" Jim is about to attempt remembering the guy's name (it's Phil, a medical student, but he won't remember that until two full weeks have passed and this evening in the Working Day has assumed legendary status) but he thinks better of it. "So, anyway," he says, waving an arm dismissively, "this guy comes in and walks right up to the bar. He's a little guy –" He turns to Meredith Lidenbrook Greenblat and says, "No offence," to which Greenblat leans over the table and nods sagely.

"He's a little guy, balding, skin that looks like he's just shaved, pant legs that could cut steak, shirt collar tight around his neck, buttoned up with a necktie, knot perfectly in place, sports jacket showing linked cuffs . . . the whole works. You notice that kind of get-up, plus the guy looks like one of the two brothers in the Tintin books . . ."

"The Thompson twins," ventures Jack from over behind the bar.

"Seems you know a lot about all kinds of literature," Fortesque says and Jack shrugs self-deprecatingly, polishes another spot.

"Yeah, right – the Thompson twins," Jim Leafman says with a big grin. "Anyways, the guy doesn't say anything but the bartender pulls him a half-pint and the guy passes him the money for it. Then the guy downs the drink – in maybe three or four swallows – wipes his mouth and strides right out."

"But he paid him, right?" Jack Fedogan asks from the counter.

Edgar says, "He paid for the drink, Jack – let's just get on with the story here."

Jack mutters something Nigel Bruce-style and returns to his polishing.

"Anyway," Jim says after taking a sip of his beer, "I didn't really think anything of it at the time. It was just, you know, a little unusual, right?"

Everyone seems to agree that such action was unusual and Jim continued.

"But it happened again."

"The same night?" the little Lorre-lookalike whispers sibilantly.

Jim shakes his head.

"Another night – maybe the next one but certainly no more than two nights later. And it was a different pub." He stops and shrugs at Edgar's frown. "Okay, we drank most nights – twenty years old for crissakes."

Edgar sits back in his chair and holds up a hand. "I didn't say nothing."

"You looked," is what Jim says to that.

Edgar takes a deep drink of beer and Jack, leaning over the counter, says, "Will you get on with it?"

"Can we get more beers over here?" says Edgar, having drained his glass.

"Same?" Jack asks, straightening up.

Everyone appears to feel that's a good idea. "They're on me if I can join you," Jack says.

Everyone seems to feel that's an even better idea.

Minutes later, Jack sets fresh glasses on the table and pulls up a chair.

"And it didn't end there," is what Jim says then, and he lifts his glass to everyone's health before taking a long sip. The others wait patiently as he drinks.

"The very next night, in a different pub again – this one another mile or so out of Headingly towards Leeds – the guy comes in and sidles up to the bar. Doesn't say anything but the girl behind the bar pulls him a half-pint which the guy sees off in short order. Then he leaves the pub. And when he leaves, he's weaving a little, you know what I mean?"

"He's canned," Edgar announces.

"Let's just say he's . . ."

"Tipsey?" Horatio Fortesque suggests.

"Tipsey?" says Jack. "What the hell's 'tipsey'?"

"Well," comes the reply, "it's what you get when you've had a few drinks but you're not yet drunk."

Everyone considers this – Jim included – while they sip their drinks.

"So," says Jim Leafman, "I go up to the girl – who's very nice, incidentally –"

"Ulterior motive, hmm," says Lorre, making it sound like Jim had thrown the girl across the bar counter and torn her clothes off. Jim ignores this and continues.

"And I ask her about this guy. You know, I seen him in the first pub – the Oak, as I recall – and then another . . . which I think was the –"

"Too much information," says Edgar.

Jim nods. "Sorry. So, it turns out that this guy, his wife died on him years earlier. She was only young, the girl told me, maybe in her mid-forties – keeled right over while they were eating their meal one evening, head-first on to the plate. So what he did, as soon as the funeral was over and done, was he went out every night to all the pubs in the area that he and his wife had visited and he had a half-pint in each one. The girl tells me this: he walked from his house – the whole round-trip would be around four miles – and he went to all the pubs on the left side of the road as he walked in and all the pubs on the right side as he walked back home. Needless to say, when he got home each night he was a little . . ." Jim looks questioningly at Fortesque.

"Tipsey," the stranger offers.

"Right, tipsey. And he had done this seven nights a week, fifty two weeks a year for –" Jim shrugs. "– three, four years?"

"God," is all Jack Fedogan can think of to say, Jack too busy casting his mind back to his beloved Phyllis, gone on ahead on Valentine's Day 1990 and Jack alone these past fifteen years. Alone apart from the Working Day. He takes a drink and glances around at the others.

"And then he stopped," Jim says, basking in the dramatic revelation.

"He stopped?"

Jim nods.

Joe Morello's laugh of relief at the end of "Unsquare Dance" signals the trio's (Paul Desmond playing only handclap in the sessions for this particular tune) "Why Phyllis" written by Eugene Wright – whose wife, like Jack's, was named Phyllis – and taken from Brubeck's 1961 album *Countdown Time In Outer Space*.

"Well, go on," Edgar says.

"I'd gotten to watching out for him each pub we went into – and, like I said, we went into a lot of pubs in those days – and I saw him a good few times. Then, one night, I was suddenly aware I hadn't seen him inside a pub for a good few nights. You know how that kind of thing creeps up on you? You kind of take something for granted and then, one day, you realize that that something has stopped?"

The consensus was that everyone knew how that kind of thing crept up on you, and Jim continued.

"I'd seen him a couple of times walking out on the street or – and I thought this was strange right off – standing outside the pub."

"Standing outside?" Fortesque asks. "Doing what?"

Jim shrugs. "Just standing there – couple of times I thought he looked kind of wistful." Jim stops and looks around the faces. "We're talking here maybe three, four weeks during which I guess I'd seen him a half-dozen times – we were always out and about at the same times so it wasn't too unusual.

"So, this one night – we'd only just gone out and we were up near West Park at the pub there – and I asked the guy behind the bar if the little guy – the Thompson twin – had been in recently. 'He died,' the guy behind the bar tells me. I was shocked but, most of all, I felt –", Jim searches the faces around him, looking for the right word or phrase. "– I felt sad. No idea why. It just seemed such a desperately sad life he'd had.

"And then, just casual, I asked the guy behind the bar when it had happened – when the Thompson twin guy had died. And he says, matter-of-factly – because why would he be otherwise – 'Last month.' So I say to him that can't be. I tell him I just saw the guy, three maybe four times just this past week–week and a half, out on the street. And the barkeeper looks at me like I just fell off of a tree. Says I must have seen someone who looks just like him. And then he goes off to pull somebody a beer."

You could cut the atmosphere with a knife.

Edgar looks nervously at Jack Fedogan, Jack looks at the little Lorre fella, Lorre looks up at Fortesque who is watching Jim Leafman. Every few seconds, one or more of them gives a little shake of their head. Even the usually confident Dave Brubeck sounds a little phased as he drifts into "It's A Raggy Waltz".

Then Jim says, "There's more," before draining his glass. "But we need refills and I need the restroom."

5 Enter Cliff Rhodes

As Jack goes to the bar, moving faster than he has done all day, the tall black man shouts, "How about another Manhattan," to which Jack nods enthusiastically. Then the black guy gets up and walks across to the table, pack of

Camels and ashtray in hand, says, "Mind if I join you? I always liked story-telling."

"Sure," says Edgar.

Jim nods Hi as he stands up.

Lorre says, "Don't be long," and there's something in there – in those three words – that sounds unpleasant and menacing.

"Pull up a chair," says Fortesque to the black man, leaning over with his hand outstretched and adding, "Horatio Fortesque."

The new arrival nods, shakes hands, and says, "Cliff Rhodes."

Introductions are then made and Jack returns with fresh beers, forgetting to charge anyone for them. Scant seconds later, Jim gets back and introductory sips are made from the replenished glasses before Jack says, "So, go on."

"You hear any of this?" Edgar asks Cliff Rhodes as Cliff swirls the olive around the Manhattan.

"I'm afraid so," Rhodes confesses. "It's not my habit to listen in on other folks' conversations but, like I said, I'm a sucker for stories."

Edgar waves never mind and slaps Rhodes on his shoulder.

"Well," Jim says, "I tried not to give it any more thought but then, that weekend – I remember: it was a Saturday evening – I saw the guy again, and this time I was sure it was him. No question. He was standing outside the Oak just as I walked across the street, standing right there outside the pub, his coat collar up, hands in pockets, still looking as smart as ever, staring through the big window they have – or used to have – in that pub.

"So, I took the bull by the horns and I called out to him. 'Hey!' I shouts to him, waving a hand in the air –" Jim demonstrates. "– like this. And he turns around, sees me and . . ." He shakes his head, checking each face individually. "And then he just kind of fizzles up into wispy smoke, smoke that's kind of man-shaped and then isn't, and that's solid for a few seconds, then less solid and then just see-through smoke. And then there's only the big window and the sidewalk, people passing by going this way and that, not one of them appearing to have seen him or seen him disappear."

"What then?" is what Cliff Rhodes decides to say to break Jim's pause.

"Well, then, I guess I just stood there looking at where the guy had been, looking at the other people, people either walking or standing – outside the Oak was a popular meeting place – and then I looked through the window into the pub. And that's when I figured out what was going on."

Sips all round followed that. Then:

"I figured that I was the only one seen him because I was the one expected to put things right."

Edgar harrumphs and takes a sip of beer, seeming agitated.

"Put things right?" hisses Meredith Lidenbrook Greenblat.

"Well, way I figured it, there had to be a reason why I'd seen him and seen him disappear while the other people all around him hadn't. And that reason was to put him out of his misery.

"See, when I looked through that window, I saw what it was that was making the guy so morose: people drinking. And it came to me that ghosts probably can't drink." Jim shrugs. "Maybe he wasn't fully aware he'd died, only that he couldn't go into the pubs and have his customary half-pint in every one. The routine had sunk its claws into him and he'd become so fixated with what he did every night that he wasn't about to let a little thing like death keep him from it. But death was keeping him from drinking."

Jim swirls the beer around in his glass and watches it make patters of froth around the rim. "And I got to thinking that 'someone', whoever or whatever keeps these things in check, had looked around for a likely candidate to put things straight again." Jabbing a thumb into his own chest, Jim Leafman says, somewhat proudly, "And I figured that person was me."

"You knew what to do?" Jack says, leaning closer over the table.

Jim shakes his head. "I didn't *know*," he says, "but I figured someone had to get it through to him that he was dead and that he should let go . . . go off to re-join his wife."

At that, Jack Fedogan grimaces, shuffling in his chair and fighting back a sudden urge to blubber. Without his letting anyone else notice, Edgar places a big ham-hock sized hand on Jack's knee and gives it a squeeze.

Cliff Rhodes, Jim and even Fortesque and the Lorre fella all see the gesture and don't let on, though Jim sees that Greenblat has seen it, has seen the little guy's soft smile tugging at the corners of his mouth, and he reconsiders his opinion of the man.

"So, I went in and ordered a pint. Didn't go to the upstairs room where my regular crowd were, and I didn't stay more than just a few minutes. I just drank the pint and moved on.

"From there, I did the Hyde Park, the Rose and Crown, the Skyrack, the Drum and Monkey, the Travellers' Rest, the Lawnswood Arms, the New Inn and, finally, the Tap and Spile . . . plus maybe a couple of others that I've forgotten about down the years."

Now Jack's grimace isn't about his missing Phyllis, it's from thinking about all that beer – eight pints at least and probably well into double figures.

Edgar looks at his friend with newfound respect.

"As you can probably guess, I wasn't too good at the end of it all . . . but we won't go into that." He takes a deep sip and rests his glass back on his coaster, pulling himself tall in the chair – maybe even almost as tall as Cliff Rhodes, sitting across from him, who wasn't trying hard at all – and he continues with his story.

"I didn't see the guy again after that, and we were out and about just as frequently as before. The way I figure it," Jim Leafman says, lifting his glass once more, "is that the guy needed to be freed. He'd gotten himself into some kind of loop, going out every night to drink in the various bars that he drank in with his wife, and then –" Jim waves a hand. "– He went and died. And, as we know, dead men don't drink too good."

He is, of course, referring to Front-Page McGuffin and both Jack and Edgar nod knowingly.

"So," Jim goes on, his voice sounding tired and kind of

resigned, "he just stood outside each of the pubs waiting for some kind of release."

Edgar snorted. "And that release was you going out and getting hammered?"

Jim shrugged. "Well, I didn't see him again."

"You ever stop to think that maybe you'd imagined you'd seen him?" Cliff Rhodes ventures.

"Absolutely!" says Edgar, loudly.

"And that maybe he wasn't there at all," Rhodes continues. "That he was just either a figment of your imagination or someone who looked a lot like him."

"It comes down to faith," Jack offers, sitting back in his chair a mite. "Either you believe in what you saw and what you did, or you don't. Simple as that."

"His was a journey of faith," Horatio Fortesque says. "The Thompson twin, I mean," he adds. And then, "As was yours," and he pats Jim Leafman on the arm.

"It's a nice story," says Lorre.

"It was a nice story," Jack agrees.

"But then, all stories about journeys are good." Edgar considers his glass for a few seconds and, sensing that there's more to come, the others remain silent. Then:

6 The man on the bus

"Back when I was a youngster we lived in Forest Plains," Edgar says, his voice slightly wistful and distant.

Jack says, "Forest Plains? Where's that?"

"I checked the mapbook once and it turns out there are several," Edgar says. "This one is in Iowa, about an hour west from Cedar Rapids.

"My first job – clerk and then teller at the local branch of First National, long since closed – was in Branton, a small town around 30 miles due north from home. There was a twice-daily bus went from the Plains straight into Branton, stopping on Main Street, about three minutes walk from the bank and then at the railroad depot where it turned right around and went back to the Plains. Same thing happened on an evening.

"In the morning, it left the Plains at seven forty-three and in the evening it left Branton at six eleven – funny how you remember the small details," Edgar says, shaking his big head slowly. "It arrived in Branton at a little after or a little before eight thirty in the morning and I'd usually be back home around seven at night.

"My dad bought me a car – an old Mercury, 1960 model, canary yellow with tail-fins and a bench seat you could've sat a football team on . . . and still had room for the cheer-leaders." Edgar slaps his knee. "Jeez, they just don't make cars like that any more."

"More's the pity," Cliff Rhodes says, the words coming out so quietly that Fortesque and Greenblat exchange frowns. But before they ask him to repeat it, Edgar is up and running again.

"But that didn't happen until I'd gotten through my proba-tion period – one month – so's the bank could decide whether they wanted to keep me on. They did and I got the car, but for that first month I used to ride the bus. In and out. Every day.

"The trip in was completely different to the trip back home. The light for one thing – morning light is just so clear and the meadows and the distant clumps of trees . . . and the little collections of houses, collections too small even to call them villages: Green Hammerton, Poppleton, Starbeck – I remember them all.

"But the evenings, well . . . they were different. The light, as I already said, was just one thing. Then there was the tiredness of the people for another. Folks have just lost their spark after a day at work. I felt that way myself – just a little – and I was only nineteen years old. But the other thing was that there were different people on the bus every now and again."

"Why should that matter?" Fortesque asks.

"Oh, it didn't matter exactly," Edgar says, "But the regular commuters, well . . . they get to know each other. There's a silent acceptance of each of you by the others – what's the old saying? Misery loves company. You know?

"So the bus in on a morning had, for the most part, the same folks on it as the bus back home at the end of the day. Oh, there were a few folks going to do some shopping in Branton – the Plains isn't exactly what you might call Fifth Avenue, though there is a mall there now, around four, five miles outside of town – but back then there wasn't diddly. And there might be a couple of people going to meet a friend or visit someone. But, like I say, most of them were commuting to work and commuting home. But even these occasional users would be on the bus in the morning and the bus in the evening – they just wouldn't be on it day after day. You know what I'm saying?"

Jim Leafman watches his friend over hands tented at his chin. "Go on," he says at last, reaching for his beer.

"Well, my first day on the bus going home, there was one passenger who stood out from the rest," Edgar says, after a big sigh. "A boy, maybe fourteen or fifteen years old. He was . . . he was, you know . . ."

"Give us a clue, Ed," says Jack.

Edgar sniffs, turns his beer around on his coaster. "He was not the brightest button in the box, you know what I mean?"

"Special needs," says Cliff Rhodes.

"Educationally challenged?" offers Meredith Lidenbrook Greenblat.

Edgar nods in a Tony Soprano way, takes a drink. "Right, those. You got the picture. So this kid, he's sitting right at the front of the bus staring at the road ahead and at the countryside on either side. All the way from Branton to Forest Plains. I got the seat right behind him so I was able to watch him all the way. And every time we stop – like to let someone off: nobody gets *on* those evening buses – every time we stop, the kid turns around and makes this noise – *wmmgmmm!*" Edgar says, hunching up his shoulders and making his hands clawlike. "And I swear he's trying to tell me something . . . something about the fields and the sky, the far-off trees, the trucks on the Interstate below us when we get into the Plains.

He swings those manic arms around, sometimes banging his hand on the bus window, making that noise." Edgar makes the noise again, and then again. And then he lifts his glass, takes a drink.

"We get to the Plains and everyone gets off," Edgar says. "Everyone except the kid. I held back because folks had gotten to standing as we got close to town and so there was no room for me to stand up. But when I did stand up and made my way to the open doors, the kid stayed behind. I looked at him and then looked at some of the other passengers and nobody paid him any attention. And you have to remember that this was my first day, right.

"So that was it. Next day exactly the same."

"What happened to the boy when you got off the bus that first night?" Greenblat asks.

"He stayed on," says Edgar. "The bus closed its doors and the kid swung right around to look out of the front window and the bus set off again."

"Back to Branton?"

Edgar gives Jim a single nod. "Back to Branton."

"No other passengers getting on?"

Edgar shakes his head. "Not that first night. There might be one or two every so often, but most nights, the bus would go back without picking up any new rides."

"So the next day," Jack says, glancing around to see how the drinks are going. "What happened then?"

"Same thing," is what Edgar answers, and there's a little chuckle in his voice. "I get on at Main Street, kid's already there at the front looking around at the folks getting on. And again, I sit in the seat behind him." He shrugs. "From there, the journey home is exactly the same. The same fields, the same sky, the same Interstate. The same stops, the same flailing arms and hands, and the same *wmmgmmm!* every time. When we get to the Plains, we all get off but the kid stays. Bus moves off and heads back to Branton.

"Next day, same thing. And the next. And the one after that. Same thing the following week. And the one after it and the one after that one. And then —"

"And then you pass your probation period," Cliff Rhodes says, "and your dad buys you the Mercury."

"Canary yellow," says Jack.

"Tail fins," adds Jim Leafman.

"And the big bench seat," says Horatio Fortesque, getting into it now.

After a few seconds silence, the little Peter Lorre-look-alike says, "Cheerleaders," making the word sound dirty.

And they all laugh.

"And that's it?" Jack asks.

Shaking his head, Edgar says, "Not quite."

"More drinks!" is what Jack Fedogan announces then. "And more music."

"More Brubeck," Fortesque says. "And –" He passes a twenty dollar note across to Jack. "– This round is on me."

7 Thick with possibilities

There's shuffling then, and leg-stretching, and visits to the restroom. But nobody speaks. When the music starts again – Brubeck, Desmond, Wright and Morello getting to grips with Cole Porter's "I Get A Kick Out Of You" – it's a relief in that it eats the silence.

Minutes later, the table re-assembles and Jack says, "So, not quite?"

Edgar nods. "Nothing else happened while I had that job. I never took the bus again, and, a little under eight months later, I got my first adviser's job down in Miami." Edgar shrugged his shoulders. "Left home and moved to the coast." He looks across at Jim Leafman and says, "Moved to the Apple in the spring of '84 – which is fifteen, sixteen years after the Branton clerk job."

"And the Mercury?"

"Ah, that went to that great wrecker's yard in the sky," Edgar tells Jack. "Transmission died on me in '71. My dad died on me in '76. I asked my mother to move down to Florida and then to New York but she refused each time.

She visited me a couple times in Miami – she hated Florida, the heat – and then New York but she just couldn't get to grips with that either. Too big, I guess. I went out to see her – birthday, Thanksgiving, Christmas – but we kind of distanced ourselves from each other.

"Then – it must have been the fall of '99 – mum got sick. You remember, Jim?" Jim Leafman nods and glances down at his clasped hands resting on the table. "I went home most weekends, stayed with her, and for a time we had hopes. But –" He shrugs matter-of-factly. "– It wasn't to be.

"We got what mom called her marching orders in the January of 2000. Three to six months, they gave her," he says, his voice sounding a little cracked. "As it turned out, she lasted barely three weeks." Edgar takes a sip of beer while the others watch him. When he starts speaking again, his voice has regained its former strength.

"I lived at home for that three weeks, the plan being to take her out, spend time with her – say goodbye, I guess – but, after the first couple of days, she went down fast. I tell you, that couple of days were wonderful . . . particularly the first one, when I took her to Branton. And, at her request, on the bus," says Edgar, pointedly, and then he takes another drink.

"Everything went fine. Didn't recognize anyone and barely recognized the countryside we drove through – so much building in just thirty-some years. Mom had a fine time in Branton – seeing where my dad used to work, visiting the cemetery out on the Canal road where her own mom and dad are buried – but she was tired when it came time to catch the bus back home.

"We got on over at Main Street, standing in line with the suits and the skirts, reading the evening papers the same way people just like them read evening papers up and down the country. It was busy when we got on but there was a seat free where, at a squeeze, we could sit together – a seat near the front of the bus, behind an intense-looking middle-aged man who was turned in his seat and, with his arms and hands tucked up clawlike around his chest, was staring into the bus interior."

"The same guy?" asks Cliff Rhodes.

"The same guy."

"Jee-zuzz," says Jim Leafman, the words partly eaten up by the big sigh that surrounds them.

"I don't think my mom noticed him right off but I did. The same actions exactly as he was doing thirty years before, the same turning around, the same flailing hands and arms and the same banshee-like wail – *wmmgmmm!* – each time the bus stopped and he turned to address his subjects.

"I couldn't believe it.

"Then, we got stuck in a jam – guys out doing maintenance work on the road up ahead shifting the two directions of traffic into just the one lane, lights controlling that – you know the kind of thing."

Everyone did and several of them took the opportunity to take drinks. Edgar did the same.

"Then," Edgar says, setting his glass down on the table again, "the guy turns around just as we pull to a stop again and *wmmgmmm!* –" He flails his arms around. "– *wmmgmmm!* he says, saying it like he's trying to tell me something. So I say to him something like, 'I know, damn traffic!', something like that. And that's when the driver leans around and says to me, 'That's the first time I can recall when someone actually said something to him.' The guy himself chuckles and turns back to face front looking out of the window. And I say to the driver –" Edgar shrugs. "I say something like, 'Oh, really?' I mean, what the hell do you say in response to something like that? And that's when I see the driver is an oldish guy, over sixty . . . and I recognize him. It's the same driver as the one used to drive the bus back from Branton all those years ago. And up to that very second, I hadn't even realized that we'd had the same driver on each of those trips back in the sixties.

"So I say to him, 'He always on the bus at this time?' And the driver nods as he settles back in his seat. 'Rain or shine. He looks forward to it,' he says to me, keeping facing forward. 'Don't know how he's going to take it when I retire,' he says. 'Retire?' is all I could think of to say. I mean, what's strange about retiring, you know? But it was the implied significance of it that puzzled me. And the driver leans back out, arms resting on the steering wheel as we wait for the lights to change again, and he says, 'He's my son.' And he looks across at the *wmmgmmm!* guy, who's jiggling his head side to side excitedly, waving his arms at the windows, and he says, 'Sure wish I knew what he sees out there that excites him so.' And that's when my mom decides to join the conversation," says Edgar.

"'He sees life,' she says. 'He sees the world and the people and all the wonder that it holds, all the promises – all the disappointments, sure, those too, but the air is thick with possibilities.' And I turn to my mom and I see her eyes are watery. She looks away and watches the *wmmgmmm!* man some more. 'And what you do when you retire,' she tells him, 'is you take the bus just the same, every afternoon, except you sit in that seat –' She nods to where the *wmmgmmm!* man is sitting '– and not that one you're sitting in right now. And maybe then, when you're able to look around and drink it all in, maybe then you'll see what he sees. And what I'm seeing right now,' she adds.

"And then the lights change before the driver gets to say anything back to that, and we make it around the roadworks and from there on in it's a clear road back to Forest Plains.

"I held my mom's hand all the way, not able to say a word. And when we get to the Plains and we get off of the bus, the driver steps down too and shakes our hands, with the *wmmgmmm!* man watching us from his window. 'I want to thank you, ma'am,' he tells my mom. But she waves him nevermind. 'You look after her,' he says then, turning to me, and I guess he saw something in my face or my eyes just then . . . and he pats me on the shoulder and nods, his mouth sad . . . as though, in that brief exchange, he'd read our minds and knew exactly what the score was. Then he gets back on the bus and we walk home.

"A couple days later, mom goes on to morphine and, as the days pass by, she slips further and further away from me until, at last, she's gone.

"After the funeral," Edgar says, "I settled up my mom's

house and set off back for Manhattan. But I drove into Branton for one last time before I got on to the Interstate. It was late in the day, after 5.30, and, on a whim, I drove down to the train depot. I couldn't park up but I could see them, the old driver and the *wmmgmmm!* man, standing in line at the bus stop, one of the *wmmgmmm!* man's arms going like a windmill and the driver standing right alongside him, holding on to the hand of the other. And, you know, the driver? He was grinning like a Cheshire cat."

Edgar lifts his glass and drains it. "End of story," he says.

8 The second parchment

Jack Fedogan reaches out a hand and places it on Edgar's shoulder, jiggling it once before letting the arm drop down by his side again.

After a few seconds of silence, Fortesque speaks. "We're all on journeys," he says, "of one kind or another. Some of them are long – or *seem* long – and some are short. But they are all journeys. And it's the journey that matters, never the destination."

"Is that why you like Jules Verne?" Cliff Rhodes asks.

"I'm not sure that I follow."

The black man shuffles around in his chair and moves his hands around in the air in front of him, as though he's manoeuvring a large package that nobody can see. "Well, I overheard what you were saying earlier – about your being a big fan of Verne's work – and it occurs to me that that's what Verne concentrated on: journeys."

"Ah, I see," Fortesque says. "I hadn't quite thought of it that way."

"More drinks?" Cliff Rhodes asks. When the unanimous response is favourable, he and Jack move across to the bar.

"So, what brings you here?" Edgar says, making the question sound unimportant as he tries to regain his composure. Jim Leafman reaches across the table and pats his friend's arm and Edgar smiles at him, taking hold of Jim's hand for just a second or two. "You said you'd met up with . . ." He says to Fortesque, looking across at the Lorre-lookalike and, with a small sad smile, shaking his head. "I'm sorry, I just don't seem to be able to remember your name."

"Meredith Lidenbrook Greenblat," says Meredith Lidenbrook Greenblat.

Edgar nods in a kind of *oh yes, of course it is* way and turns to Fortesque. "You said you'd met him in a chat room?"

"That is correct," says Fortesque, tenting his fingers atop a brightly coloured vest which only partly covers the swell of his ample stomach.

"A chat room about . . . Jules Verne, was it?"

Fortesque jiggles his head from side to side and, giving a knowing smile to his companion, he says, "Indirectly, yes."

Jack arrives back at the table with Cliff Rhodes, the pair of them carrying an array of bottles and glasses. And Jack sets down a trio of saucers containing nuts and pretzels. Without any indication of thanks, Edgar picks up a handful of peanuts, throws them deep into his mouth, and says, "So what *was* it about, this chat room?"

"It was about one of Jules Verne's books . . . certainly, as far as I am concerned, his best work and perhaps one of the half-dozen best-ever novels. *A Journey To The Centre Of The Earth*," says Fortesque. He waits for a few minutes and then says, "It's really there."

"It's really there?" Cliff Rhodes says, jamming his billfold into his back pants pocket as he sits down. "With the dinosaurs and the giant mushrooms and everything? No way."

Leaning forward across the table, Greenblat says, in that quiet Peter Lorre voice, "The central records in Hamburg do have details of one Alec and Gretchen Lidenbrook living in Bernickstrasse from 1867 to 1877. Number nineteen."

Edgar frowns. "I'm sorry but I don't –"

"It was Axel Lidenbrock who went with his uncle, Otto, a noted professor, in 1863 to the centre of the Earth," Greenblat points out. "And the professor's God-daughter was named Grauben."

"And did they live at Bernickstrasse?"

"No," Fortesque answers, "Konigstrasse. But number nineteen."

Edgar laughs, glancing at each of the others' faces in turn. "Hey, come on, guys . . . Alex and Axel? Gretchen and Grauben? Brock and brook? *Bernick*strasse and – what was it?"

"Konigstrasse," says Greenblat.

Edgar settles back in his seat and raises his hands palms up. "Well, need we say goddam *more*. There's not one damn thing that's consistent."

"N-n-n-nineteen," Cliff Rhodes says, beaming a big smile. When Edgar turns to him in puzzlement, Rhodes shakes his head. "Sorry, an old 'song' by Paul Hardcastle. What I meant was, it was number nineteen in each case, the house number – that's consistent."

"Well, please the fuck excuse me the hell out of here," Edgar says, looking for just a few seconds like he's going to stand right up and either walk out of the bar or haul off and smack someone right where they sit. "It's one thing for Jaunty Jim here thinking he's seeing ghosts staring through bar windows wishing they could get a drink and quite a-fucking-nother to tell me, based on the fact that two couples – one real and one fictional, all with different names – living at the same house number in completely differently named streets, albeit in the same town, that there's an underground sea and a bunch of monsters right below our feet. I mean, come *on*, guys!"

Greenblat says, "They married in 1864."

"*Who* did?" shouts Edgar.

"Take it easy, Ed," says Jack Fedogan.

"Alex and Gretchen. They'd been off on a long trip with Alex's uncle for much of the previous year and, when they returned, they were changed."

Edgar shrugs his shoulders. "Hell, we've all had vacations like that, right?"

Greenblat pulls a piece of paper from the inside pocket of his jacket. "Married in 1864," he says, reading from the paper. "Son Henri born 1869, daughter Eloise appeared in

1871. Eloise died in '77. Henri married an English girl, Heather Dalston, in 1904 when he was over there at Cambridge University. Henri and Heath –"

"Look, where the hell is –"

"Drink your beer, Ed," says Jack, "and settle down."

"Henri and Heather moved to Lewes near Brighton in 1908, twin sons Alain and James born in 1910. Heather didn't survive the birth."

He pauses for a minute or so to let that sink in and the others remain silent.

"Alain married Jacqueline Hay in 1938, no children. James married a Welsh girl, Johanna, in 1942 and they had two children: a son, Robin, in 1948, and, in 1952, Martha –"

"Martha was the name of Lidenbrock's housekeeper," Fortesque interjects.

Edgar almost chokes on the beer he's drinking. "Jesus Christ," he says, fending off Jack's glare with an outstretched arm. "Jack, give me a break here. Did you *hear* that? That's like saying –" Edgar affects a deep and mysterious voice. "–'And they each had four fingers and a thumb on each hand'. I mean, come on, guys – why is that *significant*? The baby being called Martha? How many Marthas are there flying around this country?"

Jack turns to Fortesque and, seemingly with profound regret, says, "He's right. How *is* that significant?"

Fortesque nods to his companion.

"Robin Lidenbrook was killed in Belfast in 1976. He was in the British Army and was stationed over in Northern Ireland – a land mine blew him and three others to tiny pieces. Martha, the last in the line, married Michael Greenblat, here in New York, in the October of 1976. Their one son, Meredith, was born the following year. In April." Greenblat looks up from the paper at the faces around the table. Then, very slowly, he reaches into his jacket pocket once again.

"My mother was not a well woman," Greenblat continues as he produces a dog-eared and well-thumbed brown envelope. "She died last year after a sickly life that culminated in a long and wasting illness. She was not a wealthy woman, not by any means. But she did have one possession which had been passed down to her over the years. And which she passed on to me."

He stops and opens the envelope, from which he pulls a folded sheet of notepaper.

Edgar Nornhoevan, for whom life comprises the solitary certainty of death – possibly from complications of an enlarged prostate – leans forward.

Jack Fedogan, jazz aficionado and one-time husband of his beloved Phyllis, leans forward.

His disastrous financial situation completely forgotten, Cliff Rhodes also leans forward.

And Jim Leafman, garbage-collecting friend of ghosts and one-time almost wife-killer, shifts sideways in his chair and stares.

With all eyes upon him, Meredith Lidenbrook Greenblat very carefully unfolds the piece of notepaper and, turning it around, holds it up for all to see.

"What is it?" is all Jack, suddenly realizing that Dave Brubeck has long since stopped playing, can think of to say.

"Is it stick figures?" Edgar offers. "Hieroglyphics?"

"That, gentlemen," says Horatio Fortesque, "is a replica of the contents of a second piece of parchment prepared by Arne Saknussemm, a sixteenth-century scholar who worked out – with the help of a book written by Snorro Turleson, a twelfth-century Icelandic writer – the way to get to the centre of the Earth. It was copied thus by either Alec or Gretchen Lidenbrook in the late eighteen-sixties."

Jim shakes his head. "You're losing me here. A *second* piece of parchment? Did we hear about the first and I missed it?"

Jack looks across at Fortesque and raises his eyebrows. Fortesque nods.

"In his book, Verne talks about a piece of parchment falling out of a copy of Turleson's book –" He looks at Fortesque. "What was it called?"

"*Heims Kringla.*"

"Right," Jack says, reluctant to attempt a pronunciation.

"Anyway, the Professor finds this book in an old junkshop and when he looks at it with Axel, a piece of parchment falls out. It's this parchment – with its runic symbols – that tells of a hidden entrance to the centre of the earth, and that's what sets off the whole adventure."

"The symbols – runes," he adds, with a complimentary nod to Jack, "tell of a secret passageway to the depths of the Earth. The parchment itself was prepared by Saknussemm who made the trip first."

"I remember the movie," says Cliff Rhodes.

Jack chuckles. "Right, I'd forgotten that." He shakes his head. "Pat Boone. Whatever happened to Pat Boone?"

"Yes," says Fortesque with obvious disdain. "There was some serious artistic licence involved in that adaptation as I recall."

"That's show-biz," Cliff Rhodes says, and he raises his glass in silent toast before taking a drink. The others follow suit.

"The first parchment – the one in Verne's book," says Fortesque excitedly, "tells of the crater of Sneffells Yokul in Iceland and how, when the shadow of the mountainous peak of Scartaris falls across it at a certain time of July, the way is revealed. This was the route taken by Saknussemm after he had written the parchment."

"But what wasn't in Verne's book –"

"Probably because he didn't know anything about it," Fortesque interjects.

"– Was the existence of a *second* piece of parchment, this one suggesting an alternative route."

Jack points at the notepaper as he gets up to bring more beers. "And that's it?"

Fortesque nods. "It's not the actual parchment, as you can see, but it *is* the same information, yes."

"And where is it, this second entrance?" Edgar asks, his tone suggesting that he isn't buying any of this.

Fortesque and Greenblat exchange glances and then face forward. "The corner of 23rd and Fifth Avenue, Manhattan," Greenblat whispers, grinning.

"Right over there," Fortesque adds, pointing to where Jack

Fedogan is standing behind the counter. "So, getting back to my original question, do you have a back room?"

9 The back room

Jack starts Brubeck off again on the PA and the drinks are set out on the bar counter.

This kind of situation is not uncommon in The Land at the End of the Working Day, as you'll know if you been here with me before. It's like the world knows when all the players needed are already assembled and there's no call for any more to come up on to the stage.

Outside, on the evening streets of Manhattan, the wind blows across the park and buffets the buildings, blowing down the avenues and across the streets, searching out points of weakness. Inside, Jack Fedogan leads his unlikely quintet across the floor and behind the well-stocked bar.

He's closed the front door and turned the sign but he's well-versed in the ways of the Working Day and believes that everyone who needs to be here is here already. Furthermore, a small voice would tell him if he stopped to pose the question, if there *were* someone else to come then he wouldn't have been able to close the door. It's probably as well that Jack doesn't pose that question because that answer would almost certainly prove to be a little disconcerting.

"You know," Edgar says as he follows Jack under the raised wooden, counter-section, "all these years and I've never been behind here?"

"Why would you be?" is what Jack comes back with to that and it's a reasonable response.

"He just doesn't like to feel he's missing out," Jim says, his smile tugging at the words and bending them out of shape.

Jim is following on behind Horatio Fortesque while, behind him, Meredith Lidenbrook Greenblat is on Jim's heels with Cliff Rhodes bringing up the rear.

To the strains of Brubeck's Mexican-sounding piano on

"La Paloma Azul" they drift, a Manhattan Wild Bunch walking in silence. Past the arrays of bottles and glasses, past Jack's collection of polishing cloths down almost to the end of the bar where Jack pauses at a closed door on his left.

"I still think you're wrong on this," Jack says, turning to face the others as he takes a hold of the door handle. Behind him, at the end of the bar, an open door leads the way to Jack's office, a small kitchen and his private restroom.

"Out of his tree, he is," Edgar adds, also turning.

"We'll see," is all that Fortesque has to say on the subject.

Jack pushes the door open on to a narrow corridor, littered along its length with crates and cartons of bottles and cans stacked two, three and sometimes even four high. As the corridor moves further from the bar, the stacks become higher and, occasionally, wider, the light dimming all the way . . . and, Jim Leafman is sure, it seems to go downwards.

"Down *there*?" Jim asks as he stares into the dimly-lit corridor. "Jack, you can hardly see your hand in front of your face." And just to prove it, Jim steps over the threshold, raises his hand and looks at it, disappointed to discover that he can see it perfectly clearly.

"Never use it," Jack says, neither proudly nor despondently. It's just a statement of fact as far as he's concerned.

Fortesque and Greenblat reach the doorway and they look inside.

"What do you think?" Greenblat whispers croakily.

"Well, according to Snorro Turleson, it's in here," Fortesque says. He reaches into his pocket and withdraws an elaborate-looking compass which he jiggles from side to side, occasionally tapping the case.

"What the hell was here in the twelfth century?" Cliff Rhodes asks nobody in particular as he leans into the corridor and then, almost immediately, back out again.

Jack shrugs. "Indians?"

"What I mean is," Cliff continues, "is what was a man from Iceland doing down here in the US?"

Meredith Greenblat says, "Well, many of the supposedly indigenous human species – Indians, if you will – can be traced back to having come down from the Arctic circle and through Canada to settle here in what was to become the United States. Perhaps –" He raises his eyebrows and jiggles his head from side to side, "– perhaps Turleson himself visited the area back when it was just a wilderness." He shrugs. "Who knows."

"May we go in?" Fortesque inquires.

Jack waves a hand magisterially. "Go right ahead."

Fortesque starts into the corridor closely followed by Greenblat.

"I must say," Fortesque's voice echoes back to the others, "it certainly is dark along here."

"You got a flashlight you can give them, Jack?" Edgar says. "The sooner we show this idea to be a looney tune the better."

"Jack, did it ever occur to you that your corridor wasn't the usual kind of corridor you'd expect to find in a Manhattan premises?"

Jack shakes his head to Cliff and then looks down at the rapidly dwindling figures. "And I don't know why," he says. "I guess it is a little strange to have so long a corridor."

"So long a corridor!" Edgar says, "it looks like it goes up into the next state. You reached the end yet?" he shouts into the gloom.

"It's getting warmer," comes back in Fortesque's curious amalgam of accents.

"Hey," says Jim excitedly.

"Don't get too excited," Jack says. "They're probably under the kitchens of the Chinese restaurant two up the street."

"Oh," Jim says, his voice dripping with disappointment.

"There's some kind of markings here," Greenblat shouts.

"The mark of Snorro!" says Cliff Rhodes, who immediately grimaces an apology to a pained-looking Edgar.

The two figures turn a bend about fifty yards distant, and Jim says, "You never checked it out, Jack?"

"Didn't need to. I just stacked boxes in there. Never used it for anything else," Jack says. As Greenblat, following his companion, disappears from sight, he adds, "I'd better get that flashlight."

Jack retraces his steps and, just for a few seconds, Dave Brubeck's version of Hoagy Carmichael's "Stardust" waft through from the bar on a gentle cool breeze. And then again, a minute later, when Jack reappears carrying a long flashlight which he immediately turns on.

"You okay down there?" Edgar shouts.

No answer.

"Maybe they didn't hear you," suggests Jim Leafman.

"Hey! You okay?" Edgar shouts, louder this time.

Still no answer.

Jack arrives with the flashlight and Edgar, already partly into the corridor, takes it from him and moves forward.

Jack follows, then Cliff with Jim at the back.

They pass a crate of Buds, a couple of boxes of Miller Lites, a case of Chardonnay, a tower of Mackeson stout.

"Mackeson stout?" Jim says as he passes it.

"Not a big seller," Jack agrees over his shoulder.

And still they move forward.

"I think I can smell the Chinese restaurant," Cliff says.

"Smells good," says Jim.

"All that beer has made me hungry," Cliff says.

By the time they've gone another fifty feet or so, the only light is from Jack Fedogan's flashlight.

"Somehow, Toto," Cliff says, "I don't think we're in Kansas any more."

"I found some scratching on the wall here," Edgar shouts back.

Jack is the first to respond. "What's it say?"

Even unseen, Edgar's shrug makes itself felt. "Just scratches," he says.

"And the corridor seems to split here."

Looking back over his shoulder, Jim Leafman is suddenly aware of two things: the first one is that someone is following through the darkness behind them and the second is a sudden need to pee. "Maybe we should get back," he says, annoyed at the way his voice seems to sound like a whine.

"Hey, Fortesque!" Edgar's voice booms. "Can you hear me?"

And still there is no answer.

10 A parting of the ways

Turning around to face the way they've come, Jim Leafman, who can feel his bladder expanding under pressure, waves an arm into the darkness in front of him. He's delighted when it doesn't connect with anything . . . such as one of those scaly mole creatures in that old black and white movie starring John Agar. Suddenly, he backs into something and someone shouts out.

"Jesus Christ, who's that?"

"Me," says Jim. "Sorry."

"You just started walking up the backs of my damn legs," snaps Edgar.

"I said I was sorry."

Jim hears Jack say, "Hey, yes: it does split two ways." He turns around in time to see Edgar shine the flashlight on a short spur to the main corridor which ends in a door. The light judders across to the left and falls on a hole in the wall. In front of the hole is a sewing machine, cobwebbed and dusty, a pair of men's shoes – a spider scurries out from one of the shoes and disappears out of the beam – a pickaxe, a length of what appears to be cable wrapped in a loop, and a clutter of broken bricks, masonry and concrete rubble.

"This is not your average bar back room corridor, Jack," Edgar says, his voice soft as he kneels down and plays the beam over the hole.

"Which way you figure they went?" Jim asks.

Cliff shouts for Edgar to play the beam over the door again and he goes across and tries the handle. It opens.

"What's in there?" Edgar asks.

"Not another corridor," Jim moans, increasingly convinced that he's going to need to add to the musky odour down here any time soon.

Pushing the door wide to expose a railed ladder set into the concrete wall beyond leading up to a circular cover some ten or twelve feet above, Cliff Rhodes says, "That must be the street." And, sure enough, the unmistakable sound of a vehicle moving over the manhole cover confirms it.

"They went that way," Jack offers, "they could get their heads knocked off."

Edgar returns the beam to the hole in the wall. "Well," he says, "I'm not even sure anyone could get through here." He reaches in and pulls at a piece of concrete. A soft rumble sounds and then another.

"Ed, I think maybe we –"

The corridor shudders beneath their feet and Jim Leafman grabs on to his crotch with both hands, applying pressure to prevent a sudden dampening of his spirits. Edgar turns the beam fully on to the hole and, way in front of them – or was it below? – they hear crashing sounds, and a cloud of dust billows from the opening.

It takes a few minutes before everyone stops coughing and spluttering. And then it's Edgar who is the first to speak. "Well," he says, "I hope they didn't go that way."

"No, they went up the steps," says Jack.

"Then why didn't they say something?" Jim asks, suddenly aware that he's shivering.

"You said before that they'd get their heads knocked off going up that way," Cliff Rhodes reminds Jack. "Wouldn't it be better if they'd gone through the hole?"

Jack doesn't respond.

"I think they went through the hole," Cliff says.

"Ed?"

"I dunno, Jack," Edgar says. "If we'd thought, then maybe we could have seen footprints or hand marks." He shines the flashlight beam in front of the hole and the steady dust-cloud still issuing from it. "But I just don't know."

"Maybe they went up through the manhole cover and just –" Jim claps his hands, one hand shooting off in front of the other. "– skidaddled."

"Without saying anything?"

"Well, they went through here," Edgar sighs, "then I reckon they're flattened by now."

"They went through the hole," Cliff says again. "And they're not flattened. They're on their way on a great adventure."

"What makes you so sure?" Jim asks. "That they went through the hole?"

"Or the adventure part," Jack adds.

"Faith," Cliff says.

"Faith? What the hell has faith got to do with it?" Edgar snorts.

Jack leans over in front of the hold, hand over his mouth. "There's no way anyone could get through that," he says, indicating the pile of rubble inside the hole.

"It wasn't like that when we first got here, Jack," Cliff Rhodes says in a measured tone. "And as for what faith has got to do with which way they want," he adds, turning to Edgar, "I can only say that faith has got something to do with everything."

"I think we're gonna start singing hymns," Jack says to Jim Leafman. And then, "You okay?"

"I need to pee."

"Let's go back," Jack announces. "We can't do anything here."

On the way back, Edgar taps Cliff Rhodes on the shoulder. "So, okay, tell me about faith."

"Faith can be interpreted as positive thinking," Cliff begins. "You heard all those stories about people lifting autos off of injured relatives? How you think that happens?"

Edgar sniggers. "That's strength, bud," he says.

"Okay, so how come those same people were unable to lift anything like what they did lift when the need wasn't as great?"

The light of Jack's outer corridor can now be seen in front of them and tensions ease . . . not to mention the strain on Jim Leafman's bladder.

"Those two guys had faith in abundance," Cliff continues. "The stories about Verne's book, the heritage of the little guy –"

"Meredith," says Jim.

"– Right, Meredith. Maybe he was the descendant of the guy who went in Verne's story – which calls for an earlier maybe, of course . . . that the story was real. And maybe the parchment was real which means that maybe the second entrance was real."

"If it was, it ain't no more!" Edgar says.

Cliff stops at the doorway back into the main corridor and, placing one foot on top of a crate of Budweisers, he says, "You know, Edgar, you're a downer."

"What the hell's a downer?"

"It's someone who has to poo poo everything that someone else says, or thinks or believes."

"'Poo poo'?"

"See?"

Edgar's mouth clamps shut.

He waits a few seconds, staring at Edgar, and then Cliff Rhodes says, "I think it's my turn to tell a story."

"Can I pee first?" Jim asks.

"I'll get more beers," Jack announces.

11 A sense of closure

Sitting back around the table, fresh beers in front of them, the four men listen intently as Cliff Rhodes begins.

"This is probably apocryphal."

"A pock of what?" a now calm Jim Leafman asks.

"An urban legend, Jim. Like the story about the escaped maniac with just one hand and a metal hook for the other . . . and he tries to get into a car while two youngsters are making out –"

"And they think they heard something so they drive off and when they get to the girl's house, the guy finds a hook hanging from her door handle."

"That's the one," says Cliff. "So, years and years ago, the story goes, a hardbitten journalist is driving through the back of beyond, somewhere in the Appalachians. You know, duelling banjos country.

"And he sees a young boy walking towards the road from the field on his right. It's only as he gets closer that he sees that the boy isn't walking through the field, he's walking towards him on water. They're right next to a small lake.

"So, the guy stops his car and gets out, calls for the boy

to come over to him – which he does. Then he asks him how he did that. The boy says, 'Did what?' And the guy says, 'Walk across that lake?' The boy looks back at the way he's just come, frowns and shrugs. 'Just put one foot in front of the other, sir,' comes the response.

"So the guy asks the boy if he does it often. 'Every day,' the boy says. 'You gonna do it tomorrow, too?' he asks. And the boy nods. 'I do it every day,' he says – because it's the fastest way for the boy to travel from his house to the tiny village down the hillside.

"So the guy tells the boy to be here tomorrow at the same time, because he's going to bring some people to take his picture and put it in a newspaper. The boy is taken aback and he asks the man why he would want to do that. The man's reply is thus: 'Because,' he says, putting an arm around the boy's shoulders, 'what you just did isn't possible. There isn't another person in this whole world can do what you just did. This makes you special. Makes you different.'

"The boy frowns and looks out at the lake. And the man tells him to be here the next day. Then he drives off."

Cliff takes a drink and carries on.

"The next day, sure enough, the man arrives at the same spot and this time he has a camera crew with him plus his assistant editor. The boy is there as well, sitting on the grass at the far side of the lake looking nervous as hell.

"The man shouts for the boy to come over and he gets the camera crew pointing in the right direction, film running. The boy starts towards them and . . . he wades out into the water. The journalist shouts for him to stop, tells him to go back and try it again. Which the boy does. Same thing.

"This happens a couple more times, during which everyone is getting pissed at the journalist. So the journalist, he goes over to the boy and he grabs a hold of his shoulder, shakes him a little. 'What you doing?' he asks the boy. 'You told me to come over,' the boy answers. 'Boy whyn't you walking on the water instead of through it?' And the boy says, 'You said it was impossible.'"

As Cliff settles back in his chair, his hands still raised up on each side of him, Jack nods, smiling. "That's a nice story," he says.

"Is it true?" Jim asks.

Edgar snorts.

"Maybe it is, maybe it isn't," Cliff Rhodes tells Jim. "It's a story, just like *Around the World in Eighty Days* or *20,000 Leagues Under the Sea*."

"Or *Journey to the Centre of the Earth*," adds Jack Fedogan.

"Absolutely. And all the stories in *The Bible*, too. Some are true and some aren't. And a lot of others have just become exaggerated over the years. But what they all do is they give hope and they provide answers and encouragement. And that's what journeys do."

"Journeys? Why journeys?"

"Well, Edgar himself said that all stories about journeys are good stories. They reach a part inside us all that other stories don't quite reach. And that's because we're each of us on our own journey.

"Jim, your story about the ghost who'd gotten himself into some kind of loop – that was a journey he undertook every night of his life, and the back-story was that he was doing it because he was so sad at the loss of his wife. And Edgar's story about the boy – and, later, the man – on the bus, that was a wonderful story, but it's the way it brought a sense of closure to Edgar's mom that makes it all the more poignant."

Cliff pauses and looks around the table. "And that's what Jules Verne was all about. He was about feeding people's need for adventure . . . making sense – and entertainment – on the journey we all make to its inevitable conclusion.

"The two men we met tonight – two adventurers in search of new experiences . . . two men who believed in what they were doing. The worst thing in the world," Cliff says, looking straight across at Edgar, "is for someone to come up to them, or to any of us, and have those hopes, beliefs and dreams flattened."

"Should we call the cops?" Jack asks.

"He didn't mean anything by it," Jim Leafman protests.

"He means for the two guys," Edgar says, slapping Jim's arm and trying to cover up his smile.

Cliff shakes his head. "I found their footprints," he says.

Edgar leans over the table. "What?"

"I found their footprints around the steps. They went out on to the street that way." He shrugs.

Everyone stares at Cliff in silence.

"Why didn't you tell us right away?" Jack asks.

"Because we made a story out of it. We made an adventure. We imagined that Fortesque and little Lorre were already high-tailing it down narrow ledges, striding through fields of giant mushrooms, discovering endless sandy beaches by the side of an azure sea and beneath the rocky dome of a gloriously high cavern before negotiating turbulent waters and watching to-the-death battles between creatures we only know about in old nature books and Steven Spielberg movies.

"We wanted them to be doing that. We wanted them to have gone through the hole. Isn't that right, Jack?"

Wide-eyed, Jack nods.

"Jim?"

Jim Leafman doesn't hesitate in saying "Yes."

And finally, "Edgar?"

Up to that point, Edgar has been staring at his beer. When he looks up, there's moisture in his eyes.

"Ed, you okay?" Jim asks.

Edgar nods. "Thinking about my mom," he says. And then, nodding, "Yeah, I wanted those two looney tunes to have gone through the hole, sure."

"Well," says Cliff Rhodes, lifting his glass to his mouth and taking a long drink, "maybe they did."

"Huh?"

"What?"

"But you –"

Cliff stands up. "I told you a story. I told you a story so's I could get your real reaction. I wouldn't have gotten it if I'd done it any other way. Truth is, I don't know which way they went. Don't know if they were who they said they were and I don't know if anything Jules Verne wrote was based on truth. But I do know this," he adds as he places his empty glass on the table. "It's been a great night. Telling stories – that's the most important journey of all."

And as Cliff walks up the stairs towards the waiting streets, the bank problem he had when he came in seems a whole lot smaller.

They're still sitting there, the three caballeros, when Cliff Rhodes shouts down, "Jack, there's a guy says his name is McCoy banging on your door. You want me to let him in?"

They exchange glances.

And smiles.

"Sure," Jack calls out, "let him in." Turning to Edgar and Jim, first one and then the other, he says, "Beers?"

"Well," Jim says, "this is a bar, ain't it? And what's a bar any good for if not beer?"

"And stories," adds Edgar.

"Guys," McCoy shouts from the stairs, "you wouldn't believe the journey I had across town."

Their laughter is so loud it blends in with that of Cliff Rhodes, striding the street, his coat collar pulled up against the Manhattan rain.

– For Hugh Lamb, Brubeck fan extraordinaire

THE TRUE STORY OF BARBICANE'S VOYAGE

Laurent Genefort

By 1864 Verne was on a roll. Having completed Voyage au centre de la terre, *and the next Captain Hatteras novel,* Le Désert de glace, *he turned his eyes to the heavens and wrote the first genuine scientific novel to explore the complex subject of getting a man to the Moon. No one had done this before. There had been plenty of fanciful stories taking man to the moon, as far back as the* True History *by Lucian of Samosata in the second century AD. His travellers are whisked to the Moon by a whirlwind. The noted French swordsman, Cyrano de Bergerac, had several ideas of space travel in* The Government of the World in the Moon *(1659), the one that worked involving a plentiful supply of firework rockets. In* A Voyage to the Moon *(1827) George Tucker (writing as Joseph Atterley) uses a newly discovered element, lunarium, which is repulsed by the Earth and attracted by the Moon, whilst in 1835 Edgar Allan Poe took his adventurer, Hans Pfal, all the way to the Moon by balloon. None of these or other writers had considered the implications of the lack of air or the forces needed to escape the Earth's gravity. Verne, though, went into immense detail, so much so that he took up most of one novel,* De la terre à la lune, *describing the plans of the Baltimore Gun Club in designing*

and building their giant gun and the projectile and needed a second novel, Autour de la lune, *to record the adventures of the company in their trip round the Moon. We are introduced to the characters Impey Barbicane, President of the Gun Club, who originally conceived the idea of an unmanned shot to the moon, the Frenchman Michel Ardan (an anagram of Verne's friend Nadar), who pushes for a manned expedition, Barbicane's adversary, Captain Nicholl, who opposes the experiment but is literally brought on board, and the mathematician J. T. Maston.*

De la terre à la lune *was not serialized in Hetzel's* Magasin *(which was intended for younger readers) but ran in the more literary* Journal des débats politiques et littéraires, *during September and October 1865. Using today's vernacular, it was the world's first 'hard' science-fiction story, meaning it was ultra-technological, drawing heavily on known sciences and projecting their development.*

Perhaps it is no surprise that the exploits of the Baltimore Gun Club inspired several contributions to this book with stories based either on the original Moon voyage, or as sequels to their other adventures, which feature later in this book. It is perhaps also not too surprising that the authors made connections with that other great pioneer of science fiction, H. G. Wells. Here then are the further adventures of the world's first intrepid astronauts.

1
What History Records . . .

The whole world knows of the voyage to the moon undertaken in 1865 by three adventurers: two Americans, Impey Barbicane and myself, Captain Nicholl, as well as a daring Parisian, Michel Ardan. The amazing project of sending a projectile to the moon was Barbicane's initiative. Ardan, that inspired hot-head, brought about our voyage to the night-star by proposing to replace the initial spherical ball with a cylindrical and conical projectile which would serve as a passenger compartment. More surprisingly, he succeeded in reconciling me with Barbicane, who had always been my enemy.

My own role is at last revealed. It is to relate what truly happened exactly thirty-seven years ago, during the six days of our inter-planetary journey. This tale will, no doubt, remain apocryphal. I have taken care that it should not be known during my lifetime, nor for several generations after me, if God wills it.

(Contrary to the usual practice of scientific memoirs, I will refrain from weighing my story down with calculations and technical notes. The reader should excuse any lack of style. Unlike Monsieur Verne and Mr Wells, my forte is not that of literature, but that of arms and armour-plating. Also, I will leave unsaid any episodes of the tale which appear accurately in the original accounts.)

Before arriving at the truth, it is necessary to return to the facts.

The events lavishly described in Monsieur Verne's *From the Earth to the Moon* and *Around the Moon* are essentially true, as are the portraits of the protagonists. Impey Barbicane is depicted as a forty-year-old man of average build, with features as severe as his character. Endowed with an unshakeable yet frosty calm, proud and enterprising, he presented the image of a Yankee cut from one cloth. He was President of the Baltimore Gun Club, a society of artillery men consumed by idleness (the war of secession was only just over, following Lee's surrender to Grant on 9th April 1865), and had the idea of launching a sphere to the moon, sending out an international call for subscription which turned a crazy idea into a reality.

As for myself, I regret to say that Barbicane resembles me on all points. I think, however, that I have a more thoughtful temperament, and perhaps, in an equal proportion, less genius. Monsieur Verne's story sensitively plays down the disputes we had with each other, and which Michel Ardan sometimes had the greatest difficulty in stopping. This Frenchman, American in character as he took a broad view of things, had an exuberant nature and could only end up by defying the experts. His moustache bristled like an angry cat at the slightest word; on the other hand, his mane of hair and his boldness resembled those of a lion. If Barbicane and I were the two wheels of the celestial chariot, he was its axle.

On 1st December at 10.46 and 40 seconds p.m., a grey cannon, set into the side of Stone's-Hill, Florida, at 27° 7' latitude north by 5° 7' longitude west shot the aluminium shell which housed us in the direction of the Moon.

Our vehicle measured nine feet wide by twelve feet high. It was endowed with four lens-shaped portholes six inches thick, and stocked with provisions for a year, water (and brandy) for several months, and fuel for one hundred and fifty hours. A Reiset & Regnaut machine would recycle the air for sixty days. Our quarters had padded walls, as well as a chest containing tools and instruments. Once launched at a speed of twelve thousand yards a second, the projectile should travel approximately 86,500 miles before reaching the Moon at the apex of its flight, four days after its departure.

I will not dwell upon the various incidents that enlivened the voyage itself while we were approaching the Moon's pock-marked face: the initial shock that caused us to lose consciousness for several minutes; the meteor that altered our trajectory enough to make us miss our objective; the death of our canine companion Satellite and his ejection from the shell, which he continued to accompany on its course – literally now a satellite; the strange moment of drunkenness due to an excessive influx of oxygen into the confined space; the equally intoxicating experience of weightlessness; the flight at low altitude across the lunar landscape; the intense cold of the moon's hidden face, followed by intense heat; the second meteor that exploded in front of us, and which we still believed to be the gift of fortune. Finally, Barbicane's miraculous discovery which enabled us to escape the circumlunary orbit destined to become our tomb.

But these few trees hide a veritable forest, for it was evidently not towards the Earth that Barbicane pointed his rockets, *but towards our original objective.* What else could be expected, indeed, of such an energetic, such a stubborn, character as Barbicane!

2

Columbus of the Moon

We studied Beer and Moedler's *Mappa selenographica*, the best map available at that time, in order to determine our landing-point. The shell flew over the lunar landscape at an altitude of less than eighty miles, so that its major configurations were visible in detail through the side windows. We admired the Sea of Clouds bordered by volcanoes, then Mount Copernicus, so high that it can be seen from Earth; then came a succession of ring-shaped mountains and palisades. Jagged and angular coastlines marked out fictional continents, vast archipelagos, oblong islands. There was no sign of vegetation or construction. The configurations of the soil indicated nothing more than the work of geology, with its stony avalanches, its mountains and its abysses, its runnels of cooled lava and its volcanic deposits. All was dead.

I reported my observations to my companions: "I can see nothing but mineral strata: no trace of an atmosphere, which would make the horizon iridescent."

Barbicane shook his long beard in a gesture of annoyance. "The atmosphere could be hidden away at the bottom of the cirques; some of them are over five thousand yards high."

"All the same," I protested, "it would not be dense enough to breathe. Experiments have proved that man cannot acclimatize himself to a pressure of less than half that of the Earth's atmosphere."

"To be sure. But we will not remain outside for long. It is time to prepare ourselves; I fear another meteor, which would certainly carry us off."

Barbicane and I covered page upon page with ballistic calculations, determining the ideal moment to ignite the twenty fire-pieces mounted in the rear of the projectile. Thanks to the fact that the Moon's mass was eight times less than that of the Earth and its diameter four times less, the fall would be six times easier to soften.

We were aiming at a vast crater in the western hemisphere. To my great shame, I must admit that I have forgotten its name. Could this be one of those effects of the "unconscious" speculated upon by Professor Freud, who is so much in fashion at present in the bourgeois salons of New England? I know not.

Following our plan, Barbicane removed the metal shutters in the rear, and replaced them with an array of cannon, already charged with powerful explosives.

At 3.50, he put his lighter to the common wick. His tone was solemn. "Gentlemen, the time has come to find out whether there is a god of ballistics."

A sharp thrust below betrayed the ignition. The visible portion of the lunar disk began to grow, its horizon to level out, as if the porthole had suddenly changed into a telescope.

"We're going to *crash*!" I cried in spite of myself.

The shell vibrated horribly, forcing us into immobility. I don't know by what miracle Barbicane managed to light the four forward-facing, braking rockets at the exact second required. The god of ballistics inspired him, no doubt. An instant earlier, and the manoeuvre would have had no effect. Three seconds later, and the lunar surface would have pulverized us. A huge impact shock shot us up to the ceiling, arms and legs all mixed together. Without the sprung leather padding, my limbs would have been broken.

"Is everyone all right?" I quavered weakly.

No light appeared through the lateral portholes; the exterior was plunged into total darkness and we had to light the gas-lamps.

"We've arrived!" Michel Ardan exclaimed, his moustaches bristling with excitement. "Us, Christopher Columbuses of the Moon!"

"Oh," Barbicane joked, "Who knows if Cyrano de Bergerac . . ."

"In that case, long live Cyrano de Bergerac and all the Columbuses of the Moon who went before him! Long live us!"

And the Frenchman went in search of the bottle of Dom Perignon that, unbeknownst to us, he had immersed in the water barrel in the depths of the hold. The shell was leaning

by several degrees. We toasted the Moon, the Earth, the Gun
Club and all the subscribing countries in one go; finally we
drank to the honour of the poor dog Satellite, first victim of
the conquest of space.

"Now we must go out and explore," said Barbicane, setting
down his glass. "If, that is, the composition and the density
of the air are suitable for us."

I regretted that we had not brought with us one of those
waterproof diving suits attached to a pump, which have
recently allowed divers to breath ten metres below the surface
of the waves. Barbicane shrugged his shoulders and unlatched
the circular door in the centre of the shell's base. I crouched
down and breathed in deeply. A dry, cold fragrance, straight
out of a laboratory, suffused my throat, but no liquid, blood
or lymph-fluid, began to run from my ears or nostrils.

"Air," I said in a hoarse voice. "Barbicane, you were right.
There is no substantial vacuum. We can go outside without
fearing illness."

Michel Ardan cheered again, and we set ourselves to
opening the exit-door. I wasn't sorry to leave the shell. At
the end of the first day of the voyage the fifty-four square
feet of its floor-space had shrunk in my mind until they
seemed much less than ten.

Barbicane claimed the right to exit first, which Michel
Ardan and I accorded him without quibble. I followed him.
A brief vertigo seized us one after the other, a sharp pain
penetrated our ears, then we breathed freely.

We had landed on a promontory jutting out from the side
of the great crater, which descended steeply for fifty metres.
The fire of the descent had blackened the portholes, so
obscuring our view. We could see, however, that the landscape was a muddle of rocks of all kinds thrown together in
powdery desolation as far as the distant walls that circled the
crater.

The vision was accompanied by a long silence. Now we
were sure: no-one had come to the Moon before us, for
literature had nowhere evoked a similar spectacle, nothing
with the power of this prospect.

Low clouds veiled part of the starry sky. A blue crescent marbled with white crested the horizon.

"Mother Earth," Barbicane murmured. "Will we ever return there?"

"Home-sickness already?" said Michel Ardan, in spurious indignation, "When a whole world awaits discovery! Don't you find that this crater lacks nothing, in dimensions or rotundity, when measured against Greek amphitheatres or Roman arenas? Who knows if the philosophers of ancient Greece were not Selenite tourists? Here, not only could thousands of spectators pack themselves in, but millions . . ."

"And the spectacles would employ myriad extras!" Barbicane said, "Certainly, you're right. The Earth is not so vast that the heavens cannot deliver us with new territories to be mapped out . . ."

Michel Ardan blushed with pleasure. "You are not a geographer, but a poet, like all scholars . . . But look!" He was suddenly pointing below. Something crept from a crevice, towards our promontory.

"A lichen," he announced, having the keenest sight among us.

There are no words strong enough to express what I felt then. "A life beyond Earth, a life beyond Earth . . ." For several minutes it was impossible to think of anything else.

Each one of us was in agreement, following Plutarch, Swedenborg or more recently Flammarion, on the possibility, and even the necessity, of life on other planets. Why should a great horologer have set a sun in place just to light mankind! What derisory vanity.

The apparent absence of atmosphere had closed the door on the subject. But here, through the window, was ample evidence of life!

The tongue of lichen reached the promontory. I bent down carefully and seized a strand, mossy, purple and scalloped . . . only to let go of it swiftly, with a kick that propelled me five steps backwards. Barbicane caught me *en route*, interrupting my grotesque leap.

"Gently, dear colleague. Don't forget that here weight is

six times less than on our native planet. What goes for the shell goes for us too. A trio of Herculeses, that's what we are."

While I was brushing my elbows and knees, Michel in turn approached the lichen with the idea of plucking a tuft of it. I immediately dissuaded him by brandishing my thumb and index finger, which were turning red and stinging with a lancing pain.

As an experienced chemist, Barbicane had, like myself, a considerable knowledge of biology, the chemistry of life.

"What would you say of this lichen," I asked him, "which grows at the speed of a crystal, moves at that of a worm, and has organic matter as its everyday fare? As what species, or rather in which kingdom, would you classify it?

"I would say," interrupted Michel Ardan, "that I wouldn't make a blanket of it!"

In the hermetically-sealed shell, closed by an aluminium panel held fast by powerful pressure screws, we had nothing to fear from the lichen. We decided to shut ourselves up there and give ourselves time for several hours of rest, as we were beginning to suffer badly from sleep-deficiency.

We had (it seemed to me) hardly closed our eyes when a shock-wave shook the shell. Scraping noises reached us through the twelve-inch-thick walls, indicating the enormous force that was being exerted on the shell. The floor began to pitch. Without wishing it, had we provoked a landslide?

I threw myself towards the porthole and let out a cry of amazement: huge claws, shiny and black, had seized our dwelling. We were flying over the floor of a crater at an altitude of nearly a thousand feet.

"Look, out of the upper porthole!"

A phenomenal abdomen, segmented like that of an insect, was wavering close to the point of the shell and covered us completely with its shadow. Through one of the lateral portholes, we could see the beating of wings like cathedral windows, overhung by wing-cases as large as ships, and, finally, part of a head with globular eyes.

I imagined the extraordinary strength of this creature, which was able to lift the 19,250 pounds of the projectile . . . But no, I was forgetting that on the Moon one had to subtract five-sixths of this weight, which left 3,208 pounds. This still remained considerable, out of all proportion for any terrestrial animal, *a fortiori* an aerian one. To be sure, we were like Hercules in this world. But it was one inhabited by Titans.

"Can this monster have taken us for one of its eggs?" Michel Ardan asked.

No-one replied, for the animal, whose general form resembled that of a *Lucanus cervus* (a beetle commonly called a flying-kite), bent its flight towards a hole, hardly larger than the diameter of our shell. It deposited us in this rocky declivity with all the delicacy of an entomologist handling a rare specimen.

The fall into the shadows was brief and, against expectation, quite gentle. Michel Ardan stood up, pulling himself together.

"This time, I think we have well and truly arrived."

3
The Selenites

"Here we are under the moon's crust," I murmured.

The portholes revealed the interior of a cavern some quarter of a mile in diameter, sealed above by a dome and pierced by holes where shadows moved. The prospect of being confronted by the larvae of a giant insectoid cooled our enthusiasm, but Michel Ardan remarked that there was nothing to be gained by remaining enclosed.

Barbicane opened the shutter and we stepped outside.

I cursed myself for not having brought a daguerreotype – or better still, a talbotype – to photograph the Selenite who was approaching us with the hopping gait of a bird. But the latter would doubtless not have allowed me to photograph it – something that was confirmed later on.

Perched on spindly legs, the Selenite was perhaps four feet high (which, by the way, reduced to nothing my theory that their size should have been in proportion to the mass of their globe, and consequently should not have exceeded one foot. Reality proved more complex: a Selenite could be either Lilliputian or Brobdingnagian, according to his role in society). It was a compact creature, which had much in common with a cockroach raised up on its back legs, from the chitinous integument that served simultaneously as skeleton, clothing, or armour, to the head capped by a helmet spiked with antennae above, and mandibles below. On its chest hung what I identified as a little fairground drum. The Selenite held out a truncated hand towards Barbicane. Automatically, the savant seized it . . . and gave it a vigorous handshake!

Visibly satisfied, the Selenite proceeded to tap on his drum. It only took me a few seconds to realize that the rhythm had nothing in common with African tribal music, but was quite simply Morse code! This was the method this individual had found to compensate for its inability to artic- ulate audible sounds. But it heard and understood every- thing we said to it.

I only had the vaguest notion of this codified language. Fortunately, Michel Ardan knew it, and agreed to act as inter- preter.

"In the name of the people of the Moon . . . I bid you welcome . . . Soon we will be able to speak aloud."

I don't know whether the greatest surprise was that the Selenite expressed itself in perfect English, or that it shook each of us in turn by the hand. But the frontiers of the absurd had been crossed so long ago that we found all of this quite natural. Our guide emitted a trill through its mandibles, at the limit of audibility. Straight away another Selenite appeared, one of quite a different make-up, resembling a horse (carriage included) and a beetle.

"One would swear that its carapace had been moulded to hold us comfortably," Ardan mumbled.

There was nothing to do but to seat ourselves on this unusual vehicle. The seats proved comfortable, endowed with rolls of chitin in the guise of armrests. The animal-vehicle set off by itself. It was silent and extremely fast. Barbicane entered into conversation with our guide, who replied without standing on ceremony. The Selenites comprised a united society, based on the perpetual progress of industry and aiming at the complete development of the Moon. They had learned our language by observing us through immense telescopes. These offered a magnification sufficient to scrutinize a fellow in the street, in London or in Peking, and to read his lips. Consequently, our arts, history and customs were by no means unknown to them. The Selenites had set up hundreds of such telescopes, spread across the surface of the Moon, which transmitted their received images with the aid of mirrors and projected them on to enormous public screens. A highly entertaining spectacle, no doubt.

It was in this way that they had had wind of our attempt to make a landing on the night star. Not wishing to be discovered, they had sent an asteroid designed to throw us off our linear trajectory. The manoeuvre had succeeded, but the plan had failed: they had hoped that we would use the shell's rockets to return to Earth, yet the opposite had occurred, despite the second meteor that their pyrotechnicians had caused to explode some hundreds of miles ahead of the shell.

"But why should you wish to remain hidden at all cost?" Barbicane questioned.

The Selenite drummed in reply that the Great Planner judged that humanity was not ready for a fruitful exchange. In the light of past history, we had been compared to a rudderless ship that no longer responded. On the other hand, certain Selenites saw the appearance of a few frail barques, but our guide remained evasive on this point. It did, however, make a comment that left me thoughtful, and a little shocked: pursuing the marine analogy, some Selenites had formed the hypothesis that the visitors – ourselves, in fact – were "rats leaving the sinking ship". Michel Ardan hastened to disabuse it. Moreover, added the Selenite, no representative of the feminine gender formed part of our expedition. I must admit that this point plunged us into embarrassment. Despite a few exceptions, science remained, and was destined to remain, a masculine affair.

Our curious equipage traversed a series of amphitheatres teeming with Selenites of different sizes, occupied with various tasks. The amphitheatre appeared to be at the heart of Selenite architecture, in imitation of the natural formations on the surface. They had known of electricity since time immemorial, and made abundant use of it. I wondered who this Great Planner could be, who was obeyed by thousands of creatures, each one different from the other.

We were quite rightly being taken to it. Before this, our equipage came to a halt in front of an incubator, a monstrous building pierced with holes of all sizes. A Selenite quite similar to the first came from it, to replace the latter.

This one was provided with a phonatory organ, a muddle of palpes and mandibles that produced a voice like an oboe. In the meantime, Michel, Impey, and I had worked out a system for naming the Selenites we met, from the noise of their carapaces as they moved. Thus, our new interpreter was called Krrak'ack.

"Krrak'ack . . . Good day," said Krrak'ack with an upper-class English accent. "I am charged with taking you to the Great Planner, so your fate may be decided."

"Our fate?" repeated Ardan, with an imperceptible frown.

"It has not been decided whether it would be better to allow you to leave, or to keep you here. It is vital that our existence remain secret."

"By my faith," said Barbicane, "if the guest quarters are agreeable . . ."

Ardan and I jumped in at these words.

"It is out of the question! We are expected *below*. Our friends in the Gun Club would be inconsolable . . . and they would definitely send a rescue expedition!"

Krrak'ack seemed responsive to this argument, as far as the frantic ballet of his antennae revealed. The reproduction of this species, which manifested a stupefying intelligence in many respects, interested me greatly. This differed from that of all other species on Earth. Selenite scientists were able to take a standard egg (and they were all so) and modify the characteristics, be they physical or mental, of the young creature prior to birth. Krrak'ack had been conceived a few days before our arrival. His carapace was as fine and supple as a leather suit, for he would do no manual work. Thanks to his enlarged brain, his learning had been accelerated, and it had taken him only two hours to master English and to assimilate the rudiments of our culture. The Selenite-vehicle that had transported us had been manipulated in the same manner. Its brain was no more than a ganglion of nerves, hardly bigger than a nut.

Their system of reproduction, or rather of production, assured the continuity of their society, as far as their descendants were concerned. Each individual corresponded to a metier, or sometimes even a specific task: there were Selenite-hammers, and even Selenites in the form of gearwheels. The disproportionate beetle that had transported our shell had been conceived with this aim. Then it had died a natural death.

Perhaps one day, with the power of technology, mankind would be able to achieve the same result. Michel Ardan stared at me, horrified.

"And would you deny your humanity? I can hardly see myself in the skin of a Selenite-tool, sensible though it may be, for I have no such calling. At least not unless there exist Selenite adventurers!"

Krrak'ack ignored him.

"That is not quite accurate," objected Barbicane, "The Selenites are tools, certainly, but also, and inextricably, blacksmiths."

When I asked to visit one of these incubator-factories, in order to examine the marvellous machines that were able to model the foetus in the egg without killing it, Krrak'ack proved intractable. Michel Ardan had a saucy smile for my complaints.

"You Americans are astounded at nothing . . . Would you coldly display a man and a woman in the act of procreation just to satisfy the curiosity of a Selenite scientist visiting us?"

"Well . . . why not?"

This time, Ardan burst out laughing.

"All the same! Scientists are incorrigible, no matter what planet they come from. I had forgotten that you were lunatic by calling . . ."

I hardly paid attention to his joke, and forgot it quickly, as our equipage had begun its mad course again. All around us, Selenites were digging galleries and amphitheatres, making greenhouses where they cultivated a kind of cactus that produced quantities of air from the rocks. For me, this industrious civilization was a marvellous symbol of progress. The variety of the Selenites seemed inexhaustible.

We were surprised to see, in the middle of an amphitheatre, a life-size replica of the White House in Washington. And, further on, an Arc de Triomphe.

"Can they have discovered the means of transporting our monuments from the Earth to the Moon?" asked Barbicane, truly impressed.

We were all impressed. And even more so when Krrak'ack told us that all these monuments had been sculpted from giant gold-bearing nodules, extracted from the heart of the satellite. These gigantic masses were of gold! I immediately tried to exchange one of them for tools and instruments from the shell. Krrak'ack remarked without irony that Selenite science surpassed ours by far. Their capacity, in terms of invention and fabrication, out-measured American industrial genius (it's quite true to say) by 100,000 times.

Michel Ardan had no more luck in his offer of the shrubs he had taken care to bring.

"In a few decades," he said, "green prairies will stretch across the Moon."

Krrak'ack declared himself tempted, but upon reflection declined the offer. The Moon's gold could easily provoke a human invasion, such as that which was taking place at that very moment in the Western United States. We should not take anything from the Moon.

The vehicle stopped at the entry to a passage, where there stood an enormous machine.

4

The Philosophical Calculator

Barbicane – as the pyrotechnician he was – identified it as an "iron bullet". It was a kind of spherical locomotive. There was no need for carriages, as a portion of the interior was fitted out with Spartan compartments. In place of bogeys, there were toothed wheels arranged around its circumference. No rails, but grooves cut all along a smooth passage, which served as a rail-track and a guide.

The passage plunged into the depths of the substratum. Barbicane and I asked Krrak'ack numerous questions, which he translated to the mechanic with much recourse to fluting whistles. The Selenite mechanic was reminiscent of octopuses and spiders, and was so much at one with the machine that it would have been impossible to extricate him from it.

A clever hydraulic system allowed the passenger section to remain always facing forward. The iron bullet reached a phenomenal speed, thanks to the lightness of its weight, but also thanks to the engine's fuel, whose name had no equivalent in our language. Always careful, Krrak'ack refused to reveal anything further about it.

"The Great Planner must be awaiting us on the other side of the Moon," Michel Ardan said with resignation, "Perhaps he will be more loquacious."

We installed ourselves as comfortably as possible. The Selenites had had the goodness to bring along the provisions stored in the shell, and so we were able to restore ourselves. Michel Ardan concocted one of his secret recipes, which he washed down with a glass of brandy as dessert.

On pouring the beverage, several drops fell on to the little table, made from a Selenite carapace. The drops drove themselves into it, bubbling furiously, melting all underneath them with the alacrity of boiling water poured on a sugar-cube.

"By God!" Barbicane swore religiously, "Alcohol attacks lunar chitin!"

"It's like the effect of acid," I confirmed, probing the holes.

"Or rather a powerful solvent. This could certainly be of use, if the need arose."

We decided to keep a litre of brandy on us at all times.

While my companions were slumbering, replete, I lost myself in contemplating the landscape which could be seen through a window, or, rather, a peep-hole.

I will not enter into detail of the tableaux which opened up as the successive strata passed rapidly before my eyes, for our journey sometimes took the form of a vertiginous fall. What I did see were fossils of monsters, each more exotic than the last, each more gigantic, such as the half-mile-long skull which served as a transit station at the centre of the Moon. Sometimes, a transparent tube replaced the rocky passage, and we plunged into huge lakes which filled immense caverns, furrowed by enormous machines with paddles. We passed through greenhouses full of giant cacti, empty, misty spaces of fearful dimensions; we passed cylindrical, bottomless wells where hoist-Selenites criss-crossed each other, using their abdomens like Montgolfiers.

Thanks to the speed of the machine, it only took us eleven hours and fifty minutes to traverse the Moon from side to side, taking account of the delays caused by the periodic changing of tracks.

On arrival at the terminus, Krrak'ack approached a kind of telegraph-machine, upon which he tapped, using his antennae. He was replied by a crackling. After five minutes of conversation, he turned his blank face towards us.

"The Great Planner is ready to receive you. He can only grant you a little time, as many tasks across the whole Moon monopolise his attention."

"Oh, what it is to be a potentate!" Ardan joked.

A new living carriage, similar to the first, came to pick us up, then deposited us in a monumental amphitheatre, opposite a kind of temple with pagodas. It took me a moment to realize that these seeming pagodas were in reality bundles of metal wires, which stretched in their millions from the interior of the tall building. A buzzing arose like a hive of bees.

As soon as we had penetrated the temple's interior, a hallowed silence fell.

Without the slightest consultation with each other, we had anticipated a Selenite with a huge head and an atrophied body. But it was not such a prodigious super-being that reigned over life on the Moon.

Nothing we already knew could have prepared us for the confrontation. The feeling that enveloped me when I saw the Great Planner (or at least a part of it) was a singular emotion, so rare that it has no name: a mixture of fear and ecstasy, of repugnance and of marvelling at the unknown. (Later, Michel Ardan confided to me that it gave him the feeling of an Iroquois at the court of Louis XIV).

The temple was no more than a wall buzzing with insects, minuscule Selenites ranged side by side, legs interlaced like the mesh of a net. The wall rose into darkness, and seemed to have no end. The first image that came to mind was that of a mechanical calculator, such as had existed for two centuries. This one was not mechanical, but organico-electrical. Each cog, each belt, each relay was replaced by a miniature Selenite whose eight or ten legs were connected to those of his fellow creatures. Individually, each would have had no more intelligence than a fly, but they had found the means to apply themselves in sequence. Each time a piece of information was transmitted to one of them, its abdomen lit up like a firefly. The wall blinked with a thousand fires.

"See their Great Planner," cried Barbicane, accompanying his exclamation with an all-embracing sweep of the arm. "Not an individual, but a colony-organism, composed of a collective brain spread out before us . . . A philosophical calculator, sheltered from all passions of the flesh, and thus able to resolve all the problems of an evolved society. Is it not amazing?"

"You mean to say that this creature exists with the aim of producing thought, as a plant produces roots and leaves? You are right, Barbicane, that is the marvel."

Michel Ardan did not share our opinion, and Krrak'ack did not give him the chance to develop his own. The creature tapped several words into the temple telegraph, and received a reply which he translated straight away. "The Great Planner has decided to keep you among us, to ensure our safety."

Temperance was not one of Michel Ardan's cardinal virtues. Upon hearing the verdict of the philosophical calculator, he swelled his cheeks with a glassful of brandy. In a single movement, he leapt in the air and sprayed a Selenite-relay, which immediately began to melt and shrivel up, a network of organs running away below it. The sudden recurrence of activity on the part of the fireflies revealed that the blow had struck home.

"What are you doing!" cried Krrak'ack, in a deluge of maddened whistling, "You are destroying the memory of the Great Planner . . ."

Barbicane had understood his friend's action. He set himself in front of Krrak'ack, with a series of appeasing gestures. Then he asked for his speech to be translated word for word.

"The Great Planner has everything to fear if he keeps us by his side. Our saliva can destroy the substance that forms your carapaces. We will be a constant menace to the community. Alternatively, if he lets us go, he has our word as gentlemen that we will never speak a word of what we have seen on the Moon."

There remained fifty gallons of brandy with which to carry out our threat.

The philosophical calculator's reply only took several seconds to reach us, and it relieved everything.

"He has decided that you will leave in two hours. The workers have just been notified."

"Two hours!" repeated Barbicane, "But that's impossible; it took us almost ten hours to reach you, and our shell is still on the other side of the Moon! How will you set us *en route* in such a short time?"

I suggested that the Selenites could re-launch the shell into orbit, and make it land on our side of the Moon. The Planner, however, had a different idea, which reflected their industrial genius: it was intending to construct a shell exactly like the *Columbiad*. No, not intending: the orders had been given, and they were already working on it. The original had been taken apart several minutes ago, and the plans had been transmitted by telegraph to the different units of production, which were at that very moment working on it.

Meanwhile, our host questioned us on the most wide-ranging subjects, from the pronunciation of certain slang-terms to our favourite colours!

"Has not a creature as ingenious and all-powerful as yourself ever had the wish to send an expedition to Earth?" Barbicane wondered.

The Great Planner told us that in the course of a past that was not counted in years, but in geological eras, the Selenites had visited the large blue planet. At that time it was covered by luxuriant forests, bereft of intelligent life except for a kind of octopus, very cunning, but with a limited consciousness. These had not survived the globe's glaciation. The Selenites, crushed by a gravity six times stronger than their own, had been incapable of leaving and had perished. The Earth had been declared a forbidden planet. Since then, only the large telescopes continued their observation.

Michel Ardan, always the practical one, asked how many Selenites there were on the Moon. The Great Planner kept us waiting for several seconds, then: "At this second, there are 1,387,180,000,512 of us."

Michel opened his mouth, then closed it, subdued.

I asked him about the formation of the Moon, which no specialist had as yet been able to demonstrate in any definitive way. The perfection of the Selenite civilization suggested the ancient nature of the globe. Once more the infinite carpet of fireflies began to shine in every direction.

"Long before the creation of the Planner," Krrak'ack translated, "the surface of the Moon was hot, and our ancestors frolicked in the sun. Then the Earth came into being, and our atmosphere began to disappear, breathed in by the new planet. We had to take refuge in the sublunar grottoes. Our survival depended upon the strength of our industry, so our

ancestors developed the machines that surround us. And they
created myself."

The idea that in times past the Moon's air had been
captured – stolen in fact! – by the Earth, affected us all.

"It is we," said Michel Ardan, cast into the deepest depths
of sadness, "we who have forced these brave Selenites to leave
their welcoming sun and live like hermits or moles. Shame
upon you, Earth, and all your generations!"

Time had run out; we had to leave. The cosmos has its
laws, stronger than those of men or of Selenites. The new
shell was ready, the provisions aboard. A cannon had just
been loaded, one sufficiently powerful to propel us beyond
the Moon's field of gravity. The fuel mixture was not of gun-
cotton, or some other derivative of pyroxilite, but a gas solution whose combustion produced nothing other than water!

We made our farewells to the Great Planner, then the
Selenite-carriage set us down in an amphitheatre. In its centre
was a steel pole which rose to a vaulted ceiling. An opening
yawned at its base. A Selenite showed us into the interior.

"But it's our shell," cried Michel Ardan.

Slight differences, in the grain of the leather, or the greater
fineness of the porthole-glass, witnessed the fact that it was
a replica. Before the door closed upon us, I saluted our guide,
Krrak'ack, with a pang. I knew that upon our departure his
job as translator would cease, and quite naturally, his existence would too. It was out of the question to take him with
us: we had promised that our voyage would leave no trace.

The Selenite who had shown us into the shell informed
us that there remained twelve minutes before the shot that
would fire us into space.

We seated ourselves, and Michel Ardan sighed, "Farewell,
Moon,"

"Yes, farewell . . ."

Barbicane expressed the despair of a geographer who will
never have the opportunity to chart the Moon.

"Others will come, who will do it," he said suddenly.

And, in a flight of fancy little worthy of a member of the
Geography and Cartography Society, he described the legions

of geographers, bedecked with instruments, drawing-blocks and pencils, surveying the craters, the dead seas and the great plains, and tracing the very latitudes and longitudes of the surface.

Other regrets gnawed at me. We had not had the time to ask whether other human expeditions had taken place before ours.

But I consoled myself: others would come, of that I was certain. Meanwhile, Barbicane soliloquised on the possibility of extracting some of the fireflies to make individual boxes of thought that could be carried on one's back . . . Then he wondered at the eventual possibility of constructing a brain greater than the Great Planner: a genial machine, to govern not only the Earth, but the rest of the universe as well!

One final thought came to me, or rather, a terrible doubt: what if the Great Planner had lied to us, and was only claiming to be returning us to Earth? What if, on the contrary, it was preparing to send us to Mars, or even to the extremities of the solar system, into infinite space?

And if . . .

5
"The Moon had revealed all its Secrets"

The return voyage was undertaken in a stupefied state, as though opiate vapours had been mixed with the air in the Reiset & Regnaut apparatus that ensured its renewal. The Moon had revealed all its secrets to us. For our good, or for bad? When I asked Barbicane, he gave me the following reply, surprising for a savant: "The Persians were convinced of the sacred nature of the sea. Why should the same not be true of space, that ocean of ether that surrounds stars and galaxies? Have we not defiled a temple, just like the ignorant traveller who enters a mosque in Baghdad without taking off his shoes?"

As everyone knows, we splashed down in the Pacific Ocean, close to the American corvette, *Susquehanna*, at 1.17 a.m.

during the night of 11th–12th December, at 20° 7' latitude north, and 41° 37' longitude west. The recovery, and our triumphant return to the United States, prevented us from consulting each other. On the train we took to tour the states of the Union, we discussed the version of our tale that would be best to present to the world. Barbicane was the last to be reasonable on the subject of keeping the secret of the Selenites.

"And why should we not tell the truth!" exclaimed this man, to whom a lie was anathema.

"All the same," began Michel Ardan, "We promised . . ."

It was I who produced the decisive argument.

"Our country has just come to the end of a war, hardly months ago. You and I, who contributed to it, know what carnage it was for our citizens. The revelation of a celestial life, within reach of a cannon's shot, would overturn the balance of power and would hurl the globe into a conflagration of unheard-of proportions, into which all states would be drawn. We Americans would incessantly strive to annexe this new continent of the air and to display the star-spangled flag on its highest summit, to make it the thirty-seventh state of the Union!"

"Don't forget," Michel·Ardan added, "that many nations, from the greatest to the most humble, offered financial assistance which gave them the right to intervene in affairs concerning their satellite. France, for example, contributed a sum of 1,253,930 francs."

I dealt the fatal blow.

"If we reveal the truth world-wide, nothing short of a world war will break out. A war of the worlds, I tell you."

Barbicane's tall frame slumped. He tugged at his moustaches without even noticing it. In a solemn gesture, he laid his left hand on Ardan's shoulder, his right hand on mine.

"You are a thousand times right, my friends. It will never be said that I threw the world into chaos. The role of science is to create order, not to destroy it. Our story will not only have the aim of astounding the general populace, it must content the most eminent scholars of Cambridge Observatory, and even our companions of the Gun Club, General Morgan,

Major Elphiston, and the unavoidable, in terms of curiosity as much as girth, J.T. Maston."

"Bah," Michel Ardan concluded, quite appropriately. "Aren't scholars, more than anyone else, subject to excesses of fantasy?"

And so it was done. In interviews for the *Tribune*, the *New York Herald*, the *Times* and the *American Review*, we each in turn repeated the same story: that the *Columbiad* had been thrown off its course by an asteroid, and consequently had circled the Moon without being able to land.

The European reviews were not content. Upon returning to his country, Michel Ardan had to reply to a flurry of questions from the young, but already famous, Camille Flammarion for his review *L'Astronomie*, and from Tissandier for *La Nature*. *La Revue des deux mondes*, *Cosmos* and *Le Siècle* had broadcast preparations for the voyage. They harassed Ardan as far as his favourite retreat – an extravagant house made of sheets of glass. Weary of finding himself always in the spotlight, he seized the first excuse to go to the East Indies, where he stayed for more than a year and a half.

He returned to see us for one last time at the Gun Club in Baltimore in February 1867, with important news: Monsieur Jules Verne was preparing to take to sea aboard the greatest (and most uncomfortable) ship in the world, the *Great Eastern*. He wished to rendezvous with us in New York the following month, in the hope of revealing to his readers the outcome of our adventure.

Michel Ardan spoke to us with the wonderful enthusiasm which was usual for him. "This Verne, whose tales of voyages to worlds known and unknown I have read with unparalleled pleasure, is just the man for the job. His *From the Earth to the Moon*, published two years ago after his correspondence with us, is a model of exactitude."

Barbicane and I agreed in concert.

"In addition, he possesses all the qualities of an adventure novelist, far from the vogue for character studies and their intimate atmospheres. He mixes fiction with an unparalleled contemporary realism, and turns the sight of a steam engine into a painting by Raphaël or Corrège. I foretell an immense and wonderful work, completely scientific. Like Edgar Allan Poe, this magician has his head in the stars, but in contrast to that fabulist, his feet remain firmly on the ground. He will produce a convincing version of our story for our contemporaries."

The motion was carried unanimously. By means of a cable sent by the brand-new transatlantic telegraph, Monsieur Verne provided us with a manuscript copy of *Around the Moon*, finished in February 1869, which appeared in the *Journal des Débats*, then as a volume two years later. This sealed our promise to the Selenites.

Until just a week ago, I did not know there would be an epilogue to our incredible odyssey. But a book lent to me by a friend revived memories which I had believed buried for ever. This book, dating from the previous year, was titled *The First Men in the Moon*. Authored by a certain H.G. Wells and, to my taste, very pessimistic, it recounted the journey of two men in a vehicle impervious to the pull of gravity, then their encounter with Selenites living in the interior of the Moon. The coincidences *vis-à-vis* the anatomy of the Selenites and their society are so numerous that in spite of the opinion of Jules Verne, who classed Wells as a purely imaginative writer (as if he knew!), I wondered whether this Englishman, born a year after our journey, had not himself carried out a voyage comparable to ours, perhaps by other means.

Reading his book convinced me, after long deliberation, to set down the true story of Barbicane's Voyage . . . and thereby liberate my conscience.

Now my hand feels lighter, and I can end my days on this Earth in peace.

Captain S. Nicholl,
Philadelphia,
26 December, 1902.

Translated from the French by Finn Sinclair

COLUMBIAD

Stephen Baxter

The initial detonation was the most severe. I was pushed into my couch by a recoil that felt as if it should splay apart my ribs. The noise was extraordinary, and the projectile rattled so vigorously that my head was thrown from side to side.

And then followed, in perfect sequence, the subsidiary detonations of those smaller masses of gun-cotton lodged in the walls of the cannon. One after another these barrel-sized charges played vapour against the base of the projectile, accelerating it further, and the recoil pressed with ever increasing force.

I fear that my consciousness departed from me, for some unmeasured interval.

When I came to myself, the noise and oscillation had gone. My head swam, as if I had imbibed heavily of Ardan's wine butts, and my lungs ached as they pulled at the air.

But, when I pushed at the couch under me, I drifted slowly upwards, as if I were buoyant in some fluid which had flooded the projectile.

I was exultant. Once again my Columbiad *had not failed me!*

My name is Impey Barbicane, and what follows – if there are ears to hear – is an account of my second venture beyond the limits of the terrestrial atmosphere: that is, the first voyage to Mars.

My Lunar romance received favourable reviews on its London publication by G. Newnes, and I was pleased to place it with an American publisher and in the Colonies. Sales were depressed, however, due to unrest over the war with the Boers. And there was that little business of the protests by M. Verne at the "unscientific" nature of my device of gravitational opacity; but I was able to point to flaws in Verne's work, and to the verification of certain aspects of my book by experts in astronomy, astronomical physics, and the like.

All of this engaged my attention but little, however. With the birth of Gip, and the publication of my series of futurological predictions in *The Fortnightly Review,* I had matters of a more personal nature to attend to, as well as of greater global significance.

I was done with inter-planetary travel!

It was with surprise and some annoyance, therefore, that I found myself the recipient, via Newnes, of a series of missives from Paris, penned – in an undisciplined hand – by one Michel Ardan. This evident eccentric expressed admiration for my work and begged me to place close attention to the material he enclosed, which I should find "of the most extraordinary interest and confluence with [my] own writings".

As is my custom, I had little hesitation in disposing of this correspondence without troubling to read it.

But M. Ardan continued to pepper me with further fat volleys of paper.

At last, in an idle hour, while Jane nursed Gip upstairs, I leafed through Ardan's dense pages. And I have to confess that I found my imagination – or the juvenile underside of it! – pricked.

Ardan's enclosure purported to be a record made by a Colonel Maston, of Baltimore in the United States, over the years 1872 to 1873 – that is, some twenty-eight years ago. This Maston, now dead, claimed to have built an apparatus which had detected "propagating electro-magnetic emissions': a phenomenon first described by James Clerk Maxwell, and related, apparently, to the more recent wireless-telegraphy demonstrations of Marconi. If this were not enough, Maston also claimed that the "emissions" were in fact signals, encoded after the fashion of a telegraph message.

And these signals – said Maston and Ardan – had emanated from a source *beyond the terrestrial atmosphere:* from a space voyager, en route to Mars!

When I got the gist of this, I laughed out loud. I dashed off a quick note instructing Newnes not to pass on to me any further communications from the same source.

Fifth Day. Two Hundred and Ninety Seven Thousand Leagues.

Through my lenticular glass scuttles, the Earth now appears about the size of a Full Moon. Only the right half of the terrestrial globe is illuminated by the Sun. I can still discern clouds, and the differentiation of ocean blue from the land's brown, and the glare of ice at the poles.

Some distance from the Earth a luminous disklet is visible, aping the Earth's waxing phase. It is the Moon, following the Earth on its path around the Sun. It is to my regret that the configuration of my orbit was such that I passed no closer to the satellite than several hundred thousand leagues.

The projectile is extraordinarily convenient. I have only to turn a tap and I am furnished with fire and light by means of gas, which is stored in a reservoir at a pressure of several atmospheres. My food is meat and vegetables and fruit, hydraulically compressed to the smallest dimensions; and I have carried a quantity of brandy and water. My atmosphere is maintained by means of chlorate of potassium and caustic potash: the former, when heated, is transformed into chloride of potassium, and the oxygen thus liberated replaces that which I have consumed; and the potash, when shaken, extracts from the air the carbonic acid placed there by the combustion of elements of my blood.

Thus, in inter-planetary space, I am as comfortable as if I were in the smoking lounge of the Gun Club itself, in Union Square, Baltimore!

Michel Ardan was perhaps seventy-five. He was of large build, but stoop-shouldered. He sported luxuriant side-whiskers and moustache; his shock of untamed hair, once evidently red, was largely a mass of grey. His eyes were startling: habitually he held them wide open, so that a rim of white appeared above each iris, and his gaze was clear but vague, as if he suffered from near-sight.

He paced about my living room, his open collar flapping. Even at his advanced age Ardan was a vigorous, restless man, and my home, Spade House – spacious though it is – seemed to confine him like a cage. I feared besides that his booming Gallic voice must awaken Gip. Therefore I invited Ardan to walk with me in the garden; in the open air I fancied he might not seem quite so out of scale.

The house, built on the Kent coast near Sandgate, is open to a vista of the sea. The day was brisk, lightly overcast. Ardan showed interest in none of this, however.

He fixed me with those wild eyes. "You have not replied to my letters."

"I had them stopped."

"I have been forced to travel here unannounced. Sir, I have come here to beg your help."

I already regretted allowing him into my home – of course I did! – but some combination of his earnestness, and the intriguing content of those unsolicited missives, had temporarily overwhelmed me. Now, though, I stood square on my lawn, and held up the newest copy of his letter.

"Then perhaps, M. Ardan, you might explain what you mean by transmitting such romantic nonsense in my direction."

He barked laughter. "Romantic it may be. Nonsense – never!"

"Then you claim this business of 'propagating emissions' is the plain and honest truth, do you?"

"Of course. It is a system of communication devised for their purposes by Impey Barbicane and Col. Maston. They seized on the electro-magnetic discoveries of James Maxwell with the vigour and inventiveness typical of Americans – for America is indeed the Land of the Future, is it not?"

Of that, I was not so certain.

"Col. Maston had built a breed of mirror – but of wires, do you see? – in the shape of that geometric figure called a hyperbola – no, forgive me! – a *parabola,* for this figure, I am assured, collects all impinging waves into a single point, thus making it possible to detect the weakest –"

"Enough." I was scarcely qualified to judge the technical possibilities of such a hypothetical apparatus. And besides, the inclusion of apparently authentic detail is a technique I have used in my own romances, to persuade the reader to accept the most outrageous fictive lies. I had no intention of being deceived by it myself!

"These missives of yours – received by Maston – purport to be from the inhabitant of a projectile, beyond the terrestrial atmosphere. And this projectile, you claim, was launched into space from the mouth of an immense cannon, the *Columbiad,* embedded in a Florida hill-side . . ."

"That is so."

"But, my poor M. Ardan, you must understand that these are no more than the elements of a fiction, written three decades ago by M. Verne – your countryman – with whom I, myself, have corresponded –"

Choleric red bloomed in his battered cheeks. "Verne indeed now claims his lazy and sensational books were fiction. It is convenient for him to do so. But they were not! He was commissioned to write truthful accounts of our extraordinary voyage!"

"Well, that's as may be. But see here. In M. Verne's account the projectile was launched towards the Moon. Not to Mars." I shook my head. "There is a difference, you know."

"Sir, I pray you resist treating me as imbecilic. I am well aware of the difference. The projectile was sent towards the Moon on its *first* journey – in which I had the honour of participating . . ."

The afternoon was extending, and I had work to do; and I was growing irritated by this boorish Frenchman. "Then, if this projectile was truly built, perhaps you would be good enough to show it to me."

"I cannot comply."

"Why so?"

"Because it is no longer on the Earth."

"Ah."

Of course not! It was buried in the red dust of Mars, with this Barbicane inside.

"But —"

"Yes, M. Ardan?"

"I *can* show you the cannon."

The Frenchman regarded me steadily, and I felt an odd chill grow deep within me.

Seventy-Third Day. Four Million One Hundred And Eighty Four Thousand Leagues.

Today, through my smoked glass, I have observed the passage of the Earth across the face of the Sun.

The planet appeared first as a mar in the perfect rim of the parent star. Later it moved into the full glare of the fiery ball, and was quite visible as a whole disc, dwarfed by the Sun's mighty countenance. After perhaps an hour another spot appeared, even smaller than the first: it was the Moon, following its parent towards the Sun's centre.

After perhaps eight hours the passage was done.

I took several astronomical readings of this event. I measured the angles under which Earth and Moon travelled across the Sun's disk, so that I might determine the deviation of my voyaging ellipse from the ecliptic; and the timing of the passage has furnished me with precise information on whether the projectile is running ahead or behind of the elliptical path around the Sun which I had designed. My best computations inform me that I have not deviated from the required trajectory.

It is more a little than a century since Captain James Cook, in 1769, sailed his Endeavour *to Tahiti to watch Venus pass before the Sun. Could even that great explorer have imagined this journey of mine?*

I have become the first human being to witness a transit of Earth! – and who, I wonder, will be the second?

It took two days for us to travel by despatch-boat from New Orleans to the bay of Espiritu Santo, close to Tampa Town.

Ardan had the good sense to avoid my company during this brief, uncomfortable trip. My humour was not good. Since leaving England I had steadily cursed myself, and Ardan, for my foolishness in agreeing to this jaunt to Florida.

We could not ignore each other at dinner and breakfast, however. And at those occasions, we argued.

"But," I insisted, "a human occupant would be reduced to a thin film of smashed bone and flesh, crushed by recoil against the base of any such cannon-fired shell. No amount of water cushions and collapsing balsa partitions would be sufficient to avert such a fate."

"Of course that is true," Ardan said, unperturbed. "But then M. Verne did not depict the detail of the arrangement."

"Which was?"

"That Barbicane and his companions in the Gun Club anticipated precisely this problem. The *Columbiad,* that mighty cannon, was dug still deeper than Verne described. And it did *not* contain one single vast charge of gun-cotton, but many, positioned along its heroic length. Thus a *distributed* impulse was applied to the projectile. It is an elementary matter of algebra – for those with the right disposition, which I have not! – to compute that the forces suffered by travellers within the projectile, while punishing, were less than lethal."

"Bah! What, then, of Verne's description of conditions within the projectile, during its Lunar journey? He claims that the inhabitants suffered a sensation of levitation – but only at that point at which the gravitational pulls of Earth and Moon are balanced. Now, this is nonsense. When you create a vacuum in a tube, the objects you send through it – whether grains of dust or grains of lead – fall with the same rapidity. So with the contents of your projectile. You, sir, should have floated like a pea inside a tin can throughout your voyage!"

He shrugged. "And so I did. It was an amusing piece of natural philosophy, but not always a comfortable sensation.

For the second journey we anticipated by installing a couch equipped with straps, and hooks and eyes on the tools and implements, and additional cramp-irons fixed to the walls. As to M. Verne's inaccurate depiction of this sensation – I refer you to the author! Perhaps he did not understand. Or perhaps he chose to dramatize our condition in a way which suited the purposes of his narrative . . ."

"Oh!" I said. "This debating is all by the by. M. Ardan, it is simply impossible to launch a shell to another world from a cannon!"

"It is perfectly possible." He eyed me. "As you know! – for have you not published your own account of how such shells might be fired, if not from Earth to Mars, then in the opposite direction?"

"But it was fiction!" I cried. "As were Verne's books!"

"No." He shook his large, grizzled head. "M. Verne's account was fact. It is only a sceptical world which insists it must be fiction. And that, sir, is my tragedy."

One Hundred and Thirty Fourth Day. Seven Million, Four Hundred and Seventy Seven Thousand Leagues.

The air will be thin and bracing; it will be like a mountain-top on Earth. I must trust that the vegetable and animal life – whose treks and seasonal cycles have been observed, as colour washes, from Earth – provide me with provision compatible with my digestion.

I have brought thermometers, barometers, aneroids and hypsometers with which to study the characteristics of the Martian landscape and atmosphere. I have also carried several compasses, in case of any magnetic influence there. I have brought canvas, pickaxes and shovels and nails, sacks of grain and shrubs and other seed stock: provisions with which to construct my miniature colony on the surface of Mars. For it is there that I must, of course, spend the rest of my life.

I dream that I may even encounter intelligence! – human, or some analogous form. The inhabitants of Mars will be tall, delicate, spidery creatures, their growth drawn upward by the lightness of their gravity. And their buildings likewise will be slender, beautiful structures . . .

With such speculation I console myself.

I will confess to a sense of isolation. With Earth invisible, and with Mars still no more than a brightening red star, I am suspended in a starry firmament – for my speed is not discernible – and I have only the dazzling globe of the Sun himself to interrupt the curve of heaven above and below me. Has any man been so alone?

At times I close the covers of the scuttles, and strap myself to my couch, and expend a little of my precious gas; I seek to forget my situation by immersing myself in my books, those faithful companions I have carried with me.

But I find it impossible to forget my remoteness from all of humanity that ever lived, and that my projectile, a fragile aluminium tent, is my sole protection.

We stayed a night in the Franklin Hotel in Tampa Town. It was a dingy, uncomfortable place, its facilities exceedingly primitive.

At five a.m. Ardan roused me.

We travelled by phaeton. We worked along the coast for some distance – it was dry and parched – and then turned inland, where the soil became much richer, abounding with northern and tropical floras, including pineapples, cotton-plants, rice and yams. The road was well built, I thought, considering the crude and underpopulated nature of the countryside thereabouts.

I am not the physical type; I felt hot and uncomfortable, my suit of English wool restrictive and heavy, and my lungs seemed to labour at the humidity-laden air. By contrast Ardan was vibrant, evidently animated by our journey.

"When we returned to Earth – we fell back into the Pacific Ocean – our exuberance was unbounded. We imagined new and greater *Columbiads.* We imagined fleets of projectiles, threading between Earth, Moon and planets. We expected adulation!"

"As depicted by M. Verne."

"But Verne lied! – in that as in other matters. Oh, there was some celebrity – some little notoriety. But we had returned with nothing: not so much as a bag of Lunar soil; nothing save our descriptions of a dead and airless Moon.

"The building of the *Columbiad* was financed by public subscription. Not long after our return, the pressure from those investors began to be felt: *Where is our profit?* – that was the question."

"It is not unreasonable."

"Some influential leader-writers argued that perhaps *we had not travelled to the Moon at all.* Perhaps it was all a deception, devised by Barbicane and his companions."

"It might be the truth," I said severely. "After all the Gun Club were weapons manufacturers who, after the conclusion of the War between the States, sought by devising this new project only to maintain investment and employment . . ."

"It was not the truth! We had circled the Moon! But we were baffled by such reactions. Oh, Barbicane refused to concede defeat. He tried to raise subscriptions for a new company which would build on his achievements. But the company soon foundered, and the commissioner and magistrate pursued him on behalf of enraged debtors.

"If only the Moon had not turned out to be dead! If only we could succeed in finding a world which might draw up the dreams of man once more!

"And so Barbicane determined to commit all to one throw of the die. He took the last of his money, and used it to bore out the *Columbiad,* and to repair his projectile . . ."

My temper deteriorated; I had little interest in Ardan's rambling reminiscences.

But then Ardan digressed, and he began to describe how it was – or so he claimed – to fall towards the Moon. His voice became remote, his eyes oddly vacant.

Two Hundred and Forty Fifth Day. Twelve Million, One Hundred and Twenty Five Leagues.

The projectile approaches the planet at an angle to the sunlight, so Mars is gibbous, with a slice of the night hemisphere turned towards me. The ochre shading seems to deepen at the planet's limb, giving the globe a marked roundness: Mars is a little orange, the only object apart from the Sun visible as other than a point of light in all my 360° sky.

To one side, at a distance a little greater than the diameter of the Martian disk, is a softly glowing starlet. If I trouble to observe for a few minutes, its relation to Mars changes visibly. Thus I have discerned that Mars has a companion: a moon, smaller than our own. And I suspect that a little further from that central globe there may be a second satellite, but my observations are not unambiguous.

I can as yet discern few details on the disk itself, save what is known from observation through the larger telescopes on Earth. However I can easily distinguish the white spot of the southern polar cap, which is melting in the frugal warmth of a Martian summer, following the pattern of seasons identified by Wm. Herschel.

The air appears clear, and I can but trust that its thickness will prove sufficient to cushion my fall from space!

"I imagined I saw streams of oil descending across the glass of the scuttle.

"I thought perhaps the projectile had developed some fault, and I made to alert Barbicane. But then my eyes found their depth, and I realized I was looking at *mountains*. They slid slowly past the glass, trailing long black shadows. They were the mountains of the Moon.

"Our approach was very rapid. The Moon was growing visibly larger by the minute.

"The satellite was no longer the flat yellow disc I had known from Earth: now, tinged pale white, its centre seemed to loom out at us, given three-dimensional substance by Earthlight. The landscape was fractured and complex, and utterly still and silent. The Moon is a small world, my friend. Its curve is so tight my eye could encompass its spherical shape, even so close; I could *see* that I was flying around a ball of rock, suspended in space, with emptiness stretching to infinity in all directions.

"We passed around the limb of the Moon, and entered total darkness: no sunlight, no Earthlight touched the hidden landscape rushing below."

I asked, "And of the Lunar egg shape which Hansen hypothesises, the layer of atmosphere drawn to the far side by its greater mass —"

"We saw none of it! But —"

"Yes?"

"But . . . When the Sun was hidden behind the Lunar orb, there was light all around the Moon, as if the rim was on fire." Ardan turned to me, and his rheumy eyes were shining. "It was wonderful! Oh, it was wonderful!"

We crossed extensive plains, broken only by isolated thickets of pine trees. At last we came upon a rocky plateau, baked hard by the Sun, and considerably elevated.

Two Hundred and Fifty Seventh Day. One Million, Three Hundred and Thirty Five Thousand Leagues.

The nature of Mars has become clear to me. All too clear!

There is a sharp visible difference between northern and southern hemispheres. The darker lands to the south of an equatorial line of dichotomy are punctuated by craters as densely clustered as those of the Moon; while the northern plains – which perhaps are analogous to the dusty maria of the Moon – are generally smoother and, perhaps, younger.

A huge canyon system lies along the equator, a planetary wound visible even from a hundred thousand leagues. To the west of this gouge are clustered four immense volcanoes: great black calderas, as dead as any on the Moon. And in the southern hemisphere I have espied a mighty crater, deep and choked with frost. Mars is clearly a small world: some of these features sprawl around the globe, outsized, overwhelming the curvature.

I have seen no evidence of the channels, or canals, observed by Cardinal Secchi, nor of the other mighty works of Mind which many claim to have observed. Nor, indeed, have I espied evidence of life: no herds move across these rusty plains, and not even the presence of vegetation is evident to me. Such colourings as I have discerned appear to owe more to geologic features than to the processes of life. Even Syrtis Major – Huygens' Hourglass Sea – is revealed as a cratered upland, no more moist than the bleakest desert of Earth.

Thus I have been forced to confront the truth:

Mars is a dead world. As dead as the Moon!

We got out of our phaeton and embarked by foot across that high plain, which Ardan called Stones Hill. I saw how several well-made roads converged on this desolate spot, free of traffic, enigmatic. There was even a rail track, rusting and long disused, snaking off in the direction of Tampa Town.

All over the plain I found the ruins of magazines, workshops, furnaces and workmen's huts. Whether or not Ardan spoke the truth, it was evident that some great enterprise had taken place here.

At the heart of the plain was a low mound. This little hill was surrounded by a ring of low constructions of stone, regularly built, and set at a radius of perhaps six hundred yards from the summit itself. Each construction was topped by an elliptical arch, some of which remained intact.

I walked into this ring, two thirds of a mile across, and looked around. "My word, Ardan!" I cried, impressed despite my scepticism. "This has the feel of some immense prehistoric site – a Stonehenge, perhaps, transported to the Americas. Why, there must be several hundred of these squat monoliths."

"More than a thousand," he said. "They are reverberating ovens, to fuse the many millions of tons of cast iron which plated the mighty *Columbiad*. See here." He traced out a shallow trench in the soil. "Here are the channels by which the iron was directed into the central mould – from all twelve hundred ovens, simultaneously!"

At the summit of the hill – the convergence of the thousand trenches – there was a circular pit, perhaps sixty feet in diameter. Ardan and I approached this cavity cautiously. I found that it opened into a cylindrical shaft, dug vertically into that rocky landscape.

Ardan took a coin from his pocket and flicked it into the mouth of the great well. I heard it clatter several times against metal walls, but I could not hear it fall to rest.

Taking my courage in my hands – all my life I have suffered a certain dread of subterranean places – I stepped towards the lip of the well. I saw that its sides were sheer: evidently finely manufactured, and constructed of what appeared to be cast iron. But the iron was extensively flaked and rusted.

Looking around from this summit, I saw now a pattern to the damaged landscape: the ovens, the flimsier huts, were smashed and scattered outwards from this central spot, as if some great explosion had once occurred here. And I saw how disturbed soil streaked across the land, radially away from the hill; from a balloon, I speculated, these stripes of discoloration might have resembled the rays around the great craters of the Moon.

This Ozymandian scene was terrifically poignant: great things had been wrought here, and yet now these immense devices lay ruined, broken – forgotten.

Ardan paced about by the lip of the abandoned cannon; he exuded an extraordinary restlessness, as if the whole of the Earth had become a cage insufficient for him. "It was magnificent!" he cried. "When the electrical spark ignited the gun-cotton, and the ground shook, and the pillar of flame hurled aside the air, throwing over the spectators and their horses like matchstalks! . . . And there was the barest glimpse of the projectile itself, ascending like a soul in that fiery light . . ."

I gazed up at the hot, blank sky, and imagined this Barbicane climbing into his cannon-shell, to the applause of his ageing friends. He would have called it bravery, I suppose. But how easy it must have been, to sail away into the infinite aether – for ever! – and to leave behind the Earthbound complexities of debtors and broken promises. Was Barbicane exploring, I wondered – or escaping?

As I plunge towards the glowing pool of Martian air – as that russet, cratered barrenness opens out beneath me – I descend into despair. Is all of the Solar System to prove as bleak as the worlds I have visited?

This must be my last transmission. I wish my final words to be an utterance of deepest gratitude to my loyal friends, notably Col. J. T. Maston and my partners in the National Company of Interstellar Communication, who have followed my fruitless journey across space for so many months.

I am sure this new defeat will be trumpeted by those jackals who hounded my National Company into bankruptcy; with nothing but dead landscapes as his destination, it may be many decades before man leaves the air of Earth again!

"Sir, it seems I must credit your veracity. But what is it you want of me? Why have you brought me here?"

After his Gallic fashion, he grabbed at my arm. "I have read your books. I know you are a man of imagination. You must publish Maston's account – tell the story of this place . . ."

"But why? What would be the purpose? If Common Man is unimpressed by such exploits – if he regards these feats as a hoax, or a cynical exploitation by gun-manufacturers – who am I to argue against him? We have entered a new century, M. Ardan: the century of Socialism. We must concentrate on the needs of Earth – on poverty, injustice, disease – and turn our faces to new worlds only when we have reached our manhood on this one . . ."

But Ardan heard none of this. He still gripped my arm, and again I saw that wildness in his old eyes – eyes that had, perhaps, seen too much. "I would go back! That is all. I am embedded in gravity. It clings, it clings! Oh, Mr Wells, let me go back!"

TABLEAUX

F. Gwynplaine MacIntyre

Despite the success and popularity of his books Verne had no time to pause. Over the next two years he strove to meet his contractual obligation of three books a year, a demanding schedule that was revised, in 1866, to two books a year. After completing the three-decker adventure novel Les Enfants du Capitaine Grant *(1865-67), also known as* In Search of the Castaways *or* A Voyage Round the World, *Verne felt he had earned a rest. During March and April 1867 he and his brother Paul visited the United States. He only had time to spend a week in America, travelling from New York to the Niagara Falls via Albany and Buffalo. He was probably surprised to find that his work was known in America. His first official American book publication was* Five Weeks in a Balloon, *which did not appear until 1869, but his work was being pirated in magazines and newspapers. His early story "A Voyage in a Balloon" had appeared in* Sartain's Union Magazine *as early as May 1852 and* From the Earth to the Moon *was being serialized at that moment in the* New York Weekly Magazine. *F. Gwynplaine MacIntyre has taken Verne's visit to New York as the focus for the following story, which is based upon authentic period records.*

The crossing was fatal. The first day out from Liverpool, the crew were hoisting the huge starboard anchor when a capstan pin snapped, throwing the anchor's full 80-ton weight upon twelve sailors. One man was killed instantly, and four deckhands were injured. On this westward crossing, the six-masted steam liner *Great Eastern* carried one hundred and twenty-three passengers bound for New York. Captain Anderson personally asked the first-class passengers to offer a minute's silence for the dead seaman as his corpse was consigned to the waves.

Among the mourners on the afterdeck were two Frenchmen: brothers, sharing a first-class stateroom; the older brother's publisher having paid 1,300 francs for their passage. The sailor's shrouded corpse was reverently carried to the rail, with no sound except the creak of the rigging overhead. Just before the dead mariner disembarked for his last journey, the older of the two Frenchmen thought he saw a movement within the taut canvas shroud. The dead sailor's hand beckoned to the passenger, and the dead sailor's bearded face whispered:

"Monsieur Verne, in your boyhood you ran off to sea. My fate might well have been your own, if your voyage had taken a different heading."

Then the shrouded form went overboard, as the ship's bandmaster piped a dirge. The passenger shuddered, and banished the thought of that dead face. The imagined voice perhaps had been the screech of the gulls overhead, or the breath of his own conscience.

The crossing took eleven days . . . and the *Great Eastern* was scheduled to begin her return voyage precisely one week from arrival. Thus, when the world's mightiest steamship reached New York City's harbour on the ninth of April, 1867, Jules Verne and his brother Paul had only seven days and nights in which to experience all they hoped to encounter of New York and Canada.

As the ship approached the Bethune Street Pier of Manhattan, Jules Verne looked across the shore to the city of Brooklyn, and he was astonished to see an immense wooden cylinder, rising twenty-one metres above the ocean's waves. "I marvel at such American wonders," he said to his younger brother, pointing over the ship's rail. "What is that tower, rising out of the sea?"

"There is no tower in the sea," said Paul Verne to his brother. "Jules, are you imagining another novel?"

"Behold the future, monsieur," whispered a voice at Jules Verne's ear, speaking French in an arcane accent. *"That cylinder is the caisson at Peck Slip, for the construction of the Brooklyn Bridge. But it will not arrive until May 1870, more than three years downstream of your present moment."*

As this whisper fell silent, the tower vanished. In the excitement of his arrival in this new world, Verne chastised himself for letting his imagination take the helm of his faculties. There were enough *genuine* marvels on this American continent to propel a score of novels.

"At least we have been made welcome," said Jules to Paul, as the brothers cleared the Customs station at quayside, summoning porters for assistance with their steamer trunks. "See, Paul? This time, I do not imagine what I behold. The streets and buildings of Manhattan are draped with buntings in homage to our French *tricoleur*. Do not tell me that this is the custom for America's streets."

Indeed, the lamp-posts and rooftops of Manhattan were garlanded with draperies striped in patterns of red, white and blue. Paul Verne – a former naval officer, now a stockbroker, and in consequence more practical than his brother – seemed sceptical. "It does indeed seem out of the common, *frère* Jules. Yet I scarce believe that these decorations are in honour of France . . ."

An officer of the English steamship, overhearing these words and conversant in French, touched his visor and explained: *"Messieurs* Verne, today is April ninth. By good fortune, we have arrived in New York on the very day when these Yanks are celebrating the second anniversary of the end to their long Civil War. You will find the Yankees more jubilant than usual, today at least."

"A pity that we have only one week in which to taste

their hospitality," said Paul Verne as his brother summoned a cabriolet.

"As we have only one day and one night in New York City before journeying north to the mighty Niagara," Jules Verne decreed, "let us billet ourselves in the finest hotel available."

This proved to be at the northwest corner of the crossroads where 23rd Street intersected Broadway: the magnificent Fifth Avenue Hotel, a six-storey edifice of white marble. As the Verne brothers strode between the six Corinthian pillars at the hotel's entrance, Paul remarked: "Let us take lodgings on the ground floor, so as to avoid any stairs."

His brother waved airily. "I am a collector of wonders! Let us have berths on the topmost flight, to obtain the best view of this magnificent city!"

Inside the hotel, an astonishment awaited . . . for it was possible for both travellers to achieve their desires in tandem: a view from a height with an absence of stairs. To their delight, the Verne brothers discovered that the Fifth Avenue Hotel contained the first and only passenger-lift in New York City. As the brothers stepped into the brass-gated cage, an attendant in mauve livery touched his cap and pressed a lever . . . and rapidly they ascended.

While Paul Verne marvelled at the counterweights enabling the brass cage to rise through the building, Jules Verne expressed astonishment at the elevator's ingenious gas-fitting. A long flexible tube of *caoutchouc* India rubber connected the elevator's twin gas-lamps to a pipeline in the hotel's cellar, where a spool on a revolving spindle paid out a reel of tubing as the elevator ascended, then shortened it again as the elevator came downwards . . . so that the interior of the passenger-lift was always lighted by a steady flow of coal-gas. The attendant explained that the elevator was steam-powered, and that the hotel's management was pleased to advertise it as "the vertical railway".

The Verne brothers' suite in the hotel's topmost storey faced east, on to Broadway. While Paul admired the bedroom's marble fireplace, Jules stepped on to the balcony and was gratified to behold a magnificent view of Madison Square Park directly across and below. Slightly north of the hotel – in the small island of asphalt where Fifth Avenue met Broadway – was an obelisk in the Egyptian fashion, more than fifty feet tall. At the foot of the spire appeared to be a tomb. Jules Verne found himself wondering who might be entombed there, and at once came a voice at his ear:

"Brigadier-General William Jenkins Worth, late of the Mexican war. At your service, Mr Verne. I died of cholera in Texas in 1849, but the good citizens of my native New York reinterred me here in '55, and now you behold my . . ."

"Are you well, brother Jules?" asked Paul Verne. Jules stared at his brother, then gazed once more at the whispering obelisk. The spire was silent now.

The two voyagers put on fresh clothes and prepared for their evening's amusement. As Jules Verne was clean-shaven, his grooming took scarcely a moment. Paul Verne, however, was the owner of a dark brown spade beard, full moustaches, and deep side-whiskers grown well past his chin, so there was much delay in the brushing of his facial topiary. "While you are pruning your hedgerows, I will descend in that delightful machine once again," Jules Verne proposed to his younger brother. "Perhaps I can reserve a *table d'hôte* for us both."

The downward journey in the hotel's elevator was nearly as pleasurable as the ascent. The attendant opened the brass gate upon reaching the lobby, and Jules Verne stepped forth . . . into the sudden thundering path of a Roman chariot, pulled by four galloping black steeds with roached manes. Verne leapt out of the way, glimpsing the contorted face and plumed bronze helmet of the charioteer as the steeds rumbled forth.

As the four black stallions galloped past him, Verne saw the leftmost horse turn to confront him. Now he heard the beast whisper: *"Your pardon, Monsieur Verne. Eight years yesterwards, where the Fifth Avenue Hotel now stands, this selfsame spot was the site of Franconi's Hippodrome, where chariot races were . . ."* The stallion's voice broke off in midsentence as black steeds and bronzed charioteer vanished into the white marble balustrades of the lobby's staircase.

"Are you ill, brother?" A familiar voice, a firm hand on his arm. Regaining his balance, Jules looked into the hazel eyes of his slightly shorter brother. The lobby of the Fifth Avenue Hotel showed no glance of chariots. Nearby, two businessmen were calmly discussing whether the United States Congress proposed to intervene in Mexico on behalf of Emperor Maximilian.

"I am . . . disoriented, Paul." The novelist smiled as a thought struck him. "You know, while we two are Frenchmen abroad in New York, we naturally say that our hearts are still in Paris. There are six hours' difference between Broadway and my little house in Le Crotoy, yes? That explains why I seem to be in two moments at once. I have fallen between the clocks."

"Then a good meal is called for, and a self-respecting wine," said faithful Paul, gently guiding his brother towards the nearby sounds of tinkling wineglasses and violin music. "And then, as we have only one night to spend in New York City, let us take our evening's entertainment in whatever place offers the greatest number of wonders in the smallest possible space."

BARNUM & VAN AMBURGH'S MUSEUM & MENAGERIE proclaimed the lettering on the roof of the three-storey clap-board building at 539 Broadway between Spring and Prince Streets.

The admission price was reasonable: only thirty centimes, or *cents* as these Americans called them. Jules Verne and his brother entered, and found themselves among astonishments. From the antechamber, a profusion of finger-posts pointed down a series of corridors: "COSMORAMAS", "GRAND AQUARIA", "THE LEARNED SEA-LION". "THIS WAY TO THE HAPPY FAMILY". To avoid the surging crowd, the Verne brothers stepped into a small vestibule to one side, from which Jules could see an adjoining salon, filled with a double row of glass exhibition cases and waxworks. Some of the gawking customers outside the glass cases seemed more grotesque to him than anything within the cases.

"Which of these miracles shall we behold first?" Jules asked his brother. Before Paul could reply, a distinguished figure strode towards them: a man in a tailcoat with a gold chain across his waistcoat. The newcomer had distinctly Levantine features – a long curly beard, a hooked nose, thick eyebrows – and Paul Verne was distressed to see his older brother cringe at this man's arrival.

"Which of you is Jules Verne?" asked the bearded man, glancing at Paul and then settling on his brother. "Ah, *monsieur!* I welcome you!" He extended his hand. "The concierge of the Fifth Avenue sent word of your visit. As proprietor of this museum, I . . . is something wrong?"

Verne had recoiled visibly from the Levantine's attempt to shake his hand. "You are . . . are you Mister Barnum?" Jules Verne asked.

Directly behind the bearded stranger, Jules Verne could see a crowd of spectators gaping at a life-sized waxwork of the famous Siamese brothers. Suddenly these people and the waxwork vanished. In their place stood a weird effigy: the likeness of a naked man, ten feet tall, carved in what appeared to be black obsidian, with arms folded across his muscular chest, his stone body contorted in a semblance of pain.

The dark effigy turned its head, and spoke: *"Greetings, monsieur. I am the Cardiff Giant: a notorious hoax that will make headlines two years from now. Well, actually I am not the genuine hoax: I am the hoax of the hoax. Mister Barnum will attempt to purchase the original for exhibition in this very hall. Upon being rebuffed, Barnum commissioned sculptors to construct me as a counterfeit of the original. In 1871, I will be . . ."*

"Explain yourself, please!" said Verne sharply to the stone giant.

"Very well. Mister Verne, you are famous where I come from . . ." the giant began.

"I am famous in a stone quarry?" asked Jules Verne.

"Nice one, monsieur. It is a pity that the humour in your novels is often lost in their translated editions," the Cardiff Giant resumed calmly. *"A more regrettable aspect of your novels is your penchant for unsavoury depictions of Jewish villains. There is one you have not written yet, which . . ."*

The giant vanished in mid-sentence, replaced by the previous spectators and the double waxwork of the Siamese brothers. "You spoke strangely, Jules. Are you well?" Paul Verne asked.

The bearded man, whose distinctly Semitic features had repelled Jules Verne, now spoke again: "Erm, you asked if I was Mister Barnum, sir. I have the honour to be his business partner, and co-owner of this house of wonders. I am Isaac Van Amburgh, of the famous menagerie."

He again extended his hand. Paul Verne clasped it, offering a half-hearted handshake. Jules merely scowled.

"VERNE!" bellowed a voice at the far end of the salon. Through the huzzabuzzing crowd pushed a self-important figure: a stout Yankee, balding, careless in dress, his waistcoat unbuttoned and his cravat undone. "How d'ye do, sir?" crowed this newcomer, seizing Jules Verne's hand and pumping it freely. "Barnum's the name: the one and only, warranted genuine." At the edge of his vision, Verne saw Isaac Van Amburgh discreetly slipping into the crowd. "Delighted to have you here among our wonders, Mister Verne!" resumed Barnum, in a rapid American accent which Paul Verne was obliged to translate for his less fluent brother. "Your novels are among my favourite reading, and . . ."

"You have read my *nouvelles?*" Jules Verne interrupted.

"Well, ah, no," harrumphed Barnum. "You must pardon a humbug. My French is not of the best. But here in New York, the *Weekly Magazine of Popular Literature* began to serialize your *From the Earth to the Moon* this past January, and . . ."

"Did they, indeed?" asked Paul Verne, who oversaw his brother's business arrangements. "I do not recall them troubling themselves with the trifling matter of copyright."

Barnum attempted a deep bow, and halfway succeeded.

"Plagiarism is the sincerest form of flattery . . . and I speak from personal experience, having been on both sides of such tributes. Ahem! May I escort your good sirs through the halls of my Museum? There are thousands of exhibits here, so permit me to show you the choicest of my astonishments."

Escorted by Barnum, the Verne brothers passed through the main salon. Between a waxwork effigy of a Chinese mandarin and a replica of the Venus of Canova was a prominent signpost reading "THIS WAY TO THE EGRESS". With a chuckle, Barnum explained this: "My museum, sirs, opens at ten sharp every day, except the Sabbath. By half-past ten, the place is chock-full of suckers, staring at my exhibits and gawping fit to kill, so's you'd think their eyeballs would bust. Plenty more people are outside the box-office, waiting to get in . . . but there's no room for 'em, on account the place is full!" Laughing, Barnum jerked his thumb towards the doorway leading to the Egress. "Sooner or later, they go through that door to find out what an Egress is . . . and find themselves in the alley, back of Prince Street." Barnum guffawed, and slapped his pinstriped knee. "They have to pay to get back in again, and meantime they've made room for a fresh crop of rubes!"

Barnum led his guests to the Cosmorama room. This proved to contain a series of displays, each depicting a life-like *tableau* of some human drama of the present or the past. Jules Verne gazed at something captioned "The Drunkard's Family". This depicted a one-room hovel. At its centre stood a broken-backed chair in which a red-faced man slumbered in soiled clothing. On the table before him, a half-empty bottle lay sideways, its amber contents spilt on to the threadbare tablecloth. In the far corner, a ragged woman covered her face with both hands, her posture grief-stricken. Starving children beckoned piteously. Near the wife stood a bare cot, with one more child dead within it. For one moment, Verne was shocked that Barnum would exploit this anguished family by putting them on public display. Then, with a greater shock, Verne realized that all of these figures were nothing more than waxworks. Even the bright puddle of liquid on the tablecloth was a *trompe l'oeil*, achieved with a polished piece of tinted glass.

At this moment a bell rang, and a bellboy spoke with great ceremony: "Ladies and gentlemen, if you please! Ten days ago our nation's Secretary of State, Mr William H. Seward, paid seven million of our tax dollars to Czar Alexander of Russia in order to purchase a piece of real estate known as Alaska." There was some murmuring among the spectators present as the bellboy spoke again: "This afternoon, at enormous expense, Mr Barnum and Mr Van Amburgh have brought to New York City, for your inspection and approval, *a genuine fragment of Alaska!*"

Cymbals clashed, and now a dainty chambermaid entered the salon, bearing a blue velvet pillow. In the centre of this pillow, slightly melted, was a large chunk of ice. The spectators laughed at the humbug, and several of the men present made discourteous remarks about Seward's folly.

Barnum bowed to the Verne brothers. "I must stage a few jests, as you see, so that my customers never suspect that they are being educated." The showman beckoned. "May I show you something to astonish you?"

There were, indeed, so many marvels in this place that it was clearly impossible to sample them all in the brief time available, so the Verne brothers permitted Barnum to escort them passed a cage containing the Happy Family – this proved to be animals of several species, carnivores placidly co-habiting with herbivores – and then onward into a wide hall, its ceiling bracketed in a double row of globed gas-fittings. And here the exhibits were *alive*, "This is my hall of Freaks and Prodigies," explained Barnum.

Jules Verne felt a rush of emotions – delight, and shock, and dismay – when he beheld the entertainment that was offered here. The dismay was for himself, as he realized the thrill of his initial delight. For each of the occupants of this room was some sort of human anomaly, displayed as a curiosity to be stared at.

There were two dwarves – one of either sex – alongside

a Circassian girl, whose pale skin was utterly milk-white. Her eyes, like red garnets, peered accusingly at Jules Verne while she absently plaited her pale yellow hair. A nearby kiosk offered something called the Leopard Child. Jules Verne peered within, and beheld a very young child, nearly naked, of indeterminate sex. The child's pale skin was stippled and piebald with a grotesque pattern of dark brown spots, covering its entire body and face. Verne shuddered.

His brother Paul had seen the horror too. "Fear not, Jules. This man Barnum is legendary for his humbugs. Perhaps the unfortunate child is one more fraud, garnished with paint."

At the sound of women's voices nearby, engaged in pleasant conversation, Jules Verne hurried onward to the next kiosk. Here a fashionably-dressed lady stood with her back to him. Her long hair was stylishly arranged, her body gracefully proportioned, and she spoke in a light gentle voice. The other woman, who appeared to be standing on a chair, was conversing in a voice that was strangely deep yet clearly feminine.

As Verne stepped closer, he gasped. The deep-voiced woman was standing on the floor, yet she towered above him. A giantess!

At that moment, the other woman turned round and faced Verne. The lower half of her face was resplendent with a chestnut-coloured beard! In one graceful hand she held a tortoise-shell comb, in her other a mirror. As she posed, she admired her own beard and combed it carefully.

A man in disguise, surely? No; the corseted figure was quite female, and her face – its unbearded portions, at least – satisfyingly feminine. In his experience as a playwright, Jules Verne was aware of crepe beards that could be affixed with spirit-gum. Perhaps this . . . ?

As if reading his thoughts, the bearded woman raised her manicured fingers to her chin. She pinched one of her own hairs, then suddenly plucked it. Jules Verne clearly saw the skin distend for an instant as the hair was uprooted. Smiling prettily, the bearded woman – now less bearded, by a single hair's worth – rolled the hair between finger and thumb, and extended it towards him. "Would you like a souvenir, sir?"

The giantess guffawed. "Go on and take it," she boomed in her deep hearty voice. "Madame Hines doesn't give a hair off her chin to just anyone."

Jules Verne now gave his full attention to the giantess. She was attractive of face and figure, except for a thick dewlap in her throat indicating a goitre . . . might that be the explanation for her prodigious size? Barely twenty years old, she seemed gigantically girlish. The giant lady stood at least eight feet tall – the upswept coiffure of her auburn hair added another few inches – and she must have weighed nearly two hundred kilos, yet the upper half of her body was elegantly proportioned. The regions below the giantess's waist were indeterminate, for she was dressed in an elaborate hoop skirt and crinoline frame that extended to the floor, entirely concealing her nether portions. Such a framework, Verne realized, could conceal nearly anything . . .

His brother had similar thoughts. "Her upper half is large enough," Paul Verne whispered near Jules's ear. "But beneath that cage of crinolines . . . who knows? She might be a woman of normal height, on stilts. She might have no legs at all, and be propped on a pillar."

The giantess confronted Jules Verne, and from her vast height she seemed to read his thoughts. With gentle mockery in her smile, the immense woman now gathered the red satin folds of her skirts, and lifted them. Raising her petticoats, the giantess revealed a trim pair of feet: each was slightly larger than Jules Verne's head, but the feet of the giantess were perfectly shaped, and daintily shod in huge slippers of black patent leather with crimson rosettes. As Verne watched, the giantess flexed one foot, her toes tapping impatiently. Then she shifted her weight to this foot, and tap-toed her other.

"You see, sir?" the laughter of the giantess rumbled from somewhere overhead. "Please mark that my shoes are not high-heeled to give me extra height. I came by my inches honestly. I am entirely . . ."

The voice of the giantess abruptly halted. Jules Verne looked up to her exalted altitude, and he saw her face shift and alter. Her features slackened, the dewlap quivered at her throat, as her blue eyes drooped and her mouth dangled open. Then she spoke again, this time with entirely a different voice:

"Monsieur Jules Verne, the young woman before you and above you is the giantess Anna Haining Swan of Nova Scotia. Only twenty-one years old, her remarkable height of seven feet eleven inches, and her proportionate weight, is the result of a thyroid tumour which . . ."

There was a click within Verne's mind. The giantess Swan shook her head as though to clear it, then she resumed speaking in her previous voice: ". . . entirely genuine, sir, in my height and my capacity. As well I sing, speak French and Latin, and . . ."

"Mister Verne!" The man named Barnum had been attending to some business, yet now he came huffapuffing back across the salon. "Or the pair of you Vernes, rather, for I have neglected your brother." Red-faced, Barnum mopped himself with a handkerchief, then pocketed this and took out his watch. "Nearly half-past! And the *tableaux vivants* begin promptly at 7.45. Would you do me the honour of viewing the show from my personal box?"

The stage of Barnum's theatre was tiled with a parquet of alternating black and white squares. Looking down upon this from his seat in the box, Jules Verne was reminded of a vast chessboard . . . and he wondered what sort of dramas might soon unfold upon it. For now, only the downstage edge of this chessboard was visible, the remainder hidden behind a huge red velvet curtain.

The audience murmured impatiently as they took their seats for the 7.45 performance, while Verne contemplated today's strange experiences. He had beheld things that did not actually exist – this Cardiff giant, for example – and he had been accosted by unaccountable voices. Was he going insane? Verne shook his head, preferring other explanations.

The excitement of his arrival in America, the astonishing wonders . . . yes, it was possible that his legendary imagination was running away with him. The apparitions had done no harm, at least. Not so far.

Verne took out his opera-glasses and consulted the printed stagebill. The current entertainment at Barnum & Van Amburgh's Museum was something called "Streets of New York, in five tableaux". Verne was vaguely surprised to encounter this honest French word in a Yankee stagebill, and he wondered if *tableaux* meant the same thing on an American stage as on a French one. Now the gas-jets in the house lights dimmed, and the calcium carbonate lamps in the footlights brightened. The audience began an eager hush as the curtain went up.

The first tableau was "The Returned Californian". This depicted a railway station, with the porters and newsboys bustling about. The effect of an arriving train was crudely achieved. From the train alighted a bearded man in buckskins, fresh from the California goldfields and clutching a valise filled with banknotes and gold nuggets. There was some byplay among the locals, as the Californian gave some money to a beggar-woman, attracting the attention of a ragged beggar who feigned blindness and lameness. The faker unfolded his bent leg and removed the bandage from his eyes to stare at the wealth in the Californian's valise. He gave the signal to an urchin. Several street-Arabs arranged a diversion; the Californian's valise was snatched, and spirited away. There was a chase, involving several constables, wearing the strange helmets that evidently were typical for New York policemen. At last, the Californian and his suitcase were reunited through the vigilance of a flower-girl, whom he rewarded.

These were not tableaux, then, as Verne knew the term from his theatrical endeavours in the Boulevard du Temple in Paris. A proper *tableau vivant* offered men and women posing motionless in a dramatic setting: statues of flesh, enacting an artist's illustration. Barnum's performers moved and gesticulated, and did everything but speak. Why not call this offering a straightforward drama, then, instead of a tableau?

The curtain descended, then rose again. The second tableau was named "Union-Square on a Winter's Night". This was a street scene, and the actors were bundled in coats and comforters. In the orchestra stalls beneath his seat in Barnum's private box, Jules Verne heard a deep awestruck gasp from the audience, as a steady torrent of snowflakes cascaded on to the stage from somewhere overhead. A most impressive counterfeit of winter!

Verne applauded the effect, but as he did so his brother Paul murmured into his ear: "See, Jules! The actors: their breath does not fog into condensed vapour, as it would in wintertime."

"And their breath would not fog upon a Parisian stage either," Verne whispered back to his brother. "We are witnessing an excellent stage effect."

Again the curtain fell. The third tableau was titled "Tenement House, Baxter Street". As the curtain rose, Jules Verne expected to see the stage still covered with artificial snow from the previous scene. There was none. The tableau now depicted a one-room hovel, with a few ragged tenants. Verne found this image unconvincing, as the large and magnificent stage of Barnum's playhouse made an incongruous backdrop for the cramped and squalid tenement scene. As the players onstage enacted their drama, Verne found his mind pursuing other matters.

What were all these bizarre encounters he had lately experienced? The first had occurred on the thirtieth of March, during the sailor's funeral aboard the *Great Eastern*. Now, the weird apparitions were arriving every few minutes. Were these due to the excitement of visiting a new country, a new hemisphere? Verne frowned. Encounters with the unexplained were all very well in his fictions, but . . .

There was a stirring in the audience, and Verne's brother Paul nudged him. The next tableau was starting. In the 437 seats of Barnum's theatre, 437 spectators leant forward expectantly. "Streets of New York" had been advertised as *five* tableaux, yet it was evident that this fourth tableau was the centrepiece of the affair. Consulting his playbill, Verne saw that this next sequence was advertised – with a crescendo of punctuation – as "The Fire! The Fire!! The Fire!!!" Now the stage's footlights suddenly went out, and all was darkness. Verne heard the creaking pulleys as the curtain began its ascent.

A sudden shaft of light – dazzling, yet flickering rapidly – burst from the gap between the footlamps and the rising curtain. As the curtain continued its climb, the florid glow became brighter. Verne gasped once more. *The stage was on fire!* He rose from his seat, resisting Barnum's attempts to clutch his sleeve and restrain him.

Now he understood. There was a fire onstage, yes . . . but it was a *coup de theatre*, a remarkable simulation. Now a wave of applause broke forth, and Verne joined into it, as he beheld stage effects far more remarkable than anything he might have contrived in his own melodramas at the theatre in the Rue du Crime, in the east end of Paris.

On the stage before him was a New York brownstone dwelling. The upper storey was engorged in thick dark smoke: Verne was aware of smudge-pots, yet he admired the ability of the stage manager who had kindled these. The smoke billowed most convincingly from the building's windows. Visible through the walls were huge sheets of crackling flame, orange and bronze-coloured. The illusion was so perfect that Verne felt the temperature rise. Now he shuddered. Was this all a stage effect, or was he experiencing one more of those peculiar visitations?

A woman appeared on the house's balustrade, clutching a squalling infant and shouting piteously for help. The fire was spreading rapidly, engulfing the brownstone. Verne bit his lips nervously, trying to decipher how these effects were achieved. The movement of the flames was very lifelike. Perhaps a sheet of butter-muslin – illuminated from the rear by means of lanterns tinted with orange-hued glass, and set to dancing by a steady current of pumped air – might counterfeit this effect without the dangers of actual fire. Verne nodded, silently vowing to duplicate this effect when he returned to his Parisian theatre.

From the wings of the stage now, a clanging of brass. Verne was seated in a side box at stage left, and in consequence he could not see anything entering from that side of the wings. The audience on the other side loosed a fresh torrent of applause, and Verne craned forward to see . . . then he gaped in astonishment.

A steam-powered fire-engine rolled on to the stage. Astride its brass fittings were ten firemen in glittering helmets. The chieftain leapt from his seat at the helm, brandishing his brass fire-trumpet as he bellowed orders to his men. The men dismounted, unfastening the cagings and ladders. On the building's upper storey, the spreading flames had nearly reached the woman and her child. Now, in a dazzling display of hydrotechnics, a burst of water gushed forth from the hoses and struck the flames, repelling them. The hiss of steam from the fire-engine's boiler was genuine; Verne could not tell if the hiss of steam from the burning building was equally real. The counterfeit flames seemed exceedingly real, yet Verne was certain he knew how this effect had been achieved. The gush of water from the firemen's hoses, the billows of steam as this water met the flames and smoke . . . Verne felt certain that these too must be false, yet he was utterly unable to determine how such effects were achieved. The chequerwork parquet of the stage of Barnum's theatre showed no sign of water. Then how did . . .

Something clicked in his brain, and suddenly Jules Verne staggered back from the heat. *The entire theatre was burning, and this was no illusion!* He found himself standing in the street, watching in horror as the giantess Anna Swan was lowered by means of a block-and-tackle from the third floor of the five-storey museum while the flames . . .

"*A glimpse of the past, Monsieur Verne. That is Barnum's American Museum you behold, at Broadway and Ann Street: considerably south of your present location, and hindwards in time.*" The flames grew oppressively hot as the voice whispered to Verne. "*The American Museum was entirely consumed*

*by fire on 13 July 1865, with great loss of life . . . although, as
you see, the giantess was rescued. The building which you presently
inhabit – Barnum's latest showplace – will be consumed by fire
less than one year from today, on March third of . . ."*

Another click. Verne found himself standing upright in his
seat in Barnum's private box, gripping the gilded wooden rail
overhanging the stage. In the makeshift tenement onstage, the
woman and her infant were now being snatched from the
flames, carried down the ladders by the valiant firemen and
ushered to safety. Now, with a roar and an inrush of air, the
burning structure collapsed, so realistically that people in the
front rows of the theatre screamed and recoiled.

Verne was suddenly dizzy. These stage effects were *too*
realistic. Desperate for air, he staggered towards . . . what
word? . . . the *egress*. There was applause; he bowed instinctively.

"Stay, brother Jules." Beside him, Paul clutched a playbill. "See? The fifth tableaux still remains. It will be instruc-
tive to observe how quickly Barnum's stagehands can clear
this wreckage from the stage, to begin the final act."

Verne glanced at the card his brother thrust towards him.
The fifth and last tableau was titled "The Home of the
Rich". At another time, this might have intrigued him. Now,
he waved his brother aside and staggered towards the door.

"You all right, Verne?" muttered Barnum, gesturing
towards a pageboy. Verne nodded, pantomiming that he only
wished to clear his head. He flung the door open, stepping
out of the private box and into a corridor leading back to
the museum.

On the second floor of Barnum & Van Amburgh's Museum,
the aisles between the glass display cases held fewer visitors
now, for most of the museum's patrons had gone into
Barnum's theatre to watch the tableaux. As Jules Verne staggered past the Feejee Mermaid and a portrait of the Earl
of Southampton, he paused to rest beside a weird
conveyance: exactly like a royal coach, but scarcely a metre
high. A brass plate on its door explained that this vehicle

was Tom Thumb's Carriage, and two Shetland ponies in convincing effigy were hitched to its traces.

"*Hel-lo, hsssir,*" spoke a voice that seemed inhuman.

Verne looked up, and beheld a face that was human in shape yet not alive. "*Hel-lo, hsssir,*" it repeated in English.

The hauntings again! Verne retreated, intending to turn and walk swiftly away when he caught another look at this interlocutor.

A man of metal stood before him on a pedestal. The counterfeit man was authentically human in his size and proportions. His limbs were gracefully jointed, although a long iron strut attached to his right leg indicated that he had difficulty standing upright.

The automaton was dressed as a footman of the French court, in breeches and livery and peruke. There were lace ruffles at his throat, half-concealing some mechanism that Verne could barely perceive. The footman's hands and face were carved wood, painted to simulate human flesh, but the colour had faded . . . and on some of the fingers it had chipped off altogether. He was perhaps five foot seven – two inches shorter than Jules Verne – yet by virtue of the pedestal he towered over Verne easily.

The footman stood in profile. Now, suddenly, his head turned and faced directly towards Verne. His eyes blinked, with mechanical precision. His jaw creaked open.

"*Hel-lo, hsssir,*" the automatic man repeated. His right arm lifted stiffly, its hand gesticulating. "*Hhhow are you?*" His eyelids blinked, revealing pale blue eyes of Essen glass.

Hearing laughter, Verne approached. At the base of the footman's pedestal stood a device resembling a harpsichord, with three banks of keys and levers: the former with ivory fittings, the latter in stained wood. A man – reassuringly human, in a hideous yellow waistcoat – was manipulating these, while two girls and a plump older woman laughed and fanned themselves.

On a brass plate near the keyboard, Jules Verne noticed a familiar name engraved: *JEAN EUGÈNE ROBERT-HOUDIN.* The great magician! Verne had met him, and attended his performances in Montmartre. The inscription on this plate disclosed that the mechanical footman was Robert-Houdin's patented Speaking Automaton. A bellows apparatus sent compressed air through the body of the Automaton, enabling him to speak as if equipped with human lungs. By pressing the manifolds of the keyboard, an operator could induce the Automaton to replicate human speech.

The waistcoated man and his companions had departed. Now the jaw of the Automaton dangled slackly and silent. Eager to reassure himself that the machine's voice was a man-made contrivance, and not some unaccountable haunting, Verne approached the keyboard. He ran his finger across several keys, in the manner of a glissando.

"Mnerghajib!" cried the Automaton.

Verne chose a key at random, and depressed this.

The Automaton emitted a loud consonant of uncertain parentage.

There was a stool before the keyboard. Seating himself, Verne now observed that each of the console's keys and levers was incised with a letter or phonetic symbol. Vowels were on the lowermost bank of keys, nearest to hand, and the letter "E" centremost. Robert-Houdin had contrived his keyboard so that most accessible keys produced the letters uttered most frequently in French. Splaying his fingers, Jules Verne located the keys that would approximate the letters of his name. He touched the keys, interposing the sequence "JULES VERNE".

"Djoo-lesss Fffvvurr-nuhh," wheezed the Automaton. Verne tried the keys again, a bit more gracefully. *"Ju-lesss Vver-nuh."* The head of the Automaton moved stiffly: chin flexing, jaw clicking. The mechanical face turned aside, the eyelids closed.

Verne nodded, impressed. The machine had spoken his name . . . but in accordance with proper spelling, not pronunciation. Which keys should he press to make the Automaton pronounce his name correctly? He surveyed the keyboard.

"Jules Verne," said someone, close at hand.

The Automaton turned its head to confront Jules Verne.

The thing's eyelids opened, and Verne shuddered as two *living* eyes regarded him, set deeply in a face that seemed suddenly more human than it had been a moment past.

"I am honoured to meet you at last, Monsieur Verne," said a voice within the Automaton, yet Verne felt an unaccountable certainty that this voice originated somewhere distant from this place. *"Pardon the imperfections of my French. Where I come from – perhaps I should say when I come from – your language is not widely spoken."*

"Who . . . no, *what* are you?" quavered Jules Verne. He was alone in this dark corridor with the apparition before him. In the Museum's adjacent salon, Verne glimpsed a shadowed group of human figures, but they stood motionless, utterly frozen. Perhaps they were waxworks.

"I am as human as yourself," said the voice within the Automaton. *"But it would cost a vast expenditure of energy for me to travel from my own abode to where you are now. You see, my address is in the future."*

Verne recoiled. "Liar! Rogue! This is one of Barnum's humbugs. Somewhere nearby, an actor is ventriloquizing . . ." As he spoke, Verne looked round for concealed speaking-tubes.

"No, Mister Verne. It has long been my wish to contact you, and to assure you that your novels will still be read many years futurewards of your own lifetime. In a future which, to a large extent, you yourself have shaped, Mr Verne." The Automaton put wooden hand to metal waist, and bowed stiffly as it spoke these words.

Jules Verne snorted in contempt. "I believe none of this! Your address is the future? In what *arrondissement* of next week do you live? In which *quartier* of tomorrow? Show it to me, then! Let me gaze upon this future."

There was another click within his mind, and suddenly Jules Verne was elsewhere. He found himself transported to a place both familiar and alien. He was standing in the Champs Élysées . . . but the world had gone mad. Cannon fire erupted, and the streets were ablaze. French troops were bayoneting women and children! Prussian squadrons trampled through the Jardin des Tuileries, laughing as the French forces slaughtered civilians. *"Behold the future: scarcely four years hence, Monsieur Verne,"* said the voice within the Automaton. *"This is Paris in May, 1871. More than 110,000 citizens of France will be slaughtered in* la Semaine Sanglante: *the Week of Blood."*

Another click, and now Verne found himself walking up a simple path. The sun's position showed the hour to be about half-past five in the afternoon, and there was only the barest sliver of a crescent moon overhead. Before him was a house he had never seen before, and yet he somehow sensed that this unknown domicile was his own residence. He was holding a latchkey in his right hand. His limbs felt heavy with age, and Verne was astonished to find his face wreathed in a heavy greying beard. At the end of the path, near the house's front door, stood a man with his back turned.

"March ninth, 1886," said the voice in the Automaton. *"This is – this will be – your own house in the Rue Charles-Dubois, Monsieur Verne. You have spent the afternoon at your club, and now a visitor awaits you."*

The man in front of Verne turned round, with anger in his hazel-coloured eyes. For an instant, Verne recognized his brother Paul. But this man was in his mid-twenties: he was Paul Verne unaccountably youthened, just as Jules Verne had somehow become unaccountably aged. And this younger edition of Verne's brother wore only a thin moustache, without Paul Verne's accustomed spade beard and side-whiskers. The young man saw the aged Jules Verne, and his eyes gleamed with the blaze of insanity.

Wait a moment. The Automaton had mentioned the year 1886. But in that distant future year, Paul Verne would be nearly sixty. This young man, the image of Verne's brother, must be . . .

"Gaston?" asked Verne, astonished. His voice felt time-worn. When Jules Verne and his brother Paul had sailed for New York in 1867, Paul's son Gaston had been only seven years old. "Gaston? I am your uncle Jules. What is happening?"

Gaston Verne raised a pistol, and aimed it squarely at his

uncle. Jules Verne heard two shots ring out. At the second gunshot, his left leg exploded . . .

In agony, Verne staggered back . . . and found himself once more in the corridor of Barnum's museum, in 1867. His face was beardless. His left shin, just above his ankle, tingled unpleasantly but appeared unharmed.

"Is that enough future for you?" asked the Automaton. *"Now, sir, I will explain. In my century – far ahead of here – the novels of Jules Verne are still read and admired. I wish I could say as much for your plays. In my century, we have a limited ability to look yesterwards, and to witness the past . . . even to send some information backwards through time, although such things are strictly rationed. To send* myself *into the past would have required far too much energy, so I have contented myself with briefly occupying other vessels . . . such as this impressive Automaton of your countryman Robert-Houdin."*

Jules Verne rubbed his left leg angrily, and listened.

"The process of witnessing the past is a difficult one," continued the Automaton . . . or rather, the unseen visitor who spoke from within the Automaton's mechanism. *"I have one opportunity, and only one, in which to see the great Jules Verne: only one occasion, in the span of your lifetime, in which to witness your actions and audit your words. Naturally, Monsieur Verne, I chose to observe you in April 1867: during the one week in your life when you visited New York and Canada. Specifically, I chose this particular night – April ninth – so that I could get my money's worth of marvels. This is the night, sir, when you met Phineas Barnum, and when you visited his Museum filled with miracles and humbugs. The opportunity for me to observe Jules Verne* and *Phineas Barnum in a single yester-glance was too good to pass up."*

"Very well, monsieur," said Verne, regaining his composure. "You have seen me. What of it?"

"Simply this, sir. The process of gazing backward from my century to your own is imperfect. I have stirred up a few distortions in the time-stream, some chronal overtones. This was unavoidable."

Jules Verne rubbed his left shin, unable to relinquish the

sensation that he had actually been shot. "So, then. Those things I saw and heard? The bridge to Brooklyn that has not yet been built? The hippodrome that no longer stands?"

"My fault, I confess," said the visitor within the Automaton. *"In attempting to reach across the centuries for a glimpse of 1876, I have muddied the currents of the time-stream . . . and inadvertently given you a few glimpses – let us call them tableaux vivants – of the adjacent past and future."*

The pain in Jules Verne's leg was no longer there, as if the injury had never occurred. Perhaps it never had, and never would. Now he stood defiantly, confronting the Automaton. "You claim to be the future? *My* future?" Verne snapped his fingers, as if dismissing a waiter. "I reject you, whatever you call yourself. I am Jules Verne! I *create* the future, and you are not part of it! Those things you showed me: Paris in flames? My own nephew a homicidal madman? *Non, monsieur.* One week from tonight, when my brother Paul and I set sail for Brest, I will set down my account of this New York adventure . . . and I will take care to leave you out of it altogether. You have now been unhappened, sir!"

As Verne spoke these words, he touched the keyboard of the Automaton, pressing several keys without knowing their functions. The mechanical footman's arms gesticulated, as if warding off an attack. The footman's eyelids clacked shut, and his mechanical mouth emitted one last gust of speech:

"Au revoir."

There was movement in a nearby corridor. The night's tableaux had ended, and now the audience were departing Barnum's theatre. Jules Verne stood between the waxworks, and he pondered what he had seen tonight. These phantom yesterdays and threatened tomorrows: Paris besieged, Gaston Verne a madman. Were these things real, or merely part of Barnum's humbugs?

At least one portion of tonight's entertainments had been honest enough to confess its fakery. Verne recalled that the tableau on Barnum's stage – the burning house – had been indeed quite convincing. The steam-driven fire-engine had been genuine, but it had employed counterfeit water to extinguish artificial fire.

"Perhaps the pasts and the futures which I witnessed tonight are merely . . . *tableaux vivants,*" Jules Verne decided. "Performances contrived for my benefit, to entertain me. In that event, they have succeeded." He shuddered once more, at the memory of witnessing Paris in flames. "But I choose not to look behind this particular curtain, to see the stage machinery that has trundled these tableaux into place."

Now the theatre doors were opened wide by the ushers in gilded brocade, and Paul Verne came forth with Barnum at his arm. With a deep bow, Phineas Barnum invited Jules Verne and his brother to come backstage and view the scenery-changing apparatus.

"Thank you, but . . . no," said Verne sadly, stepping away from the pedestal of Robert-Houdin's talking Automaton, and slightly surprised to find himself walking with a faint limp in his left leg. "The illusions, Mister Barnum, are more enchanting if one does not see the wheels turning behind the scenes. I have a long voyage ahead, in unexpected and uncharted regions." Verne nodded graciously. "But I shall never forget the tableaux that have been shown to me tonight. I do not think that I will pass this way again."

Taking his brother's arm, Jules Verne moved towards the egress of Barnum & Van Amburgh's Museum, and the night air beyond. Already, in his mind, Jules Verne was imagining a wondrous new procession of tomorrows . . . and fictional characters arrayed before him in an infinite range of tableaux.

THE SECRET OF THE NAUTILUS

Michael Mallory

Even before he went to New York, Verne was thinking about his next book, which had the working title Un Voyage sous les Eaux, *but it was not until he returned that he had the time to develop it. The result would arguably be his best book, probably his best known, and certainly with his most famous character: Captain Nemo in* Vingt Mille Lieues sous les Mers *– 20,000* Leagues Under the Sea *(1869/70). Verne had to revise his original draft because Nemo had become too strong a character, too full of revenge, aimed solely at the Russian Empire, because of their treatment of the Polish. Hetzel persuaded Verne to tone down this hatred and make Nemo more of a Robin Hood character who fought against all oppressors. Hetzel was probably right because Verne made Nemo far more enigmatic, a mystery man whose origins and motives are not entirely known or understood. This gave him a fascination that has intrigued readers ever since. Even Verne could not leave him alone as he brought him back in a sequel,* L'île mystérieuse, *in 1874.*

Perhaps equalling Nemo for fascination in the story is his creation, the submarine Nautilus. *There was nothing new in describing a submarine – they had existed for many years and the inventor Robert Fulton had even named his* Nautilus *in 1797. But none were like Verne's remarkable machine, powered by electricity, and with every comfort, able to tour the entire underwater domain. A vengeful enigmatic commander with his all-powerful invention was a successful formula that not only Verne would exploit again, but which has become a staple figure in science fiction and techno-thrillers ever since. We will encounter both Nemo and the* Nautilus *again in this anthology.*

November 23, 1894

As I take up my pen to record these events of the past, I consider how many times I have previously sat down to do so, only to reconsider and crumple up the first page without bothering to go on to the second. Perhaps this account will be dismissed as fiction; perhaps it will go unnoticed altogether. I have no control over any of those eventualities; I am but the teller of the tale. As to whom I am, it is of little consequence. Were I to release my name, the reader might indeed recognize it, but that knowledge will add to neither the truthfulness nor the strangeness of the story. I am not the hero of this particular tale; rather, it is a man of remarkable abilities and intellectual capacity, a man known to the world as Captain Nemo.

How I came to be in the service of Captain Nemo is as immaterial to this history as my identity. Suffice it to say that I became a crewman in his submersible vehicle, the *Argonaut*, in the year 1876, during my twenty-sixth summer. Those familiar with two popular literary works in which Captain Nemo appears may protest that his great sub-aquatic vessel was not called the *Argonaut*, but the *Nautilus*, and they would be right, at least in part. They may also feel that they know the history of this amazing personage, but as I discovered during my time with the captain, the written record as it has existed up until now constitutes a deliberate fabrication. Until now, the truth about Captain Nemo has never been set down.

The most remarkable adventure of my life began in late August of that year, when Captain Nemo and I had

consigned First Mate Willett to his Maker at the bottom of
the Indian Ocean. Willett and I represented the sole crew
of the *Argonaut*, which was a much smaller vessel than the
Nautilus, and his untimely demise – not, ironically, the result
of one of the sea's inherent dangers, but rather a burst
appendix – cast a pall over the ship, so much so that when
Captain Nemo appeared before me several days later with
expression graver than any I had yet encountered, I initially
assumed it was a late reaction to the tragedy. That, however,
was not the case.

"Louis, we are changing course immediately," he
announced. "We will be heading for latitude 150° 30' and
longitude 34° 57'."

"Where is that, sir?" I asked.

"The site of a former land mass in the South Pacific. I
only pray I am not too late."

"Too late for what, Captain?"

I could see a thunderhead forming on his face, and began
to fear that my rampant curiosity, which occasionally served
to annoy this man of indecipherable moods, was about to
raise his ire. Within a moment, however, the storm passed.

"You might as well know," he said, sombrely. "The time
may come when I am in need of your assistance in this
matter. Come with me while I reset our course."

I followed him to the ship's navigational room and, not
for the first time, marveled at the directional system he had
installed, which literally steered the submersible through the
depths of the ocean in automated fashion, based on his
calculations. While the system's finer working points were
known only to the captain, I knew that it operated on the
same mechanical principle as a music box, with a slowly
revolving cylinder that held movable and removable dots
that, depending on their placement, controlled the instruments that governed depth, speed and direction. I waited
until he was finished, at which time he astonished me by
inviting me to join him in his private study, as though I were
an equal on board the *Argonaut*! After offering me a cigar
made from seaweed, which I declined, he lit one of his own,

savoured the greenish smoke, and began. "As of this moment, Louis, we are in pursuit of a man named Ludovico Divenchy," he said. "Have you heard that surname before?"

As he pronounced it – *DEE-von-SHEE* – I was not familiar with it, and said so.

"The name is a modern derivation of the original spelling, which might be more familiar to you: *da Vinci*."

"You mean, as in Leonardo da Vinci?" I asked.

"I do, though you will not find the Divenchy branch of the family on any official records. The spelling and pronunciation was altered by the grandfather of Ludovico Divenchy, and subsequently retained by Ludovico's father Beniamino and his brother Cesaré. They alone know of the family connection."

"How, then did you learn of such things, Captain?"

"I should think that would be obvious, based on what I have told you."

"You mean, you are . . . ?"

"I am Cesaré Divenchy," he acknowledged, "and the man we are pursuing is my brother."

I sat stunned at this revelation. "What has he done?"

"What I have prayed was not possible, even by my brother, whose knowledge of engineering surpasses my own, despite his youth," he replied. "He has raised the *Nautilus* from its place of rest, that is what he has done. The signal sounded this morning."

"Signal?" I uttered, now hopelessly lost.

"Before sinking the *Nautilus*, I installed on its dorsal fin a device that operates on the principles of electro-magnetic waves. The wave it emits is contained underwater, but in the open air it is programmed to sends a message to a receiver, which I keep here on board the *Argonaut*. Receipt of that signal means that the *Nautilus* has surfaced, and there are only two men in the world with the knowledge to facilitate it. Since I have not, it has to be Ludovico. Believe me, Louis, it is in the best interest of mankind to keep the *Nautilus* hidden at the bottom of the ocean."

"But why?"

"Because of what it contains. Buried within the *Nautilus* is the body of my father, Beniamino Divenchy. Not only does he rest there, but his legacy is there as well – a legacy for which the world is not ready."

"I do not understand, sir," I said.

"How lucky you are, Louis," Captain Nemo said ruefully, "for understanding my father and the consequences of his work has not offered me many peaceful days. Father was a scientist, and a brilliant one, but he did not so much leave footsteps as craters which were impossible to fill, at least by me. It was as though there were two men co-existing within his body: one of them benevolent and caring, and the other driven by his work to the point of inhumanity. Ludovico inherited Father's driven side. He was brash and daring, never for one second doubting himself, even as a child. For that reason, Father favoured him at all times. I say this without bitterness, for I was quite content upon the day I could be free of them both. As a young man I traveled the world; I wed a beautiful Nepalese woman and had two wonderful children; I had little to do with my father and brother, until the association was forced upon me."

"Forced by whom?" I asked.

"By those who wanted my father's discovery." He rose and began to pace in agitated fashion. "You may see fit to call me mad, Louis, but what I am about to tell you is the truth. My father discovered a way to make gold. I do not mean *earn* gold, I mean *make* it, create it from a base element."

"He found the Philosopher's Stone?" I gasped.

The captain shook his head impatiently. "There is no such thing. The transmutation of iron into gold is a chemical reaction involving extreme heat and molecular bombardment."

"What a boon to mankind that could be!" I enthused.

Captain Nemo smiled sardonically. "So it might seem. So father wished. Alas, there was a dangerous side to it. Through Ludovico's indiscretion, word of my father's discovery filtered out. Most refused to believe it; however a few dangerous and powerful men sought to verify the rumour, and did so. Once confirmed, these men never gave us a moment's peace, they hounded us for father's notes." He sat back down and regarded me through sorrow-filled eyes. "I was the weak link in the chain of familial stubbornness because I had a family. I took my wife and children out of Italy, but no matter where we went, we were pursued by these evil men. Eventually we fled to India, a country we loved, but were soon discovered. These human monsters did not even try for me. Instead they went straight for my innocent family. They murdered my wife and babes in cold blood and over their precious bodies told me to go to my father and tell him that they would not be deterred in their campaign to gain the secret of transmutation."

After swallowing down a lump in his throat, the captain continued: "I did travel back to my father to deliver a message, but not the one my tormentors were expecting. I told him Cesaré Divenchy was dead, murdered as thoroughly as my wife and children. I told him I cared not if he also died at the hands of these criminals. And then I forcibly expelled him from his own laboratory and used his damnable discovery for my own good. I worked for two full days, never stopping to eat or sleep, the heat of the forge searing my flesh, until I had created enough gold to buy the city of Rome. I'd have made even more, had not Father summoned Ludovico to the house and told him to break down the door."

The captain again fell silent, casting the cabin into an eerie stillness. At last he continued: "I left him, not caring a lira for his fate, took my gold and used it to finance the *Nautilus* and my escape from the world. Six years later he came to me, ill, weary and disillusioned, a broken relic of a once indomitable figure. He was tired of being pursued and knew there was only one place he could truly hide: on board the *Nautilus*. I dismissed my crew and took him in, and for the first time began to develop something of a filial relationship with my father. I took the *Nautilus* to an uncharted island in the South Pacific and vowed to remain there with him, hidden from the eyes of the world. And then the impossible happened: that infernal balloon filled with castaways landed on the island! I wanted to go elsewhere, but Father would not hear of it. By then the admirable side of his personality had gained dominance over the dark side, and he wished only to help others. It was he who aided the castaways while I remained in the shadows.

"After three interminable years of blundering about, they made their way into the *Nautilus*. By then, my father was dying, and in his last moments on earth he managed to put forth the greatest prevarication of his life: he claimed that *he* was Captain Nemo. He spun a fabrication of his supposed early days as Prince Dakkar, which, despite glaring inconsistencies, the fools accepted without question. On his deathbed, Father created a lie to throw our constant pursuers, who had begun to suspect that the missing Cesaré Divenchy was Captain Nemo, off the trail. He thought only of protecting me, and thus died for me. I secretly recovered everything I needed from the *Nautilus* and then sent it down to become the grave for both my father and his papers. How I hated to consign my glorious ship to oblivion. I went on to build the *Argonaut*, which is smaller, less personal, harder to love, but which has given me ten years of peace. Until now."

He then fell into a silent, almost trance-like, contemplation that I was unable to penetrate. Even though I still had questions about his story, there was nothing I could do except leave him to his mood and go back to my cabin and my journal. Except for what communication was necessary for the continuance of life on board the *Argonaut*, the silence continued until we reached the designated latitude and longitude coordinates.

The sun was high when we surfaced and all I could see on any horizon was water. But using a telescope, Captain Nemo spotted a small dark shape protruding from the water to the east. "There," he said, pointing. "It has drifted some." Going below, he steered the *Argonaut* toward the object, and as we came closer, I could see fins on the back of the shape

– steel fins. It was the *Nautilus*. As soon as the *Argonaut* had pulled up against its hull, the captain reappeared on deck and threw a noose of rope over one of the metal dorsal fin spikes, then swung himself aboard and waited for me to do the same.

He opened the hatch of the *Nautilus*, and as we descended into the vessel, I was struck by both the design of the *Nautilus* and its beauty, and I could easily see how a man could live here indefinitely, the laird of his own self-created, tranquil castle. In the dim light of a single candle, I followed him into a chamber that was clearly designed as living quarters. On the bed was the well preserved, if emaciated, body of an elderly man with long white hair and beard, and I could see the facial resemblance between the remains of Beniamino Divenchy and his son. "I am sorry, Father," Captain Nemo said quietly. Then looking to the wall opposite, he added: "Even from here I can see that the safe has been opened." Hastening to it, he found it empty.

Before he could comment, though, a low, unearthly moan filled the *Nautilus*, and for a moment I stopped breathing, for it seemed to be coming from the body of Beniamino Divenchy! Captain Nemo's face paled as we cautiously approached the ornate bed that served as the corpse's bier, and only when close enough to touch it did we notice a figure lying on the floor on the other side of it. It was a man – a brawny man of about thirty years of age, with dark hair and beard.

"Ludovico!" the captain exclaimed. Then, handing me the candle, he dashed to the figure and pulled him upright. The man gave forth another moan. "Help me get him above," the captain ordered.

As best I could, I aided him in dragging Ludovico Divenchy to the main hatch stair and struggled to hoist him upwards, though the burden of the task fell onto the captain's strength, not mine. Once we got him on to the deck of the *Nautilus*, the captain reached down and took a handful of seawater and flung it into his face. It took several dousings before Ludovico began to stir. He opened his eyes and squinted in the glaring sunlight. Seeing the captain, his face darkened. "You," he muttered.

"Yes, Ludo, it is I," the captain replied.

A look of rage came over Ludovico's face, and he attempted to lash out at Captain Nemo. Despite his weakened condition, the blow could have done a good deal of damage, had it connected. "You have come back to the scene of the crime, eh, Cesaré?" he said.

"What crime, Ludo?" the captain protested. "The only crime that has taken place here was committed by you. Your very presence here attests to that. To whom have you given Father's papers, Ludo?"

"Oh, that is rich," Ludovico spat, struggling to his feet on the deck. "First you lure me here, and then –"

"*I* lure *you* here?"

"Yes, and I do not appreciate being played for a fool, least of all by you!"

"Gentlemen, please!" I called out in desperation.

"Who in hell are you, whey-face?" Ludovico Divenchy demanded, giving me a vicious glare.

"He is my crewman," Captain Nemo said, "and while you are on board this vessel you are to treat us both with civility. I will not countenance any of your –" He stopped suddenly and appeared momentarily lost in thought, then said: "Ludo, are you under the impression that I summoned you to the *Nautilus*?"

"You know damned well you did!" Ludovico roared. "I saw the letter!"

"What letter?"

"The one you sent to –" Now it was Ludovico Divenchy who stopped mid-sentence as a realization dawned upon him. He slapped a hand to his forehead and wailed, "Oh, my God, it was a forgery!"

"What did this purported missive of mine say?" Captain Nemo asked.

"It instructed me to return to the *Nautilus* and raise it," Ludovico answered. "Cesaré, it was in your handwriting. I

recognized your signature. That was the only reason I acqui-
esced. What a fool I was!"

"Agreed," his brother said, "but nothing can be done
about it now. Come, we have work to do."

Ludovico required only a little help descending into the
Argonaut, and no help whatsoever consuming the three
brandies his brother offered him in the vessel's salon, though
they did not serve to put him in a more congenial mood.

"Now, Ludo," Captain Nemo began, as his brother
finished his third drink, "it is imperative that I know who
has the secret."

Looking with some embarrassment at his brother,
Ludovico Divenchy said: "A priest named Father Saldana."

"A *priest*?"

"He came to me and claimed to know everything about
Father's notes, and said that it was the will of God that
the church be in control of the discovery before any government of the world obtained it. He said that it was the only
way to prevent worldwide strife. You must admit, that is a
reasonable argument. Then he presented me with that letter
purportedly from you, stating that I should trust and help
him. And when I had managed to bring that sunken coffin
to the surface and handed over the papers, I was offered
a congratulatory drink for my efforts – a poisoned one.
Forgive me, Cesaré, but I assumed it was your doing all
along."

"Have things so deteriorated between us that you would
really think I would seek your death?"

A silence fell between them, which I broke to say: "If, as
you say, the drink was poisoned, why are you still alive?"

Ludovico Divenchy's withering gaze reduced me to the
status of a gnat. "I may be a fool at times, boy, but I am
not an easy man to vanquish."

"That quality, brother, can only aid us," Captain Nemo
said, "for we must get those papers back!"

My mind was still raging with questions. "Forgive me,
Captain, but I fail to see how a formula for creating gold
carries with it such dire consequences."

"Do you possess the mental capacity to understand?" Ludovico challenged.

"How can I tell if I do not even know what it is I may not understand?" I snapped back.

Captain Nemo gave a deep sigh, and said: "What do you know of atomics, Louis?"

"Atomics? Nothing, sir."

"You see?" Ludovico said.

The captain stifled his brother with a gesture. "Listen to me, Louis; the ability to create gold carries with not simply the potential for economic havoc. When one element changes into another, it is because its atoms move and regroup, but that very atomic movement produces an extreme form of radiation. Father discovered ways to control the process to minimize the danger. However, if used improperly or ignorantly, the transmutation process could create a force of heat and fire that could consume cities and destroy every living thing for tens, if not hundreds, of miles. It could lay waste to entire countries, perhaps even mankind itself."

"Good God," I muttered.

"The invocation of God is more than proper, for in the wrong hands my father's discovery could unleash Armageddon."

I studied the faces of the two men, both of whom, I knew, were not given to levity. Their present expressions confirmed the fact that Captain Nemo was not exaggerating the danger of metal transmutation. "God help us," I muttered, fearfully.

"We cannot wait for His intervention," the Captain said. "We must retrieve the secret and destroy it ourselves. Ludo, do you have any idea where to find this M. Saldana, whom I doubt very much is a man of the church?"

"None," Ludovico said, shaking his boulder-like head. "Wait . . . at one point he used a strange word in such context as to indicate a place: Rakata, he said. Do you know where that is?"

"That is the name of an island in the Flores Sea, in Indonesia," Captain Nemo replied. "There is very little hospitable there, though."

"Isn't that area volcanic?" I asked.

Upon hearing my query, the heads of both brothers snapped up. "Heat!" they cried in unison.

"With the heat of a volcano, they could manufacture a ton of gold," Captain Nemo said, "but at what consequences?"

"We must get there at once," Ludovico said.

"We can be there in less than two days."

"If we only had a flying ship, we could arrive there in one," Ludovico mused.

"A flying ship?" the captain retorted. "Come, Ludo, that is sheer whimsy. Even you cannot conquer the skies."

"What a pity, brother, that your imagination does not match your intellect."

After that, the two men ceased conversation. Captain Nemo stood watch over the *Argonaut*'s control instruments, never resting or even stopping to eat. Under normal circumstances it was impossible to detect the sense of motion on board the submersible; however, traveling at a constant maximum speed, as we were doing now, gave me a slight sense of dizziness. Luckily, I had to endure only one more day of it before we arrived at the captain's coordinates of 9° 23′ longitude and 114° 49′ latitude. Calling both Ludovico and I into his private study, Captain Nemo unveiled the glass panel set in the room's ceiling. It was early evening in this part of the world, and there remained enough light on land above us for us to see the shadow of the ship a dozen or so fathoms overhead. "We will surface immediately," the captain said. "I wish to see the colours the vessel is flying."

We rose a fair distance from the ship, which appeared to be a schooner, and once we had climbed onto the deck, the captain took up his telescope to examine it. There have been times when I felt that nothing on earth, and probably few things in Heaven, could actually take Captain Nemo by surprise. But as he scanned the ship through the glass, he appeared to be at a loss for words. "What country is it, Cesaré?" asked his brother.

"See for yourself," he said, handing him the telescope.

After a lengthy look, Ludovico said: "I have never seen that flag in my life!"

I was permitted a look next, and, like them, had never before seen the banner, which was half green, half golden-yellow, surrounding a white diamond shape.

"We must get closer," the captain said, and ordered us below. Sinking just under the surface, we proceeded over and through the jumble of levels formed by the underwater bases of the volcanic cones. At last we were below the unidentifiable schooner. "We will wait for darkness," the captain instructed.

Under the sea the hour of the day loses its relevance, but the passage of time does not. The next three hours seemed endless. With nothing else to pass the time, I took to my cabin, where I recorded notes in my journal until a knock on the door signaled that it was time to make our move.

The *Argonaut* surfaced close to the hull of the schooner. The evening was warm and the full moon provided enough illumination for us to see, but cast an eerie yellow glow over the sea and ship. Since the only weapon to be found on board the *Argonaut* was a harpoon, we would board the ship as unarmed as we were uninvited. Attaching a rope to a grapnel, Captain Nemo skillfully threw it and hooked it on to the deck of the mysterious ship, permitting us to climb aboard.

No helmsman stood at the wheel of the schooner; in fact, the deck of the ghostly ship appeared to be deserted. "What do we do now, sir?" I asked the captain.

"We came for answers, Louis," he replied, "so let us waste no time in posing our questions." He then lifted his foot and stomped on the deck as forcefully as possible. Below, I could hear a confusion of voices. Then various forms began to appear on the deck. One of them approached us with a lantern, and when he saw Ludovico, he stepped back. "Good Lord . . . Divenchy!"

"Well well, my friend, the holy man!" Ludovico said, and reached for the throat of the man I presumed to be the deceitful Saldana. Only the unmistakable sound of pistols being cocked at close range stopped him. "There is no need for this," a voice said. "Come below, Signor Divenchy. The rest of you as well. God alone knows how you got on board this ship, but now that you are here, no immediate harm will come to you unless you invite it." We were marched below and ushered into what normally would have been the captain's quarters on a ship, but in this case appeared to be a meeting room, for seated around a table was a dozen or so men, each one dressed in the garb and hair fashion of a different nation. "This is why we could not recognize the flag," Captain Nemo commented.

At the head of the table was a nondescript fellow whose nationality became clear only when he spoke: "We fly our own flag," he said, revealing an American drawl. "We represent each of the major countries of the globe, though before long, our flag will be the only flag, and there will no longer be separate nations."

"And you will be in control, I suppose?" Ludovico sneered.

"Yes, and who better? We are the elite of the world," the American replied. "We will provide the masses with their basic needs, and they, in turn, will work to provide us with ours. For the first time in history, there will be order in the world."

"You cannot be serious," Ludovico said.

"Utterly serious," the man said, and despite the madness of his plan, his eyes betrayed a deadly earnestness.

"You expect the nations of the world to sit back placidly while you take them over?" Captain Nemo asked.

"Come now, Captain Divenchy . . . or do you still prefer Nemo? Yes, we know who you are. Our agents are nothing if not thorough. Anyway, ninety-nine per cent of the world's population was born to be serfs and vassals. They are sheep constantly in search of a shepherd."

"May I ask the shepherd's name?"

"Collectively we are the One World League, Captain. My name is Walker."

"Walker, the oil baron?" Ludovico Divenchy said.

The American smiled. "You've heard of me, how gratifying," he said. "Soon, my friend, I shall be President Walker of the World, thanks to you. The League has been planning this venture for some time, but we lacked one key ingredient for success: the means of limitless wealth. You, Mr Divenchy, provided that."

Suddenly the meaning of the strange flag on the ship came to me: a diamond surrounded by gold and green, which is the colour of American currency . . . the flag itself symbolized wealth!

Pistols or no, Ludovico Divenchy looked as though he was going to lunge for the man, but his brother prevented him by placing a hand on his arm. Then he stepped forward and said: "I have but one question for you, Mr Walker, for which I demand an answer: are you the men who killed my wife, my children?"

"I know nothing of that," Walker answered. "There are a lot of bad men out there, Captain, but we are not among them. Our goal is noble. We will bring order to a chaotic world, and said world will thank us."

"You will annihilate the world," Captain Nemo charged. "The transmutation of iron into gold releases a dangerous amount of energy. I suggest you burn whatever notes you took from my father and forget you ever heard of the process."

"Oh, why, yes, of course!" Walker said with a hearty laugh. "Sure, we'll just throw this miracle away and simply forget about the possibility of creating our own wealth and power. Good god, Captain, you would do better to tell a rooster to ignore a henhouse!"

"What is your plan for us?" Ludovico demanded.

"Treat you as guests, of course," Walker replied, "for a while. Our workers are now inside the volcano on this island, preparing to make the first transmutation. You, gentlemen, will be privileged to watch. Until then, however, you will be held in the brig, for everyone's safety. Take them away."

Guards took us to a tiny cell in another part of the ship and locked us in. The captain sat quietly and I sat frightened, but Ludovico paced as best he could in the small quarters. "Why could not Father have left well enough alone?" he raged. "We would not be in here if he had never made that discovery."

"Neither would we be here if you had been able to keep quiet about it," the captain rejoined. "Since the ability to achieve a great discovery at the exact moment the world is ready for is a matter of chance, not genius, I can forgive Father."

"So I am to blame for this? I, who nearly lost my life aboard that damned iron barrel of yours?"

"I have lost more because of you and your reckless tongue than you will ever know, Ludovico!"

For a moment I feared the two men would come to blows, but after a few tense and hot moments, both slumped down. "What's done is done," the captain conceded. "We must direct our energies toward finding a solution."

"There is only one solution, Cesaré, you know that," Ludovico replied. "Let them conduct the experiment and blow themselves into oblivion."

"And what of us?" I asked, but neither had an answer.

None of us slept that night. Shortly after dawn, Walker and two of his crew appeared to open the doors of the cell and free us – at least as free as one can be with pistols directed at their hearts. We were led to a lifeboat, lowered and rowed to the edge of Rakata Island and then marched up to an entrance to what looked like a small tunnel in the side of the volcanic cone. Walker lit a lantern and entered first, and the guards beckoned us to follow.

After squeezing inside, we descended over an incline of roughly two metres and landed on a natural trail, which we followed downward through heat and closeness that increased with each step. Eventually we came to a gigantic natural chamber inside the cone, on the floor of which was a solid, white hot, steaming line – a crack in the surface of the earth, through which could be seen the magma flow! Saldana and a gathering of workmen were already down there, as close to the crack as they dared get, sweltering, some even staggering, in heavy protective outfits that in some measure resembled diving suits. Surrounding them were hundreds of bars of pure iron. "They are attempting too much, far too much," the captain uttered. "Neither Father nor I ever attempted more than a few ounces at a time, and that offered danger enough."

Marching past us now came the other members of the One World League, each one holding a small box, which they lowered down to the workmen. "What are the boxes holding?" I asked.

"It can only be an element called *cerilium*,[*] Louis," Captain Nemo replied. "Its molecular structure is highly unstable. It is the trigger for the transmutation."

Walker gave the signal to begin, and Saldana instructed the workmen to edge the iron bars closer to the crack in the earth, which was steaming like a locomotive engine, making the air almost too sultry to breathe. The members of the League looked on intently as the bars and began to soften and glow red, then white. Then in an instant, the iron melted completely, creating a pool of molten metal. With a gasp, I watched as the pool actually caught fire!

Now the heat inside the volcano was almost too intense to bear. "It is time!", Walker shouted. "Throw on the cerilium!" Beside me, Captain Nemo tensed. Under his breath, he said: "The first concussion will likely result in total chaos and that will be our chance to flee and escape . . . providing we survive the blast."

We did not have long to wait. One workman opened his box and threw the contents into the pool of molten iron, and what happened next I can only describe in terms of abject horror. An explosion shook the very walls of the cone and a pillar of fire – for that is the only way to describe it – rose up from the floor and consumed two of the workmen, reducing them to bones in seconds, and within another second reduced the bones to ashes. The remaining workmen

---

[*] There is no such element as cerilium, but in the interests of safety, the true name and nature of the element used to transmute iron into gold is being withheld from this record.

leapt back in terror, as did Walker and the members of the League. "Now!" Captain Nemo shouted, and the three of us turned and ran back up the trail to the tunnel opening. The path was slick and ashy, making it hard to climb, though I was spurred on by the memory of the workmen's annihilation. Ludovico, the strongest of us, had the least problem, and once we had reached the steep incline leading out, was able to push the captain and I upwards to safety, after which the two of us hauled him through the opening from the outside.

Salt air never smelled so welcoming!

As we raced for the boat to take us off the island, a cloud of steam rose from the volcano. We leapt into the boat and Ludovico took the oars, rowing like a madman until we reached the *Argonaut*. Behind us, a white plume of smoke – this one shaped like a toadstool – emerged from the volcano. "They will not be emerging," Captain Nemo said, climbing on to the deck of the *Argonaut*.

Ludovico went into the submersible first and I followed next. No sooner had I set foot on the bottom when I heard the crack of a gunshot and saw Captain Nemo plummet through the hatch and crash to the floor below! "Captain!" I cried, attempting to sit him up, and discovering with horror the spreading bloodstain on the back of his jacket.

"The damnable cowards!" Ludovico cried, climbing back on deck, while I attended to the wounded captain. I heard another gun retort, followed by a mighty curse from Ludovico. He sprang back down into the *Argonaut* bleeding from his shoulder.

"There is still a man on board that damned ship!" he cried, fingering his wound, which was but superficial. Then looking at his brother, he asked: "How is he?"

"I'm afraid . . ." was all I could get out.

Captain Nemo opened his eyes and looked at Ludovico. "A brother shall die for a brother," he uttered. "It is the law of the *Nautilus*." With his eyes still on Ludovico, he smiled wanly . . . then he breathed his last. Cesaré Divenchy, scion of the house of da Vinci, alias Captain Nemo, lay dead.

Ludovico appeared at first to be in a state of shock. Then he rose with a look of determination so fierce that it made my skin turn cold. "How do you operate this bucket?" he demanded.

I led him to the control instruments in the captain's cabin and attempted to explain their operation, as best I could. At a glance he absorbed their workings, and immediately took charge of *Argonaut,* pushing it into full speed. "Hold on to something, boy," was all he said, and, sensing what he was about to do, secured myself as best I could.

.Seconds later we rammed into the hull of the schooner, and despite my best efforts, the impact knocked me to the floor. Ludovico reversed direction enough to turn the submersible around, traveled back to where he had started, and then charged and rammed the ship again. It took three punishing impacts before the schooner of the One World League had a hole in its hull large enough to send it, and whoever remained on board, to the bottom.

When he had finished, he ordered me to take over control of the *Argonaut.* "Where do you wish to go?" I asked, tentatively.

"First, back to the *Nautilus,*" he said. "Then you may drop me off on land anywhere, and do with this ship as you wish."

"I believe the captain would have wanted you to take it."

"The sea holds no interest for me," Ludovico Divenchy said. "I look upwards into the clouds. It is there I wish to be, and now it appears that I must."

"You must?"

"What if some of these wretches survived? What if this blasted League of theirs still exists somewhere else in the world? What if they once more attempt to use my Father's discovery? The world may never be ready for this knowledge. Cesaré was correct in blaming me. I *am* responsible for this business, so it is now up to me to end it. I must patrol the earth, looking for signs of its misuse. I may have to visit every volcano on the planet to make certain this does not happen again. But for now I must rest. Let me know when we have arrived at the *Nautilus*." He strode into the closest cabin – the one that had been occupied by Willett – and I did not see nor hear from him again for nearly two days.

When we had reached the site of the *Nautilus*, I alerted him, and he emerged from the cabin, asking, "Where is he?" I had placed the body of Captain Nemo in his study, and told Ludovico so. "Get us beside the *Nautilus*, so close that I can step from one deck to the other," he instructed, as he went into the study. Once I had so positioned the *Argonaut*, Ludovico Divenchy reappeared carrying the body of his brother in his arms. He refused any help in lifting the body through the hatch of the *Argonaut* and down into the *Nautilus*, where he lay Captain Nemo down to rest with their father. He then opened the reservoirs' stopcocks and sent the *Nautilus* back to the realm for which it was designed for the last time, a uniquely fitting sarcophagus for its creator. From there we traveled to the coast of New Guinea, where Ludovico Divenchy muttered a terse goodbye to me and strode out on to land without so much as a backwards glance. I never saw him again.

The *Argonaut* was now mine, and even though I grew more experienced in its operation, I began to long for life once more on land. I decided to retire the submersible permanently near the Samoan Islands, and after a brief stay there, took a conventional ship back to Scotland (a journey paid for through the discovery of Captain Nemo's treasury). Years later I returned to Samoa, and it is from here that I write this history.

The world at large continues to endure chaos, strife and war, but remains innocently ignorant of the devilish plot of "President" Walker and his One World League to "solve" the problems. Some years after this adventure, however, the world most definitely heard about the isle of Rakata, which in 1883 was virtually wiped from the map through the violent explosion of its primary volcano, Krakatau. Whether this globe-affecting event was an act of nature, a whim of the Almighty, or the effect of the remaining quantities of cerilium finally reaching that pool of molten iron, I have no clue. All I can state with certainty is that not long after Krakatau's eruption, the world began to hear reports of an amazing man flying about in a "cloud clipper." No one knew the true identity of the mysterious genius who called himself Captain Robur . . . no one except me.

I conclude this testimony in the hopes that, for the sake of mankind, this self-professed "conqueror" will be successful in his mission. It is unlikely I will ever know for certain for even now, as I pen these words in my beloved paradise, surrounded by loved ones, I can feel the night coming. I am spending my remaining time in prayer, not for my own soul, but for that of the blustery genius who was the brother of the most remarkable man I have ever known.

> *Here he lies where he longed to be,*
> *Home is the sailor, home from the sea,*
> *And the hunter home from the hill.*

The sailor is indeed home, though the hunter will maintain his vigil over the hills. I pray the hunt be successful.

DOCTOR BULL'S INTERVENTION

Keith Brooke

After the creative energy needed to produce 20,000 Leagues Under the Sea, *Verne rested on his mental laurels for a while. He was no less productive. He completed his sequel to* From the Earth to the Moon *with* Around the Moon *(1869), plus a short novel inspired by his voyage on the* Great Eastern, Une ville flottante *(A Floating City) (1870). His next long novel was the uninspiring* Aventures de trois Russes et de trois Anglais dans L'Afrique australe *(1871/2) – a work almost as tedious as its title. It is sometimes known as* Measuring a Meridian, *because that's what the six men are trying laboriously to do. He also began work on a long novel set in the polar regions of northern Canada,* Le Pays des fourrures *(1872/3),* The Fur Country.

In the midst of all this, Verne's father died and it was almost as if Verne needed some light relief. He wrote a short humorous story, "Une Fantaisie due Docteur Ox" (1872), usually translated as "Dr Ox's Experiment". Quiquendone is a small sleepy town where nothing happens and the town council do their best not to rock the boat. Under the pretext of installing street lighting, Dr Ox intends to give the town a jolt in the arm by feeding them pure oxygen and then sit back and enjoy the consequences. The story, all too often dismissed as minor, was a satire on the dull

and complacent, those who would hold back the advance of science.
Once in a while Verne believed they should be taught a lesson.
In the following, Keith Brooke takes a leaf from Verne's book.

1

How it is pointless to seek, even on the best maps, for the small development of Sunny Meadows

Sunny Meadows? Huh! Don't give me that Sunny Meadows crap. It's a dump. Don't waste your time looking for it: it really isn't worth it. You could call up a map on your Visionscreen and eyeball it for Sunny Meadows but you're wasting the effort. It's just urban-suburban sprawl. Get a satellite view and it's all the same: Sunny Meadows has nothing to distinguish it from anywhere else. It just *is*, although nobody really cares whether it is or it isn't. GPS would find it: this one, and all the other Sunny Meadows in existence – look it up on Routemaster and you'll find something like eight entries, in the Thames Gateway, the M4 corridor, Coventry, Hemel Hempstead . . .

If you don't believe me, just go there (nobody goes there, it isn't worth it). Get in your car and drive to good old Sunny Meadows. You probably won't realize when you get there, because Sunny Meadows looks much like its neighbouring suburbs, all drive-through fast food churn-outs and identikit houses set back from the roads. You can park in the Wal-Mart car park. Nobody will mind. Nobody much goes there any more, since NutriMent UK came to Sunny Meadows and started piping orders right into the home so you never even need to get off your fat backside if you don't want to.

Sunny Meadows wasn't always Sunny Meadows. In fact it wasn't Sunny Meadows until fairly recently, but urban sprawl has a habit of sprawling, bringing places like this into existence. Before it was Sunny Meadows it was what they called a "grey field development zone": shells of old factories and warehouses, acres of dead tarmac and concrete, a few scraggy patches of bramble and nettle growing where the polluted soil permitted. But now it is transformed: this is a modern place to live and, on the whole, the people are contented here.

Much of modern life here, as elsewhere, is automated: the dreams of early sci-fi made flesh, or rather, plastic and metal. No need to go out, for everything you need comes to you who wait; those still carrying the mixed blessing of working for a living usually do so from home, while the majority live off inherited investments in automated factories and virtual trading cooperatives and other abstruse financial constructs. Such an economy is precarious, built as it is from many layers of carefully-stacked cards, but as yet no-one has found the right card to pull so that – ker-plunk! – down it all falls.

So what to do in this world of inherited leisure? Some might choose to study the arts, or refine their skills of contemplation, dwelling on those philosophical puzzles which still beggar our understanding. Others might devote themselves to physical improvement or to travelling to see the many wonders of the modern world (for not everywhere is as unappealing as Sunny Meadows).

Most, however, watch the vee.

They sit on sofas, with a NutriMent outlet to hand, three, four or even five metre Visionscreens in front of them. They sit and they watch. The *Bud and Suze* channel is a popular one: 24/7 you can watch the ever-controversial couple, joking and laughing in their any-place-anywhere apartment, the two of them watching the vee and bitching with their friends in buddy windows. You can bitch to your own friends in buddy windows, while you watch Bud and Suze doing exactly the same thing on the vee. Everything's voice-activated, so you just have to bellow for Trish or Asif or Jeremy and if they're on-vee you'll pop up for each other in buddy windows and bitch. You can yell at Bud and Suze, too, along with forty million other yellers, and your input will be calibrated and entered into the script machines guiding the daily lives of your two idols.

It's not all *Bud and Suze*, of course – they may be there 24/7 but you can hardly be with them for all of that; you have to spread yourself around. You can flick the vee to another channel with whatever voice-prompt you've pre-set. *Flick*, and you're on one of the games shows: On which family quiz did *Street Throb* winner Davey Bruce win three days in a row before getting his last question wrong and losing everything? *Flick*, you're on one of the wet channels, anatomy blown up and in your face on the four-metre, so much it takes a few seconds to work out which bit you're looking at. *Flick*, animals, all fur and teeth; must be from somewhere far, far away.

Sunny Meadows? Come on . . . why come to Sunny Meadows when you can live this life anywhere you choose? So nobody ever comes to Sunny Meadows.

Apart from Dr Bull, of course, and his bright young assistant Gideon Eden. They came to Sunny Meadows a couple of months ago, but nobody really noticed, at first.

2

**In which Maddy and Nicholas consult about
the affairs of the town, and Maddy adjusts
her position ever so slightly**

Maddy Wheatfen sat on her sofa, legs tucked up underneath her. It wasn't as well-placed as the armchair, but the armchair was just a little too snug a fit these days. She'd been telling herself for weeks that she'd have to rearrange things in here: move the furniture around so she'd have the perfect view from the sofa; or, at the very least, tilt the vee more in this direction. She would take care of it one day. There was no hurry.

"Screw him!" she yelled at her three-metre screen. Then, realizing that her words were open to misinterpretation, and conscientious as ever about her input into the script machines, she corrected herself: "I mean tell him where to get off, Suze. He's a no good, cheap jerk."

There. That would show him. She felt good now. "Hey, Nicholas," she called, and a buddy window popped up on-screen. Her good friend, Nicholas van Pommel beamed out at her.

"Hey, Maddy," he said. He paused for a couple of minutes, as if weighing the import of his next words. "Looking good," he said, finally.

Maddy reached down for a toffee-cream smoothy from the NutriMent outlet and took a long slurp, licking the thick mixture from her lips afterwards. "Likewise," she said.

Nicholas's eyes didn't stare straight out of the buddy window, so Maddy knew he was watching something on his vee. She took another slurp.

Nicholas was something on the town Advisory Board. Maddy liked it that at least one of her vee buddies was Somebody. He would even consult her when big issues came up. Things to be dealt with. They usually agreed that matters could safely be deferred. Let them blow over. If they were important, they'd come up again. She liked to think that she and Nicholas were a good team: a town Somebody and his focus group of one. She liked to bring him into her world, too. "I yelled at *Bud and Suze*," she told him now.

They sat in shared, distant silence.

"I told Suze that Bud was a no good jerk."

Nicholas nodded.

"You watching them?"

Now, he shook his head. "Just a wet," he said.

It was Maddy's turn to nod. "You yell at it yet?"

He shook his head.

She finished her smoothy and asked for another one. Seconds later, the NutriMent outlet churned out her order. She realized her leg was getting uncomfortable, tucked up under her as it was. She was still getting used to her relocation to the sofa. She realized that more space can be harder to cope with than too little, in some ways. She would have to move. Not yet, though; give it a few minutes.

"That Bud's a jerk," Nicholas said, eventually.

Maddy nodded. She couldn't agree with her friend more.

She studied him more closely, his bushy moustache drooping down around his mouth, the folds of skin under his eyes, those sad dog eyes. If Maddy's mother hadn't passed away three years ago she'd be telling her she could do a lot worse. It was true: she could do a lot worse.

"Yeah," she said. "He's a jerk."

They let another long silence pass.

"They say the Queensbury flyover is looking a bit shaky," said Nicholas.

"The Board really should do something about that," advised Maddy.

Nicholas shifted, scratching somewhere just beyond his buddy window. "Hmm," he agreed. "It should be a priority item, of course. Top of the list."

"I do hope someone raises it," said Maddy, revelling in the cut and thrust of town governance. "It might fall down one day."

"Hmm," said Nicholas. "We have other matters to deal with, of course – the state of the fire service, for a start. Buildings could burn to the ground before anything was done. But the flyover should be a priority matter after that. Before it falls down, at any rate. Let's just hope it doesn't catch fire . . ."

Maddy realized that her leg had gone to sleep, which could hardly be excused when she was dealing with such elevated matters as agreeing that something should be done eventually, when all other matters had been dealt with. This was important business. But now . . . she leaned to one side, and regretted it, for a needle of pain stabbed her previously dead leg. She shifted again, and eased her leg out further along the sofa so that it was not trapped under her. There. That was much better. She would get used to this arrangement before long. Maybe all she would have to do was tilt the vee a little.

3

In which Tracy butts in, uninvited, and plays gooseberry to Maddy's voluptuous melon

Tracy buddied on to Maddy's veescreen. She wasn't really Maddy's buddy, but when she had called Nicholas he'd made it a threesome, as it would have been rude of him to talk to her and leave Maddy dangling. So up on to her screen, just below Nicholas's buddy window, Tracy Wordsworth pinged into virtual presence.

Tracy was a good ten years younger than Maddy's mumblety-mumble years, and she came in at comfortably less than a hundred kilos, which was just plain unfair in Maddy's reckoning. She had good teeth, and full lips, and long, black hair that curved just enough to frame her face in a really pretty way. She was Nicholas van Pommel's personal assistant. Maddy smiled at her, hoping that neither she nor Nicholas could detect the steady grinding of her teeth.

"Nicholas," said Tracy, in her girly voice. "You'll never believe me when I tell you there's been a fight!"

Maddy saw Nicholas come to attention, his eyes peering directly out of his buddy window, one eyebrow raised all of a couple of millimetres. She had not seen him so alert since the final of *Whose Breakfast?*

"A fight, you say?" Nobody ever fought in Sunny Meadows, other than the street kids, and they didn't really count because the mall mood sprinklers kept them subdued easily enough.

"Well . . . not so much a fight," said Tracy. "More an altercation. Nothing physical. But voices were raised. In Dr Bull's house. At the presentation."

Ah, the presentation. Dr Bull had bought out the local NutriMent UK franchise, and was proposing some significant improvements to the home delivery system. This afternoon he had been demonstrating the system to a few select guests at his home on the other side of Sunny Meadows. Nicholas had been invited, of course, but he had deferred a decision on whether to attend or not, and now, well, now it was too late, which was just as well by the sound of things. An altercation . . . Such things did not happen in Sunny Meadows, always such a peaceful place, where nothing really happened at all.

"It was Mr Green and that Mr Darley. They were getting very hot under the collar. It was after the sampling. They just started disagreeing with each other. It was most unseemly."

Maddy knew from what Nicholas had told her of Town Board affairs that such behaviour was quite out of character for the two misters. She wondered what could possibly be behind it.

"Thank you, Tracy. I think that will be all for now." Nicholas's eyes had wandered back to the main panel of his veescreen, but he was clearly perturbed by these happenings. "My associate and I were dealing with pressing matters."

So, she was his associate, was she? That must be good. Tracy's buddy window popped away.

Pressing matters . . .

"That Bud's a jerk," said Maddy.

After a long pause, Nicholas nodded. "Yes," he agreed. "He certainly is."

4

In which Maddy and Nicholas pay a visit to Dr Bull and it emerges that the good doctor may not be all that he seems

Who, then, was this man who went by the name of Dr Bull?

He was, it's fair to say, something of a one-off. In an age of sitting back and having the world come to you, Dr Bull was a man who went out and instigated things. He was a doer. A thinker, too; in fact, it was in the area of scholarly endeavour that his star shone the brightest. He had presented papers to the Royal Society, and published in the world's leading journals – unusually, ranging across a wide spectrum of specialisms, from physiology through psychology and sociology to logic and telecommunications. He had studied at the finest institutions, and challenged some of the greatest scholars of his time; certain observers had even described him as the great revolutionary thinker of the age. To any onlooker aware of the doctor's background, his current occupation as proprietor in chief of Sunny Meadows' NutriMent feed might appear to be something of a departure. Such an onlooker would not be surprised to learn that Dr Bull had assumed this position in order to make improvements and refinements to the system, or even that he was treating such intervention as a grand experiment, upon which he and his able assistant Gideon Eden were making copious notes.

Dr Bull was a man of medium height, and he would also have been of medium build were it not for a slight tendency to over-indulge. Now, he sat back behind his deep oak desk and plucked another marshmallow from a silver dish. "Well, Gideon, well indeed!" he said, biting a quarter from the marshmallow. "These people of Sunny Meadows – we know from our preliminary study that they are the dullest, flattest, least animated people in the land. For animation they are midway between sponges and coral! And yet, at my little demonstration – transformed! They bickered and they questioned. They expressed opinions! We have seen the first ripple in a dull, flat expanse of water."

"You heard Darley and Green?" asked young Gideon.

The doctor nodded. "No harm was done," he said. "That two men, normally so close to comatose, should come close to blows was an interesting outcome, this early in the game. We will have to monitor the inputs, I think."

The assistant dipped his head in agreement.

Dr Bull beamed at him. "I think the time has come to extend our trials," he said. "We should tackle a public space. Just think, Gideon: if things carry on like this we could transform the world!"

Gideon smiled back. The two were, quite clearly, very pleased with how things were progressing.

As, too, was Maddy Wheatfen. Very pleased indeed! For, right at this moment, she was on her way to visit Dr Bull himself. The previous evening, after well over an hour's buddy chat with Nicholas consisting of little more than half a dozen remarks by each, Nicholas had suddenly become more animated. Daintily licking cream from his fingertips, having just consumed an oversized eclair from his NutriMent outlet, he had fixed Maddy's gaze and said, "We shall confront him! That's what we will do."

Caught out, Maddy tried desperately to think back to the last remark either of them had made. Confront whom? Why? How? She gave up and simply nodded. It seemed like the right response.

A few minutes later, Nicholas added, "In the morning, I think. One can't rush in, after all."

Right now, as she fussed with her appearance, and tried to remember the things she needed – keycard . . . well, that was about it – Maddy felt that they were rushing things nonetheless, and then she realized that she quite liked the sensation. She couldn't remember the last time she had seen Nicholas *in actuo*. She sucked her lips in to moisten them, remembering gorgeous Tracy's pout.

She went outside.

The sun was bright. Too bright. The air moved, and smelled different. It all seemed so . . . *uncontained*. When was the last time she'd seen *anybody*? She stood on the threshold, unsteadily. Had he actually meant this? Maybe Nicholas had been talking about confronting whoever was to be confronted on the vee. Did you know that you don't have to call it a buddy window? It's really easy to change the labelling, so some people might be buddies, others slaves, or heart-throbs, or subhumans; maybe Nicholas was meaning to confront this person via an arch-antagonist window? Last night, Nicholas had been in a sweetheart window, not that he had known.

But no. He had been quite clear. He had wanted Maddy to come for him, in person.

She liked driving, although she could barely remember

the last time she had done so. She liked the sense of power, of control. She liked to be actually doing something, participating instead of merely viewing. Her car rolled out of the parking niche and a door opened. "To the home of Nicholas van Pommel," she told it, when she was settled in the driving seat. As the car set off, she adjusted the seating position to give herself a little more room. She wondered what it must be like to have to do steering and speed and directions, all at the same time. It was hard to imagine. No wonder people used to need training before they could drive.

Soon, Nicholas was climbing in to join her. "Thank you so much, Maddy," he said. "So kind of you."

Dr Bull lived in a house that was older than those around it. It had probably been here before even Sunny Meadows. The two stepped out, and Maddy told her car to go park. Dr Bull's front door did not respond to their voices, but there was a sturdy-looking bell suspended to one side. Nicholas nodded towards it and said, "Do you think we should?" Maddy shrugged. They could, she supposed, but was it necessarily the right thing to do? What if it were there for show and there was some more subtle means of getting a response from the door?

The door opened while they were still deliberating, and a rather handsome young man bowed in greeting. Maddy was just adjusting her mental image of what Dr Bull must look like when she learned that this was, in fact, the doctor's assistant, Gideon Eden.

"You would like to see the doctor?" he said. "Of course. Please follow me."

They did so.

"Please, wait here," said Gideon, gesturing towards two chairs and a tray of pastries. They were in the doctor's study.

They sat, but the silence between them was not the normal comfortable silence of vee buddies: Maddy saw in the occasional glance around the room, and the clumsiness with pastry crumbs, that her friend was . . . yes, she was sure, he was getting impatient. That was not like Nicholas, at all.

She found herself glancing at the door, as if that would speed things along. Where *was* the stupid man?

The doctor entered the room, apologising for the delay; he was accompanied by his assistant, who remained standing by the door. Dr Bull was almost exactly as she had pictured him, which she realized was probably because she had seen him on the vee at some time. He was an eminent man, after all.

The doctor seated himself behind his wide desk. He placed his elbows on the wooden surface and steepled his fingers in front of his nose. Finally, he said, "Yes?"

Nicholas nodded. "It has been some time since we had the pleasure," he said. He took another cake and bit deeply.

"So it has," said Dr Bull. "Although I don't believe *we've* had the pleasure," he added, nodding towards Maddy.

As Nicholas was busy with his confectionery, Maddy decided to make the introductions. "I'm Maddy," she said. Then she decided to elaborate: "I am an associate of Mr van Pommel."

"My pleasure," said the doctor.

"Mine too," said Maddy. This all seemed to be going terribly well.

"I had hoped to attend yesterday's demonstration," said Nicholas. "But you know how it is. These things can't be rushed." Then he leaned forward with his hands on his knees. "In fact, that's exactly it, Dr Bull. Here in Sunny Meadows we never rush what can be done at a sensible pace. We like to measure ourselves, and deal with things in their own good time. I hear that your demonstration caused something of a controversy, and in my role as Deputy Chair of the Town Advisory Board I feel it is my duty to investigate. We can't be having these . . . these *reactions* in Sunny Meadows."

The doctor seemed amused. "And yet, here you are, in my study," he said. "That seems very spontaneous."

Nicholas drew himself up. "We considered the matter at length before rushing here to see you," he said.

"Go on, go on," said the doctor, waving a hand at the pastries, having seen Nicholas's gaze wandering back to a particular cream and jam extravagance. "I'm glad you're here," continued Dr Bull, leaning forward. "You strike me as both fine examples of the upstanding citizenry of Sunny Meadows."

Maddy felt a surge of pride at this. She didn't upstand often, if she could help it, but it was nice to know that her qualities had been recognized.

"What would you two say if I told you that we of Sunny Meadows are on the verge of something revolutionary? Something that would have our community leading the way instead of sitting back and watching? What would you say to that?"

Maddy quite liked the sound of the words, even though she had no idea what he meant. She looked at Nicholas, expecting him to have that slightly-raised eyebrow of angry resistance. It wasn't there. He nodded instead, and said, "It would be our proper place!"

"My little demonstration yesterday was a success. And now I must confess that you have been part of a repeat. The cakes – you like them?"

Nicholas looked at them. Now his eyebrow was just a little raised, out of curiosity. "My favourite," he said. "Particularly after the exertion of travel."

"I know," said the doctor. "Or rather, *I* don't know: the system does. Over the last few weeks my modernised NutriMentPlus system has modelled your preferences, and ninety-nine per cent of the time it knows what you want before even you know it. When the system is fully operational it will do this wherever you go: stop off at anywhere with an outlet and it will recognize you and deliver what you want without you having to do a thing."

"Not have to do a thing, you say? That seems a very Sunny Meadows approach."

Dr Bull smiled.

"When will it be available to everyone?" asked Maddy. It seemed unfair that only a select few should be benefiting from this revolution.

"Oh, you know," said the doctor. "We can hardly rush

into these things. We must proceed cautiously, at a sensible pace."

"We should consider such matters at length," said his assistant. Maddy had forgotten he was there, standing by the door.

"In the fullness of time," said the doctor.

Nicholas leaned forward and banged his fists on Dr Bull's desk. "I want it *now!*" he cried.

The doctor seemed amused by this uncharacteristic outburst. He paused to make a note on a block of paper, then glanced at his assistant.

"Perhaps," said Gideon, "we could tighten up the schedule. Move critical points forward, that kind of thing."

Dr Bull nodded. "Then it is agreed," he said. "We will proceed with all possible haste."

5

**In which the risen come,
blinking, into the sunlight**

All returned to normal in Sunny Meadows. The altercation at Dr Bull's little demonstration was soon put aside as Messers Green and Darley resumed their amicable acquaintance by vee. Nicholas van Pommel's outburst in the doctor's study was easily forgotten, as Maddy would tell no-one, although she stored the memory of her friend's animation for moments of personal recollection.

Maddy had signed up for ExerThighs™ classes, every Wednesday in the Sunny Meadows Amenity Centre, starting this week. She drove there, telling the car to park as close as she could get, and then went into the building. There were lots of kids here, and for a moment she thought she had come to the wrong place. They stood around in small, grunting groups, heads hung low, eyes glazed from too much vee. Then she remembered that there were games sessions today, too, and she understood why they were here: while she was upstairs thumping about to some ancient disco beat, these kids would be playing shoot-'em-ups on the vee. It got them out of the house, she supposed.

She went up and was dismayed to see Nicholas's personal assistant, Tracy Wordsworth, already changed and limbering up. She almost turned and left, but then Tracy saw her and smiled and it was too late, she was committed.

It was murder! If this was what it took to get down to a slim ninety kilos like Tracy then maybe Maddy would be better off sticking to her natural weight. After barely five minutes she hurt. Deep inside, her muscles were trembling with the effort of moving and stretching in ways the body just wasn't designed for.

"It gets easier every time," Tracy reassured her, as Maddy resorted to watching from the side.

Thank goodness for the cakes. Or rather, thank goodness for Dr Bull's new NutriMentPlus, which was being trialled in the Amenity Centre today. It knew exactly what she wanted, and almost as soon as the interval started, Maddy was drawing deeply on a toffee-cream smoothy (with extra choc-shavings). She looked around at the shabby interior of the gym. The high windows showed blue sky. She remembered the feelings of being uncontained when she was outdoors, and she remembered the taste of the air. "I'm going outside," she told Tracy. Fresh air would be far more beneficial than sitting here feeling guilty and looking at svelte young women doing things she could only dream of. You could get that on the vee, after all.

Tracy hesitated, then said, "I think I'll join you. If you don't mind, that is."

Maddy smiled. It was a mad kind of day. Things were just happening, unplanned, unpondered.

Out in the main concourse, the kids seemed to have given up on their games early. They were drifting out of the great darkened rooms lit only by vee screens and going . . . outside. The ExerThighs™ escapees followed.

"It's a lovely day, isn't it?" said Tracy.

Maddy looked around. It was. The air and sun were good.

This was far better than sitting in the gym and feeling bad. Out on a grassy area, some kids had a ball. Maddy recognized it from the vee: the sims of the old greats playing against each other. The kids were playing soccer. They stopped to watch, part of a growing crowd drifting out to enjoy the sunny day. It was really quite exciting . . . quite revolutionary.

After a while, the ball came towards them and, as if by instinct, Maddy swung a foot at it. She made contact, and the ball flew back into the melee. Tracy squeezed her arm and winked at her. "Come on, Maddy," she urged. "Let's show 'em!"

They trundled out from the crowd of onlookers and, more by surprise than skill, Tracy took the ball off the feet of one of the young lads. She kicked it roughly in the direction of Maddy, who lumbered towards it. A kid chest-high to her, but almost as broad, got there first and paused with a foot triumphantly trapping the ball, then he saw that she was not going to stop and raised his arms protectively. Maddy barged into him and some part of her made contact with the ball. A big cheer went up, and then she realized that others from the watching crowd were joining in, too.

One, however, remained aloof. One member of the crowd stood back, watching, making notes, talking into a phonemic stuck to his jaw. Gideon Eden had a job to do, an experiment to observe, to report upon. Outbreaks of spontaneity have to be observed minutely if they are to be understood.

6

In which Nicholas van Pommel is consternated and Dr Bull and Gideon, his assistant, reach a critical point

She woke. She wished she hadn't. She felt as if she had been dragged back and forth over a cattle grid (she was a great fan of *The Farm*). It hurt when she moved. It hurt in different ways if she lay still.

She filled the bath. She would need to get a bigger one, if her ExerThighs™ regime made no difference. The hot water helped a little. She had grass stains on her knees, grass mowings in her hair. Bruises. One big one on her shin from where one of the little buggers had caught her.

She slumped on the sofa and called up the vee. She really must tilt the screen a little. Some day. "Nicholas?" He popped up in a buddy window – still labelled "sweetheart" instead of "buddy" she saw, with a mixture of guilt and amusement.

"Maddy," he said. He seemed quite animated today. "Are you okay? Did you hear about the uprising?"

"Uprising?"

"At the Amenity Centre. People just upping and leaving their screens. Going *outside*. Rowdiness! Unruliness! Anarchy!"

"I was there," she said softly, wondering what had happened to their long silences.

He stared at her. "You were there? You were affected?"

She nodded, feeling slightly defensive. "I went outside. It was a nice day. Tracy was there, too." She wondered about mentioning the football, but decided to defer that in the good old Sunny Meadows fashion.

"What's happening?" Nicholas said, shaking his head.

It was only then that Maddy, too, wondered what was happening, or more specifically, what had happened the day before at the Amenity Centre. So many people, just getting it into their heads to do something different . . . It wasn't *bad*, though, was it?

"What if this insanity spreads?" he added.

What indeed?

"Bud and Suze are back together again," she told Nicholas. "She should know better by now."

He paused to think, then nodded. "You'd think so, wouldn't you?" he said.

Over in Dr Bull's old house, they were discussing matters more weighty than the state of Bud and Suze's half-scripted relationship.

"Well, Gideon?"

"All is ready. Preliminary trials are complete. The technology appears robust enough to cope, and we have observed the impact on the populace."

"At last. Now we can extend the experiment to all of Sunny Meadows. Let operations commence!"

7

In which it will be seen that the epidemic invades the entire town, and what effect it produces

In the following weeks the madness, instead of subsiding, became more widespread. No corner of Sunny Meadows remained untouched by moments of spontaneity and enthusiasm, by altercation and dispute and simple acts of *doing*. The streets, normally deserted save for the automated delivery vehicles, saw people out in the fine weather. Walking. Adolescents gathered in great crowds to play football with the one football known to exist in Sunny Meadows. Screen buddies visited each other, in person, and they watched *Bud and Suze* or *Celebwatch* or *Truth or Dare?* together, all in the same room.

Maddy's neighbours, old Mrs and Mr Oliver, started having rather noisy parties with their good friends the Blanchards. In a very short matter of time, Maddy's neighbours were Mrs Oliver and Mr Blanchard, although the parties continued apace. Maddy didn't know what to make of it all (although it rather tickled her to see the colour back in her neighbours' cheeks), but Tracy told her that this kind of thing was happening all over. "Life is speeding up," Tracy told her. "People aren't just sitting back – they're grabbing their opportunities with both hands. Have you seen Nicholas lately?"

Maddy shrugged. They were outside the Amenity Centre again, the ExerThighs™ class having moved outdoors to take advantage of the extended fine spell. Not that anyone really knew if this weather was unseasonably good or merely typical – whatever, they could still make the most of it. She wondered what Tracy meant by her mention of Nicholas. Perhaps she was planning to seize him with both hands. Maddy looked at her new sort-of-friend and knew she couldn't possibly compete.

"Okay, exergroup, time to get back to it!"

Maddy scrambled to her feet, not wanting to be last into position. Claude, their Thinstructor™ (PENDING), thumbed the soundbox and the beat started pumping out. Copying his actions, as well as she could, Maddy shifted from foot to foot with the music, pointing to the sky, pointing to the thigh, pointing to the sky . . .

The music drew unwanted attention. Some kids who had been playing soccer now stopped and shuffled over to watch and gesture and gurn, and then . . . point to the sky, point to the thigh . . . a whole crowd of them aping the rigorous, scientifically-devised routine of the ExerThighs™ programme.

It came to a head when Denise Mackay (down ten kilos since starting the programme, but still packing a mighty haunch) stopped in mid ab-flex and yelled, "Will you kids just fuck off and die?"

They stared at her. Everybody stared at her. Denise was the mildest, meekest, most god-loving grandmother you ever could hope to meet, in Sunny Meadows or almost anywhere else. She did flowers in vases and she always took trouble to smile at everyone she passed, just to be sure she covered all the ones whose faces she half-recognized but whose names wouldn't come.

She stood there, hands on hips. Just daring any one of them to be stupid enough to react.

Someone is always stupid enough. Indeed, Dr Bull, although not present at this incident, had many years before published a paper that empirically demonstrates this very point: if a situation requires someone to do something stupid, you can always find someone stupid enough to do it.

Little Danny Rogers burst out laughing. He couldn't contain it. He was there at the front of the crowd, and this old, round woman was glaring at them all, using language she must have learnt from the vee because oldies didn't speak like that in the normal run of things.

Her eyes locked on him.

She screeched and took a great stride towards him, and then another. She was on him in seconds, an impressive act in itself. Danny Rogers barely knew what had hit him, let alone what had landed on top of him, squeezing the air from his lungs and the urine from his bladder.

After a second or two of rather bemused silence, broken only by an old woman's squawking and a small boy's rather muffled protests, one of the gang of youths tried to haul Denise Mackay off their compatriot. The old woman swung an arm and caught him in the jaw with a fleshy elbow. As he stumbled back, all hell broke loose. Teenagers piled in, at least a few of them subsequently staggering back shortly afterwards; then Claude bellowed at his class, "That's one of ours, that is!" and threw himself into the battle in support of Denise.

Maddy followed Tracy in, body-checking a dreadlocked young girl as she did so. She would have more bruises in the morning. And aches, and pains, and she would have to try to soak it all out in the bath, and she would both regret it and puzzle over it. She knew all this. "Take that, fuckwit!" she yelled, punching a tall, barrel-bellied boy in the chest.

Back in Dr Bull's grand old house, he and his assistant were somewhat removed from events. They thought this advisable because, while it is not possible to predict the detail of spontaneous chaotic flourishings, the generality can be all too predictable.

"There is fighting at the Amenity Centre," Gideon told his master. "And I believe a young people's rave event is to take place in Festival Fields this evening. The Advisory Board have reached three decisions at their latest vee-meeting—"

"Unprecedented!" gasped the doctor, his eyes flaring with excitement.

"—and someone has painted the entire frontage of Dewberry Mall."

"Colour?"

"Many, Dr Bull. Many."

The doctor chuckled.

"Doctor . . ." Gideon hesitated, as if about to broach a sensitive subject. "Do you think that, perhaps, and in the light of current happenings, we might have misjudged the levels? Do you not think that they are a trifle high?"

Dr Bull fixed him with his staring eyes, and the young assistant might easily have seen in that look just a hint of the madness that had spread through Sunny Meadows. "We have only just begun, my boy! If anything, I'd say that the levels are too low. This is an experiment, not a humanitarian exercise."

8

In which the Sunny Meadownians adopt a heroic resolution

It was not long afterwards that the long-running, off and on (although mostly, it must be said, off) dispute with the neighbouring New Town development was fanned into sparky life, once again. New Town, which was both older than Sunny Meadows and not really a town at all, but more a sprawling suburban stain (pretty much like Sunny Meadows, after all, then) had, until this point, been blissfully unaffected by the madness recounted in these pages. Indeed, many residents of New Town must, by now, have long since put aside any memory of what was, for those of Sunny Meadows, a festering *casus belli*.

As a great man once said, winning is not everything, it's the *only* thing. He also said that a game of football is hardly a matter of life and death – it's more important than that. And what's more, you only sing when you're winning. On that bitter day in February 1974, New Town Athletic won, and then they sung about it and forgot. But Sunny Meadows Wanderers lost, by a single goal, scored from the penalty spot after a decision made by a short-sighted, dim-witted, one-sided, black-shirted representative of Beelzebub.

"Wilkins dived like a bleeding Stuka," yelled one belligerent fan now, as, many decades on from that fateful day, a crowd of newly-invigorated Sunny Meadownians gathered to watch the local youths (those not injured in the ExerThighs™ incident of two weeks before, at least) kick a ball around an area of grass. The said Wilkins, did, it must be said, go on to play a season and a half of professional football in League Division Three, but his reputation as a divebomber followed him wherever he went.

There were general mumbles of agreement.

"So what are we going to do about it, then?"

"Demand a re-match!" cried one, and then several more.

"And what if they refuse?"

"We'll deal with that if we have to," said one ominously rumbling voice. "Just let 'em dare."

9

In which Gideon, the assistant, gives a reasonable piece of advice, which is eagerly rejected by Dr Bull

"Was I not right?" Dr Bull popped a fat pink marshmallow into his mouth.

Gideon dipped his head in acknowledgement. "Of course, Dr Bull. Your hypothesis has been emphatically supported. The solution to the problem of our current malaise is merely a matter of devising the appropriate biochemical stimulation. The experiment has been a success."

Dr Bull nodded. "Exactly! Biochemistry, I tell you."

"Do you not think that matters have gone far enough, now?" asked the young assistant, rather tentatively. "Do you think, perhaps, that these poor fellows should not be excited any further? It would be a simple matter for me to re-set the parameters."

Dr Bull had that look in his eye again. That glint of the popular madness. "Just you try!" he growled.

10

In which it is once more proved that a distant view can sometimes be all the clearer

Maddy drove Nicholas out over the Queensbury flyover.

"Do you think we should?" he asked nervously. "The structure is unstable, you know. One day . . ."

"Then do something about it," she told him. "You're on the Advisory Board. Take action. Until then . . . well, let's live a little!"

He pulled himself up in his seat. "I'll have you know that the Advisory Board is looking into the matter. And I'm going to advise them to take action, what's more."

He said it as if he didn't realize he was agreeing with her. He said it as if he was putting her right on a matter of grave importance. Maddy glanced across at him, and wondered what had happened to them . . . what had happened to her town. It was all very well that people seemed to have a bit more drive about them these days, but you could take a thing too far.

For a moment, from the top of the flyover, they could look back over Sunny Meadows. Maddy couldn't tell which part was hers, where her street was, her little maisonette. It all looked the same.

They found the countryside. Maddy had seen countryside on the vee – she was a big fan of *The Farm*, after all – but all these square fields and manicured hedges seemed so wild to her. She wondered whether this picnic was really a good idea.

The car found somewhere to park that was right by the river, so they didn't have to go far to eat. Maddy had been baking. She had made a quiche, and she had made a salad from Wal-Mart; she had made eggs, too. Perhaps that was too much egg for one meal, she had thought, when she was packing the bag this morning, but by then it was too late. They spread a blanket, just like she had seen, and put the food out on it. The ground was uncomfortable, but she wasn't going to complain. Nicholas seemed to be calmer out here, and she didn't want to stir up his animosity again.

It was peaceful, apart from the insects and the stones in the ground. It was unlike anything Maddy could quite recall.

Nicholas had a small box with him and, after they had eaten, he placed it on the blanket with a flourish. When Maddy opened it up she saw that it contained a selection of cakes, courtesy of NutriMentPlus. She could tell that from the way they were square, to make packing and delivery easier.

He must have sensed her disappointment. "Maddy? What is it?"

It was hard to put into words. It was a feeling she hadn't quite recognized herself until now. "I'm sorry," she said. "I thought we could do it differently today. Eat differently. So I made everything. None of this came from the outlet." NutriMentPlus was supposed to give you everything you wanted, before you even realized you wanted it, but Maddy had fumbled her way towards the realization that what she really wanted was to be the same side of a hundred kilos as Tracy Wordsworth. And she wanted this lovely man as he was now, in the flesh.

Spontaneity struck again. Nicholas reached for a rectangular chocolate eclair and hurled it into the river. A jam tart followed.

Maddy took a doughnut and hurled it out into the middle of the flow. She collapsed back on her elbows, laughing more than she could ever remember laughing. This was turning out to be quite a memorable day!

11

In which matters go so far that the inhabitants of Sunny Meadows, the reader, and even the author, demand an immediate denouement

The Advisory Board of New Town thought the demands of their neighbours some kind of practical joke. Indeed, they thought it quite a funny one, and laughed each time someone

mentioned it. Then, a member of the Board, or perhaps a
family member, looked up the records and found that it was
true that New Town Athletic had beaten Sunny Meadows
Wanderers 1-0 in February 1974, and that Bomber Wilkins
had scored from the penalty spot. They found it even more
amusing that this absurd challenge was actually based on
historical fact! How charming a conceit! But a re-match . . .
Why actually *play* football when you can watch the sim
matches on the vee? Why play when you can see recon-
structions of Pele, Best, Platini, Zidane and the Nevilles
battling it out on the big screen?

This response did not go down well with the newly invig-
orated citzens of Sunny Meadows. "They're rubbing salt in
the wounds," one grumbled. "They're scared," said another.
"And what about the Challenge Shield in '93?" said another.
"That was a clear off-side!"

And so, the good people of Sunny Meadows gathered
before the rainbow-hued frontage of the Dewberry Mall. Dr
Bull had a good view of this, for the mall was just across
the street from the NutriMent depot, the very heart of his
operation. He and Gideon went out on to the street, to
stand on the fringe of the crowd. He wanted to see how far
this would go.

"We'll show them!" cried someone near the front of the
crowd. "We'll march on New Town and beat the living crap
out of them."

"Anyone got a car?" asked a more sensible voice nearby.

"Fascinating," mumbled the doctor. "They're really going
to do it, Gideon. I may have to refine my models. They're
really going to take action . . . Gideon?"

His assistant was no longer there.

Suddenly, at the front of the still-growing crowd, a young
man stepped up on to something so that he was head and
shoulders above his fellows. "Stop," cried Gideon, for it was
the doctor's assistant who now addressed the crowd. "This
should not be happening. It has gone too far. You are under
the influence of an altered biochemistry. This must—"

He was going to say "stop", but the word was prevented

from escaping his lips by Dr Bull's very firm grip around his assistant's windpipe.

The crowd fell on the two. It looked like being a good scrap, and they were all up for a good scrap right now. Nobody understood what the fight was about, but they all started to land blows and kicks when—

12

In which the denouement takes place

When a formidable explosion blasted them into silence. They stood, and turned. What had been the NutriMent depot was now a burning shell of a building.

And Maddy Wheatfen stood just outside its hanging gates, looking rather self-conscious at having so much attention focused on her. Her skin was blackened, and her blouse was in tatters, which only compounded her self-consciousness. She hadn't meant the whole place to blow up, when she set fire to the outlet feed vats . . . it just, kind of, *did*. In a particularly satisfying way.

"Let him go," she said, waving towards the biggest heap of struggling bodies and hoping they would work out what she meant. "Dr Bull."

Maddy had realized, while throwing NutriMentPlus cakes at the birds on the river the other day, what it was that had happened to her community. It was the feed, the pipes carrying NMP supplies direct to the consumer, exactly what you need before you even know you need it, wherever you are. What a sophisticated way of getting other substances to each individual in exactly the right dosage! What a marvellous means of experimenting on an entire population. She had done some reading on the vee. Journals and stuff. She had understood enough to confirm that Dr Bull was capable of such an arrogant act.

"He got carried away," she said. "We all got carried away." She saw Nicholas in the crowd, looking almost as shamefaced as he should for getting so worked up over a silly little ball-game. "It's good to get carried away sometimes, but just not too much, okay? I think it's time we all got back to reality, just a bit, don't you think?"

But reality would never be quite the same again for the good folk of Sunny Meadows (which could, really, have been almost anywhere). All had been transformed by recent events, and Maddy found it hard to believe that a single person here would return to the ways of old.

Released from beneath the crowd, Dr Bull lost no time in slipping away, followed by his ever-faithful assistant. Maddy wasn't sure if the expression on his face was the chastened one of someone who had learnt a hard lesson, or if he was simply planning to claim the insurance and go off and set up elsewhere. To tell the truth, she wasn't sure which of those outcomes would be best.

She caught Nicholas' eye again. He smiled, and she smiled back. He came to her, and kissed her, and wrapped her in an embrace so powerful that she had to rise on tiptoes and then her feet even left the ground for a moment. Or maybe she imagined that part.

It was all chemistry, she thought. That's what Dr Bull would argue, and she was happy to believe him for now.

THE VERY FIRST AFFAIR

Johan Heliot

Doubtless the satire of Dr Ox helped recharge Verne's own batteries for he now embarked on the book that comes closest to rivalling 20,000 Leagues Under the Sea *as his best known and most popular –* Le Tour du monde en quatre-vingts jours, *or* Around the World in Eighty Days. *The novel was serialized in the Paris daily magazine* Le Temps *from 6 November to 22 December 1872, which apparently tripled its circulation during that period as readers waited anxiously to find how Phileas Fogg had overcome his latest problem and whether he could meet his deadline. The book, published early the following year, outsold all of Verne's other titles during his lifetime.*

The idea of circumnavigating the globe in eighty days was not entirely original to Verne. Several sources have been suggested, including the 1871 edition of Bradshaw's Continental Railway Guide, *which not only suggested the journey could be completed within "78 to 80 days" but also described a route almost identical to that undertaken by Fogg. Verne's genius was not only to combine this with a series of cliff-hanger adventures and fascinating characters, but to add the twist of the extra day arising because of crossing the International Date Line, a fact that Verne cleverly keeps hidden until the end. The idea had first been used by Edgar Allan Poe in a short story "A Succession of Sundays"*

(1841), which Verne had reviewed in 1864, but whereas Poe used it as a puzzle, Verne used it to considerable dramatic effect.

The character of Phileas Fogg, like Captain Nemo, is mysterious and enigmatic. We never really get to know him, despite our closeness to him throughout the adventure. Verne created two other fascinating characters in the novel, Fogg's servant, Passepartout, and the stupid Detective Fix who, on the trail of a bank robber, pursues Fogg around the globe. We shall meet both these characters, and learn a lot more about them and Fogg, in the next two stories.

You can call me Passepartout, since I've already gone by that name. But you may rest assured that's not my true identity. Furthermore, I'm not the only one who has lied in this respect in this tale. The masks will come off when it's time. Don't you worry about that.

Phileas Fogg's crazy wager had everyone in the world on the edges of their seats for eighty days, at the end of 1872. I was at the peak of my form at that time. Despite my tender age, I had already practised numerous trades – acrobat, fireman, gymnastics instructor – all of which required perfect physical condition, muscles and flexibility. I was in such good shape that, despite my modest stature, I easily defeated larger men in most of these disciplines. It was for that reason that the French Information Services, founded in June 1871, after we lost the war to Prussia, contacted me. The *Statistics and Military Reconnaissance Section* (for that was its true name) was responsible for obtaining any information France considered vital, using any means available. For that purpose, the Section needed vigorous, strong-willed men, with a taste for adventure.

That suited me to a T, although nothing could have prepared me for the most remarkable adventure that could possibly be imagined.

At that time, you see, few people were aware that travel between worlds was possible. Even fewer were able to make such trips.

So, when I was assigned to the service of this unusual Englishman for my first mission, I had no idea about Phileas Fogg's true nature. Yet, his very name should have aroused my suspicions! What could be more nebulous than "Fogg"? What could be more inconsistent, more deceptive?

The man I met on Wednesday 2 October 1872 appeared to be in his forties and in relatively good physical condition, apart from a slight stoutness. He towered head and shoulders above me and his hair was a blonde mop. In other words, he could have been anyone, since there was absolutely nothing particular about his appearance and certain specialists were already highly skilled in the art of disguise.

Everyone now knows the conditions in which the wager concerning the journey around the world was placed, that very day, in a hall in the Reform Club, in Pall Mall, not far from another famous club – I'll return to this later. Obviously, there was nothing of chance about it. The *Statistics Section* could never have guessed the form in which the challenge would be issued to Fogg, since no one had even heard tell about the eccentric Englishman just a few days earlier!

At this point, I would like to provide some clarification about traveling between worlds and the information collected by the secret services in this respect. Those who specialized in communicating with spirits, namely famous metapsychics such as Camille Flammarion and mediums of the calibre of a Daniel Dunglas Home, all agreed that, although there was nothing difficult with respect to traveling in the form of an astral body, they still knew nothing about the theory that made this "common marvel" possible. For some time, it had been accepted that the entities with which the metapsychics communicated were not the souls of the deceased, but rather spiritual residues of individuals who were quite alive, yet living in other worlds. The mediums' abilities to concentrate and certain mental predispositions granted either by Nature or Chance provided invaluable bridges between our inaccessible neighbours and ourselves.

In short, when the *Statistics Section* got wind of Fogg's extravagant project, my superiors' hearts skipped a beat. I was immediately assigned to get as close to the Englishman as possible and collect as much information about the man as I could.

I have no intention of going into our expedition in any detail at this time. Everyone knows our itinerary, the methods of transportation we used, the successive ports of call on our journey, from London to Suez, from India to China, from San Francisco to the Far West, and so on. The fictionalized versions of our adventure (particularly that of M. Jules Verne), the theatrical adaptations (I'm thinking of Adolphe Dennery's wonderful play) and, more recently, Mr Méliés' unparalleled screenplay have all popularized the 'terrestrial' episodes of our tribulations.

But that is not the main point. Far from it. As is so often the case, we have to dig through the silences in the story to get to the heart of the matter. After all, that which is written, which is left to posterity, is only a general consensus. That which is left unsaid, intentionally, because we fear that it will fly in the face of common sense, deserves the full attention of enlightened minds.

Initially, I was overwhelmed by the frantic pace of the race, the haste with which we left London for France. I played the role of the zealous servant, inasmuch as possible. Fogg appeared satisfied. For my part, I was glad that his finickiness required me to remain close by, since that facilitated my true mission which was, as I remind you, to seize the moment when my "master" would deploy a portion of his inexhaustible energy to contact another world.

As for my employers, no one doubted that Fogg was a talented medium, since he had taken up the gauntlet cast down at the Reform Club. Now, and I am returning to this matter because the time is propitious, it appears that this august gathering was known in occult circles for the quality of its members, a quality that owed nothing to birth, nothing to fortune, as in the case of most gentlemen's clubs – with the noteworthy exception of one other club, also located in Pall Mall, which I will touch on soon. No, as you see, what brought the members of the Reform Club together, apart from their allegiance to the Crown, was their passion for the Journey. A passion which all could appease, depending on the purity of their gift. These gentlemen met to turn the tables and communicate with foreign spirits, in the intimacy of their downy nest. We obtained this information from a servant who, although he officiated with the required discretion inside the Club, led a life of debauchery outside it. His turpitudes had led him into the arms of highly unscrupulous trollops, and it was a matter of no consequence for the *Section* to exert a little pressure on the libertine flunky by threatening to reveal the details of his escapades to his wife.

Now you understand how this whole matter started, the first in a long series, yet the only one that was kept secret. The state of agitation that reigned at the Reform Club in the days following Fogg's appearance was sufficient to alert the *Statistics Section*. Something was about to happen that would involve the most powerful metapsychic society of the day and a perfect stranger – no matter what M. Verne says! My adoptive land could not refrain from reacting; she sent me to London so that I could pierce through Fogg's mystery. Here is what I discovered . . .

The first incident occurred in the train that we took to cross through France and Italy, on our way to Brindisi. At one point, Fogg left our compartment, claiming that he needed to 'stretch his legs' and charging me to rest since, he added, before too long I would have no time for idling.

I nodded and allowed him to walk down the corridor of the car. Then, once I was sure that he would not detect me, I slipped out behind him. I saw him calmly walk through the doors to the next car. I was on the verge of abandoning my tail, so that I would not lose my cover so early on, when Fogg started behaving in a most unusual manner. I saw him as he stopped in the middle of the corridor, took out his pocket watch, and watched the hands turn for three long minutes, as if nothing else could possibly be more important. Then, he suddenly put his watch back into his pocket and disappeared into the closest compartment, so quickly that I doubt anyone other than myself saw him.

The velvet drapes were drawn, preventing me from observing. I approached the compartment on tiptoe and placed my ear against the wooden wall. In vain. The clackety-clack of the train wheels bumping along the track and the huffing and puffing of the nearby locomotive masked the echoes of any potential conversations. Disappointed, I returned to our compartment. Fogg reappeared there less than ten minutes later. He looked radiant and found it difficult to hide this.

I allowed a few minutes to pass before I stood up and declared, "If you please, I too would like to stretch my legs a bit."

"Go ahead. It will be several hours before we reach Brindisi, unfortunately."

He smiled as he made this last remark. I nodded and left the compartment. I immediately headed for the car where Fogg had had his mysterious rendezvous. The door of the compartment was still closed and the curtains were drawn. I caught the eye of a railway employee and said, "I have to take a message to Mr Dugenou. Is this his compartment?"

Obligingly, the fellow, who sported a bushy goatee and eyebrows, consulted his log. After a quick glance, he shook his head.

"You're mistaken. There's no Mr Dugenou on my list. And, in any case, this compartment is unoccupied."

"It wasn't reserved?"

"I didn't say that. Only that the passengers weren't here when the train left."

I tried my luck. The man looked amenable enough.

"You're certain there's no Dugenou?"

"Absolutely. The reservation was made in the name of . . ." Once again he glanced at the log. "Ah, here it is, in the name of Smogg. An Englishman, of course."

I was dumbfounded. The employee tipped his cap at me and walked off. I rejoined Fogg, who was dozing. Smogg!

What nerve! Choosing such a transparent pseudonym was tantamount to provocation. Did he know who I was? Had he set such an obvious trap for me – and, I admit, one into which I had all too readily fallen – in order to remove any shadow of a doubt as to my person?

In any case, Fogg demonstrated no change in his behaviour toward me. As soon as we reached the heel of the Italian boot, we boarded a steamer, the *Mongolia*, heading for Suez and then Bombay.

More than willingly, I will say nothing of that professional nosy-parker who had dogged our heels from Suez. Fix, since that is who I mean, has no role to play in this story, despite the fact that Verne and his cohorts gave him a rather important one.

On the other hand, I will provide details about an episode that was either unknown to the novelist, or hidden by him, much like the compartment reserved by Mr Smogg. The *Mongolia* was steaming across the Arabian Sea with the Indian peninsula in its sights. We had been on board five days and a certain routine had taken over our activities. Yet, fewer than twenty-four hours before we were to arrive at Bombay, Fogg started to look nervous. Oh, there was nothing spectacular in the case of this man who controlled his emotions superbly . . . But I did see the pocket watch reappear on several occasions, up to ten times in a single hour, and for no apparent reason. That is until that evening, when Fogg decided that it was time to head off to the captain's table for dinner. I presumptuously decided to inform him that we had been taking our meals in our cabin and that I was perfectly content with that arrangement.

"It's a simple matter of courtesy," he retorted. "This is our last evening on board. The captain has informed me that he would be honoured by our presence."

I said nothing and we went outside to take some air to stimulate our appetites. Fogg consulted his watch yet again as we strolled along the upper deck of the ship. Suddenly he stopped, pretending to be vexed. And I must admit he was an excellent actor.

"I don't have my calling cards with me," he exclaimed. "A most unfortunate omission on my part. This dinner will most likely be an excellent opportunity to exchange cards with the captain's guests."

"I'll go get them," I offered.

"It's getting late," countered Fogg. "You go to the dining room, instead, and tell them that I will be late."

What an elegant way of getting rid of me! I pretended to continue on my way to the dining room, but I quickly walked around the upper deck and returned to our cabin, just in time to see Fogg closing the door behind him. I pressed my eye to the keyhole, but the key was still in place. I pricked up my ears. This time there was no racket to prevent me from overhearing the conversation. But it was all in vain. The cabin was silent. One long minute passed. Then another. I was starting to believe that Fogg had actually gone back to look for his cards when a muffled detonation made me jump.

There was no question about it. It came from the other side of the door. Fearing the worst, I knocked and then called out, "Mr Fogg? Is everything all right?"

No one answered. So I slipped the thin iron hook, which served in part to justify my pseudonym, from my sleeve and a few seconds later I had unlocked the door. I opened the door and entered, an explanation prepared in case I had to face Fogg's anger.

A pointless precaution. The cabin was empty.

Impossible, yet true. Fogg had disappeared. The perfect closed door mystery. The cabin had no other exits, not even a ventilation shaft through which a skilful contortionist could wend his way. And Fogg's circumference prohibited any such fantasies.

I took care to close and lock the door behind me and quickly inspected the few square yards. Everything was in its place as I had arranged it when we took possession of the rooms. I resolved to wait for Fogg to return, hidden in his trunk. I was small enough that this was quite simple. A hole cut in the wicker with my pocket knife gave me a clear view of the small cabin. All that remained was to wait patiently . . .

It wasn't long. I barely had time to feel the first cramps in my calves when a flash of lightning lit up the interior of the cabin, as if someone had launched a distress flare. Once again, I heard the distant detonation. I blinked, my vision blurred by a thousand phosphorescent specks. Fogg's voice came to me, distorted by a metallic echo, as if he were speaking from the other end of a lead pipe. Despite this, I was able to make out his words.

"Until we meet again, dear brother!"

When I looked again, he was there, standing in front of the small writing table that was affixed to the back wall, adjusting the knot in his tie. He looked exhausted, yet delighted. He started to whistle a tune that was unfamiliar to me (and for good cause, since it had been composed in a place to which I could never travel), while straightening his attire.

I knew immediately that I had just witnessed a brilliant demonstration, in all meanings of the word, of travel between worlds. What concerned me above all was what I had heard. Who had Fogg been speaking with? Who was this 'brother' whom he had promised to meet again?

I had no time for further questions. Once he had freshened up, Fogg went out. I squeezed out of my hiding place, inserted my hook into the lock once again (which was locked from the outside this time), stepped outside, closed the door behind me, and took to my heels in an effort to beat Fogg to the captain's table.

Fortunately for me, the Englishman was in no great hurry. I bolted into the dining room, barely out of breath, greeted the guests, who had already been seated, apologized to the captain for my master's tardiness and sat down just as Fogg entered, radiant and nonchalant.

The dinner was delightful and Fogg was a most charming guest.

The next day, we landed in India.

★   ★   ★

Once again, I will skip over the circumstances that lead to the rescue of the beautiful widow of the Rajah of Bundelkund. M. Verne provided sufficient details in his account. Aouda Jejeebhoy was a magnificent woman and that is all that matters. If Fogg fell under the spell of her charms and then enjoyed a mutually beneficial relationship with her, of which I have absolutely no doubt, the affair was conducted in the most complete secrecy – at least in my opinion – in a world where this type of relationship between a white man of high social standing and a woman of colour, even though she was a princess, did not infringe on good manners. As for Aouda, I only know what I saw and what M. Verne reported, which was not much at all.

Together, we boarded the *Rangoon* and headed for Hong Kong from Calcutta. Fogg reserved a second cabin for Aouda, and I found a company employee who assured me that he had made no other reservations. With a few well distributed banknotes, I had confirmed that there was no Mr Smogg on board. I was convinced that he would not attempt anything during the crossing. Yet, when Fogg informed me, as we approached Singapore for a brief stopover there, that he was taking the princess for a ride in the country, I knew that he considered that an ideal opportunity to act in all quietude since a Frenchman would never be so boorish as to interfere with a blossoming romance.

A Frenchman wouldn't, but I would. After all, my blood contains various exotic influences . . . But, enough said about that. Let us return to what concerns us. Therefore, Fogg managed to give me the slip for long enough for a carriage ride through Singapore. I let him take a small lead and then followed. I found it amusing that I was not alone since that policeman, Fix, had had the same idea.

It was just that Fix was not sufficiently interested to follow the couple into all of the sites they visited, much like newly-weds on their honeymoon who are curious about everything. Most fortunately, I did not share that imbecile's scruples. In the old city of Singapore, in the heart of the Chinese community, there is a temple with elegant, gilded curves, in imitation of ancestral and continental models. I cannot swear to this, but I think Fogg checked his watch. Then he ordered his carriage to stop at the entrance to the building and invited Aouda to follow him. I followed in their footsteps, behind Fix, and was in turn intoxicated by the rich fragrance of the incense – and something else, more bitter, sharper, that I suspected had something to do with the poppies that grew a few leagues from the island, in China.

My suspicions were confirmed when I discovered, in an area where altars dedicated to the gods were usually found, a row of stalls, separated by paper screens. In each small space, a silhouette slumped languorously, pipe in mouth, possibly dreaming, eyelids fluttering under the effect of the opium.

Never for a single second did I imagine that Fogg had brought Aouda to such a place to partake of the pleasures of the drug. I was only half surprised when I saw him convince the pretty princess to take a puff on a pipe, which immediately put her to sleep. Then, abandoning her to the supervision of a young Chinese man with a shaved head, he strode through the pearl curtain at the back of the room.

I made the most of the welcome darkness to steal a tunic and pointed hat from a smoker and, thus disguised, I followed suit. My small size gave me an advantage since I was easily mistaken for an employee of that strange temple and I was allowed to come and go in peace.

I witnessed the most extraordinary scene which even today, almost half a century later, remains engraved in my memory. Fogg had gone into a modest room, lit by an oil lamp, where the temple accessories were stored. Votive statuettes stood next to rolls of paper covered with frescos painted in old-fashioned colours; crates of moth-eaten tunics framed the most impressive object, a superb Buddha in the lotus position, covered with gold from his belly to the top of his head, as smooth as could be. I crouched down behind a crate, not far from the single door, ready to note the slightest suspicious sign. Fogg, glanced quickly around the room, making sure that he was quite alone and then kneeled in front of the Buddha.

Was he about to pray? I was filled with doubt. Would he secretly invoke the pot-bellied idol of the Asian peoples? But the pretence of prayer did not last. Removing his gloves, Fogg ran his hands over the statue's belly, which was as round as a globe of the Earth. In a low voice, he started to chant in a language that I did not recognize. Then, to my great surprise, the effigy of the 'Enlightened One' shone with a gentle light, which increased in intensity as Fogg recited his rosary.

Under the direction of Camille Flammarion, I had attended a few séances held to communicate with another world. As a result, I had already looked upon the luminescent nimbus of the creatures that had been contacted by the metapsychic. Yet the halo of energy connecting the universes had never been so bright! I was completely dazzled and had to close my eyes for a second. The distant detonation caused me to jump.

When I opened my eyes, Fogg was no longer alone.

He was embracing a large, thin man wearing a loose tunic embroidered with gold thread. The hands of the new arrival, which rested on Fogg's shoulders, were impressive. Long and knotted, they ended with claw-like fingernails, covered with a silvery polish. The embrace continued. Then Fogg took a step back, revealing the face of the apparition.

I bit the inside of my cheek to keep myself from crying out.

The face was a perfect replica of Fogg's, apart from the skin colour, which was similar to that of the Natives, and the fine, black whiskers that hung from the corners of his mouth, much like those of a catfish.

"Welcome, my brother!" Fogg exclaimed.

I then saw that they were about to leave the room. I withdrew, with the required amount of discretion, on tiptoe, and returned to the smoking room where I hid behind a screen.

Fogg and his 'brother' arrived a few seconds later. After embracing once again, Fogg left his curious twin. Then, he gathered up the sleeping Aouda and left the temple.

I followed suit and took to my heels to return to the wharves, still wearing the local dress. The *Rangoon* would soon get underway for Hong Kong. Neither Fogg, nor Aouda for that matter, ever referred to their detour into the opium den.

At this point, I would like to remind you that we ran into a storm and arrived a day late. It was there in Hong Kong that Fogg decided to take Aouda to Europe. I'm convinced that he had already planned the outcome of this decision – marriage – but he never once breathed a word of it.

That imbecile Fix chose this moment to interfere and sidetrack me from my mission. After a number of misadventures, I was able to join Fogg in Yokohama, Japan. M. Verne provides an uplifting account, with the occasional exaggeration.

Still, we finally found ourselves together on board the steamer, the *General Grant*, on our way to America. There, a train would take us from San Francisco to New York, where our trip around the world would be almost over.

I concluded that I would have to force Fogg to reveal his intentions before we arrived on the East coast of the United States. Obviously, I had no way of guessing that he had, in turn, decided to submit to my requirements, in a most spectacular manner!

Using the pretext that we might eventually have to ward off an Indian attack as we travelled through the American Mid West, I purchased some Enfield rifles and Colt revolvers. Fogg accepted the weapons without comment. He didn't even take the time to inspect them. This was fortunate for me since the models I had given him were loaded with blanks – unlike those I had kept for myself.

I was fully prepared for the final scene when I would force Fogg to reveal his true identity, just when he least expected it, namely when he would once again contact a "brother" from another world, something I was fully convinced he would do. Let me explain. The first contact had taken place, and I am convinced of this, in the compartment of the train that carried us across France. In Europe, as a result. The second, on the ship that carried us to India, near the Arabian peninsula, not far from Africa. The third took place in Singapore, taking care of Asia. And we had just landed on the final important continent in our trip around the world: North America. Thus, it was inevitable that a new 'brother' would be contacted there.

However, first hours then days passed and Fogg appeared to take no interest in anything but the interminable whist games played with certain passengers. We did have quite a few adventures (encountering a buffalo herd, crossing a bridge that threatened to crumble under the weight of the train . . .), but nothing perturbed Fogg particularly. We passed through state after state as we inexorably continued on our way towards the East Coast.

Then we arrived in Nebraska. There, after that stupid duel Fogg fought with a certain Colonel, what had been just a pretext for me became reality. A tribe of blood-thirsty Sioux attacked our train. This was followed by a violent battle in which my sole concern was to hope that Fogg did not notice he was shooting blanks!

I'll skip the details. However, I would just like to say that I had to use all my skills to distance the Indian threat from the train, taking steps to disconnect the locomotive from the cars. Just as I was about to return to the train, which was rolling freely, I received a brutal blow to the back of my head and fell unconscious.

This was one thing M. Verne did not mention, since he preferred to imply that I remained a prisoner in the tender as a matter of bad luck! As a result, everyone believes that Fogg reacted heroically, and like a perfect gentleman, organizing a hasty rescue mission to Sioux territory.

But, here's the truth. I regained consciousness inside a teepee, one of those large pointed tents that housed entire Indian families. Two stolid braves, with skin as red as brick, stood guard, armed with rifles. Yet, I was not mistreated and I was even fed well during the time I was confined there.

Then, rifle shots broke the silence. Shortly thereafter, the buffalo hide that covered the entrance to the tent was raised and Fogg came in.

"How are you doing, my old friend?"

He had slipped the Colt I had given him a few days earlier into his belt. The Redskins had given up their posts. Faking anger, I leapt to my feet, and moved as close as I could to the rifle held by the Brave who stood next to the door

"What's the meaning of all this, Fogg?"

"Calm down. You'll be given all the explanations you need shortly. But, before that, I have one last ritual to complete. This place will be fine."

I wanted to protest, but Fogg raised his index finger to his lips and murmured, "Shh! Let me concentrate."

He took off his gloves, as I had seen him do in Singapore, and then consulted his pocket watch, as he had done in France and on board the *Mongolia*.

"Yes," he said, "The time is right. And the location is fitting," he added after another glance at his watch, which he then put away.

Next, Fogg's hands appeared to dance in the air, painting complex figures in the void, similar to Japanese calligraphy. Each movement left a luminous residue in its wake, much like the energy halo mentioned by the metapsychics, but even brighter. I noticed that the Sioux, who were impressed, had closed their eyes. I took advantage of the opportunity to slip over to the rifle I had noted earlier and grab it without being noticed.

When I returned my attention to Fogg's incandescent sculpture, I noticed that it was "inhabited". I was no longer surprised by the famous detonation, much like the sound of a gun being fired into eiderdown. I was familiar with the phenomenon by now and showed no emotion. Fogg repeated his Buddha trick. But there was one difference. The "brother" he contacted appeared to be no more than a child, judging from his small stature. (I easily towered head and shoulders above him).

I understood my error when the last remnants of the halo dissipated. The individual who had thrown himself into

Fogg's arms, who was kneeling on one knee, was definitely a full-grown man, as could be seen in his features, which were the same as Fogg's, emaciated, with a hint of trickery in his eyes.

A dwarf! Fogg's American brother was a dwarf!

"My dear Passepartout," Fogg started, "Allow me to introduce the final member of the Moriarty tribe, the adorable Loveless . . ."

He stopped there. I had cocked my rifle. The small click had its usual effect. I held everyone off, the Sioux, Fogg and the dwarf – Loveless Moriarty. What a dance card!

"You promised me some explanations. I believe the time has come. Unless your curious watch has something to say about all this?"

"This device is much more than a simple timepiece," Fogg started. "It enables me to keep track of the brief periods of time when a breach is opened between two worlds and to locate the areas where the energy required for a transfer flows at its purest."

I had guessed as much, but I preferred not to interrupt him, particularly since what interested me most was still to come.

"This technology is the fruit of the information that is constantly exchanged between the Reform Club and certain scientists from other worlds. I joined those amateurs to take advantage of it. If they only knew the potential of what's available to them! But those Pall Mall imbeciles prefer to lend a hand to Her Majesty's secret services, rather than turn a profit. You should know all about that since you're an agent for France, aren't you?"

I nodded in agreement. What was the point in lying?

"And as for me . . . Well!" He sighed. "Good grief, I fear that my tale is both terribly trite and terribly complicated. Of course, my name isn't really Phileas Fogg. In some circles, I'm known as Professor Moriarty. Use that name, if you prefer."

I learned no more. What was the true identity of this

"Professor Moriarty"? Believe it or not, I still have no idea today, fifty years after our first meeting!

"As you may have noticed," he continued, "I'm rather skilled at contacting other worlds. For a time, I trained with that medium Daniel Home, when he officiated in London. But I soon came to realize that my talent far surpassed his. I could have put my talent to good use for profitable purposes, and I would have succeeded beyond my wildest dreams. But money or rather money *alone* holds no interest for me . . ."

Oh, now we're getting to it, I thought. With a shake of my rifle, I ordered him to continue.

"As a result of the contacts I made with other worlds, I learned one fact that the metapsychics have yet to learn: each of us, you and me alike, has as many doubles as there are universes."

"As many brothers, you mean?"

Fogg/Moriarty nodded.

"Almost twins, with a few slight differences, depending on their environment. As you see, the unfortunate Loveless was stricken with a serious illness in his youth and didn't grow as he should have. But what does that matter?"

The dwarf, in fact, was smiling, not the least bit inconvenienced by his disability.

"Although the body may have undergone certain modifications, the mind, my dear Passepartout, the mind of each double reverberates in unison with the same concerns. There's no chance that a nice boy from the London we know would behave like a boor anywhere else."

"Or vice versa."

Moriarty burst into laughter.

"Of course, you're right. And vice versa!"

I changed the topic abruptly. "How many of you are here, now?"

"You crossed paths with my first brother, dear Fantomas, in France, without realizing it," replied the fake Fogg.

"That can't be!" I exclaimed. "They're so much like you that I would have noticed!"

"Except that that particular brother is a master of disguise. Imagine him with a goatee, fake eyebrows and dressed as a railway porter."

I jumped. The blackguard had duped me thoroughly with his "Mr Smogg"! He had pulled the wool over my eyes with the audacity of the master criminal he actually was.

"All right, I'll let you have that one," I admitted. "But as for the transfer on the *Mongolia*, I stand firm. You reappeared alone *down below* and then I locked the cabin door!"

"My dear friend, you're not the only break-in artist around. There are others who can pick locks too, you know. The individual you saw reappear was my brother, the admirable Nemo. And as for me, I waited until you left your hiding place to go to the upper deck and peacefully join the captain's table, while my twin slipped off on board the submarine that was waiting for him."

"So, you knew I was there, watching you."

"But, of course. Just as I knew that you were following me in Asia, when I set out to meet my Asian brother, the refined Fu Manchu."

I admitted that this point astounded me. But the reason for all these masquerades was still beyond me.

"Why did you allow me to observe the successive arrivals of your brothers without making any attempt to stop me?"

"First of all, because I didn't want to alert your employers. It's far easier to keep an eye on a single agent. Then, too, because I wanted a worthy witness. And I think you are one, my dear Passssepartout, if that really is your name."

I couldn't believe my ears. "A witness? Whatever for?"

The Moriarty twins laughed like little children. They seemed to find my puzzlement quite amusing. Loveless continued with the explanations.

"To make the game worth it, my dear chap, we need adversaries who are worthy of our talent. What point is there in sowing chaos if we have to remain in the shadows? No, what we want to do is make sure that our exploits burst into daylight! And for that, we need this world to recognize our intentions. The report you will be handing in will help with that. Consider it the first move in the game between ourselves and Good, starting now!"

I was dumbfounded, as I'm sure you must realize. So, Moriarty and his diabolic doppelgangers considered this whole thing a game!

Hesitantly, I asked, "And just what are your intentions?"

"Some pillaging, an assassination or two, a little bit of extortion, definitely some terror, and a couple of abductions or so. How would I know?" "Fogg" admitted. "Put yourselves in our shoes for a just few moments, my dear fellow . . . Your world is such a magnificent prey, with its vast wealth and potential! We all come from places that are so poor, so sad, so desolate, that our criminal genius is wasted. Who would fear the name Moriarty in the world I come from? No one at all, no one at all . . ."

So, he admitted that he came from another world. Which one? I never found out.

"On the other hand," added the dwarf, "America will tremble and quake before Loveless!"

"And Europe before Fantomas!"

"China before Fu Manchu!"

"Africa and the East before Nemo!"

That seemed to be everything that had to be said. I aimed my rifle at the "professor's" chest and declared, "I won't let you."

And I fired. The detonation exploded in the tent, causing the diabolical brothers to convulse in laughter.

"Come on now, old man. Don't you recognize that weapon? It's the one you gave me in San Francisco. Loaded with blanks. Quite unlike this one."

He brandished his Colt. Rage filled me as I realized that I could have escaped from the tent without the least risk of getting shot.

"The game has started," Moriarty repeated.

Loveless nodded and added, "And *you* will be our adversary. You and your brothers. We'll help you transfer them here. We'll have so much fun!"

★ ★ ★

And that's the entire story of the very first case in which I found myself fighting against that devil Moriarty. After the Sioux episode, I was drugged and I completed Phileas Fogg's incredible trip around the world in a state of unconsciousness. Fogg then disappeared from circulation, making way for Moriarty, after first marrying Aouda. I'm convinced that he put her away safe from harm in his original world, since I never heard mention of the beautiful princess after that.

I submitted my report to the *Statistics Section* and resigned. From that time on, I was driven by a single obsession – the need to organize and coordinate the fight of Good against Evil, on a planetary scale.

And that's exactly what I have done, from my Pall Mall HQ, a stone's throw from the place where it all started. I did promise, at the beginning of my tale, that I would get back there. Now you know the real reasons behind the Diogenes Club.

But I know you're dying to ask THE question.

You know the one I mean. The one about my brothers?

Well, Loveless Moriarty kept his word. Taking advantage of the fact that I was at his mercy, he used me as bait to lure his first adversary to America, which he took for himself. Then the professor proceeded in the same manner, using the watch he had stolen from the Reform Club, and other brothers appeared, here and there.

They all looked just like me, except for a few details: James, the American, shared my small stature and energy; Fandor, the Frenchman, enjoyed my athletic prowess. Yet, the most famous of all had nothing in common with me, except for a vague expression in his eyes. Just as I remained short and my waistline swelled with age, Sherlock was lean and lanky . . .

And the Moriarty brothers? Unlike *my* brothers, unfortunately, they're not all dead. If you have any doubts about that, just ask yourself who placed the gun in the hand of that Serb student in Sarajevo, in June 1914.

In one manner or another, the game is still being played.

But without me. I'm tired, old and worn out by the fight.

This object in my hands . . . perhaps you recognize it? Yes. It's Phileas Fogg's famous watch, just as I collected it from the Reform Club storeroom.

I'm planning another trip around the world. I don't know exactly where I'll wind up, but I'm sure you'll understand that I would truly like to meet a certain individual, someone I met in the jungle fifty years earlier.

Treat me like an old coot if you like.

That's not a problem.

Meanwhile, you have no business stifling my confession or disclosing it, as you did so admirably well in the case of Sherlock's exploits, dear Dr Watson.

With kind regards from Mycroft . . .

Translated from the French by Sheryl Curtis

EIGHTY LETTERS, PLUS ONE

Kevin J. Anderson & Sarah A. Hoyt

Letter #1

30 September 1872
London, England

My dearest Elizabeth,

I leave this note for you, as the house was empty when I came home to pack. Doubtless you're out enjoying a quaint diversion with your women friends. As for me, I am unexpectedly off to the Suez, my dear. I've been dispatched to intercept a notorious thief who stole fifty thousand pounds from the Bank of England.

The villain is sure to leave the country and use his ill-gotten fortune to live extravagantly abroad. Detectives have been dispatched, one to each major port, and I have been chosen to keep a sharp eye on all British travellers who come through the Suez. I have a clear description of the thief, a well-dressed man with fine manners. Should I find him, I will shadow him till a warrant can be dispatched.

I'm sorry to leave you with nothing more than a note on this, our first anniversary, particularly since you never had the proper wedding you deserved. I still feel a bit of remorse over our brash elopement to Gretna Green, but you know your parents would never have consented to our love match. I still remember how haughtily your mother said that, because I need to work for a living, I should come in through the tradesman's entrance.

I trust you will keep a stiff upper lip while I'm away. The bank has offered a substantial reward to the detective who captures the thief, and I am convinced I'll get him if he comes my way. All that's needed in law enforcement these days is flair. You have to know how to nose these vermin out. And I, of course, have excellent flair. As I've told you many times, I have a veritable sixth sense for these things.

Two thousand pounds will allow us to buy a better home and to hire a servant to do the housework for you. I know you expect such things out of life. It will also prove to your parents that, though you disobeyed them, you were ultimately right to choose me as your husband.

Meanwhile, I will write to you every day I possibly can. I'm sure you'll hardly notice I'm gone.

> Yours, with much love,
> Herbert Fix, Inspector, First grade

Letter #9

> 9 October
> Suez, Egypt, Africa

My dear Elizabeth,

Good news! After all these days of waiting, the thief has finally come to the Suez.

Today, when the steamer *Mongolia* docked at the quay in Suez, I spotted a passenger forcing his way through the clamouring and stinking crowd of locals. You would not believe the mob of natives and black Africans that press around every passenger, offering to sell monkeys, unguents, jewellery, and the most grotesque pagan idols. One wretch even had the temerity to offer me some ground mummy which, he said, would strengthen my virile parts! I shudder to think, my dear, of you having to witness such sights.

By great luck, the fellow who came out of the *Mongolia* was in search of a government official. He nosed his way directly to me and held out a passport, for which he wished to procure a visa from the British consul. He was a wiry, dark-haired Frenchman, but he carried an Englishman's passport – his master's. Of course, I immediately glanced at the passport, and the description was exactly that of our thief! I could do no less than try to stop the man.

I told my suspicions to the consul and begged him to delay this man until I could get my arrest warrant. To my great disappointment, however, the consul said that I had no proof the traveller – Phileas Fogg – was guilty of any crime, and that without such proof he could not be detained.

I must therefore follow this rogue to his next stop, which is Bombay. I have talked to his servant, Passepartout – a good sort of fellow, but French and therefore garrulous. The man is convinced his master means to circle the globe to win a preposterous bet. Apparently the cunning devil made a wager with the gentlemen in his club that he could go completely around the world in a mere eighty days. With my keen intellect, I realized immediately that this outrageous boast is nothing more than cover for his escape with the stolen money.

Hoping to pry more information from the talkative Frenchman, I took him on a shopping expedition to the bazaar. There, merchants offer all types of goods, including a very expensive perfume called Attar of Roses, of which a single drop can be mixed with oil or water to make many concoctions prized by the local ladies. Since you are always in my thoughts, I meant to buy you a dram of it. I also saw a fly swatter made from an elephant's tail, which I thought might amuse you. But, as I'm sure you'll understand, I had scarcely any time for frivolous purchases.

Passepartout wished to obtain new shirts and other accoutrements for his master. Due to the haste with which they left London, they had brought no more luggage than a carpetbag! Tell me, what man – not a thief and not in possession of $50,000 – would thus abandon his home and everything in it? The loquacious Frenchman continually bemoaned the fact that he had left the gas burning in his room and that his master wouldn't allow him so much as a moment to run back to turn it off. This is not the natural behaviour of a man who truly intends to return home.

I have applied for a warrant, which should catch up with us in Bombay. My dear Elizabeth, the reward money is as good as ours. I have not had the time to pick up any souvenirs for you just yet, but I am sure to buy you something in Bombay, once the villain Fogg has been arrested.

Yours affectionately,

Herbert Fix

Letter # 20

20 October 1872
Bombay, British India

My dear Elizabeth,

Here I am, once more, fulfilling my promise of writing a letter a day to you. I will also post at once the letters I wrote aboard the steamer.

Unfortunately, we have made such rapid progress – Fogg bribed the owner of the liner to have the engine stoked with extraordinary zeal – that my warrant is not yet with the police here. I am more certain than ever of my quarry's guilt. What man but a fleeing criminal would throw away money in such a way?

Only those who have not had to work for their income view it as of little importance. I know you do not like it when I speak of the extravagance of the lace on your sister's gowns, but were it not for your parents' private income, she would surely weigh her expense more carefully and not burden herself with so much expensive frippery.

But worry not, my dear. Soon you'll be able to afford dresses as good or better than hers. In fact, time permitting, I might pick up some fabric in Bombay, which is a city of goodly size and filled with all manner of strange things.

The streets are extraordinarily crowded with dark people attired in cotton robes. On the way to the police station, I saw a man who lay completely at ease upon a bed of sharp nails. Imagine! I also saw a man hypnotize a deadly snake by playing his flute.

I'm rather upset at not having received the warrant yet, but you may be confident in my abilities, my dear. Rest assured – Phileas Fogg, who really has no intention of going around the world, will no doubt remain several days here, which will certainly be sufficient time for me to arrest him. Meanwhile, maybe I'll find you an appropriate gift . . . perhaps some silk with which the native women wrap themselves. Something called, as I understand it, a sari.

Oh, I almost forgot to acknowledge that I received your letter, which you sent ahead to Bombay. It is extraordinarily kind of you to say that you'd gladly forego the two thousand pounds for the sake of having me near you again. Your female emotionalism is quite charming, in its own way, but I know you are not serious. If I obeyed you, I have no doubt you'd soon resent our poverty. And, more importantly, I cannot let the villain Fogg go unpunished.

Bear my absence with fortitude, for I'm sure the arrest warrant will come soon, and I'll return to you in glory and bearing the reward money that will start your climb back to the sphere you abandoned in order to marry me.

With my regards,

Herbert Fix

Letter # 21

21 October 1872

Dear Elizabeth,

The warrant is not yet here. I write in haste and frustration. It turns out that Phileas Fogg intended to leave Bombay for Calcutta via the Great Peninsular railway. I was at the point of stepping into another train carriage, when Fogg's servant Passepartourt arrived breathless, hatless, barefoot, and bearing the marks of a scuffle.

Though I fear you'll reproach me for my rudeness, I confess that I eavesdropped on the conversation between him and his master. The Frenchman had lost his shoes and barely escaped after violating the sanctity of a heathen pagoda on Malabar Hill – which is forbidden to Christians (or, at any rate, to anyone wearing shoes).

I was, as I said, on the point of stepping into the train carriage when I realized that, rather than waiting for the warrant from England – which might not reach us in time – I could simply find the temple and give the heathen priests the name and destination of their transgressor. Then *they* could press charges.

You see, the British authorities are extraordinarily careful never to offend the native religions – it is part of keeping control over this great uncivilized mob – and therefore, what that fool Passepartout did was an offence before British law. I'll get a warrant for that crime, too, then meet them at Calcutta, and have both men properly arrested.

I will write to you soon and announce the date of my return home with the reward money.

> Yours, in haste,
>
> Herbert Fix

Letter #25

> 25 October 1872
> Calcutta, British India

Dear Elizabeth,

At last Fogg and his servant have arrived. I was in some anxiety that something had befallen them in the jungle as they crossed the subcontinent. I could not stop thinking of the thief and all those bank notes rotting away in the verdant wildness of India, and my reward unclaimed! I was truly in despair – but now they've arrived at last, and the magistrates had them arrested at the train. Everything was going so well.

Unfortunately, Fogg bought his way out of the situation by posting an exorbitant bail of £2,000, as if it were nothing.

Two thousand pounds – the same amount that could have made the two of us comfortable for so long, thrown out like so much rubbish!

As I've said before, money that one has not earned is easy to discard.

Sadly, it appears that the thief will escape once more, and I must continue my relentless pursuit, even if it takes me all the way around the world. He is boarding the *Rangoon*, which lays at anchor and is to depart in an hour for Hong Kong.

I have no choice but to follow, despite your half dozen letters imploring me to come home, which I recently collected from the consulate. I'm a little puzzled as to how you seem to be sending your letters ahead to my next destination. Perhaps you believe the extravagant story of a trip around the world in eighty days. Yes, doubtless it's been published in every newspaper in England, and it appeals to your romantic female imagination. I must dissuade you from continuing for soon the thief will stop his travels and your charming letters will be lost forever in some city to which I'll never travel.

And still the warrant hasn't caught up with me. Bureaucracy can be truly exasperating.

My greatest worry now is that Fogg is flinging money about with such abandon that the reward – being a fixed percentage of the recovered money – is shrinking visibly before my eyes.

I'm sure it will still be enough to make you happy.

I shall get him in the British colony of Hong Kong. Fogg and Passepartout are now traveling with a beautiful and clearly genteel young lady they picked up somewhere in the jungles of India. I suspect an elopement, and though you might call it unworthy of me – considering that we also eloped – I should be able to arrest Fogg for *that*, too, because elopement, until sanctified by marriage, can be prosecuted as a crime. I will question Passepartout for details about this woman.

Yours,

Herbert Fix.

Letter #37

6 November 1872
Hong Kong

Elizabeth,

We arrived in Hong Kong after much adventure. In your letters you expressed the wish that you could join me in my pursuit. You must realize that this travelling abroad, though exhilarating for a man, would be much too demanding for a delicate woman such as yourself. You are much happier at home.

Just before we landed we met with a hurricane, the greatest storm I've ever seen. It was as if the heavens themselves were on my side, whipping the seas and the wind into frenzy to delay us. And while I was gripped by the most horrible nausea, I hoped we'd have to turn and run before the squall, which would slow our journey to Hong Kong. This made it more likely the warrant would arrive, and would also disrupt whatever plans this scoundrel has for escaping the law.

Alas, the vessel braved it, and we made landfall shortly after.

Meanwhile, I learned that the relatives of the mysterious woman are not likely to chase Fogg for besmirching her honour. Aouda is a mere native, despite her pale skin – an Indian princess, whom Passepartout and Fogg supposedly rescued from being burned with her husband's body, a barbarous tradition of immolation. Now she is travelling with them.

They have already reserved berths on the *Carnatic*, which was scheduled to depart tomorrow for Yokohama. But I met Passepartout on his way from the quay to his master's hotel, and he told me the *Carnatic* has unexpectedly changed its departure time to this evening instead. The Frenchman was in a great hurry to tell Fogg about it, but I waylaid the simple-minded and naive servant and got him intoxicated in an opium den, a very common establishment in these parts.

The man will sleep for at least a day, till long after the

Carnatic has sailed. I am sure Fogg will not leave without his man. If my plan succeeds in delaying them, I shall go to the embassy and see if there are any forwarded letters from you.

Yours,

Herbert Fix

Letter #45

14 November 1872
Yokohama, Japan

Elizabeth,

Once more I write in haste. Fogg, having missed the *Carnatic*, engaged a small sail boat, the *Tankedere* – and he allowed me to travel with him. He does not even suspect that I am his nemesis! And Passepartout refuses to believe his master might be a thief. Either he is a wily accomplice, or a fool.

It is maddening to be so near him for so long and yet not to have the warrant that would stop him in his tracks. But there is nothing for it, as we're no longer in British territory. My only hope now is that he'll indeed go around the world in such a fashion hoping to confuse pursuers. I shall arrest him as soon as he lands in England again. Fogg intends to pursue travel to America aboard the *General Grant*.

I've already engaged a cabin in the *General Grant*, and I've now read the latest batch of your letters which, if you'll forgive me, are rather tiresome in your insistence that I return to you at once. I have a job to do. Despite the rate at which this scoundrel is spending the stolen money, think of the renown his capture will bring me, and how much easier it will make my rise in the world.

Only minutes ago I saw Passepartout being dragged into the boat by Fogg. Passepartout wore a most extraordinarily fanciful oriental uniform, with wings and a false nose which would have sufficed for a family of twelve. People on deck say this is a costume worn in theatre for the glory of some god or other. Foolish native habits and abominable idolatry, of course, and one wonders how even a Frenchman could bear to mix himself in it.

While I take a moment to catch my berth, let me tell you something about Yokohama. It is a city of good size, and the native quarter is lit by many-coloured lanterns. There are astrologers everywhere using fine telescopes. Scientific instruments to enhance their superstition. Most ironic. For fun, I thought about having a horoscope cast for you – an unusual and exotic gift – but I had no time to delay. I must catch Fogg.

Sincerely,

Herbert Fix

Letter #64

3 December 1872
San Francisco, United States of America

Elizabeth,

We are in San Francisco, the wild city of 1849, with its bandits, incendiaries, and assassins who all came here in the Gold Rush. The city looks more civilized than you'd expect, with a lofty tower in the town hall and a whole network of streets and avenues. It also has a Chinese town, that you'd swear came from China itself.

We found ourselves caught in the middle of some incomprehensible political rally – a dispute for the post of Justice of the Peace involving two men – and soon it turned into a brawl. I could not make head nor tail of it, nor why anyone would seek to harm anyone else over such a silly squabble. I think these Americans are just hot-tempered.

In the turmoil, I actually protected Fogg from what might have been a disabling blow. Don't worry. Other than my clothes, nothing was hurt. Fogg insisted on buying me new garments, which are of a quality and cut to which even your parents could not object.

In your latest letters you reproached me for my "despicable Opium plot." I must say that you simply don't understand the business of men. Some deeds, though unpleasant, are necessary. Don't concern yourself about the matter any further.

You'll be heartened to know I'm now wholeheartedly working to speed Fogg's travel. Indeed, now that the thief is heading back to England, I am more than glad to help him. The sooner he gets there, the sooner I can arrest him. (And be back home with you, of course.)

And now we are to catch a train on the Pacific Railroad, headed for New York, from where we shall sail for London. I must rush to the train, so I don't lose sight of Fogg.

Herbert Fix

Letter #70

11 December 1872
New York, United States

Elizabeth,

Sorry for not writing for two days. Ran out of paper. You'd never believe what we've done in our trip across the United States. We rushed over a bridge mere moments before it collapsed, and in the process we'd stoked up such a head of steam that we didn't even stop until we'd passed the station! Then there was a herd of animals so large that they impeded the movement of the train. We had to wait until the beasts moved before the train could pass. Only imagine! The Americans call them buffalo, though Fogg said that such a classification is absurd. Not sure why.

The wonders of this continent. This world.

At one point, Fogg nearly engaged in a gunfight duel with another passenger, but they were interrupted by an attack from the savage Sioux, who kidnapped three passengers, including Passepartout – which, naturally, necessitated a rescue. Afterward, we caught an express train at Omaha station. Fogg, apparently imagining the demons of justice after him, is not fond of sightseeing, only rushing onward and onward. All the better, for that means I'll collect my reward sooner.

Now we've reached New York at last – but alas the vessel

in which we expected to cross the Atlantic sailed forty-five minutes before our arrival. Fogg will no doubt find some boat to purchase or coerce. I very much fear there's not much money left out of the £50,000 he stole, but I shall still reap fame for apprehending him. Wouldn't you like to be the wife of a hero?

Herbert Fix

Letter #80

21 December Friday
Liverpool

Elizabeth,

We have made landfall, and I served Phileas Fogg with the warrant, but – how could misfortune befall me so? After all my labours, after pursuing him round the world, I am not to enjoy success. Despite every indication, it appears that Fogg is not the thief after all, for the man who actually stole the £50,000 was apprehended three days ago, whilst I was travelling.

Worse, that upstart Passepartout punched me when he learned my true purpose in accompanying them on their long journey. Now I am bruised and tired, humiliated, disappointed – but at least I'm home, where doubtless you'll be waiting for me.

Herbert Fix

[On embossed letterhead identifying it as belonging to the law firm of Everingham, Entwhistle and Brown – on the fireplace mantel of Fix's home.]

London, 18 December 1872

Dear Mr Herbert Fix,

This letter serves to notify you that your wife, the honourable Elizabeth Rose Merryweather Fix, has returned to her parents' home and is suing you for divorce on the grounds of abandonment.

Our client has further instructed us to inform you that she did not object to your poverty or even your low upbringing, but she cannot forgive your obsession with career at the expense of her peace of mind and felicity. She further instructs us to inform you that you married her under false pretences, always having characterized your marriage as a love match, when it is clear you love nothing more than your reputation and the pursuit of your own ambitions.

Lord and Lady Merryweather advise you to pose no argument and seek no reconciliation with their daughter, as they have the means to see you dismissed from your employment.

> Sincerely,
> Nigel Entwhistle, Esquire.

THE ADVENTURERS' LEAGUE

Justina Robson

Fresh from Around the World in Eighty Days, *Verne returned to the character of Captain Nemo, believed dead at the end of* 20,000 Leagues Under the Sea. *L'île mystérieuse* or *The* Mysterious Island *had had a long genesis. Verne had written an early version before he wrote* 20,000 Leagues, *and this was essentially a novel of castaways who survive on an island by using their ingenuity and scientific knowledge. It was derived, to a large degree, from one of Verne's favourite books,* Swiss Family Robinson *(1813) by Johann Wyss. By the time he returned to it, though, Verne was able to weave into it characters from other novels. We find that the survivors of a balloon accident on a remote island have some kind of mysterious protector who turns out, at the very end of the novel, to be none other than Captain Nemo. He reveals, in his final moments, the truth about his origins and motives. With his death the castaways obey his last wish and scuttle the* Nautilus *which bears its body to a watery grave. We have already seen from Mallory's story that there might be another interpretation of Nemo's final days. Now we look ahead to the inspiration that the character and story gave to future generations.*

Riba leant out of the window and looked up. His body was at an awkward twist because he dare not let go of the ledge. It was twelve floors down to the pavement. Just above him and to his right, outside the Newsdesk window, the summons' posts of the Avian Messenger Service jutted out of the brickwork. One of them was occupied by the sturdy form of an external maintenance Parrokeet who was testing the wirework for the new satellite dish the editor had just had installed. The other two were empty.

Riba pulled his head in and ran a hand through his hair reflectively. The posts and local environs were crusted with foul-smelling bird muck which had a habit of flaking loose. He lived in dread of inhaling the stuff, but he seemed to have escaped this once.

"Go stir up some trouble, Riba, you're spoiling the view." Slattery, who was supposed to be writing the minority sports column, had his feet up on his desk. A printed magazine was laid over his face as he leant back in his chair, arms behind his head.

"Something's going on," Riba told him, stuffing his hands into his pockets and leaning against the wall so that he could look out across the city towards Downing Street. "I can tell by the way everything's flying."

Slattery snorted. "Mmn, yes, maybe in some uncharted corner of the universe there still exists some angle on the day's big story that's not entirely shredded and bedded. The small pets of the world may be bursting to give you their reactions to the reactions on the reactions so far. I can see it now. Impossible Space Journey – a hamster speaks. *I was in my wheel, you know, just doing a few laps, when suddenly . . .*"

But Riba was already out of the door and moving out of the paper's network footprint. In a café a half a mile distant he sat down and opened his Abacand – a handheld device of infinite practical use. Using the money from his last major investigative assignment he pump-primed his account with DarkNet, the non-governmental AI communications service.

He drank his way through four espressos and oiled, smoothed and bribed his way through all but a handful of dollars in the next few hours. Finally, as lights began to come on across the city, he felt that lifting of the hairs on the back of his neck as an old contact from the Forged Uluru network came on line. Using the café's integral holographic units they projected their avatar into the empty chair opposite Riba's.

Forged people, whose bodies might be far distant or in a form not suitable for talking, in order to manifest themselves in the form of Original, or Unevolved human beings, used Avatars as a matter of course in order to communicate more effectively. Their appearance conventionally revealed much about the personality behind their design. This one took the form of an ancient Chinese man with a pot belly. He wore orange robes, had a shaved head, and smoked a meerschaum pipe that gave off a fierce blast of smoke every so often, like the funnel of a tug-boat. Riba knew this avatar, even though he knew nothing about who it really was, and he was used to the fact that it never spoke. Instead it gave him an amused smile and sent his Abacand the time and departure point of a trans-Atlantic flight. Then, with an extra-large puff of smoke, it did the genie-thing and vanished.

The notes included a brief description of a person. Riba had used this contact before, when it gained him access to a file that revealed the identities of a half a dozen businessmen involved in financing interplanetary piracy. Upon receiving this new instruction he immediately called in a couple of favours from other journalists to borrow enough money to buy a ticket and by the time Slattery was ploughing his way through the volleyball scores Riba was stepping aboard the helium airship *Byzantium*, bound for New York.

The *Byzantium* was a passenger craft ideally suited to extending journey time beyond the practical and into the realms of affluence. No vehicle appealed less to Riba personally but, if it led him to definite information on the peculiar circumstances of Voyager Lonestar Isol's return to Earth space, then it was the best transport in the world. That this return was a matter that required serious investigation was beyond question.

The Voyager was an early type of Forged human being, an engineered mind in an engineered body which was suited for the long years, great speeds and incredible tedium of interstellar exploration. Her Manifest Photograph was currently showing on every newscast in the system. Riba flinched instinctively every time he saw it. Isol looked like fifty different kinds of assassin bug wedded to the toughest machinery money could buy. She was as inhuman as he could imagine, on the outside at least. On the way to catch his flight he did his best to forget it although it was the kind of thing that had a way of stamping itself on the mind.

Isol had returned only yesterday from a journey of over thirty years' duration. According to the official story she had followed a single, accurate trajectory out of the Sol system towards its near neighbour, Barnard's Star. All had been well. There were some nice photographs of nebulae, some pertinent observations on planets, black holes, the galactic hub and other such matters of importance to science. There were also many transmissions to and from the Forged Independence Party Headquarters.

Riba re-read these and their latest updates with the feeling that at last here was something he could get his teeth into. Isol was a political agitator and a radical of the out-there order. She wrote vehemently about the obsolescence of Old Monkey – the humans like Riba who were as nature had made them. It was Isol's view that the Forged should create an independent state beyond the legislative and economic grip of the present Solar Government so that they could pursue their own reproduction and evolution unhindered by "historical and unsympathetic" views of their destiny.

Riba viewed the looming prospect of a civil war with mixed feelings. For the last few years the Forged Independence movement had grown. Together with an increasing lawlessness out in the wider system it had built an ominous momentum with incident after incident of piracy and assault out on the frontiers of Solar space. The Unevolved fear of their stronger and faster gengineered cousins had grown and on Earth there were daily incidents of violence and misunderstanding between the two. The Forged resented their slavery. The Unevolved envied the Forged their power. But the Forged supplied the Unevolved settlements with essential resources from the wider system, and the Unevolved . . . well, sometimes it was difficult to see exactly how the Unevolved fit into the macroeconomics of it all, but you could safely say they still had the dollars to buy in. They were a big market and the Forged had a lot to sell.

That was the big story as it was being broadcast, but Riba was more interested in what the little newsnets and the independents had to say. Their reporters had rounded on the fact that, for anyone with an Abacand and a half decent recollection of secondary education, you could see that it was clearly impossible to return to Earth within three years when you'd been travelling away from it as fast as possible for thirty. Besides, General Machen, the commander-in-chief of all Solar military and police forces, had issued a statement that morning in Riba's very paper, warning against action until a thorough and full account of Isol's journey could be published. And that level of explanation meant there was something very bad going on.

By the time Riba took his seat upon the *Byzantium*'s viewing deck and observed the tedious rituals of Buck's Fizz before cast-off and salutes to the captain, he was already planning an in-depth exposé. He would write carefully of what facts he might find and he would argue with meticulous daring for the case of allowing the Forged complete freedom to self-govern – an angle his editor and the paper's owner were also not averse to because they hoped it would mean that most of the Forged would disappear from Earth.

They were an hour into their flight and had just begun the low-altitude portion of the journey to allow a spot of whale-watching when Riba decided to take himself on a tour of the ship. But after a few minutes he was sure that he was being followed. He thought it might be his contact. He took a few turns that led him into the relative privacy of the luxurious upper deck accommodation corridor and waited. Thirty seconds later a man approached him and Riba's neck hair stood on end for a second time that day. Not a woman in a green coat holding a leather bag but a man with long blond hair bound back into a queue and dark glasses, his powerful form almost entirely covered by a grey trenchcoat with its collar turned up high.

"Regrettably your investigation must end for the time being," this young man said without preamble. He took Riba's hand and arm in the semblance of a casual conversational hold though it effectively prisoned Riba in a vicelike grip. "I have been sent to send you to your contact." He began to tow Riba along the corridor at a swift pace.

Riba struggled, at first without trying to appear in trouble, but then more violently. He didn't like changes and he really didn't care for the strength that so easily overpowered his own.

"Don't make this difficult," the man warned him in a low tone and Riba realized that he wasn't the only one who was nervous.

"You are interfering with the lawful free press!" Riba asserted loudly in the textbook style. He was ignored in the same vein and found himself hauled along the ramp towards the aft gliding decks where wind-hangers and the elegant lines of individual air-yachts were moored by rope to the smooth flanks of the *Byzantium*.

"Yes, yes," said the agent. "That's my job."

"Help! This man is robbing me!" Riba shouted, but the *Byzantium*'s crew were busy at distant posts and the few passengers who were within earshot were of the kind who sank deeper in their seats or hurried away, afraid and embarrassed. Within moments both he and his captor were standing on the air deck, nothing in front of them except ten metres of beautifully finished hardwood landing strip and the blustery air over the ocean.

Riba scrabbled with his free hand in his pocket and signalled out with his Abacand, cuing emergency messages he'd had in place for just this awful moment. To his dismay a flat beep informed him that they were all blocked.

"It's nothing personal," said the agent, dragging him

towards the edge of the launch pad. "And nothing perma-nent," he added as he anchored his own feet with miracu-lous traction and pushed Riba over the side. Riba thought he saw bare feet not boots in that instant, and that the soles of the feet were covered in suckers.

This impression was wiped from his mind by complete terror as Riba understood that he was falling more than a hundred metres towards the unbroken waters of the Atlantic. He heard screaming and felt a searing pain in his throat as the gigantic hull of the *Byzantium* passed over him. His limbs flailed. He thought of helpless mice he'd held by the tail at pet shows, of Slattery's high-pitched hamster saying *I bet you didn't ask the mice* . . .

Riba turned gently in the airstream and saw the sea rushing to meet him. As he marked the likely spot of his demise he saw something that almost made his heart stop prematurely.

Something was rising up through the water.

A great beast, pale and vast, more massive even than the largest whale – he couldn't make out its exact shape. There was a centre, solid and near-white, but then there were great reefs and rafts of less tangible matter, tentacles and sheets of flesh that ballooned and snaked about in the surface water. For miles they seemed to reach out, a billion arms . . . He thought he saw a single enormous eye staring up at him and at that instant tried hard to die.

He fell and beneath him the creature suddenly thrashed and convulsed, stirring up a mass of bubbles into a frothing whirlpool where the simple sea waves had been. There was then no more time for thought. Riba met the ocean – not the hard, unyielding density of solid water, but the soft foam of the creature's ferocious wake.

He felt himself falling still. To his astonishment the water accepted him in a gentle way. It drew him down unharmed into the cold of itself. Thoughts of the creature instantly made him kick and thrash. Riba stared wildly about him, seeing only dim greyness and the leisurely upward race of a trillion bubbles, feeling the pressure of endless water in his ears and against his lungs, just like the man's hand on his arm – hard and merciless. He was deafened to everything but the sound of his own panic.

Riba made the surface choking and coughing and saw the awful pale hulk of the creature again as the shield of bubbles dissipated around him. Huge arms and fingers of translucent jelly, pocked with pink-edged suckers the size of saucers, reached towards him through the water. He turned and began to swim, hopelessly, but the tentacles were everywhere, some breaking the surface and turning their tips towards him where he saw, with horror, the distinct shapes of primitive pigment patches – yet more eyes.

Something cold and powerful snaked around his legs and bound them tight. He opened his mouth but was pulled under. His last sensations were of cold water, cold strength in flesh that wasn't remotely like any flesh he knew. His last impression was of stealthy and nimble fingers making a thorough attempt to pick his pockets.

When he woke Riba found himself lying on solid ground. It was so unexpected that he gave a start and discovered that, all things considered, he didn't feel that bad. His skin was sore from salt water abrasion and he felt battered but he was able to move to hands and knees and then climb to his feet with almost ordinary ease. His solid ground turned out to be a long white sanded beach, fringed by tall palm trees which stretched up to the sky and out over the baby blue shallows of a small lagoon. Not four metres away from him he could see the rivulet of a fresh water stream cutting a shallow groove through wet sand to the sea. He moved towards this and bent down for a cautious handful. In moments he was on his hands and knees, drinking and splashing.

He impressed himself with his resourceful skills as he remembered to take off his clothing and rinse it out, spread it to dry on the sand, clean off the salt on his skin and then move quickly into some shade. The day was hot and the sand even hotter. A few flies came and gathered around his wet skin and then left him alone. It was only as he took a rest and began to notice more of his surroundings that it occurred to him to wonder where he was and how he had got there.

A search of his clothes proved what he already suspected – his Abacand was gone. Now he had cause to wish he had taken up the subdermal kind of machine, but he had never fancied a permanent link to the digital world until this moment. Its loss made him feel twice as naked and a thousand times more vulnerable.

The giant squid thing must have taken it before abandoning him here. Riba didn't like to think of it as a thing, but without a name or a clade to place it in he couldn't help thinking of it that way. Of him. Of her. Whatever.

Riba sat back and tried to think. What had the blond man promised? Ah yes, this was not personal and not forever. So he had some hope of returning to his old life after all, even if he was the subject of a peculiar kidnapping as it was beginning to seem.

Riba waited impatiently for his clothes to dry so that he could make a full inspection of what he guessed might be an island. He hoped that even without the Abacand he might remember some of the very clever survival skills he'd so often admired in documentaries and that maybe he would outfox his captors and figure out where they were holding him before they picked him up again. Even so, could the squid have carried him all the way from near Ireland to the Caribbean? Squid had prodigious powers of speed and agility in the water and it had been a mighty monster but, even with the potential of extra powers from engines and the like, it was no quick journey.

He set off on his reconnaissance at an eager pace which soon became more cautious. The sandy lagoon rim gave way to rocky headlands which required a lot of effort and patience to climb over. Soon he was very hungry and very tired. He took another drink from one of the many rivulets escaping to the sea and lay down in the shade beneath two palm trees for a rest.

When he woke it was late afternoon. He found a green stick and went digging for clams in the sand. Within an hour or so he had collected a reasonable plateful – enough for a paella – and he had also, pleased with his cunning, decided that if he couldn't get them out alive he would get them out roasted and hot after baking them in a fire.

There followed a most trying several hours. There was no dry wood. There was no dry tinder. Stupidly he had been travelling without a magnifying glass. After two hours of failed efforts at making fire he gave up and, one by one, began to fling the shellfish back into the sea. Halfheartedly he tried to crack one in his teeth but his teeth would have cracked first.

Riba wrote in his head, "Without his tools to help him Man loses the evolutionary arms race to a humble mussel." But it was hard to laugh.

A moment or two later he began to hear unmistakable sounds of the progress of something inside the woods that backed on to the sand. Too tired to feel very afraid just yet Riba turned to watch, thinking of pigs or deer.

To his complete surprise what emerged from between the palm trees was a man with white hair and a thick white beard. He wore a rather severe suit and a high white collar tied up with a white cravat. All the white things stood out clearly against the darkness of the forest and the indigo of the sky behind him. What interested Riba most about him however, was not his clothing, or his cane, with which he had parted the last fronds of green before emerging, but the fact that in his other hand he was holding what looked like a china plate with something on it.

The old man waved his stick at Riba in a friendly way. "Hello there," he called out. "You must be Arnau Riba. A tricky man to find it seems. Don't trouble yourself so much, dear fellow. Here, I've brought you a sandwich."

Riba would remember for the rest of his life the taste of that sandwich – it was cheese and pickle – and the way it felt to eat it, so salty and tangy and indescribably wholesome as he stood and studied the face of this peculiar stranger. The eyes beamed at him. The tweed suit – he did not know how to explain the mirage of colours in that lovely wool or how prickly and hot it seemed, or how it sat upon the cotton shirt beneath the thick beard or how the sandwich and the man both merged into a curious saving grace that was quite ridiculous to him in the same instant that it was perfect.

"Forgive me," said the man with another smile, "I have you at a disadvantage. I am Jules Verne, the Right Hand of Pelagic Bathysaur Island Iukina. At your service."

Riba stared at him, eyes bulging, cheeks bulging, chewing. He thought about asking the obvious questions – who?, why?, what? – but took another bite instead. It seemed likely that answers would appear in time and they were less important right now than eating.

"Yes, Mr Riba," said Verne cordially, taking a deep, satisfied breath. "You are upon a living island afloat on the breast of the Atlantic. Me, in fact. And as such you are my guest. Welcome. I hope that you will forgive the delay in my locating you, but my eyes and ears, the flies, are easily diverted, and by the time they had told me of your whereabouts and I had made the journey, you were no longer at the location they remembered. A fly's memory, you know, is a strange and marvellous . . . ah –" Verne glanced down at the empty plate as Riba took the second half of the sandwich. Verne looked down, gently brushed off a few crumbs on to the sand. "I wonder if the crabs here will enjoy bread? No doubt they will. The water on this side is also very good of course, but many more refreshments are available a short journey away at the Club. I hope you feel able to manage a short walk?"

Riba, feeling the first hit of sugars arriving in his bloodstream had concluded, by the time that Verne began to speak of flies, that if the man were really a Hand – a physically human component of a greater human composite being – then he could be as dotty as he liked so long as there really were more sandwiches. Riba found it hard to believe in Forged like this one; that is, he had known intellectually that they existed, but he had never really thought about them in any practical fashion. He could not bring himself to quite believe that what he had stood on, sheltered on and been thwarted and restored by was a single being and not a volcanic atoll. But it made sense – there were no islands like this anywhere near the airship's course.

To the old man's question about walking he simply nodded. The old man smiled and turned, beating back stubborn bits of jungle with his walking stick as they retraced his steps. In less than two hundred metres Riba found himself standing on a hard dirt road. A small battery-powered car was parked there, looking neat and very red against the darkening green of the jungle. As the sun went down, and Riba sat feeling the roll of precision suspension carry him silently through the deep blue twilight, his surprise began to turn to curiosity.

His astonishment was completed when they rolled up towards the soft yellow lights of a large hut built on stilts. An expansive verandah ran all the way around it and the steps down to the car were lit with the twinkle of many small citronella candles to greet their arrival. Walking up and on to the smooth boards Riba felt a rush of gratitude for civilization in general. As he turned in through the doorway he saw a large room panelled in dark wood and furnished with the most beautiful and expensive furniture he had ever seen. At the heart of the room a fire burned within a stone bowl and near this fire a group of chairs were drawn close, each different, and each supporting a different figure with the exception of a tall wing chair which he assumed was Verne's.

A soft breeze blew in at their backs as Verne ushered him forward. As they approached Riba saw one of the others stand up and draw another chair forward to place within the circle next to the empty seat. This man then turned and came to greet them. He wore a well-cut suit, like a uniform, and carried a cap beneath his arm. Like Verne he had white hair and a white beard, but by contrast this man's beard was clipped neatly short and his hair was a great length that fell around his shoulders. Dark walnut skin crinkled around brown eyes as he held Riba with his gaze.

"Arnau Riba, I am a longtime admirer of your feature articles, if not your methods of investigation. I regret you found your introduction to the ocean so traumatic." He held out his hand and Riba took it, shook it, felt its strength and resilience as he wondered at the choice of words. He must mean Riba's fall.

"Permit me to introduce you," Verne said, putting the sandwich plate aside. "This is my good friend Captain Nemo, Hand of Bathysaur Nautilus Kalu."

"Nemo?" Riba repeated, finding the name ringing bells in his head. Then he began to understand. He stared at the merry smile of the man whose hand he still held. He saw the great eye of the huge tentacled monster that had churned the ocean up beneath him. It was only with the greatest willpower that he managed to keep a semblance of cool.

"No doubt you are wondering at our choice of Hands, Mr Riba," Nemo said. "Those who meet us often remark upon it and perhaps, to a person not as keenly aware of their intellectual and imaginitive forbears as ourselves, it must seem strange. Jules Verne was a Frenchman of the nineteenth century, one of the first great science fiction writers. He also lived in a time of great change and his studies of engineering and the natural world gave rise to stories of great adventure and the heights of invention to which human minds might aspire. Kalu and I see ourselves as the literal conclusion of the work of Verne and his contemporaries including the architect of your hometown, Barcelona – the incomparable Antoni Gaudi. In our physical forms you may witness the work of millions of scientists and artists, designers and engineers inspired by the works of these great minds. In our minds we hope you will discover the same unbridled imagination, and in our hearts the same abiding wonder, curiosity and love of the Earth and all her works. It is why we are here, Mr Riba, and it is also why you are here."

Riba looked from one of the old men to the other. "Jules Verne, the island's voice. I see. But Captain Nemo?"

"Why," said the captain, continuing in their peculiar and elegant way of speaking, "this is both by way of an homage and a small joke in one. Captain Nemo is Verne's most well-known hero. Like myself, Nemo is a scientist-explorer. He is also the captain of a submarine, named *Nautilus*, which is mistaken for a giant sea-monster when it sinks ships bent on acts of war. I myself am a Nautilus Class Forged, created to investigate and protect all the life of the oceans, in particular its greatest depths and, like Nemo himself, I seek peace."

"We appear as old men. Although we are nothing of the sort we think of ourselves as Jules Verne and Captain Nemo because the conceit has improved us and connects us by heart and mind to both the past and the future, history and dream. But here," Verne continued, taking Riba's arm and sweeping him onwards to the waiting circle. "Here are our other friends also glad to make your acquaintance. Allow me to introduce to you the illustrious Sinbad, Hand of the Wind-Drifter Velella of the same name – he was always named after the hero of the seas."

Riba shook hands with a young man dressed in flamboyant pirate colours, his hair beaded and a rapier-thin moustache on his top lip matched by a dagger of beard on his chin. He had no idea what manner of creature a Wind-Drifter might be but as the young man's green eyes sparkled he grinned and whispered to Riba, "I am the sailor and the boat, the crew and captain all in one. Look me up when you get home."

He sat down then and with a splash the lady of the group stood up from her rest, legs immersed to the knee in a porcelain tub of salt water. She was taller and more willowy than Riba, and looked like someone who has really gone to town on fancy dress for a party themed around fish.

"This lady is WaveRider Mermaid Silene, and she is here herself." Verne said.

Silene inclined her head regally, "Look, no hands!" she joked and then gave Riba her long, cool hand to clasp. Against his palm he felt the slight roughness of scales. The soft feather lines of gills on her neck lay demurely closed, like lines of paint. Only her hair gave it away – it was not human hair at all but fleshy and fibrous and deep crimson, like a kind of kelp. Then she sat and Riba moved along.

"Here is Ahab, Hand of MekTek Orca Moebius, fish-marshal."

Riba was sure that there was another joke in this, but he would have to look that up too. Ahab was a rough-looking individual whose clothing wouldn't have passed muster anywhere Riba knew. He looked as though he spent his life beachcombing and living on what he could find. He clapped Riba on the shoulder and gave him a stiff nod, without getting up.

"And last but by no means least the pioneering scientific documentary-maker and populist, Sir David Attenborough, Hand of ArchaeoTek Legion Ketier. Ketier is like a kind of Hive, Mr Riba – in the oceans, he is everywhere."

Riba shook hands with an ordinary looking kind of man in clothes much like his own. Then he was allowed to sit in his own seat, at Verne's right hand, and Verne sat also, completing the circle. Riba felt strangely moved, without understanding why. His throat was taut as Verne said, "Welcome, Journalist Arnau Riba, to the Adventurers' League and Dance Club of the Ocean. We are of the sea and pledged to defend her wealth and nurture her children. We adventure in body and spirit within her. We dance to her music."

They all smiled at his discomfort and puzzlement as a machine servant provided him with iced tea, but Nemo handed him back his Abacand, so he didn't mind it. He was too carried away with the itch to start collecting stories and the amazement that such a thing as the League existed, unknown to the Original and Unevolved humans.

"That's all great, Mr Verne," Riba said after a drink of tea, "but what about that agent who pushed me out of the *Byzantium*? I call that unfriendly. And why was it necessary to bring me here?"

"Do you mean this agent, Mr Riba?" Verne asked, and he gestured outside the circle to a door in the far wall of

the room where a tall, blond man had just entered. Although
he now wore much less clothing – only a pair of shorts –
which revealed his true skin to be the silver, blue and black
of a fish, his blond hair was unbound and he was clearly
the same individual. He carried his shades in one hand.

"This is the Pelagic Triton Mephisto, another member of
the League," Verne told him. "Don't be alarmed by his name
if you know it. He does not aspire to seize your soul."

Riba at least did understand this reference to Faust's demon.
"Only my arm from its socket," he said, standing up.

Mephisto held out his own hand. His eyes were unusually large and dark and in the dry air of the house they
teared rapidly so that he appeared to cry. "I regret the circumstances of our . . ."

"Yeah, whatever," Riba said. He glanced at the man's
silver and blue shining skin – warm and human around his
hands, face and feet, but as miraculously metallic and decorated as a mackerel elsewhere. The luxuriant blond mane
moved of its own accord now it was unbound. It was Tek.
"But what's this all about?"

"We have been trawling the same conversations on the
underground newsnets," Captain Nemo said as Mephisto
sat beside Silene on her wet bench. He put his feet in her
footbath and slid the special eyeglasses on to his face where
Riba saw they acted like reverse goggles, covering his eyes
with salt water.

Nemo continued, "We have drawn similar conclusions to
yours, Mr Riba, concerning the nature of Voyager Lonestar
Isol's return. We also have access to the Forged Uluru
network, which you and the Unevolved human world do
not. Your contact is known to us through the dream net of
Uluru and it was she who decided that you should meet us
here. I hope you will forgive her."

"That depends on what's going on," Riba said, amused
to think of his Chinese pipe-smoker as a girl. "Mind if I
record?" He held out his Abacand.

"We wouldn't have given it to you otherwise," Silene said
with a roll of her pretty blue eyes. "You're here to write."

"I don't write for . . ."

"Please," Verne held up his hand. "Let us be civilized. Nobody seeks to pocket you, Mr Riba. If you will permit me to explain?"

Riba shrugged and set the Abacand down between them on the polished surface of a marble-topped table, picking up his tea glass. They'd played hard and they'd played nice, he was stuck here, he might as well see what they'd got. And besides, it was so hard not to like them and their aspirations to nobility, in spite of everything.

"We know that Isol has returned with alien technology," Verne said quietly into the silence that followed Riba's assent. The only other sounds apart from his voice were the soft, distant wash of the ocean and the occasional snap from the fire. He had Riba's full attention now.

"We do not understand its nature or what it promises, but it must be responsible for her faster-than-light journey home. You were hoping to discover this and reveal it to be the cause of Solargov's silence on the matter, but of course, had you discovered this story, you would not have lived to tell it to any kind of conclusion. In sending you to us your contact has saved you from an untimely end at the hands of Machen's agents. Isol has promised the Forged freedom from the bonds of Earth, you see, and it is too soon to reveal this to the Unevolved masses. On that the League and its allies are in agreement with General Machen. Unfortunately most of the Forged are aware of it and it is likely that the Forged Independence Movement will soon trumpet it from the rooftops, so it's only a matter of days before it becomes common knowledge."

"So why deny me the story?"

"We would like you to *write* the story," Nemo said. "But we thought that if you were going to do so, you should have the benefit of a fuller picture, and not have to try to piece it together from little parts. There should be no misunderstandings here of the kind that led so many to war in the past. Civil war and insurrection must not take place within the system, nor on Earth itself. Not between the Forged and the Unevolved, which is what we fear will happen if this is handled badly. There are too many uneasy people on all sides with too little understanding."

"And what kind of understanding would this be?"

"Your paper is noted for its anti-Forged sympathies," the Triton said. "And you have written extensively yourself of how alien we seem to most Unevolved human beings; that we have created ghettos and cultures of our own which seek to exclude the Old Monkeys. You accuse us of racism, Mr Riba, although you do not use the word. It is implied by all your writings that that you see yourself distinguished from us in fundamental ways which deny our humanity. In recent editorials, not written by you, your media group have been advocating segregation as a solution to the tensions on Earth between Forged and Unevolved."

"I prefer the term Original," Riba said, although he was rankled.

"As you wish," Mephisto shrugged – a simple gesture that provided all the Gallic inferences of contempt that Riba had ever seen made. "It was our decision to invite you to spend some time with us in the hope that you might review your Original position."

"And if I don't?"

"Please do not become bullish," Verne said gently, but with great firmness, to both of them. "You are free to leave, Mr Riba," he leant forward and picked up the Abacand, "with or without your story."

Riba didn't like the direction things had taken much but he could see the sense of staying. "It isn't racism," he said, feeling a kind of devilish urge. "Racism is history. You and I are very different. That's all. People need their own kind around them. Why else do you even have this club?"

"Well that's the point!" Silene said irritably. "We aren't the same kind at all. Each one of us has as much in common with one another physically as we do with you, Mr Riba."

"I thought you and he . . ." Riba pointed from her to the Triton.

"It is a gulf of a mere two hundred or so genes and a

handful of proteins. More than separates you from a chimpanzee," the Triton said and added with a dryness that could have turned the Atlantic to a desert, "We do not breed in the wild."

"Mr Riba is playing with you," Nemo said. "He is no racist, are you?"

"No," Riba said, trying not to be sullen about it. "The differences are just an angle, that's all. And the coin flips both ways. Until the Forged came along there was no such thing as a real sense of generic human identity in the Originals, not one that could unite them over and above their religious and cultural differences. Now that's changed. We've got you. And you've got us, babe."

"And the MekTeks are out in the cold," Mephisto said, although he switched off his frosty demeanour. "But that's for another day. Today it is essential that Isol's radicalism and her determination to separate the Forged from the Sol government does not precipitate war, not least because most of the big guns these days are all Forged citizens and many of them are sympathetic to Independence. This prevention cannot come down to a single story of course, but much can be changed by a timely story – witness Mr Verne's effect on the world. More immediately, Isol's discovery of an alien presence so close to home could be exactly the generic constraint we have been needing to create a union between the Forged and the Originals."

As Riba thought it over Nemo revealed the details, "Tupac, the great Mother/Father of us all, says that the alien material is a substance against which Sol has no defences. Though it appears benign it is extremely powerful – changing shape at the user's will – and its true purpose cannot be fathomed. To our knowledge Isol is in voluntary quarantine at the Idlewild station out close to L4. But we suspect that the material is not confined to her possession. If the extremists in the Independence movement were to come into contact with it the effects could be devastating. Quite final in fact. They are single-minded."

"Can you get me an interview with Isol? With Tupac?" Riba asked.

"We speak for Tupac here," Silene said and touched the side of her head gently to indicate that she shared a digital link into the Uluru net where all the Forged communed. Riba saw that her long dark fingers were webbed although her thumbs were free. What he had taken for nicely painted nails were mother-of-pearl claws which expanded and retracted to enhance her gestures.

Riba sat and considered. Now here was a story for the ultimate conspiracy and paranoia theorist to feast on! A kidnapped journalist is given secret details of a potential weapon . . . He was already planning ways of presenting it, so that it would seem like matters were under control and so no one would panic, but at the same time he wondered how much Verne and the League were controlling him. With information and vested interests, one could never be sure.

"No doubt you suspect our agenda," Ahab said as they watched Riba thinking. It was the first time this wiry old sea-dog had spoken and Riba was surprised by the growl of his voice. "We have nothing with which to convince you of our information's pedigree and of our honest intent but one thing. Would you care to take a tour?"

Riba assented, got up and followed Verne, first to a room where he was provided with fresh, clean clothing and then outside on to the verandah at the back of the building. Nemo came with them, leaving the others inside. As they walked on to a long gangway that led off through the trees Riba heard calypso music begin to play behind them and wondered if they really meant the part about dancing.

The gangway took them down gradually to ground level in the dark of the forest but the way was lit by electric lights here, set like torches at the sides of the path. Soon they reached a door in a low stone archway which opened as they approached. Riba slapped a mosquito as they began to descend a staircase down and down into a well of rippling, water-cast light. After twenty metres the narrow stone came to a flat floor and they walked out under the sea beneath a protective shield of polycarbonate. They were under the lagoon, Riba guessed, as small fish darted in and out of the range of the light whose reach gave the illusion that they were captured within a greater cavern of water, forested with weed.

"This lagoon, along with my other specialised habitats, collects and protects the most endangered marine life," Verne said as they passed along the way. Frequently he stopped to point out an individual fish, animal or plant and relate its physiology to Riba, its habitat, its behaviours. It seemed there was nothing about them he didn't know.

As they left the lagoon proper and changed direction Riba saw a silvery flash in the corner of his eye and looked up and to his right. There he saw the Triton and the Mermaid wave lazily to him – that single flourish of their arms the only remotely true human gesture, for in their natural element they were transformed. Their legs, though still disjoined, fit together as smoothly and with as much fluid grace as a true tail. From their calves and backs elegant spines lifted and fanned fins. Between them swam the largest shark that Riba had ever seen.

The huge fish glided along with a relaxed, half-asleep momentum and passed barely inches over Riba's head.

"This is one of only fifteen Great Whites left on Earth," Nemo said as they watched the three pass into the dark again, the trailing fins of the Triton last to vanish as he shepherded the huge creature back into the deeper waters. Softly, softly, sweet calypso tunes filtered through the water as Riba listened to the sound of his heart and put his hand to the clear dome, to try and feel what might be out there, still unknown and almost lost.

They did not only show him sharks in the lagoon, but crocodiles at home in the small mangroves, saltwater ones with beady eyes and skins like pebbly beaches. They showed him a reef off the coast, of rainbow corals and the floating arms of sea urchins, the prickly spines of starfish and the darting fizzes of colour that were the billion fish, all facing into the gentle currents of the Island's smooth passage through the deep ocean. Silene swam to the viewing ports with a fish or a sea cucumber in her hands now and again, and Mephisto persuaded deeper-water beasts to show themselves in the light for a time; hammerhead sharks and the diamond shapes of rays with their aerial-like tails; huge conger eels with savage grins; bass and groupers. He brought in a shoal of mackerel and became almost invisible among them as they turned and darted in a single cloud.

"Even the fish that were most common are now much reduced, although the conservation measures mean that mackerel and tuna and the great so-called product fish, anchovies and sardines, are much more successful these days," Verne told him. "They're welcome passengers when the seas are rough, but we don't trouble them much unless our sharks are hungry."

"The true deep ocean is something I cannot show you personally," Nemo the Nautilus said as they walked out of the reef area and back towards the surface. "But my work there is bent on discovering the life and history of the oceans and the geology of the Earth beneath."

"Each of you are one of a kind," Riba said. "Why aren't there more?"

"An Island and a Nautilus are not easily made," Verne said. "The cost of Forging is always high. But we are worth the taxes, I hope you find. Together we form the marine conservation and research unit of the Earth. From the deepest to the most shallow, wherever the water is salt and creatures live off the sea we are there. And it is our intention that the oceans here, the only saltwater oceans in this system, possibly in existence, survive this encounter of Isol's. For that we cannot have a war. In war our energies would have to dissipate and we must choose a side – the Forged or Earth. We are bound to the Earth, how could we fight against it? Maybe some would, and so you see it would never be a simple matter of the Earth Forged leaving for new worlds, as Isol wants to promise and your media wishes to say. We will never leave the ocean. And we are not your enemy."

They had come outside again on the surface and took Verne's smart car. It drove them to the far side of the Island

and Riba saw the colonies of seabirds that girt the Island's windward side, vast cliffs of them clustered against the protecting shield of the mountainside.

Riba could stand on this island, and speak to it. This, above all, he could not get over. The Island was a habitat and a researcher, a scientist and a human being, a creature of the ocean who was land and sanctuary, a dreamer – so many things at once. He looked at Verne and then at Nemo as they returned to the car, the Island and the Monster of the Deep, walking together. He looked up through clear skies to the stars and the quick sweep of gleaming satellites. Out here there was no light except the small ones marking the car and the galaxy was visible, milky and rich across the roof of his world. How small was this ocean, and how large, he thought, with only the Forged themselves to shepherd us out there into the vastness of the true sea.

"I'll write your article," he said, joining the old men in the car. "What's the angle?"

"Jules Verne himself wrote not only to spread the wonder of scientific knowledge but also to raise awareness of its dangers," the Island said, through Verne the Hand. "Not that knowledge was dangerous, but that misapplication of it would always have serious consequences, both for the person who applied it and for the world. He lived at the beginning of the age when humans were to get their hands on the greatest powers and the greatest wealth. Many evils we might consider footnotes in history were current at the time – slavery among them. I propose that you consider presenting our information in the light of this perspective: to treat properly with any alien world we must strive to understand ourselves and the way that we create our own, and that to ensure our survival we must apply ourselves closely to the study of threats that lie both without and within."

"Doesn't sound like the kind of stuff that grabs the head-lines," Riba said.

"The headlines are up to you," Verne said as the car took them through the jungle back towards the house. The moon was out and the skies clear. Tupac shone like a star close to its side from her place in orbit. "I'm sure you'll think of something."

Riba was already planning his full-virtual Time magazine spread of *The Adventurers' League*, never mind his brief half-life in the global newsnets when it came to setting out the full story of Isol's trip and what she'd found. For good magazine sales you need a stable, literate population who want to talk. Wars were always good for that, but he could live with the peace, he thought, as he followed Verne up the steps and into the Club. He could live with the idea of noble adventurers on a secret island, eternally afloat, watching out for everyone.

"Hey, do I get membership here?"

"That depends on what you write, Mr Riba. It all depends . . ."

HECTOR SERVADAC, FILS

Adam Roberts

With The Mysterious Island *we see the end of an especially productive period of Verne's writing. Few of his next sequence of novels would capture the imagination in the same way as* 20,000 Leagues Under the Sea *and* Around the World in Eighty Days. *Verne seems almost to have lost his faith in mankind. Unlike his castaways in* The Mysterious Island, *who use their ingenuity to survive, the survivors on an open raft in* Le Chancelor *(1874/5) resort almost to cannibalism and murder before they are saved.* Michael Strogoff *(1876), about the war between Russia and the Tartars and envisaging a Tartar invasion of Siberia, was popular in France and remains well known if little read today.*

With his next novel, Verne's growing misanthropy turned upon science. Until now all of Verne's scientific novels had been assiduously researched to ensure painstaking accuracy. Hector Servadac *(1877), on the other hand, is clearly a fantasy. The Earth is struck by a comet and a chunk of it, including parts of Gibraltar and North Africa, are carried away into space complete with its occupants. The scientific consequences of such a collision are ignored, and the attempt to return to the Earth by balloon is equally preposterous. At the end it is suggested that the whole episode is a dream. In fact the book, which also contains some* of Verne's most racist views, has to be read in the same vein as Dr Ox's Experiment, *and that is as a satire upon isolationism and prejudice. It is a book that tells us far more about Verne himself and his views of the world than almost any of his other works.*

The strange dreamlike quality of the novel has been captured wonderfully in the following story which looks deeper into the nature of reality.

1

Hector flew in. It's OK, he caught breakfast on the plane. He doesn't need anything to eat, he's good. But there was a wait at the hire car desk, and the wait brought speckles of sweat to his face and torso. His flesh, having been starved of Californian sunshine, and having been seduced by French food for a year, had assumed the colour and consistency of mozzarella. He tried this line, self-deprecating and he hoped witty, on the woman seated next to him on his connecting flight. He smiled, sticking his lower jaw out and showing his teeth. His teeth, he admitted to her, had become Europeanized during this last year. That red wine, that ink-dark little coffee in the dainty little cups, those *gitanes*, the very air in Europe, it tends to stain. Stains the dentine. There are reasons, you see, why everybody in Europe has such crappy teeth. But what can you do? And you know what? he asked the woman in the seat next to him. Avignon has more Italian restaurants than French. I hadn't expected that. And Montpellier has more *American* restaurants than anything else.

"You mean," the woman asked, "McDonalds?"

But Hector could tell she wasn't really interested.

"Some," he said. "But, you know, Steak Houses. Of course, it's a big university town, Montpellier. Students love to eat American, fast food, steaks. That's the reason I was there, actually, doing some work at the university."

But she wasn't interested, she wouldn't be drawn, and when she started talking herself it became apparent that she was married, that she had a kid, and that Hector was on a hiding to nothing. He smiled and nodded as she talked, but not sticking his jaw right out, not the big beaming grin, just a polite smile, and a polite nod, and behind his eyes he was thinking, you could at least wear a damned ring on your finger, you could at least give me some heads-up.

At the airport he had to queue at the hire car desk. He told himself that a year in France had accustomed him to queuing; but as he stood there, looking through the glass walls of the terminal at the wide Californian view, the perfect blue of the Californian sky, the cars with their broad paneled paintwork glistening in the sunshine as if wet, some of his American impatience started to return. He fidgeted. He started sweating a little. Anger started warming inside him, although of course he kept it in check. At the head of the queue he was told that there would be a twenty-minute wait before he could be given the keys to his hire car. At least twenty minutes, we're sorry sir.

"Why?"

"There's been an unforeseen eventuality, sir," said the clerk. "I do apologise, sir. We can offer you a coupon for a complimentary breakfast in *Home Cookin'* whilst you wait, sir."

"No, that's OK," said Hector. "I had breakfast on the plane, I'm good."

2

When he finally got his car, when he finally drove out, he got lost on his route to the ranch.

The car's air-con was either too cold, or else not cooling enough. He kept fiddling with it. He made a pit stop, picking up a couple of cans and something to smoke, and then drove on out, drove east into the desert. The signs of human habitation became poorer, sketchier; the gaps between buildings opened up, and soon he was leaving the major roads and driving lonely tarmac under the cyanide blue of a perfect Californian day. He fiddled continually with the radio tuner as he drove. None of the stations seemed capable of playing two good tunes one after the other. One good song, one shit song, that seemed to be the playlist of every music station within broadcast range.

He got lost. It was probably deliberate, on an unconscious level. He told himself this with some self-satisfaction at his powers of auto-psychoanalysis; getting lost was his own passive-aggressive response to his father's passive-aggressive actions, his own subconscious way of saying "how am I supposed to find your fucking ranch? It's in the middle of *nowhere.*" To sell a perfectly good house, and buy a stretch of desert miles from anywhere – how could that be construed as anything *but* passive aggression on his father's part? Hector circled so completely, still, even at thirty-eight, in the symbolic orbital of his father, or rather circled the space his father occupied in his own cognitive map of the universe, that he could only understand this action (selling a house, buying a ranch) in relation to himself. What other explanation could there be? Dad was free to buy and sell what he liked, *of course*, he was free to dispose of his home, which only happened to be the house in which Hector had grown up, the house in which his mother had died – *of course* he could do that, if he wanted to. He could buy some waterless ranch miles from anyway, if he wanted to. He could join some cult, or whatever the hell it was, and spend all his money on subterranean whatever cables, if he wanted to. But why would he want to? Except to piss with Hector's head? And the lady on the radio was singing the song that told him, Hector, that he – made – her – *feel*, that he made her *feel*, like a nat-ur-al woman.

Hector sang along. But the next song was some Nashville crap, and he fiddled with the tuner again.

He stopped in a small town, in which there didn't seem to be a single building more than one storey high. He asked in the drugstore for directions, but the guy serving there couldn't help him. He stood on the main street for long minutes, in the heat, looking vaguely about, thinking maybe a cop could help him, but he couldn't see a cop.

Above him the sky was a deep blue, a dark lacquered blue upon which a handful of high feathery clouds looked like scuffs. And there, tiny as a bug, was a plane, drawing two tiny, scratchy lines after it, crawling over the sky. Just visible was its boomerang wingspan, its missile fuselage. It looked like a Christmas ornament.

He bought a map at the gas station and spread it on the passenger seat. He'd parked in the sun, and the material of the seats was hot as if it had just that minute been ironed.

3

The two-hour drive took Hector four and a quarter hours, but finally he rolled up to the gates of his Dad's new place. Hector senior had thrown a fence around the whole area, but most of the land was in a dip or depression in the land so pulling up at the gate afforded a fine view of the ranch. There were half a dozen buildings, including several tall barns. Several heavy machines were visible, diggers, tractors. Huge spools of cable lay piled in the shade of one of the barns. Round-shouldered apricot-coloured hills dominated the horizon.

Hector pulled out his mobile and called his Dad's landline. After a dozen rings his Dad picked up.

"Dad? I'm here. I'm at the gate."

"Yeah," replied his father. He always, or so it seemed to Hector, began his sentences with this drawly, emphatic assertion of positivity. More than a tic it had become a self-caricaturing habit. "Why didn't you use the intercom?"

"I'm using my mobile."

"Yeah. Well, the gate's open."

And so it was. Hector got back in the car and nudged the gate open with the fender; and, not bothering to stop, get out, shut it again, he drove straight down the side of the little hill into the declivity where the ranch house was. Pulling up to park alongside a grey four-by-four, itself parked beside a truck, he could see his father standing on the porch with two other people.

Hector climbed out of the car, and pushed a smile to the front of his face. "Hi Dad, hi" he called, energetically. "Hey, you look *great*." But he didn't look great; his hair had thinned across the crown, and large amoeba-shaped freckles, horribly expressive of advancing age, had come into being across his broad brow and scalp. Old, old. But as he came up the steps of the porch one at a time, Hector was also aware of how he must look to his father; podgy, nervy, pale.

They hugged, Dad's face swimming up close like an asteroid ready to crash into the world of Hector's head, but swerving to one side at the last minute. The old man clapped his son's back, and Hector returned the gesture, but there was little heat in it. Hector had seen something, something almost imperceptible, in his Dad's eyes the fraction before they had actually embraced. It occurred to him, as if for the first time, that his father was actually scared by his son.

Not physically scared, of course; this tall, lean, still-muscular man could face no plausible physical threat from his shorter, jellied, breathless offspring. Not that, but something more abstract and therefore even more startling. Because Hector's father was not one to spend too much mental energy on abstracts; and yet it was as if, looking at his son for the first time in a year and a half, the older man had experienced a sort of unnerving, a tremor in the soul. It was a revelation for Hector, who had always completely taken it for granted that his father was much stronger than he in character as well as in body; that this seemingly self-sufficient man might look nervously upon the arrival of his son to his house; that he might not know what to say; that he might be anxious about making a fool of himself, of simply having to interact with this other human being – this had literally never occurred to Hector before. And he had the miniaturely vertiginous sense of himself as his father must see him: not merely out-of-shape and fidgety, but as

his own flesh and blood rendered implacably and impene-
trably other by the process of growing up, of a monstrous
hybrid between his father's self and the safely alien other
people in his father's life.

The old man stood back, and looked at his son. "Yeah,
guys," he said, apparently talking directly at Hector but in
fact addressing the two people standing behind him on the
porch, "this is Hector junior. Hec, that's," he added with a
hitchhiker's gesture of his right thumb over his shoulder,
"Tom Brideson and Vera Dimitrov, we call her Dimmi.
She's," he went on, after an awkward little pause, "Bulgarian."
And then, after another pause, as if the thought were belatedly occurring to him that he should warn his son away
from her, he added, "yeah, she's with Tom, they're a couple."

"I'm delighted to meet you," said Hector, relishing his
chance to try on a little bit of his newly acquired, flouncy
old-European manner.

"Good to meet you," said Tom.

"Yes, nice to meet you," said Vera, in accentless English.

Father and son stood looking at one another. The
awkwardness was palpable, almost painful. "I got your book,"
Hector senior said, shortly. The book had been, in fact, one
issue of an academic journal, *Art and Aesthetics*, in which
Hector had published an article about late Cézanne.

"Great," said Hector, adding, superfluously, "I hope you
didn't read it. You didn't need to read it."

"Yeah," said his father, meaning no. And then: "Marjorie
not with you?"

Hector took this, almost eagerly, as an excuse to talk
about himself. "To tell you the truth," he said, rocking back
on his heels, "Marj and I are going through a more distant
period right now. We're still amicable, we're still on dinner-
and-wine terms, but she's in London now. I think she's
seeing a guy there. We parted on perfectly amicable terms.
I mean, it was never as if we were going to get *married*."
But looking again at his father's face he could see that these
details were of no interest to him at all. A realization dawned.

"Oh," he said, his shoulders slumping a little. "Did you

ask that in our self-appointed capacity as the new frigging Noah?" He started into this sentence thinking it a witty observation, a chirpy son-to-father thing to say; but as soon as the words were spoken he realized how much *venom* he was expressing, how angry this ridiculous new phase in his Dad's dotage was making him. His own rage unnerved him. "Two by two into the ark, Hec and his mate, is that it?"

Hector senior didn't flinch. "Yeah," he said.

4

He heard the whole story, but not in one continuous narrative: instead it came out in a couple of separate interchanges with his father, and with some of his father's disciples. Hector junior took his small suitcase upstairs to a bare room with a single bed, and unpacked whilst his father stood in the doorway. The room had white walls and a plain crucifix over its single window. There was a deal dresser with glass handles screwed into the wall. There was no TV. "Yeah," said Hector senior, "there's a radio in the bottom drawer. It's a wind-up radio."

"Thanks," said Hector.

"You hungry? We had lunch already. But – if you're hungry?"

"So," said Hector, "those two, the Bulgarian girl and the other guy, they are living here?"

"They live out back."

"Out back?"

"The second building. There's a group."

Hector put a folded shirt in the top drawer. "I see," he said. "Like a commune?"

"Yeah," said his father, but he was shaking his head. "You might jump to that conclusion. But they're allsorts. A dozen or so. Mix of genders."

"This end of the frigging world," said Hector, not looking at his father. He couldn't bring himself to say *fucking* in his father's presence. "It's an extreme thing to believe, isn't it?

It's old, Dad. It's bent out of shape, don't you think? Are they all religious, the ones staying?"

At first it seemed as if his Dad wasn't going to answer. "I couldn't lay the cables without them. Besides, we'll need them later." And then: "You want to have a look round the new place?"

"Sure," said Hector.

They walked together around the half dozen buildings; the ranch house, and a newer barn-like building with a dozen rooms inside it. Another barn was filled with an astonishing mass of supplies, tinned food, seeds, huge drums of something or other, electrical equipment, mysterious crates. "You got a storehouse here," Hector said, "that any survivalist would be proud to own."

"Yeah," said his Father.

The sun was so hot it felt like a heated cloth wrapped around Hector. It made his eyes water.

A group of half a dozen men and women were working out the back, spooling a fat serpent of cable from a large mechanized wheel on the back of a truck. The cable was going in the ground. Away in the direction of the lay, on the side of hill, a second group were digging a hole. Hector senior introduced the cable-laying workers to his son, and Hector junior forgot all their names straight away.

As they walked back to the ranch house, Hector asked, "The cable?"

"A special carbon bond," was the reply. "It's a strengthening thing, yeah. It binds the land, strengthens it. The clever thing is that it has some *give* in it, it's not too rigid, see, so it helps absorbs the tremors. It'll keep the ranch in one piece."

"OK," said Hector, wincing inwardly to see his father so evidently throwing his money away on this crank end-of-the-world notion, "I see. For earthquakes, is it?"

"Any kinda tremor," said his father.

Inside they fetched two mid-day beers, and sat down on the porch outside to drink them together. They talked about the book. "I read the book," Hector told his Dad. "After I got your email. The end of the world is nigh!"

"Yeah," said his Dad.

"Took me a while to track it down," said Hector. The sentence didn't come out as rebuking as he'd thought, or hoped, it might. "That title *Off On A Comet*, that's not the title in French. I," he added, preening a little, "I read it in French, you know."

"Yeah," said his Dad. The bright sunlight brought out the lines in his face, like acid resolving the grooves and gouges into an etcher's plate. They fanned from the corners of his eyes, like the route-maps provided by airlines from a hub, Atlanta say, to a hundred destinations. His left cheek had a deep fold running from his eye to the corner of his mouth, but there was no corresponding fold on his right cheek. Perhaps he slept always on his left side, always pressing the crease into that side of his face, every night.

"It's a crazy book," he told his father.

"Yeah," said his Dad. "It's some book."

But this was not what Hector had meant. "So," he said, breezily, "the hero, this guy you reckon is an ancestor – he's in the French army in Algeria. And this comet hits the earth, and he's there with his batman and at first he thinks it's resulted in this great flood, since he's surrounded by sea which he wasn't before." Hector's father stared impassively at his son during this recital of a story that he knew perfectly well. But Hector junior wanted to stress the absurdity of the adventure, and hence of his father's new craze. "He searches about and finds some more survivors of this comet-hit, and they all band together, but something's gone screwy with the heavens, the sun's rising in the west –"

Hector paused, loitering over this point for reasons he didn't wholly fathom within himself.

"Rising in the west, and Venus looming large, and so on. Then it turns out they're all living on a chunk of land – *and* sea, which is I think we can agree *pretty* tough to swallow – that's been knocked off the earth by the collision of the comet and carried away *on* the comet . . ." Hector shook his head. "You see how crazy that is?"

"Yeah," said his Dad. "Tell me – how is it crazy?"

"Well for one thing, this comet crashes into North Africa, scoops up a chunk of the ground, and flies on . . . but the people on the chunk of land can still see the sky, they're not you-know *embedded* in the comet, so the chunk of ground must somehow have been flipped over through one-hundred-eighty . . ." He grinned a goofy grin to emphasize how stupid this was. "Then they fly through the solar system, with – you know, gravity, and with atmosphere, and with the sea freezing rather than boiling off into space, it's daffy."

"Yeah," said Hector senior.

"And then they return to the earth at the end and they plan to float off the comet in a balloon, and then they just float into the Earth's atmosphere, *phhhw*." Hector raised his hands, palms upwards, in front of his chest, as if lifting two fragile, invisible spheres. "Crazy. And then they get home, and nobody's noticed that they've even gone, and nobody seems to have figured that a comet carried off half of Algeria. I mean, what is that? Is it one of those, And I Awoke and Behold it was a Dream things?"

His father was staring into the middle distance. How he could look so long, without sunglasses, without even wrinkling his broad blue eyes, was beyond Hector.

"Then I figured the name of the guy, the title of the book in French, is Servadac, and that's '*cadavers*' reversed. You see? So I figured it was a trope," and as he spoke, he revised his words *en courant* to an idiom more appropriate for his father, substituting, "a manner of speaking, a metaphor rather than a literal account. It was Verne deconstructing, you know, Verne criticizing and playing around with the conventions of nineteenth-century science fiction. I wondered whether it isn't all about death, and spirit journeys, what are they called, astral journeys, and heaven and hell and so on. I'm not hugely experienced in reading these sorts of texts. Books I mean." Hector had minored in English, but it had mostly been Shakespeare and African-American literature. He had majored in History of Art.

"It's kind of a shame," said his father, in a low voice with a burr underneath it, as if he needed to clear his throat with a strong cough, "that you didn't bring Marjorie with you."

5

Outside, alone, Hector walked over to a low concrete structure, three feet in all directions, perhaps some sort of bunker or store, and sat on the edge of this and smoked a cigarette. The fact that the ranch was in a declivity gave it a weirdly foreshortened, film-set feel; the horizon looked close enough to touch. The sky above was pure, cyanide blue. The sunlight felt heavy and hot. He wondered, absently, whether he shouldn't borrow a hat from his Dad.

No cicadas spoiled the perfect silence.

At Yale, where he'd majored in Art History, Hector's room-mate had been a theology student, a lawyer's son from Pennsylvania called Orwell Matthiesson. Hector remembered his own astonishment, imperfectly hidden behind a bottle of beer in a dim-lit bar, when Orwell had described – laughing, as if it were the biggest joke in the world – *punching* his own father during a fight. "You actually hit him?" Hector had asked, goggling. Orwell was a beanpolish, sharp featured guy with long arms and big hands. "Sure," he had replied. "I whaled him in the stomach. He saw the blow coming, he was able to tense up, no harm done. He was *mad*, though. Man he was mad with me. But you know how it is when you're having a fight with your Dad, you know how fierce it can get."

But Hector didn't know. He had never once fought with his Dad, never so much as raised his voice, or stormed out of a room. He had barely even contradicted his father, during all the long years growing up in the LA house. In fact, as he looked back on his childhood and adolescence from the vantage point of Yale freshmanship, he could barely remember talking to his father at all. What did they have to talk about?

He had decided to study Art History because, he told himself, he loved art; but his first year at school had been a process of fastidiously unlearning his visual tastes; or if not unlearning (for the sorts of paintings that moved him as a teenager still stirred something in him as a student, against his better judgment) then rather a carefully modulated process of systematic repression of his gut-responses. His mother had been an artist, producing brightly coloured figurative canvasses depicting lush natural landscapes, or animals, or nudes with animals, or sometimes, Hector shuddered to recall (for these were the paintings that sold in California in the seventies) unicorns, dolphins, pumas, starscenes, zodiacal interpretations. As a child Hector had almost worshipped his mother's ability to conjure these images out of two boxes of paint and a stretch of canvas. As a teenager, he had of course acquired distance from them, which out of her presence sometimes took the form of disdain; but his taste in the fine arts was indelibly marked by his childish immersion in those images: he loved Gauguin, he admired (without true heart's yearning) Van Gogh, he thought Chagall beautiful. At Yale, however, after some over-enthusiastic partisanship, it dawned on him that these sorts of artists marked him as insufficiently aesthetically sophisticated, and so he conditioned himself to love abstract art, to prefer Leonardo's sketches to his completed paintings, to drop names like Ben Nicholson and Karen Waldie. He had settled on Cézanne as a doctoral topic in part as a compromise between the figurative and the abstract. Compromise was one of the badges of his life, like stretch-marks on his soul. Coming to terms with the world, the world meeting him less than half way. It was the realization that growing up was, beyond a certain point, a kind of shrinkage.

He had never really known what his father did for a living. Something in business, it seemed. Something involving selling, or speculating, with the now-wealthy ex-hippies of San Marino and Silverlake and Los Feliz.

Hector sat on the concrete cube in front of the ranch house and pondered as the smoke scraped into his lungs with its delicious thousands of miniature hooks, and his skull relaxed minutely. When he said to his Dad, about the Verne novel, "You see how crazy that is?" he had actually been saying "you see how crazy your life is now, Dad? You see how insane you were to sell the house and buy this ranch and move here with these weird followers, these cultists, whatever they are?" But if his Dad had deciphered this particular communication, he didn't show it. There ought to be a way, Hector thought to himself, that I can tell Dad what I really feel.

The Bulgarian woman (Hector had forgotten her name) had come out of the house and was walking over the dirt towards him. As she approached the sound of an industrial drill started up, from somewhere well away, behind the main building. The distance shrank it to an amplified mosquito noise.

"Hello," she said. "Do you mind if I sit with you?"

By way of response Hector offered her a cigarette. "Smoke?"

She didn't reply, instead settling herself on the edge of the concrete, disconcertingly close to Hector. Their hips were touching. Her legs, as long as Hector's, stretched straight out. Even in heavy-duty jeans, he could see that they were good legs, shapely legs. Trying to be surreptitious, he glanced up and down her body. His intimate from-above perspective of her breasts gave her a shelf-like forcefulness of figure. Her curling hair was dark brown. It smelt faintly of candy. Her face, which had struck Hector earlier as conventionally pretty in a broad-set sort of way, looked better in profile: the clean lines of her nose running down to a proportioned tip of flesh at the end, lines at the edges of her mouth suggesting a laughing personality. Despite his Dad's warning, Hector's libido, or perhaps it would be more accurate to say his mere habit of bodily response, perked up at the prospect represented by this woman. He imagined her undressing. He imagined placing his hand, purposefully, on the spot where his hip had accidentally achieved contact with hers. He speculated about the way her flesh would feel under his fingers; not too taut, not too slack. And straight away, without thinking about it, without weighing the propriety or even likelihood of success, he began wondering about the best way to get her into bed – a direct address, a sly insinuation, a slow seduction. His cigarette had burnt into a drooping hook of ash. He dropped it in the dirt.

"I'm sorry?" he asked. She had said something to him, but he'd been too preoccupied with the entwining physicality of her presence, and he hadn't properly heard.

"*Je pense que vous cherchez*," she said, looking straight ahead, "*une simple question qui n'exigera qu'un oui ou un non. Mais c'est n'pas ça facile.*"

The fact of her speaking in French further confused Hector's fidgety, jetlagged mind. "I'm sorry?" he said again.

"You have," she said, turning her head enough to see him out of the corner of her eye, and presenting another attractive half-profile, lips that Hector felt an actual physical itch to reach over and kiss, "just come back from France, I think?"

"Yes," he replied. And belatedly, he added, in his flat American-accented French, "*c'est vrai. C'est simplement que votre mots prononcés . . .*"

"It's alright," she said, smiling warmly and thickening the laughter lines prettily at the edges of her mouth. "Only I wanted to say that this question does not exist. It is more complicated than a simple yes or no, is all I wanted to say. If you could stay here longer, you'd maybe understand."

This puzzled Hector; and piqued him too, as if he were being banished from the sexual possibilities of this woman as soon as he had been introduced to them. "I can stay," he insisted. "Why can't I stay? Does Dad want me to go?"

She was still looking at him out of the side of her eyes. "You misunderstand. I have not expressed myself well. You will stay as long as any of us. Only, if you could have come earlier, it would have perhaps been better."

Hector had an insight into what she meant. "Is it happening soon, then? This end of the world stuff?"

"Tonight," she said.

The sound of the drill rose and fell in the hot air.

"Well," said Hector, trying to think of something witty and ingratiating to say to this woman, whose hip was still pressed so suggestively against his, "I guess I'll get an answer to my question soon enough. Tonight, I guess." He fiddled a new cigarette out of the packet, and slipped it into his mouth. "What happens when, or if, I should say – if tomorrow dawns and everything's still the same as it was? I mean, like the millennium. I often wondered how the people who really believed the world was going to end in 2000, how they felt waking up the next day and realizing they were wrong."

Instead of answering this, the woman said, "I said *if you could stay here longer* because we hoped you could have come weeks ago, and then we could have persuaded you of the inevitability of this thing. But your father thought you would get into a temper and leave, and then you would be away from the ranch when it happens." Her accentless English slowed over these last three words, to give the unspoken "it" an appropriate weight. "So it is better that you are here only today, although it will be a shock for you when it happens."

"*If* it happens," said Hector. He clicked his skull-topped metal lighter and placed a knob of fire on the tip of his cigarette. "I'm sorry," he said, drawing and blowing off a lungful of smoke before removing the cigarette from his mouth and holding it away from her, "I should have asked – do you mind?"

She was looking away from him now, which gave Hector licence to peer closely at the interwoven fibres of her curly brown hair, at the snuffbox indentation in the exact centre of the back of her neck. She smelled sweet, the heat and light squeezing wafts of whatever conditioner she used out of her hair straight to Hector's nose.

The drill stopped its noise, and sudden silence was almost as startling as sudden loudness. Hector looked hastily to the front, not wanting to be caught staring.

"I love Hector," the woman said. And for a moment

Hector's heart scurried in his chest, and he could sense the blood pumping in his head; but she meant his father, of course. The downstroke of this realization, with its release of petty annoyance, almost tipped Hector into vindictiveness; he almost asked, *and are you sleeping with him then?* But he did not ask this question. Instead he dragged on his cigarette, and looked away to cover his confusion.

"If you'd been able to stay for a few weeks," she said, "you might have had one of the visions yourself."

"Oh," he said, scornfully. "Visions, is it?"

"They are very eloquent visions."

"Yeah?"

"Without your father," she said, simply, "I would be, now, in Europe, and tomorrow I would be dead. You also."

"Everybody dies," he said; but although he intended this as debonair and fearless, it came over merely as flip and rather callous. He sucked too strongly on his cigarette again, and had to stifle a cough. "I used to imagine," he said, spontaneously, with a tingling in his chest of the sort he felt when he was doing something reckless, something filled with the possibilities of huge triumph and huge disaster mixed together, like asking a beautiful woman out, or attempting a risqué answer to a crucial question in an important interview, "I used to imagine exactly what it would be like to fight with my Dad. I used to lie awake at night, when I was at college, planning exactly what I'd say, exactly what his response would be, how I would cut him down to size, everything. But it never came to the right moment in actual life. There are so many things," he went on hesitantly, although in fact exaggerating his hesitancy of expression because he felt this was something he ought to express in a circumspect fashion, "so many things that I've never been able to communicate to him, about how I feel."

"Your father thinks," she said, as if replying to this confession, "that it is merely a random matter that he got the visions. That it could have happened to anybody. But I don't think so. I think he got the visions because of who he is."

She hopped off the ledge and turned to look at him. Her

breasts moved just out of synch with the rest of her body, a fact of physics that sent jangles of electric excitement along Hector's nerves.

"Hey," he said, uncertain what to say.

"I think you like me," she said, and smiled.

Hector simply stared at her.

"Perhaps you are worried about Tom, but after tonight it won't matter so much. The first child I have *will* be his, and maybe the second. But genetic mixing is an important part of this, of this whole thing, and there are only a few men here, and it would be foolish to be too exclusive."

This, Hector thought, wide-eyed, was perhaps the most extraordinary speech a woman had ever spoken to him. "Christ, you're forward," he said, gruffly, suddenly aware of his own Adam's apple, like an unswallowed lump in his throat. "Christ."

"You do not remember my name," she said, smiling again. And then she turned and went back inside.

6

He ate that evening with the whole group, sitting on the porch, scooping beans and fried potatoes and hot dogs western-style, and watching the setting sun polish the distant round-shouldered hills a startling lobster-red. He still couldn't remember anybody's names, but the mood of the group was chatty, informal. "Isn't the world supposed to be ending in a few hours?" Hector asked nobody in particular, loudly, after his third beer. "You're all mighty jolly." But his only reply was laughter.

He only spoke to his father for a few minutes in total that evening. "I was just wondering, Dad," he said, emboldened by the booze, and by the strange social environment (and with the Bulgarian's strange words still buzzing in his brain from earlier), "about this Jules Verne book."

"Yeah," said his Dad, looking levelly at him.

"I was just wondering. I don't see how it can be, you

know, *real*. It's so wacky."

Hector senior nodded. The Bulgarian woman's boyfriend, whom Hector now knew, after what she had said, was called Tom, was sitting close to him; and he leant in at this point. "Servadac knew Verne," he said, smiling. "Had worked as a crewman on his yacht. When he had *his* vision, he went to Verne. That's what happened."

"Yeah," said Hector senior, nodding sombrely, as if he knew what the hell this was about.

"Verne wrote it up, published as fiction of course. But, as a novel, it's so far removed from his usual thing – his usual thing, you know, is *thoroughly plausible* machines and inventions, it's all very much feet-on-the-ground stuff. But *Off On A Comet*, man, that's strange. *Servadac*. Didn't you think it was strange?"

"Sure," said Hector.

"That marks it out. Its very strangeness is the badge of its truth."

"I guess I don't understand what you mean by true."

"It came to him, to Servadac, *as* a vision, a vision so intense he felt he was *living* it," Tom said, with unnerving vehemence. "It was a warning. It came a little early, yeah. But it was a true warning."

Hector played with his beer, picking at and peeling away the Budweiser label, rolling it up between his finger into a skinny cigarette, and then unrolling it. He could not think of a suitably forceful manner of expressing how absurd this sounded to him. Once Tom had moved away to talk to somebody else, he leant closer to his Dad and asked: "You really believe that?"

His father only nodded.

The light faded, the red hills becoming cigar-coloured, and then they were black against a carbon-purple sky fantastically replete with stars. Some people, as if to preserve the wild-west mood, were lighting actual oil lamps and suspending them from the overhang.

Hector took himself off to bed.

He had slept on the plane over from France, and had

been able to stay awake all day without much bother. This was his patented failsafe technique for dealing with jet-lag: to push through the first full day, to resist the urge to nap in the afternoon and then to go straight to sleep at the proper time. Nevertheless his body clock was operating according to a different logic than the daytime-nighttime of California, and he did not feel sleepy at this point.

He undressed, naked in the heat, and sat in bed to read for a while. There was no bedside table, or bedside lamp, so he was forced to read by the main ceiling light. Attempting to move his bed to be better placed underneath this light source he discovered that all four legs were screwed into the floor. This annoyed him. And so instead of reading his book, he sat up, with the cotton sheet over his naked body, and fumed mentally. He wanted to masturbate, but at the same time he half-hoped, whilst more than half-disbelieving, that the Bulgarian woman would come to his room; in which case he wanted to keep himself in a state of appropriate readiness.

The lightshade threw a wineglass shaped shadow over the ceiling.

If Dad had been possessed by the Bible, he thought to himself, would that have been better or worse? Possessed by the book of Mormon, and visions that told him to build a temple in the desert, something like that? But that would have been worse, because his Dad had always been thoroughly practical and material; it was his Mom who had been artistic and mystical. And his Mom had died, and floated away to some mystical realm, beyond Hector's reach, whilst his Dad had stayed right here, thank you very much, slap in the middle of the material, physical realm, living and breathing and smelling of sweat. *Jules Verne*? It was too outlandish even to be weird, like something so cold it feels hot.

He ordered the thoughts in his brain. He told himself: I'll put these thoughts in some sort of order in my brain, file them away, and then I can go to sleep. And, glancing at the inside of his bedroom door, if this woman comes, she can damned well come and wake me up.

It was the *particular* book that galled him. For his Dad to think that – say – *20,000 Leagues Under the Sea* was a true story would be one thing, surely batty but within the realm of possibility. Maybe some nineteenth-century billion-aire could have secretly constructed a submarine, and blah-blah-blah, and maybe it had been hidden from the world and blah-blah-blah. But *this* book, with its kooky Hale-Bopp-cultist air, its fly-away-on-a-comet-to-paradise nonsense? And his Dad had had visions, telling him *this* book was true, that the world was going to end this way?

He had not, he realized, ordered his thoughts. He had made himself more annoyed. He got out of bed and turned out the main light and got back into bed. He lay in the dark for a *long* time, thank you very much.

7

So, he went to sleep. It was dark, and he went to sleep. Despite the fact that his body thought it was mid-morning rather than late at night. In fact, he fell asleep just as he was telling himself that, in a minute, he'd get out of bed and turn the light back on so as to be awake when the world ended. But, with the perversity of the unconscious, it was this that acted as a trigger and propelled him into sleep.

So when the world indeed ended, he was asleep.

He was woken because somebody was shaking him, rocking him from side to side in the bed. The sheet was on the floor beside the bed.

Nobody was rocking him from side to side. He was alone in the room. But he was rocking from side to side.

He yelped, and woke up, or, more precisely, came to an approximation of consciousness. Grains of sleep made his eyelids sticky and unresponsive.

He jumped out of the bed. At some level of his half-awake brain he knew this was an earthquake. He'd grown up in California, so he knew about earthquakes, and he told himself that the thing to do was get out of the house as fast as possible, to get the *hell* out of *there*.

He stumbled to the door and pulled it open. It felt like a live thing in his hands, trembling and shaking as if afraid. He flung it open, but it bounced and juddered back and forth on its hinges. The floor heaved beneath him as if the room were about to vomit. The straight rectangle of the doorframe warped as he staggered through it to a parallel-ogram, and then flicked back to a rectangle.

The carpet wriggled underneath his naked feet as he rushed at the landing. In the funhouse surrealism of this jelly house, and in his half-awake, panicked state, Hector acted instinctively. He ran as if he were in the Pasadena house; not this strange new ranch, but the house he knew in his bones, the place where he had grown up. He ran in the dark and turned right to bound down the staircase. But there wasn't a staircase. Instead he received a smack across his stomach, as if somebody had thwacked him fairly hard with a pool cue, and suddenly he was falling.

His mind clarified with extraordinary suddenness. The earthquake tremor vanished from his senses. He understood instantly what he had done; he had run right through the railing along the top of the landing and was falling through space, such a *stupid* thing to do, such (he immediately believed, with complete conviction) a stupid way to *die*. He thought two thoughts in rapid succession: one, an annoy-ance that he had never even learnt the name of the Bulgarian woman; the other, more self-remorseful wail, *I'm thirty-eight and I'm going to die without even getting* tenure *for fuck's sake*.

He was weightless for the second, or second-and-a-half, of the fall.

Then he collided with something that jarred his ankles painfully. He felt a tumble of further motion, up-down, diffi-cult to make sense of in the dark, and then he was standing upright on the trembling floor. It took considerably longer to understand that he was still alive than it had done to realize that he was falling. His heart was gulping repeatedly in his chest, and his nerves burned along his limbs and up and down his torso.

In his mind came one thought, with bell-like clarity: her name is Vera Dimitrov and they call her Dimmi.

The earthquake was still going on, but it seemed diminished in comparison with the intensity of Hector's own aftershock and fear. He turned on wobbly legs, and looked behind him. In the extreme dimness of the hallway he could just make out the crescent shape of the sofa that had broken his fall. He had burst through the railing at the top of the balcony hallway, and happened to land exactly on the central cushion. He had bounced up and forward and come to rest where he was now standing. It was a fluke.

A light went on. Hector flinched.

His father came in. "Are you up?" he asked.

"It's an earthquake falling," said Hector, through a gummy mouth. "We should get outside."

With a precision of diction that only added to the sense of unreality pervading the night, Hector senior said, "The house is reinforced. The house is the safest place to be right now. Go back to bed, Hec. Go back upstairs to bed."

Still trembling, Hector obeyed his father, pulling himself up the stairs by the shuddering banister and retracing his steps to his room. As in a fever-dream he clambered back onto his juddery mattress, and pulled the sheet back over himself, and lay there whilst the world shimmied and shook all around him.

8

He fell asleep again, despite all the shuddering. When the earthquake subsided he woke, with the unexpected stillness of the earth; but an aftershock ruffled through the ground, and another one, and he started counting them, and soon was asleep again.

He dreamt, for some reason, of a fireworks show. He was in the Pasadena house again, with the Bulgarian woman, Vera or Dimmi or Hot Momma or whatever she was called, and she was smiling at him over her shoulder as she walked away. But as she stepped through the door she was a different person, and dream-Hector believed she had removed her face Mission-Impossible-style, to reveal somebody else underneath. The door of the house opened, with the impossibly concertinaed topography of dreams, directly into Griffith Park. It was dusk, and many people were milling about underneath a sharkskin-coloured sky. Hector tried to catch up with Vera, but placing a hand on her shoulder she turned and was a stranger, somebody he didn't recognize. "Your point?" this stranger asked. "Your point is?" "That's a pretty fucking deep question," replied dream-Hector, trying to throw a laugh into the statement but only managing an insincere gurgle. Somebody else (the connection wasn't clear, it jumbled) was talking to a crowd, and dream-Hector trying to push to the front, and the speaker was saying "these fireworks are special, they are the true nature of things." Dream-Hector thought to himself, "that sounds like my Dad", but it wasn't his Dad, it was some dark-skinned, dark-eyed man no older than Hector was himself. The sky had dimmed abruptly into a clear desert night-sky, flush with stars like dustings of static electricity, and in between the sparkles was a purple so dark it was barely distinguishable from black. "These fireworks," the speaker was still saying, "are special, they are the true nature of things. You've heard of the Big Bang? That was exactly like these fireworks." Dream-Hector tried to contradict, because this didn't seem to him right at all, the Big Bang being ancient history not current affairs, but he couldn't remember when fireworks were invented, the Chinese wasn't it, and his mouth was gummed up, he couldn't form the words. He turned to the person next to him in the crowd, but everybody's face was angled upwards, looking at the dark sky, and above him the fireworks were bursting in glory, marvelous sunflower- and lily-shaped expansions of light occupying the sky hugely, flowering with intense illumination, and then breaking into crumbs of neon red and white.

He woke to a bright window. After the end of the world.

The shaking house, and himself falling from the first storey. "Well," he said, to his empty room, "was that a *fucking* weird dream?" But he knew that it had not been a dream. He knew it had all happened. The palms of his feet felt tender, as if they'd both been slapped hard. Otherwise he was unhurt. But his mind was dancing, one-two-three, one-two-three.

Fin, as it says at the end of French movies.

As he was dressing he realized that the whiteness of the window was the sign of a general fog. Fog in high summer in the Californian desert. How weird was *that*?

He went downstairs, but the house was deserted. The sofa looked somehow smug in the daylight; the whole scene shrunk by its perfect visibility to a comical rather than a tragic arena. Had he really believed he was going to die, just falling one storey? The most he'd have suffered would have been a twisted ankle, maybe, at the worst a broken bone. Yet the terror was still there, in mental aftertaste; the genuine death-is-here terror.

An aftershock rumbled and gave the floor an odd number of shakes. Hector flung his arms out, like a high-wire artiste, to steady himself. The shocks settled.

Out on the porch the world was milky and immediate, with an oceanic tang to the air, salty and ozoney. The view had been perfectly opaqued; Hector couldn't even see the parked cars a few yards away.

Tom was sitting to the left of the front door, cradling what Hector at first thought was a cup of hot coffee, but which, looking twice, he saw was a pistol. The gun brought an automatic hey-I'm-your-friend grin to Hector's face.

"Hi," he said.

Tom looked up, his grin already broad. "Good morning," he said. "Some night, yeah?"

"Yeah," said Hector. "That was some quake."

"You could say that," said Tom, blinking with what looked like suppressed glee. "You could say that."

"That one wasn't predicted," said Hector. "At least, I didn't see it in any papers. It wasn't on the TV."

"No."

"My Dad, is he about?"

"He's checking the perimeter with Pablo and Esther. They'll be an hour more, I'd say."

Hector said nothing for several minutes. He took a seat next to Tom and stared at the blankness of the fog. "This is pretty freaky weather. It was so hot and clear yesterday, and now so white and chilly. I mean, I lived in California most of my life but never saw anything like this. I mean, this far inland."

"It's very striking weather," said Tom, almost grinning with delight at the joke which he had a portion of, but which Hector didn't yet get.

"But," said Hector, groping inwardly for a laugh to lighten the words but not finding one, "hardly the end of the world . . ."

The fog sat, motionless as cataracts. After it became clear that Tom wasn't going to reply, Hector said. "I mean, *fog* is hardly the end of the world, is it?"

"It's the Pacific," said Tom.

"What is?"

Tom gestured with the pistol. "All this."

"The fog is the Pacific?"

"What's left of it. Much of it boiled away to space, I guess, but a fair proportion of it ended up here. Most of it will distil out again, eventually. It depends how close we come to the sun."

Hector tried to listen to this, and the words made sense, of a sort. But they did not lodge in his consciousness in a meaningful way. He could have been listening to an engineering specialist explain some complex process in a technical language of which Hector was himself ignorant. Forcing a laugh, that sounded accordingly more like a bark, he replied, "so a comet hit the earth last night and boiled the Pacific?"

"Something hit," said Tom, in a clear, low voice. "Not a comet."

They sat in silence for a while. The sound of two people talking became audible, somewhere away in the fog, but

Hector could not pick out the words, only the fact that one speaker was a man and one a woman. That conversation, whatever it was, came to an end, and everything was quiet again.

Eventually Tom began speaking. "Something hit," he said. "Something very dense. *Ve-ery* dense, and relatively small, and traveling fast. And something intelligent, I think. That's what *I* think. When – it – realized it was going to collide with the earth it sent ahead, somehow, broadcast something to communicate with the inhabitants, to warn them maybe, or maybe – who knows? – to brag."

"Who knows?" repeated Hector, amiably, trying not to hear exactly what was being said, but not succeeding.

"I think it tried in the 1870s, to communicate I mean, which resulted in the strange and rather garbled vision that Monsieur Servadac experienced."

"I see," said Hector, thinking with focused fury and anxiety on an imagined mental picture of Vera, called Dimmi, naked, stark naked. He tried to pour all his attention, his mental energy, into that image. He tried to divert all his fear and incomprehension into that inward vision, so that he could present an unruffled and fearless visage to Tom. He fiddled in his pocket for cigarettes, but he'd left the packet upstairs.

"The whatever-it-is," said Tom, "hit last night. Somewhere a little east of India, in the sea, *through* the sea and, thwack, into the earth. It penetrated pretty deep, breaking up the globe, shattering it into myriad lumps, before losing its speed and stopping – somewhere below us now. Not too far, couple of hundred miles I think. Maybe a thousand."

"Directly below us?" asked Hector.

"The world was broken apart, of course. But the lump we're on, it's in the best position. In terms of survival. Maybe a sixth of the globe's mass in size, but the – object – is so massive, though small, that its gravitational pull is three times that of the rock it's embedded in. If the fog cleared, you'd see. We're on a strange shaped planetoid now, my friend."

Hector wanted to say: *I can't believe you could speak aloud a sentence like that.* But he didn't say anything.

"If the fog cleared, then it would look as though the horizon were rearing up all around us. If you tried to walk to Frisco, it would get steeper and steeper until eventually it'd be more like mountain climbing. But that's good, because it means that we're in the bottom of the concavity, so the air, and eventually the water, will settle here."

"It's a good story," said Hector, eventually.

They sat in silence a while longer.

"And this object, stuck in the soil below us, *spoke* to my Dad, did it?" Hector asked, eventually. "It communicated with him? Warned him?"

Tom didn't answer.

"And," Hector went on, finding at last, with a sense of gratitude to the gods of the subconscious, reserves of scorn inside himself after all, and able to give his words a withering tone, "and this intelligent super-heavy whatever-it-is is happy just to sit embedded in a huge fragment of a broken planet is it? I mean, why didn't it swerve and avoid the earth, if it's so intelligent?"

"We've most of us had visions," said Tom, mildly. "Since we came here, although none as detailed as Hector's. Why didn't it swerve? Who knows? Maybe this is part of its alien life-cycle. You know, a mole's gotta dig in the earth, salmon've gotta swim upstream to spawn, this thing's gotta crash into planets and embed itself, destroying them in the process. I don't know. You don't know."

Hector stood up, reaching for anger, although actually all he felt was fear, the other's emotion's close kin. "But I *do* know," he said. "I know you're all wacko. There was a quake last night – big deal, it's California for fuck's sake. I *know* that I'll get in my hire car and drive back to LA and get a room in a fucking hotel. Tell my Dad I'll call later."

"Go for a drive, sure," said Tom, with infuriating patronage. "Only, belt up, and take care. The roads'll get steep sooner than you realize. Roads you think should be flat'll get steep."

"Right," said Hector, meaning *no way*. Meaning *never*.

The light was thinning, the fog growing darker. It was dusk. Hector could see the dial on Tom's watch, on his wrist, sitting in his lap on top of the pistol; it said eight-oh-five. He must have slept right through the day, which unnerved him, because he had thought it was morning. Still, he could drive through the night if he had to.

Yet he stood there havering, on the porch.

"Things," he tried, "don't feel any different to yesterday."

"We're on a curious ellipse, orbitally speaking," said Tom, looking into the fog, as if talking to himself. "I've been trying to calculate it, but it's tricky to do the numbers. I reckon we'll move away from the sun for seven months, and up from the ecliptic, but not too far, not so far that the fog would freeze solid. Or so we hope. But then we'll swing back in and down, and things'll warm up. We need to plan to have the first children by then."

"Yeah. Right," said Hector. "I'm getting into my car now."

"You go ahead," said Tom.

"I will. I'm driving away."

"Have a drive around, sure. But be sure you can find your way back."

"I'm going now," said Hector. But he was still standing there on the porch, with the fog in every direction away from the house, as if the ranch had been wrapped in mother-of-pearl.

THE MYSTERIOUS IOWANS

Paul Di Filippo

Most of Verne's novels over the next ten years, 1877–1886, have largely been forgotten. Only a few of their titles, listed here in English, will raise more than a little recognition – The Black Indies *(1877),* A Captain at Fifteen *(1878),* The Begum's Fortune *(1879),* The Tribulations of a Chinaman in China *(1879),* The Steam House *(1880),* The Giant Raft *(1881),* Robinson's School *(1882),* The Green Ray *(1882),* Kéraban the Inflexible *(1883),* The Southern Star *(1884),* The Archipelago on Fire *(1884),* The Waif of the *Cynthia, written with André Laurie (1885) and* The Lottery Ticket *(1885). Perhaps only* Mathias Sandorf *(1885), in the style of Alexandre Dumas is remembered, and this includes another mysterious scientist, Dr Antekirtt, who has a super-scientific castle on a remote island. Possibly this work was enough to inspire Verne again because in 1886 he created another of his great characters, Robur in* Robur le conquérant, *also called* The Clipper of the Clouds. *Robur, like Nemo, is on a vengeful mission against the world, except that whereas Nemo achieves his aims with his submarine, Robur works through a massive flying machine, the* Albatross.*

By the time of this novel Verne's attitude to scientific advance was changing. He still saw the need to progress but was aware of its dangers and warned that we needed to move cautiously.

Robur, who would return as an even greater avenger in The
Master of the World *(1904), knew that mankind was not ready
for advanced science. Paul Di Filippo takes that cue for the
following story.*

"I am inclined to think that in the future the world will not
have many more novels in which mind problems will be
solved by the imagination. It may be the natural feeling of
an old man with a hundred books behind him, who feels
that he has written out his subject, but I really feel as though
the writers of the present day and the past time who have
allowed their imaginations to play upon mind problems,
have, to use a colloquialism, nearly filled the bill."

> – Jules Verne, "Solution of
> Mind Problems by the Imagination."

On the morning of 24 May 1898, Mr Bingham Wheatstone
disembarked from the transcontinental train famously
dubbed "The Grey Ghost" for its swift and whisper-quiet
mode of propulsion, alighting at the very doorstep of the
city known far and wide as Lincolnopolis, the capitol of the
enigmatic sovereign empire known as Lincoln Island, a
dominion incongruously situated in the vast heartland of
the United States of America, bounded roughly by the
borders of what had once been the state of Iowa.

Descending the automatically unfolding steps of the
streamlined railcar, Wheatstone glanced about the several
platforms of the Lincolnopolis station for a brief moment.
He saw a bustling scene, as thousands of brightly dressed
visitors and natives mingled beneath the great vitrine-roofed,
adamantium-girdered enclosure, which dwarfed any Old
World cathedral in its spaciousness. Despite a constant flow
of trains, the air within the station remained fragrant and
wholesome, thanks to the clean gravito-magnetic engines
that pulled the various expresses.

Although a young man of only twenty-nine, and thus too

youthful to more than dimly recall the era of coal-powered propulsion that had been the rule up until 1875, Wheatstone was a student of history sufficiently well-versed to realize that such a pristine environment had not always been associated with rail travel. His parents, for instance, would have been forced to endure the soot and smut and cinders belched by coal-burning steam engines.

But all such inconveniences had been eliminated by a genius named Cyrus Smith, President-for-Life of Lincoln Island, and his many capable comrades-in-invention.

Hefting his single valise, Wheatstone leisurely traversed the space separating him from the nearest egress, threading his way among the many exotic specimens of humanity thronging the platforms. Sheiks from the Holy Land, Zulus and Watusis from darkest Africa, Laplanders, Muscovites, Mongols and Manchurians.

Lincolnopolis as a general rule during any period of the calendar attracted numerous representatives of every nation on the globe, diplomats, tourists and business folk eager to experience the wonders of the city or to conduct negotiations or to facilitate trade. But this day was unlike any other, and had occasioned even greater numbers of foreign visitors. For this very day marked the inauguration of the grand festivities connected with the thirtieth anniversary of the founding of Lincoln Island.

But even more startling than the cosmopolitan mix of humans was the presence of innumerable ape-servitors, all neatly garbed in red vests and pillbox hats, busy trundling steamer trunks, polishing brightwork, and sweeping the immaculate tiled floors. These intelligent quadrumanes belonged to the same race as the legendary Jupiter, the anthropoid servant who had been a loyal member of the household on the original Lincoln Island. Jupiter and his tribe had perished in the destruction of the ocean-girt Lincoln Island, but his cousins had been discovered on neighbouring Tabor Island in subsequent expeditions to that region, adopted and brought back to North America. Although not widely employed outside sovereign Iowa, the quadrumanes formed an essential component of that nation's working class.

As Wheatstone drew closer to his chosen exit, the travellers bunched into a line focused on the portal, one of many such queues. When he drew even with the customs station, holding his credentials expectantly, he immediately encountered the famous efficiency of the Lincoln Island government.

Teams of inspectors, their impressive white linen uniforms featuring the governmental crest that depicted the starfish-shaped outline of the original Lincoln Island, were rapidly and dispassionately going through the luggage of each visitor. While this procedure was underway, another official verified the identity of the person seeking entrance via his ordinator console.

Soon it was Wheatstone's turn. He surrendered his valise and handed over his passport. He watched as the ordinator operator – a competent-looking young fellow with a spray of freckles across his face lending a schoolboy charm to his person – expertly stroked the complicated controls studding the surface of the big mahogany cabinet that bore its proud brass plate identifying it as a "Saml. Clemens & Co. Mark Two" model.

Once the unique code attached to Wheatstone's citizenship in the USA had been translated into a format sensible to the ordinator's machine intelligence, the information was transmitted telegraphically to the central clearinghouse of such data. In less than a minute, the response returned, activating a piece of attached equipment that featured a scribing pen moving over a continuous sheet of paper. With remarkable speed, the pen engraved a likeness of Wheatstone with all the verisimilitude of any illustration from, say, *The London Illustrated News*! Following the portrait, the pen dictated some text.

The ordinator technician ripped the inscribed paper off its roll and studied the picture and text, frequently glancing at Wheatstone's visage for purposes of comparison. At last he seemed satisfied, turning to Wheatstone with a smile and a handshake.

"Welcome to Lincoln Island, Mr Wheatstone. I note that you are a journalist."

"Yes indeed. I am employed by the *Boston Herald*. I have been dispatched to report on your grand anniversary celebrations."

"You'll need a press pass then. One further moment, please."

"Of course."

The second response to the ordinator operator's fiddling took but an additional ninety seconds, at the end of which a solid *thunk* signalled the arrival of a capsule delivered through the pneumatic-tube system that threaded all of Lincolnopolis. The capsule disgorged a wallet-sized, flexible sheet of adamantium inscribed using a diamond stylus with the particulars of Wheatstone's employment and the terms of his liberty in Lincolnopolis.

"Once you are settled into your hotel," said the customs official, "present this at the Bureau of Public Information at the intersection of Grant Boulevard and Glenarvan Way. They will have further instructions and counsel for you."

Wheatstone took the flexible rectangle of adamantium. "Thank you very much for your help." The reporter collected his valise, neatly repacked, and strode off toward the broad exterior doors of the rail station. Within a few seconds, he found himself outside the crystal transportation palace.

Avenues lined with stalwart buildings in marble, granite and travertine stretched away radially from the hub of the train station. The wide sidewalks were thronged with bright-eyed, happy, strong-sinewed citizens of both sexes, all clad in pleasant modes of costume suitable for the Iowan spring climate; with awestruck tourists goggling at the sights; and with scuttling quadrumanes busy running errands for their masters.

The avenues themselves boasted a steady traffic of wheeled vehicles of every elaboration, all propelled by clean magneto-gravitic engines. The slices of sky visible above the urban canyons featured the occasional passing light aircraft. So far the sciences of Lincoln Island had managed to permit the construction only smallish atmospheric craft capable of hosting one or two riders at most, and not useful for much more than aerial observation or pleasure jaunts. But there was already talk in such gazettes as *Scientific Iowan* of scaling up these vessels into long-range behemoths that would revolutionize travel.

As Wheatstone hailed a passing jitney, he was already mentally casting the lead paragraphs of his first story, a paean to this tiny nation.

"Hotel Amiens, please."

"Sure thing, mister!"

The Hotel Amiens proved to be a superior establishment, from its natatorium and billiard rooms to its corps of quadrumane bellhops. Every room featured ordinator-mediated communication outlets and piped music from the central Lincolnopolis chamber orchestra, which performed twenty-four hours a day, thanks to an extensive complement of musicians.

After refreshing himself and replacing his travel-sweaty shirt collar and exchanging his informal checkered coat for a more sombre black one, the young reporter set out for his appointment with the Bureau of Public Information.

The impressive columned government edifice at the corner of Grant and Glenarvan bore an inscription chiseled above its entrance: INFORMATION WISHES TO BECOME DISSEMINATED.

Presentation of his adamantium press pass to a Bureau concierge earned Wheatstone swift admission to the office of one Andrew Portland, an under-secretary responsible for foreign reporters. Portland sported a magnificent set of muttonchop whiskers and a vest-covered cannonball of a gut that hinted at certain large appetites. On the wall behind the under-secretary's desk hung a portrait of Cyrus Smith, President-for-Life, looking fatherly and compassionate as he gazed off into some half-apprehended future.

Mixing probing questions with hearty chatter – Wheatstone found himself talking at length about the charms of his fiancée, Miss Matilda Lodge – Portland eventually satisfied himself as to Wheatstone's bona fides.

"Well, Mr Wheatstone" said the under-secretary, "I'm pleased to grant you the freedom of our city and countryside, with the exception of certain military installations. Of course, I expect you'll want to spend the majority of your time at the exposition itself. Over five hundred acres of exhibits located on the outskirts of town and easily reached by public transportation. You'll hardly be able to exhaust the various pavilions during your stay here, and your readers will be insatiable, I'm sure, for all the details you can provide."

Wheatstone arose, sensing the interview was over, and extended his hand. "Thank you very much, Mr Portland. I'm sure that with your assistance I will be able to convey a vivid sense of Lincoln Island's unique character to the *Herald*'s readers."

Out once more on the street, Wheatstone pondered his next actions. As the hour was well past noon and he had not eaten since breakfast on the train, he considered a meal quite appropriate. With the aid of a passing citizen, he managed to find a nearby chophouse, where he enjoyed a thick T-bone steak, an enormous Iowa spud, and a pitcher of beer. Pleasantly sated, smoking a post-prandial cigar, Wheatstone let his gaze rest benevolently on his fellow diners, many of whom were handsomely accoutred Negroes.

One of the founders of North America's Lincoln Island in 1868 had been Cyrus Smith's manservant, Neb, who had always been an equal member in the workings of the original castaway colony. Consequently, Negroes had enjoyed full suffrage in Lincoln Island from the country's inception. This model of interacial equality had served as a beacon to the United States during its painful postwar Reconstruction period.

And this doctrine of the universal rights of mankind had been spread further by a policy which Lincoln Island promulgated once its ascendancy had been cemented. Any nation which desired to trade with Lincoln Island and benefit from its technologies had to eliminate legislated racial biases within its own borders. With this combination of carrot and stick, the Iowans had managed to transform much of the world's attitude in only three short decades.

His cigar finished, Wheatstone contemplated his next step. Although the Hotel Amiens and its luxurious bed beckoned for a nap, Wheatstone hitched up his braces and resolved to head out to the fairgrounds for his first look at the exposition that had drawn him and so many others hither. It was no difficult feat to hop aboard one of the many special bunting-decorated trolleys ferrying people for free to the fairgrounds, and within half an hour Wheatstone was disembarking with dozens of other eager sightseers at the gates of the exposition.

The massive entrance was flanked by two groups of statuary depicting the founders of the republic. On Wheatstone's left loomed the titanic figures of Cyrus Smith, the lusty sailor named Pencroff, and humble Neb. At their feet lay the equally gigantic form of Top, Smith's loyal dog. Matching the formation on the other side of the gates were representations of journalist Gideon Spillet, Ayrton the ex-mutineer, and young student Harbert Brown. The animal totem in their tableau was Jup, the original quadrumane.

It was these six brave souls who, having found themselves dumped, weaponless and without tools or provisions, from a runaway hot-air balloon upon the bountiful but rugged Lincoln Island, had through sheer ingenuity, perseverance and hard manual labour created a small utopia which, regrettably, met its end due to a volcanic explosion.

All six of the men, Wheatstone knew, were still alive, with Smith being the oldest at some seventy-eight years of age and Brown the youngest at forty-eight. Together, they formed the ruling council of the current Lincoln Island, with Smith as first among equals. Wheatstone felt particular affection for the figure of Spillet, naturally, who had turned the *New Lincoln Herald* into one of the most formidable gazettes in the world.

Joining the mass of his gay fellows – women in long gowns and ostrich-plumed hats, children in kneepants and caps, men handsomely besuited – Wheatstone soon passed through the gates and was greeted by an astonishing vista. On these several hundred acres, the magnificent Iowans had constructed what amounted to a second city, one dedicated not to mere habitation but the nobler cause of displaying the wonders of Iowan science and the promises it held for an even brighter future. The architecture of this city-within-a-city recalled such fabled past metropoli as Babylon, Nineveh and Alexandria, but with an ultra-modern slant.

Feeling somewhat at sea, Wheatstone resolved to attend the introductory lecture advertised to occur half-hourly in the hall nearest the gates.

Once seated on a velvet-covered chair in a large darkened amphitheatre with scores of others, Wheatstone was treated to a show of magic-lantern slides accompanied by a very entertaining speech given by one of the many trained actors who served as guides to the fair. He thrilled once more to the famous tale of the castaways, an abbreviated saga which was followed by an account of the subsequent thirty years. The act of Congress in 1875 which had reluctantly but decisively allowed the petition of the Iowans asking to secede from the rest of the United States; the attempted invasion of the fledgling country by a cabal of European powers, launched from their base in Canada, which had been efficiently and mercilessly repelled by uncanny weapons of a heretofore unseen type. The signing of various peace treaties and the establishment of Iowan hegemony in several areas of international commerce and trade. The immigration policies which encouraged savants from all corners of the globe to flock to Lincoln Island –

After this, Wheatstone toured several exhibits, taking copious notes. From the Hall of Gravito-magnetism to the Chamber of Agricultural Engineering; from the Arcade of Electrical Propagation to the Gallery of Pneumatics –

Finally, though, even the exciting speculations failed to compensate for Wheatstone's natural fatigue after such a busy day, and, after consuming a light snack of squab and sausages from a fairground booth, he returned reluctantly to his hotel room.

There, to his surprise, a blinking light on the ordinator panel in his room signalled that a message awaited him.

Triggering the output of the electronic pen produced a cryptic sentence or two that lacked all attribution of sender, as if such information had been deliberately stripped away.

Mr Wheatstone – have you noticed the absence of a certain name from these festivities? I refer to the appellation of "Nemo." Would you know more? Meet me this evening after midnight at the Gilded Cockerel.

As a journalist, Wheatstone was used to such anonymous "tips." In the majority of cases, they led precisely nowhere. But every now and then, such secret disclosures did produce large stories of consequence. The young reporter could feel his blood thrill at the possibility that he would bag such a "scoop" from this message. This was an outcome he had hardly dared hope for when he had received his current assignment. But if he could manage to distinguish his reportage from all the other laudatory profiles that would be filed from this dateline, both he and the *Boston Herald* would benefit immensely. And proprietor William Randolph Hearst could be most generous to his successful employees.

Checking his pocketwatch, Wheatstone determined that he could snatch a few hours' sleep before making the rendezvous with the mysterious informant. But before he stretched himself out, he fired off an ordinator message of his own, to his ladylove back in the land of the bean and the cod.

Dear Matilda – I have arrived safely in Lincoln Island and already find myself embroiled in matters of some significance. If I succeed in making my name as I suspect I will with this assignment, perhaps you and I may finally get married. As you well know, my resolve not to ride on the Lodge family coat tails necessitates my obtaining a certain stature within my chosen profession before any nuptials can proceed. Please send all your kindest thoughts my way.

Having dispatched this message, Wheatstone stripped down

to his undergarments, set the alarm clock by his bed to sound at 11:30 p.m., and was soon deeply asleep.

The clanging of the alarm seemed subjectively to occur almost simultaneous with his descent into the realm of Morpheus, and Wheatstone awoke with a start. Yet it was but a matter of minutes for him to refresh himself, dress, and descend to the lobby of the Hotel Amiens. There, he inquired of the concierge the address of the Gilded Cockerel. The rigorously circumspect fellow looked askance at Wheatstone, as if his query were somehow improper, but supplied the address nonetheless.

Outside, the thronged streets of Lincolnopolis were well-lighted not only by the permanent electric standards, but also with numerous strands of coloured bulbs celebrating the exposition. Wheatstone had no trouble hailing a jitney, and soon found himself standing outside the door to the Gilded Cockerel.

Judging by its exterior, the tavern, situated in a shadowy, mirey lane totally incongruous with the rest of Lincolnopolis's civic splendor, seemed somewhat louche. But Wheatstone had been obliged to frequent worse places, and he entered boldly.

The interior of the establishment confirmed Wheatstone's original estimation. Gimcrack decorations could not conceal the shoddiness of the furnishings. Odours of spilled ale and less savoury substances clogged Wheatstone's nostrils. Raucous laughter and shouts indicated a total lack of public decorum. But what was more offputting than any of the sensory assaults were the figures of the patrons of the Gilded Cockerel. To a man – and there were no females present – the customers were clothed as total fops. The amount of lace and brocade present would have outfitted the vanished court of Louis the Fourteenth.

Wheatstone knew instantly that he had fallen in with sodomites. Their generic resemblance to the infamous Irishman Oscar Wilde was indisputable.

Bracing his spine, careful not to make any physical contact with the seated, simpering deviants, Wheatstone advanced toward the barkeep, a burly chap whose sleeveless shirt afforded a view of his numerous tattoos.

"I am supposed to meet someone here tonight."

The barkeep's mellifluous voice was utterly at odds with his appearance. "What's your name, honey?"

"Mr Bingham Wheatstone."

"Ah, of course. Your date's awaiting you in one of the private rooms. Last door on the right, dearie."

The nominated door opened to Wheatstone's touch and he stepped inside. Not electricity, but a single candle illuminated the small room: rickety table, two hard chairs, an uncorked, half-full bottle of wine and a single glass. A man stood with his back to the door. At his feet bulked a large carpetbag.

Hearing Wheatstone's entrance, the man turned, and Wheatstone could not suppress his exclamation.

"Harbert Brown!"

"Quiet, you dolt! I trust everyone here, but there's still no need to announce my presence to the world. Now, have a seat."

Wheatstone took one of the chairs, using the time to study the familiar yet altered face of Brown. The man's lips appeared to be painted, and his eyelids daubed with kohl. Taking a moment now to light a slim cigar, Brown exhibited a limp-wristed effeminacy. Although the youngest member of Lincoln Island's ruling council, Brown was still middle-aged, with all the attendant sagging flesh of that stage of life, having been an adolescent stripling during the castaways' adventures, and today his unnatural airs reeked of a jaded degeneracy.

Wheatstone ventured to paint the picture presented by Brown's appearance in the most charitable light.

"Sir, you have adopted a most convincing disguise –"

"Oh, you know as well as I do that's stuff and nonsense, Mr Wheatstone. This is the real me. It's when I appear in public as a moral and responsible politician that I am actually in disguise. And what a trial it has been, maintaining that façade all these years. Little did I imagine when I became

Pencroff's catamite as a youth that I was embarking on a tedious charade that would last decades."

Wheatstone felt his mind whirling in a tornado of overturned conceptions. "But what are you implying?"

Brown languidly expelled a cloud of cigar smoke. "Need I spell it out for you. Mr Wheatstone? What kind of relationship did you suspect existed between a lusty sailor and a young boy who inexplicably accompanied him everywhere? Pencroff and I were lovers during our imprisonment in Richmond, Virginia, and we remained so for three years on Lincoln Island after our balloon escape. In fact, in the absence of females, I was able to provide carnal solace to all our little band during that period. Although none of the other men were bent that way originally, they all gladly succumbed to my charms when their natural urges reached a certain crisis point."

"But, no, this can't be –"

"Oh, don't be so shocked, Mr Wheatstone. It's not becoming in a supposedly seasoned reporter. And anyway, this is not the matter I invited you here to discuss. The sexual habits of Lincoln Island's rulers have little import outside the narrow confines of our tiny elite. No, the topic today is the very future of human progress. You see, Mr Wheatstone, I fear that Lincoln Island has become a positive blockade to technological advancement, and that its continued dominance in the global scientific arena will eventually doom mankind and actually induce a long, hard fall back to savagery."

"How can you assert such an impossibility, sir? It contradicts everything I know."

Brown sighed, took a seat, poured himself some wine without offering Wheatstone any, sipped, then said, "Ah, that is the problem, Bing. May I call you 'Bing'? You most assuredly do not know everything. What, for instance, do you make of the name of Captain Nemo?"

"This is the name you mentioned in your message to me. Well, I seem to recall that a brigand once roved the seven seas under that *nom de guerre*, harrassing shipping and so forth. Were his quixotic campaigns not chronicled in some musty old volume early in this century? *Beleaguered Below the Seas*, or some such title? If this is the fellow you refer to, his relevance is not immediately apparent."

"Indeed, you recall the broad, distorted outlines of Nemo's career. I'm surprised you apprehend even that much. During our Robinsonade upon Lincoln Island, Nemo had already been absent from the public scene for thirty years. Nowadays he is hardly even a phantom. And much of that public nescience regarding him and his works is deliberate, fostered by us here. Yet such was not the case three decades ago, when his name was still on the lips of the cognoscenti. You can imagine our surprise when we discovered this notorious criminal genius to be a fellow resident of our little island."

"He was cast away, like yourselves, then?"

"Not at all. He had retreated to the island purposefully, to spend his final bitter days in peace and seclusion. We witnessed his death from natural causes, and buried him there."

"How then can his name play any part in the current discussion?"

"Nemo was a wizard, Bing. And he was buried in his wizardly craft, the *Nautilus*, a submersible vessel. We sank it with his corpse, as per his last wishes. But the trouble – the trouble is, the *Nautilus* did not remain sunk."

"I am beginning to see the vaguest hints of the direction in which your story is heading. Pray, proceed."

Harbert Brown took a long meditative swig of wine before continuing. The guttering candle caused shadows to warp eerily across his bleary-eyed visage.

"Can you envision the ambitious dreams and lofty expectations which the six of us repatriated survivors held, once we were transplanted to Iowan soil, Bing? On primitive Lincoln Island we had struggled against all odds and created a semblance of civilization out of nothing but our wits and the abundant raw materials present. True, we had benefited from the secret interventions of Nemo at certain crucial junctures. And even now, with his final gift of a casket of riches, he was underwriting our mainland venture. But despite his bolstering, we had firm faith that we six alone could still establish a beacon of superior living in the midst of these United States. Imagine then how our hopes were dashed when so much went wrong in the first few years. Crop failures, natural disasters, cut-throat competition from neighbours, prejudiced merchants who refused to deal with us because of the presence of Negroes such as Neb, governmental restrictions, a poor quality of lazy immigrant workers from the sewers of Europe – all these factors and more conspired to render our Utopia a stillborn shambles. And at the head of it, our leader, Cyrus Smith, despondent and despairing for the first time in his life. Now you must realize one thing, Bing. Cyrus is not the genius the world thinks him. He is clever, and well-versed in engineering lore. But he hasn't an original bone in his body. He can re-create, but not create."

"But all the flood of inventions that have come from his fertile brain –"

"They did not come from Cyrus Smith's brain, Bing! They came from Nemo's!"

"You mean – ?"

"Yes! In eighteen-seventy, using the last of our wealth in a desperate gamble, we mounted an expedition back to the site of the vanished Lincoln Island, back to that small remnant crag of rock from which we were rescued. We sent a primitive submersible down to the sea floor – providentially shallow – and found the *Nautilus*, miraculously intact. Pencroff in his undersea suit entered through her open hatch, and managed to get her miraculous engines going again. Luckily, the indestructible machines had shut themselves down in a programmed fashion when we scuttled her. We crewed the *Nautilus* and brought her back to the East Coast. There, we lifted her into drydock, sundered her into sections, and carted her back to Iowa. Then began in secret the plundering of her real wealth, all the marvellous inventions she contained."

"Suppose I credit this tale, Mr Brown. What of it? You

have disclosed the ignoble reality behind the myth of Cyrus Smith's genius. I suppose we could concoct a three-day scandal out of such material and sell a few extra papers. But how does this revelation materially affect the grandeur of what you Iowans have achieved? And how can you possibly deduce the end of civilization from your tawdry tale?"

Brown leaned forward intently, all foppishness banished by earnestness. "Are you the same fellow who wrote that series of articles entitled 'Some Thoughts Toward the Manifest Destiny of Our Arriving Twentieth Century'? That's why I picked you, Bing, because of the speculative acumen you exhibited in those writings. You seemed to recognize that the continued success of our present planetary culture is based on a perpetual flow of advancements. There can be no such thing as holding still. The growing interconnectedness of the world, the demands of a surging population, the rising expectations of the common man as to what life will bring him – all these factors and more conspire to demand a flood of fresh inventions from the world's laboratories. And the world looks to Lincoln Island to lead the way. If we were to stagnate, the worldwide system would collapse in a Malthusian disaster of rioting, starvation and savagery."

"Agreed. But surely the risk of stagnation is next to nil –"

Brown banged a fist upon the table, sending his tumbler of wine toppling. "Don't you get it, Bing? We've copied and slightly improved all of Nemo's technology. If I may coin a term, we applied 'reverse-engineering' to his devices. Smith's talents were perfectly adequate for that. But we don't understand the first principles of any of it. We've engaged scores of brilliant men from around the globe – Edison, Bell, Ford, Michelson, the Curies, and many more whom I could name – and none of them have had an ounce of success at unriddling, say, gravito-magnetics. We're like primitive witchdoctors recreating effects by following formulae passed down from the gods."

"Surely you judge yourself too harshly," Wheatstone protested.

"Not at all! It's taken every iota of ingenuity we possess

just to translate Nemo's devices into automobiles and trains and such. That's why large-scale manned flight has baffled us. Nemo's engines were never designed for such applications. And we've just about reached the limit of what we can mine from the last scraps of the *Nautilus*. But what's even worse is how we've fatally detoured the destined course of scientific history. By futilely investing generations of talent in following Nemo's bizarre avenues, we've allowed the foundations of science circa 1870 to crumble and molder. The world of 1898 is not what it should have been. There is no organic path left for us to follow from here out. To re-organize the scientific establishment that existed thirty years ago is nigh impossible. Yet our only hope for the future is to attempt such a thing. But we cannot even make such a last-ditch effort until we first tear down the sickly monster we have erected. And your help is essential for that task."

Wheatstone felt torn between a host of contradictory impulses. His affection for what Lincoln Island had created vied with his desire to make a journalistic splash. His belief in Brown's sincerity – the man appeared to truly believe everything he had said – warred with his incredulity at the enormity of the long-standing hoax.

"How can I accept what you tell me without some kind of proof, sir?"

Brown got tipsily to his feet and secured the neglected carpetbag from the corner of the room. He hoisted it to the tabletop, unclasped it, and reached within. From the bag he lifted a fantastical helmet with thick glass plate for a visor, bearing an ornate capital N. This he thumped down on the table.

"Here is one of the diving helmets from the *Nautilus*."

Brown examined the headgear with interest. "Intriguing, sir. But this could be something intended to deceive me."

"Thought you might say that." Brown reached again into the bag and removed another exhibit.

Wheatstone's knowledge of human skeletal anatomy had been buffed by various professional interviews with leading anthropologists. The skull now flaunted before him displayed odd configurations of bone that seemed to hint at larger mental proportions than the human norm.

"Yes," Brown confirmed, "this is Nemo's very skull. The fishes had picked him quite clean by the time we returned. He claimed to be an Indian prince, but I suspect that he was much more. Perhaps a visitor from the future, perhaps a stranded traveller from another star. Or perhaps a human sport, a forerunner of some species of mankind yet to come. In any case, he possessed qualities of mind the likes of which are all too seldom encountered."

The skull formed a shocking weight in the pan of the scales that favoured Brown's story. But still Wheatstone hesitated. So much was riding on his decision –

Brown sensed this hesitancy. "Damn it, man! I had been hoping to avoid this, but I can see I've got no choice. Come with me. I'm taking you to see the carcass of the *Nautilus* itself!"

Brooking no resistance, Brown grabbed Wheatstone's sleeve with one hand and his bottle of wine with the other, and they departed the Gilded Cockerel. Outside, they strode off, Brown leading. He continued to swig from his bottle, muttering all the while.

"We're rotten at the core, Wheatstone! Nemo was the worm in the apple of the original Lincoln Island, and he remains so today. Our whole existence is predicated on a lie!"

Wheatstone refrained, wisely he thought, from either agreement or dissent.

After half an hour of progress through the deserted streets of a manufactory district, the pair arrived at an innocuous warehouse. Brown pulled Wheatstone down an alley and around to a side door.

"No one comes here any more. The *Nautilus* was stripped long ago, its components distributed to various laboratories. We should be perfectly safe venturing inside."

"I take it then that you are playing a lone hand. You have no fellow conspirators to rely on?"

"Hah! Who among those self-satisfied drones wants to

rock the boat? They're all frightened old men. But poor little
Harbert Brown, the baby of the group, still has some hot
blood in his veins! They'll all be dead soon, the duffers! Not
me! And I don't want to live in a desolate future. That's
why I'm doing this, Bing!"

After employing a key on the padlocked door, Brown led
Wheatcroft into the stygian interior. "There should be an
electric-light switch somewhere near this entrance – Ah-ha!"

The blaze of illumination that flooded forth following
Brown's simple action caused Wheatcroft to fling up an arm
across his face against the glare. When his eyes had adjusted,
he lowered his limb.

The vast open floor of the warehouse held just what had
been promised. Like a slaughtered whale strewn across a
beach, the segments of Nemo's wonder-vessel reared ceil-
ingward. Steel arches and ribs trailed bits of truncated wiring
and pipes and bits of decoration. The shattered pieces of
the *Nautilus*'s staterooms – slabs of mahogany and tile,
broken chandeliers and armoires – were heaped in a corner.
The whole panorama was morbid and desolate in the
extreme.

Wheatstone moved forward for closer inspection, but was
arrested in his tracks by a shout.

"Stop right there! We are from the council!"

Across the room, framed in another doorway, stood a
short, gnarled yet feisty old man surrounded by quadrumanes. The surly apes wore not the vests of their servant
cousins but rather leather brassards, and carried truncheons
belligerently.

"Pencroff!" exclaimed Harbert Brown.

"Yes, you cocksure little fool. Did you actually think your
plotting went unnoticed? We've known all along about your
treacherous scheme. And now you'll have to face the consequences. Secure them, boys!"

At Pencroff's command the apes bounded forward and
cruelly pinioned Wheatstone and Brown. Within seconds the
prisoners had been placed in the claustrophobic back of a
Black Maria wagon, which motored off.

Brown was too devastated to speak, and Wheatstone found himself similarly dejected. How had he come to such a fix? Ambition had undone him. He could not delude himself that high-minded principles had played any part in his involvement.

Their windowless conveyance eventually came to a stop. The rear doors opened, and a rough-handed quadrumane escort hustled Brown and Wheatstone out and into a new building. Inside, the conspirators were separated. Soon, much to his surprise, Wheatstone found himself deposited in a spacious library. His animal captors left him then, and he collapsed into a chair.

Not many minutes passed before the library door clicked open. Wheatstone shot quivering to his feet and found himself face to face with the president-for-life of Lincoln Island.

At age seventy-eight, Cyrus Smith still possessed all the charisma of his youth. His stern, bearded countenance radiated a patriarchal aura not unmixed with a sly humour. He smiled at Wheatstone, and extended a hand.

"Come, come, Mr Wheatstone, you're not among ogres here. If at all possible, no harm will come to you. I think you'll find us more than reasonable when it comes to straightening out this imbroglio you've stumbled into."

"Sir, you have foisted an imposture upon the world!"

"Have I, Mr Wheatstone? Yes, I suppose I have. But consider the benefits that have accrued thanks to my little charade. The living standards of much of the world's population are higher than they've ever been before. Cowed by the weapons we have liberated from the *Nautilus*, the nations of the globe have learned to value diplomacy over aggression. The Sons of Ham are fully enfranchised and valued, both in North America and elsewhere. I venture to say that this version of 1898 is, on the whole, a more just and admirable one than any other merely hypothetical branch of history that would have resulted had Lincoln Island never existed."

"But your paradise is balanced upon the tip of a needle! It takes all your efforts to keep it from toppling. And as

Brown has revealed to me, you are soon to run out of strength."

"Ah, poor Brown! We will see that he gets the kindly care and attention he needs to overcome his alcohol-sodden delusions. No one is going to harm him. He is one of us."

"Are you claiming that his presentation of the situation is incorrect?"

"No, not at all. But Harbert was not privy to our secret search, a quest that has now borne fruit. We have secured the allegiance of a new savant, a mastermind whose fertile brain will more than compensate for the absence of our beloved Captain Nemo."

"You believe then that this newcomer can stave off that day when science reaches its natural limits?"

"Indeed, he will, I am certain. And may I say that you have a fine way with words, Mr Wheatstone. I'm certain you will do justice to the exclusive interview we intend to grant you with our new saviour."

Exclusive interview? Wheatstone began to feel for the first time in hours that he might yet emerge from this deadly affair with both his hide and reputation intact, even enhanced.

"Would you care to meet him now?"

"Why, yes, if the hour is not too late."

"Not at all. Our new comrade is almost superhuman in his endurance and vital spirits."

Wheatstone used an ordinator to issue his summons. Within a few minutes, a man strode boldly into the library. And what a figure of a man! Of middle height and geometric breadth, his figure was a regular trapezium with the greatest of its parallel sides formed by the line of his shoulders. On this line attached by a robust neck there rose an enormous spheroidal head – the head of a bull; but a bull with an intelligent face. Eyes which, at the least opposition, would glow like coals of fire; and above them a permanent contraction of the superciliary muscle, an invariable sign of extreme energy. Short hair, slightly woolly, with metallic reflections; large chest rising and falling like a smith's bellow; arm, hands, legs and feet, all worthy of the trunk. No mustaches, no whiskers, but a large American goatee.

Even Cyrus Smith seemed to shrink a little in the presence of this newcomer, who remained forebodingly silent. But Smith soon recovered himself and said, "Mr Wheatstone, may I present our new friend, Robur. With his aid, I believe we can conquer all such problems as our aerial delays at last. With Robur at our side, progress need never end."

Wheatstone shook Robur's hand and felt a galvanic charge.

The young reporter suspected that things were really going to get interesting now.

OLD LIGHT

Tim Lebbon

From 1886, Verne entered a long period of depression. It was probably started when Verne's nephew, Gaston, in a moment of madness, shot Verne, wounding him in the leg. The injury left Verne with a limp that severely reduced his mobility and though he was still only fifty-eight, he began to feel "geriatric". It was not helped by the deaths of several friends and relatives, including Hetzel, who died in 1886, and Verne's mother who died early in 1887. This depression was apparent in a series of lacklustre and rather negative novels, including North against South *(1887),* The Flight to France *(1887),* Two Years' Vacation *(1888, better known as* Adrift in the Pacific*) and* A Family Without a Name *(1889).*

In the midst of this he completed, but then put aside, a very personal novel about loss and love. Le Château des Carpathes *(*The Castle of the Carpathians*) is usually dismissed as an over sentimental gothic romance. Set in Translyvania (and written several years before Bram Stoker completed* Dracula*), it tells of strange events happening at the eponymous castle once owned by the Barons de Gortz but long believed to have been abandoned. The villagers suspect that the manifestations are supernatural but two more pragmatic locals set out for the castle to discover the truth. We eventually learn that the Baron de Gortz had fallen in love with the voice of a great singer, La Stilla, who had died.*

*The scientist, Orfanik, had invented a recording device that
captured La Stilla's voice and, using her portrait, de Gortz
arranges for Orfanik, to project the vision and sound of La Stilla
throughout the castle, where de Gortz retreats to be alone with
his memories. Biographers believe that the novel is a projection
of Verne's own views at this time as his friends and loved ones
died. In the following story Tim Lebbon captures that mood
admirably as he explores the further work of Orfanik.*

In the beginning, I turned away.

I'm not sure why. I'm normally a helpful person, compassionate, and the sight of a man in such a state would usually
urge me to aid him as much as I could. He was injured,
though still alive; the twitch of an eyelid, a foot moving in
circles as if dreaming a dance. Before I realized what I was
doing I was back on the pavement, seven steps and a lifetime of guilt separating me from the prone figure.

Perhaps it was the shock of what I had seen. Walking
along the canal the last thing I expected to come across
was someone lying across the towpath, apparently bleeding
to death. Maybe it was the sight of flies buzzing around
him. Or perhaps subconsciously I had already realized the
danger. He exuded strangeness like the warmth of a dying
breath. I must have picked up on that long before my morals
kicked in.

Even then I did not return straight away. I looked around
for help, but there was none to be had. The countryside was
quiet, its solitude broken only by the bleating of new-born
lambs and the mournful cries of a single buzzard circling
high overhead. I wondered where its mate had gone, and
whether it regarded this man as a possible source of carrion.

Standing at the top of the steps leading to the towpath,
I was suddenly certain that the man would be gone. When
I skirted the wild undergrowth and reached the level of the
canal once more there would be nothing there; no body, no
blood, no promise of pain. I would be left with the fact of

my hallucination, but I would rather live with that than be marked by this stranger's blood and problems. And then there was that guilt again, flicking at my memories with its stale breath. I would much rather be without the guilt.

If he *had* been an hallucination, should I still feel remorseful for turning away? The thought troubled me, as if someone else were thinking it.

I went back down to the towpath. The man was very old. His forehead was badly gashed and bruised, and I saw the splash of blood on the rock he must have hit when he fell. But it was the weirdness of this fallen man that shuffled my thoughts, and fear was yet another consequence of my shock.

He was foreign, perhaps Eastern European, and his clothing set him aside. I had never seen clothing like that beyond a movie screen. His trousers were of sackcloth, rough and snagged, held up by a belt of rough animal skin. His shirt was colourful and bright, even though it was obviously aged and weathered. Cuts here, rips there, all of them added to the garment's mystique. I could see no bottle, but I was already certain that he was not a drunk. Nearby on the towpath a long, heavy coat lay like a slaughtered shadow, arms askew, the material so strange that I could not place it. Not cotton, not wool, it reminded me most of rough elbow skin.

The man coughed. His eyes sprang open and fixed right on me, as if he already knew I was there. He smiled.

I stepped back. There was so much blood on his face, and his smile looked fearsome. Something scurried in the bushes beside the towpath and I turned, ready to face whatever came out. Perhaps it was a wild animal drawn by the smell of blood; a rat, a fox. But it was only a bird startled by my movement.

The man was still smiling at me. Ridiculously I smiled back, having no idea what else to do. He was bleeding copiously from the head. It can't have been more than a few minutes since he had fallen.

"Here," he said, "take this." He sat up awkwardly, swaying. He looked so *old*. I thought of broken ribs or crushed hips, but there was little I could do about that right now. He held up a long object wrapped in an oily cloth, and beckoned me over with a tilt of his head.

I obeyed. It was that or turn and run, and I could not allow that a second time.

"Lie still," I said, "don't move, I'll go and get help."

"Hmph!" He tried to laugh, but it descended into more coughing. He looked up at the trees and down at the canal. "I'll be fine. My time's not just yet." His voice was heavily accented and distorted by pain, but still I understood every word.

"What happened?" I asked.

"I fell. I'm tired. I've been looking for weeks."

"I don't understand. Looking for what?"

"For you, Alex Norfan. Take it. You'll understand."

"I . . . I don't think I can."

"You must!" His vehemence brought on more coughing, and blood dropped from his nose on to the ground between his knees. "This is no simple trinket," he whispered, trying to remain calm.

"It's not mine," I said, unable to ask what I was really thinking: *Why was he looking for me?*

"It is, it is." Still he proffered the object.

"What is it?"

"The future," he said. "It's been mine for so long, and now you're the last of the line, so it's yours. It's from the old castle in the Carpathians . . . haunted, haunted by miracles from the past . . ." He closed his eyes. He looked so pale, so ready to die, and suddenly so familiar. The shape of his brow, the curve of his cheek, the hook nose. I put my hand to my own face, and wondered.

"But –"

"Alex Norfan? Orfanik?" the man said, and he must have seen the reaction that name inspired in me. "There are more things than you know," he continued. "You're a man open to mystery, yes? To exploration? And I came here for you, because this is yours by birthright."

I shook my head to dislodge the strangeness, but it only

tangled it more. "I need to get you to a hospital."

"I've never been to one all my life, and I will not start now. It can do me no good. Now take this, curse you!"

I held out my hand and touched the thing he was offering. It was cold, even through the rag.

"I don't want it —"

"Don't you want to know . . . about when . . . you will die . . . ?"

"What?"

The man seemed to sink back into himself, as if shrivelling by the second. The flow of blood lessened and he lay back down as if to sleep.

"The future . . ." the man whispered, and I had to lean in close. "I saw the future in a beam of light. That tree! That bird! That smell and sound! Now . . ."

He died. One second he was there, the next he was nothing but a ruined heap of flesh, blood, bone. I stepped away. The canal fell silent but for the calling of the buzzard high in the sky. It had drifted away above the fields, as if the man's death had ended the bird's interest.

The corpse's arm was still raised. The weight of his offering should have dragged it to the ground. There was so much wrong here that I expected him to rise up at any moment, confound me some more. But he remained motionless, the arm raised, forbidding me to leave without at least looking at the object he held.

I snatched it away, and his arm sank slowly to the ground. *I should report this*, I thought, *I should tell someone*. But there was more to this than normality could bear; the canal and the woods surrounding it were painted with a bizarre hue, as if the man's final exhalation had landed everywhere.

I had always known the presence of mystery. And now I would find it for sure.

Inside the oily rag lay a torch.

I fled the scene of death and ran into the woods, clutching the torch to my chest with one hand. I had yet to switch it on.

Birds called out, ruffled by my crashing through the woods. I made no attempt to keep quiet.

I've been looking for weeks . . . for you, the dead man had said. I must have misheard him. I had only decided to walk here this morning, and even then I had almost changed my mind.

I dodged between trees, keeping to rough paths which dog-walkers had trodden into the woods over the years. I met no one. If I had, perhaps I would have said something about the body on the canal path. Or perhaps not. There was something so otherworldly about what had happened that I had already set it aside from earthly concerns.

I tripped and fell, gasping as the wind was knocked from me. Kneeling up, assessing my bruises and scrapes, I realized that I had dropped the torch. It had rolled, shedding the oily rag like a snake's skin, and fetched up beneath a bank of brambles. The thick carpet of pine needles pricked at my hands and knees as I forced my way beneath the bushes. I winced as thorns pricked my shoulders and scalp. The torch lay tantalisingly close, yet however hard I stretched I could not quite reach it. I had a choice: leave it for a while and try to find something with which to haul it out; or force my way into the thorny bush, and accept the pain that would entail.

I thought of the dead man, his bleeding head, his comments that I was open to mystery.

I pushed into the bush.

The torch was cool in my hands, heavy, a weight in the world that should surely not exist. As I sat beneath the tree in my back garden, turning the item back and forth in my hands, I realized that the dead old man was right. There were more things . . . *always* more things, more than anyone could ever know.

Either the torch was a brilliant forgery, or it had been made hundreds of years ago. Its shell was beautifully wrought in iron, patterned with swirls of flowers and strange sigils which could have been letters, or pictures representing letters.

Running my fingers over these designs I could almost feel time inlaid in them, cast into their patterns like air bubbles trapped in metal. They spoke of ages passed, and though there were no revelations here, the weight of the torch's age was obvious.

I opened the end. It unscrewed easily, as though it had been made yesterday. *Such craftsmanship*, I thought, *such care, none of that nowadays*. As I tilted the torch and looked inside, time whispered around me. It flowed through the tree, leaves kissing though there was no breeze. It ruffled the grass, shifted the air around my garden, as if to gain a better view of whatever I was about to see. The world had shrugged in defeat at something it sought to hide.

"Maybe it's all true." Silence was my only answer as nature withheld its secrets.

Inside the torch was a battery. It had the appearance of granite inlaid with large buttons of quartz. It was fixed, not replaceable, bound in by thin strips of twisted steel. If this was truly that old . . .

"It *can't* be true." But inside, I knew that I had been living my life a lie. The dead man had sought me out, spoken that mysterious name, and given me this weird and wonderful creation for a reason. I knew the story of the Castle of the Carpathians, and my own alleged common ancestry with the fictional inventor. But now, sitting holding this torch, readying myself to turn it on and see what it would reveal, I tried the name in my mouth.

"Orfanik."

It sounded so familiar.

I did not switch on the torch that evening. It rested by my bed as I tried to sleep, and in those dark hours strange dreams visited me, whether nightmares or oddities of my waking mind I could not tell. I saw flashes outside the uncurtained window, though the sky was bare of clouds. They forked across the glass again and again, and I began to believe that they were inside the room. I tried to close my eyes but still I saw them, blood-red wounds etched against my inner-eyelids.

I remembered my father telling me these tales when I was a teenager, handing me Verne's classic novel to read, and the weird feeling I had upon finishing it. "It's only a story," I said to him, and he smiled and nodded, then shook his head. "There's always doubt," he replied. His appearance changed to that of the dead man with his severe Slavic looks, and in my dream their faces were not dissimilar. The dead man spoke to me again, and though I could not hear the words I knew that he was angry at my doubt.

You're a man open to mystery, yes? a voice said from the dark. I nodded in my sleep, shook myself awake, not sure whether the owner of the voice was actually there.

I reached for the torch to find out.

The beam of light that sprang out shocked me. I had not expected the old torch to work. My surprise set the beam quivering across the walls, furniture and reflecting from the window, and I rested my hand on my raised knee to keep the torch steady. There was something about the beam and what it revealed, as if this old battery made old light.

There was a spider on the wall, a huge wolf spider, its legs curled up to its body in death. I shifted the torch and sensed sudden movement in the dark, aiming it back at the spider again. Light passed across the window.

There was someone outside. Someone with a melting face.

I shouted and dropped the torch. It struck the floor and blinked off, leaving the bedroom in darkness. I closed my eyes for several terrifying seconds, letting them adjust to the dark again before opening them to stare at the window. I could see nothing, and somehow I reigned in my fear long enough to go and close the curtains.

"Orfanik." I whispered that name again, the fictional character whom my father had often claimed to be real. "Orfanik, what have you made this time?"

I retrieved the torch and hid it beneath a pillow. Come daylight, I would see if it was still working. But not now.

Sleep eluded me as images of the melted face combined

with my memories of the dying man. They were not the same, and yet surely they were linked

At least, my imagination was making me believe so.

As dawn broke the darkness I was still sitting on my bed, aware of the weight of the torch lying beside me. Daylight bled some of the fear, and my conviction that I had had a supernatural experience faded away. There was an explanation for what I had seen, I was convinced of that. Orfanik has supposedly been an inventor, not a conjuror, and whatever the torch had shown me had been through science, not super-science.

I opened the curtains quickly, jumping back as a huge spider scurried away behind them. Maybe it had just been asleep.

As the sun poured in I mused on the speed of light. Outside there were still a few stars fighting the dawn, and I wondered whether they were even still there. I was seeing them as they had been thousands, even millions of years ago. As a child the prospect of travelling faster than light, then looking back and seeing *myself*, had disturbed me greatly. It knocked me from the centre of things, which is where every child believes itself to be, and it was that more than my realization of death that marked the point when I started growing up.

And now light was playing with me again.

I decided to return to the canal to find the dead man. Even as a corpse, he could have answers.

The man was gone. I was not really surprised. What did surprise me was the total lack of evidence that he had ever been there. No blood soaked into the towpath, no impression in the grass, no barriers, tape or fences erected by police.

Here was yet another mystery. This weekend seemed rich with them.

I started walking along the towpath, the torch heavy in my pocket. I had yet to turn it on again, although the chance of it being broken seemed remote. It was old. If it had been made by Orfanik (and acceptance of my ancestry had come without my being able to identify the point at which doubt turned to belief), then it was hundreds of years old. Unlikely – hell, impossible! – but still there it was, hanging in my trousers and banging against my leg with each step.

I saw the future in a beam of light. The dying man's words rang inside my head, and I thought of the brief image of the face I had seen outside my bedroom window. I shook my head. Light glinted from the surface of the canal and blinded me for a few seconds, and when I looked at the woods the world had changed. Of course it had. It changes every instant.

I took out the torch, bent down and found a snail crawling along a twig.

I turned on the torch. The circle of yellow light was weak in the daylight, but it was still there. I lifted and lowered it, pleased that the light behaved as it should. Then I moved it over the snail.

Instantly the snail's body vanished leaving a hollowed, brittle shell behind. It was holed, probably by a bird.

I shifted the torch away and the live snail was still making its way along the twig. Back again, empty shell. Away, live snail.

I was seeing two times. The only question was, just how far apart were they? I could turn off the torch and wait to see when the snail would meet its end . . . but it may be days or months from now.

Amazed though I was, understanding still seemed to come easily to me. Perhaps it was the open mind handed down from my father, the belief in things we could not see, the acceptance of more things than we could ever know. Or maybe it was the face I had seen in my bedroom window, and the familiarity in its eyes.

I stood and walked away, pocketing the torch once again. Surely it must have its uses. I simply had to figure out what they were.

★   ★   ★

Back home in my sitting room, I sat in the leather rocker and looked around. All about me were hints to my heritage, yet I had never taken them seriously. A few trinkets my father had bequeathed me; a pocket watch from the last century that ran backward, a voodoo doll supposedly from Haiti, a crystal ball that could fly, or so it was said. Some of the pictures hanging on the walls showed scenes of technological genius from the past; the Wright Brothers on their first flight, Armstrong taking his first steps on the moon. The book-lined walls contained at least a hundred volumes on popular science, and many more on sciences not so well known. I was surrounded by the wonders of discovery and the vicarious pleasures in confounding expectations.

The torch showed time, and the man had wanted me to have it. He must have been a relative, perhaps a distant cousin from Eastern Europe, descended from Orfanik or some distant branch of my wild family tree.

I suddenly felt the need for company. I had become very aware of my own death, and knowing that the flick of a switch may reveal it to me – however far in the future it may be – made me feel very vulnerable.

Outside in the hallway I called Marlene. As I dialled I hoped that she would shed some light on the subject, and I found myself giggling at the literal image.

"Marlene," I said, "I think I'm going mad."

"*Going?*"

"Ha ha. I mean it." There was silence for a while, and I heard her drawing on her ever-present cigarette. She used the time to think.

"Alex, you sound strange," she said. "Seen a ghost?"

"Not exactly. Well . . . are there ghosts of the future, do you think? Can the dead haunt themselves?"

"Erm . . . ." Another pull on her cigarette. She never had been able to understand the way my mind worked, and that had driven us apart. It was hardly surprising. I barely understood it myself.

"Honey, the last day has changed everything, and I need grounding, I need pulling back down."

"I'm painting for the next hour, but we could meet at Cicero's if you like?"

"That would be good. And Marlene . . . thanks." Marlene and I had been separated for almost six years. I adored her.

Being outside made me feel better. I had brought the torch with me; perhaps that was a bad idea, but behind all the threat it still felt so precious. Leaving it behind would have felt like denying the point of the journey. I could *tell* Marlene about it, or I could *show* her. And there was a small sense of smugness at her anticipated reaction.

Cicero's was a great little café, and Marlene and I had continued meeting there ever since our break-up. It felt like neutral ground, somewhere we could discard our gripes at the door and sit in the pleasant, informal atmosphere with a latte and a slice of peach cake. After every one of these meetings I hated going outside on my own, feeling the familiar hurt descending again as I glanced back at where Marlene sat inside, waiting for me to leave. There was something calming about Cicero's. Nothing bad ever happened there.

Marlene was waiting in a window seat and she waved as I walked by. I raised the torch in greeting, and her eyes tracked it as I lowered it to my side once again. She looked more worried than interested.

The café was buzzing already, and I had to weave my way between occupied chairs to reach Marlene.

"Hey honey," I said, leaning down to kiss her cheek.

"Hi." She smiled as I sat down, but I could see her gaze drawn again and again to the torch in my pocket. "That it?"

I had not even mentioned the torch to her on the phone, and for a second her question threw me. "What?"

"The cause of all your troubles."

I grabbed the coffee menu from the table and scanned the list, even though I had the same drink and cake every single time we came here together. I liked the regularity; it seemed to preserve something of our past, hold back the change.

"You look tired," she said, suddenly sounding truly concerned.

"I am."

"Been up late? Anyone I know?"

I snorted and shook my head.

"You spend too much time thinking about time."

I glanced up at her, surprised yet again at how perceptive she could be. "What do you mean?"

"Dwelling on the past . . . on us. Thinking about what the future may bring. You should live in the here and now. Every moment is an instant in your life that you can live without worry."

"So when did you become the great psychologist?"

"I'm a painter. I philosophise, I don't psychoanalyse."

"Very droll."

Marlene must have ordered for both of us. The waitress brought over our coffee and cake and we sat silently for a moment, sugaring, pouring cream, enjoying the familiar smells and processes.

"So are you going to tell me what that thing is?"

I took the torch from my pocket and laid it on the table. It looked so old set against the clean, crisp furniture of Cicero's. "What does it look like?"

"It's a torch," Marlene said. "A bit ostentatious, isn't it?"

"That's how they built things two hundred years ago."

She snorted. "Yeah, right."

I did not care about her disbelief. There was no need to persuade her as to the age of this thing, nor even its origins. Once I showed her what it could do, all such doubts would evaporate.

I took a sip of my coffee, looked around at the other people in the café. Hands waved, smiles were given, a dozen stories were being told, and everyone here was unaware of their future. I could shine their fates upon them, but would they really want to know? Would anyone, given the chance, truly wish to know the moment of their death? I doubted it. But being *able* to know would be a terrible temptation.

"What would you do if you knew you were going to die?" I said.

"I *do* know."

She'd seen! She'd seen the torch!

"Everyone dies," Marlene continued. "Most people just don't think about it that much. You're not ill, are you?"

"I don't think so," I said. "But with this, I could find out."

"I thought it was a torch."

I stirred my coffee unnecessarily, watching the bubbles spin on its surface. "You remember me telling you about my father's thoughts on our family heritage? The fact that he connected us with a character in a Jules Verne book?"

"Orfanik," Marlene said.

"Yes, the inventor. A mad genius. He made things that no one understood at the time, but reading the book now it's so easy to see what he was doing. I always thought that was the book's fall-down. It didn't age well."

"But you never believed your father."

"Not really, no. But now . . ." I rolled the torch on the table, back and forth, trying to imagine the source of the power that lay inside.

"You're confusing me," Marlene said, and she hated that. Her confusion over my thoughts and interests is what essentially ended our life together. She did not have a mind receptive to mystery.

"What if you could see your future. What if you could see the moment you were going to die. Would you choose to see it?"

"No."

"Even if you could? Even if seeing might help you prevent it?"

"How could it?"

"I don't know."

I rolled the torch. It grumbled over the table.

"And you think this thing here can show you the future?"

"It shows the moment of your death. Orfanik made it, for whatever strange reasons he had. It found its way to me. And now I have the power —"

"Oh for Heaven's sake!"

"Marlene –"

She snatched up the torch and flicked it on. It slipped from her hands, hit the table and dropped to the floor. And in those couple of seconds, as the beam of light span across the café, I saw two briefly illuminated images of Marlene.

The torch hit the floor and went out.

"*No!*" I stood quickly, knocking over my chair. Heads turned, but Marlene was the only person I could see, the only pair of eyes I could face looking into. Ironic, as I had just seen them melted away by fire. "Oh, no!"

Something in my voice convinced her. Doubt was extinguished, her anger faded, her face paled, and for those few quiet seconds after the disturbance she wanted to know what I had seen. I could see it in her eyes. I shook my head, trying to dislodge the image that had stuck there like a subliminal message.

those flames that scream the cries . . .

Marlene gasped out loud, stood and fled the café. As the door swung shut behind her I thought, *I'm the one who should be running.* I watched her cross the street and disappear behind a building, waiting for a car to run her down and explode at any second. None came. Her image had been of no definable age. Perhaps we had years left yet, meeting at Cicero's and mourning a past that had not worked out.

Or perhaps I would never see her again.

I snatched up the torch. I had intended following Marlene, but as I left the café I turned in the opposite direction and ran.

What use was a tool that would let someone see their own death? Why would someone strive to invent such a device? Where would Marlene encounter the fire that would kill her? Had my seeing Marlene's death brought it closer in any way? Had Orfanik used the torch himself? How had it left his possession and found its way through the centuries to me? Was I really related to a fictional character, or was this some cruel cosmic joke?

Sitting in the park, the answers to these questions – and many more besides – eluded me. I ascribed each question to a garden opposite my bench, and watched as bees went from one to another, unable to provide any answers. Time would take these flowers and make them mulch, and in time perhaps my fears and questions would fade as well. But for now – this exact moment, the one instant in life that held greatest importance – all I had were more questions. Soon, I would need to find a larger flower bed.

Guilt took me home and stood me in front of my bathroom mirror.

I held the torch, pointed it up at my face, fingered the button.

I looked into my eyes, seeing myself as no one else ever had.

And like a suicide seeking only attention, I could not go through with the act. If the torch had been a .45 I would have thrown it away then, but it was too precious to damage like that. I lowered it, continued staring into my own eyes, watching the tears form and flow.

I stayed that way for a long time. I cried because I wished my father had known the *truth*, rather than the *myth*. The tears were also for what I had seen of Marlene. I hated the selfishness of that, the thoughtlessness, but I was already grieving for her, even though I still had no idea of when she would meet her horrible death.

In the end the torch slipped from my grasp and fate visited me again. It hit the floor, snapped on and bathed me with its strange light.

I saw through my tears.

Over the next few days I fell in love with Marlene all over again.

I eventually persuaded her to meet me at Cicero's and we sat there for hours, talking about everything except what had happened. I was never sure whether she truly believed that I had seen something, and I did my best to keep the haunting truth from my eyes. I think I succeeded. In all that time, I never saw the shadow of fear cross her face.

We met again a day later, and three time the following week, and the week after that we sat outside at a pavement table. This was a huge step for us, eschewing the neutrality of the café's interior, and it turned the meeting into a date. As I rose to leave Marlene stood up, closed in and kissed me on the lips. It did not surprise either of us, yet my heart paused for long seconds.

I walked away smiling and stepped carelessly into the street, knowing that no car would knock me down. That was not my way.

We take it one day at a time. The image of Marlene's death haunts me still, but there is an unspoken agreement that it will never be mentioned again. Mystery cannot come between us, as it did before. Love holds so much more power over me.

Especially knowing what I know.

Having seen my own old, weathered face wither and bubble in flames, at least I know that we will be together until the end.

THE SELENE GARDENING SOCIETY

Molly Brown

Gradually writing himself out of his depression, Verne produced another sequel. Sans dessus dessous *(1890), translated as* Topsy-Turvy *but better known as* The Purchase of the North Pole, *brings back the members of the Baltimore Gun Club, twenty years after their moon venture. The Gun Club acquire the land at the North Pole where they believe are vast mineral deposits. In order to get at them they need to melt the ice cap and decide the best way to do this is to shift the axis of the Earth. Despite the cataclysmic consequences the Gun Club continue in their project only to fail because of a mathematical error in their calculations. While it appears to be another preposterous novel, it is in fact, like* Hector Servadac *and* Robur the Conqueror, *another parable about the potential irresponsibility of man in trying to act like God.*

Although Verne did not write again about the fellows of the Gun Club there is no doubt that these individuals would stop at nothing. We have already learned of their further adventures in space in two earlier stories. In the next two we learn of their later escapades.

Chapter One
J. T. Maston takes up gardening

An open-topped carriage turned up the long drive to one of the grandest houses in New Park, Baltimore. The mansion's doors flew open, a stream of servants filing out into the afternoon sun to greet their mistress, the former Mrs Evangelina Scorbitt.

Evangelina patted the large box on the seat beside her. It contained her latest purchase: a wide-brimmed hat garnished with a cluster of tall feathers. Despite having invested – and lost – nearly half of the late Mr Scorbitt's fortune in the Baltimore Gun Club's failed scheme to melt the polar ice cap, she was still one of the wealthiest women in Maryland, well able to afford the occasional new hat. And this hat was something special.

At the age of forty-seven, Evangelina was painfully aware that, even as a girl, she had never been a beauty. But the moment she'd tried on that hat, she'd felt transformed. The milliner insisted she looked ten years younger, and for the first time in her life, this overweight middle-aged woman with hair the colour of dirty straw had actually liked what she saw in the mirror. It was the most wonderful hat in the world, and she couldn't wait for her new husband to see her in it.

Her driver was slowing the horses to a walk when the ground beneath them was rocked by an explosion. Evangelina was thrown back in her seat as the horses reared up, then bolted across the lawn.

She calmly grabbed hold of the side of the carriage as it careered across the grass, pursued by a gaggle of uniformed servants. And every dog in the neighbourhood was barking. "You'd think they'd be used to it by now," she sighed.

She was sitting in front of her dressing table when the house was shaken by another explosion. The maid standing behind her jumped, nearly skewering her with a hat pin. "Sorry, Ma'am."

Evangelina shook her head. The staff were as skittish as the horses. And the neighbourhood dogs were at it again. She told her maid to close the window.

Melting the North Pole had seemed a good idea at the time. There must be limitless supplies of coal in the Arctic – once you got past all that ice. So a plan was devised to straighten the Earth's axis by firing a gigantic cannon set into the side of Mount Kilimanjaro, the idea being that the recoil from the shot would nudge the planet into the desired position.

Despite the cannon's failure to affect the Earth's orbit – due to a slight mathematical error involving the accidental erasure of three zeros – and the loss of all that money, Evangelina continually reminded herself that everything had worked out for the best in the end. Everyone now agreed that melting the polar ice would have drowned half the civilized world, including Baltimore. And so the mistake in calculations became a cause for celebration, and the man who had made it became a hero. And that hero was none other than Mr Jefferson Thomas Maston, generally known as J. T.

J. T. Maston was nearly sixty, with an iron hook at the end of one arm (the result of an accident with a mortar during the Civil War), but he was a great man: not only a renowned mathematician, but an inventor (he'd designed the mortar that removed his hand himself). It was not long after their first meeting that Evangelina had decided she wanted nothing more than to be this great man's wife, and it was now a little over three months since Evangelina had got her wish, and had become Mrs J. T. Maston.

She should have been deliriously happy, if not for one thing: J. T. Maston had taken up gardening.

She found her husband bending over a howitzer in a far corner of the grounds. "I thought that would be a good spot for the azaleas," he said, pointing at a patch of cleared soil between the fountain and the grotto.

She positioned herself directly in her husband's line of sight. "Well?"

"Well what?"

She did a little twirl, raising a hand to indicate her hat. "What do you think?"

"About what?"

She stopped twirling. "Never mind."

Her husband shrugged and turned his attention back to the cannon. "Stand back."

Evangelina covered her ears as the gun went off, discharging a cloud of seeds.

Chapter Two
In which a solution is suggested

"I wouldn't even mention it," Evangelina said, "but the neighbours are complaining, the staff are threatening to leave, and now he's dug up all my rose bushes and is talking about turning the ornamental pond into an onion patch."

The monthly gathering of the New Park Ladies' Gardening Society burbled their sympathy. They were meant to be discussing their annual "Best Delphiniums" award, but the conversation had drifted off-topic.

It was a warm day, and the various scents of lavender, musk, rose, and vanilla emanating from the ladies around her seemed to be fighting a losing battle against the reek of garbage wafting in through the windows of the Methodist meeting hall.

"And he didn't even notice my new hat," she added, fanning herself. This was greeted with such an eruption of clucking and tsk'ing that Fiona Wicke was forced to bring down her gavel.

Once the most beautiful woman in Baltimore, these days the thrice-widowed chair of the gardening society contented herself with being the most fashionable. She leaned back in her seat – at least as far back as the stiff horsehair-padded bustle beneath her dress would allow – and formed a temple with her lace-gloved fingers. "I take it Mr Maston and Mr Barbicane are still not speaking?"

It seemed everyone in Baltimore knew about the rift between J. T. Maston and the president of the Gun Club. It all went back to those three silly little zeros. The one thing Mr Impey Barbicane refused to forgive was an error in calculations – even an error that had saved the world – with the end result that Mr Maston had not only resigned his position as club secretary, but had completely forsworn mathematics. And taken up gardening instead.

"Therein lies the source of your problem," Fiona said, "and also the solution. Find a way to reconcile those two men, and you shall have your garden back."

"But how?"

"You might distract the men from their quarrel by providing them with a new goal on which to focus their attention."

"As you might distract a vicious dog by throwing it a piece of meat," the society's first vice-chair (and one of its youngest members), the forty-three-year-old Hermione Larkin, added.

Fiona raised an eyebrow at her vice-chair before turning back to address Evangelina. "Give them a new project to work on and all past differences will quickly be forgotten."

"As your garden will also be forgotten . . . by your husband, I mean," added Hermione.

"A project?" Evangelina said. "What kind of project?"

Prunella Benton rose to her feet. "Wasn't your husband involved in that expedition to the moon some years back?"

"That's it!" a voice at the back of the room exclaimed. "That's your project, a return to the moon!"

Chapter Three
A delegation

"There is no point in returning to the moon," Mr Impey Barbicane stated categorically, the beads of sweat on his upper lip betraying his discomfort at being confronted by a delegation of middle-aged women. "The moon is uninhabitable."

"Baltimore was uninhabitable a hundred years ago," Prunella Benton said, dismissing Barbicane's argument with a wave of her hand. "No society to speak of, at any rate."

"My house was uninhabitable until I replaced those awful curtains," Hermione Larkin added, rolling her eyes.

Barbicane, exasperated, turned to his compatriot, Captain Nicholl. Though it was only a few months since Evangelina had last seen them, both men looked older than she remembered. The face below Barbicane's trademark stovepipe hat seemed thinner and more haggard, while Captain Nicholl seemed pale and tired.

Even the room seemed different from how she remembered it. The formerly gleaming clusters of muskets, blunderbusses, and carbines that adorned the walls now seemed dingy and uncared-for, the glass display cases of ammunition were covered in a layer of dust, and the exuberant atmosphere she recalled from her previous visits had been replaced by an air of gloom.

It felt as if everything in the place had somehow become smaller. Even the men seemed smaller.

"It's not the same thing at all," Captain Nicholl stepped in. "There is no air or water on the moon."

"And there are no sandwiches in a forest," Hermione responded. "If you wish to have a picnic in the woods, you bring the sandwiches with you!"

"Sandwiches?" said Barbicane.

"What Mrs Larkin means is: if a place is not inhabitable, you find a way to make it so," Evangelina explained.

"May I remind you," said Captain Nicholl, "Mr Barbicane and I have actually orbited the moon, and in our close observations of its surface, we saw no sign of life, and no sign of anything that might sustain life."

Fiona Wicke spoke up at this point. "If, as you say, there is no air on the moon, it is worth bearing in mind that vegetation produces oxygen."

"But there is no vegetation on the moon," Mr Barbicane responded, a trace of irritation creeping into his voice.

"And there was precious little vegetation in my garden until I planted it," said Hermione.

"Ladies," said Captain Nicholl. "From what I have seen with my own eyes, I am forced to conclude that the lunar soil is incapable of supporting vegetation. You must believe me when I tell you that nothing can survive there. Nothing."

Hermione seemed about to speak again, but Fiona silenced her with a discreet shake of the head. "Just one last question," Fiona said. "Why did you send a projectile to the moon in the first place?"

"To prove it could be done," said Barbicane.

"They were laughing at us," Fiona said as the women emerged into the sunlight. "Not aloud, but inwardly; you could see it in their faces. And they had every right to do so. We were not prepared, we had not thought it through."

A sudden gust of wind sent several sheets of discarded newspaper flapping about the square. Hermione grimaced in disgust as one of the dusty sheets plastered itself across the front of her carefully draped and bustled skirt. "When is someone going to do something about the garbage problem in this city?" she demanded, shaking her skirt free.

Fiona watched the paper blow away down the street, her face creased in thought.

Chapter Four
Fiona thinks it through

"Is Mrs Wicke at home?" Evangelina asked, handing the maid her card.

Evangelina was left to wait in the front parlour while the maid went to see if her mistress was at home. She was admiring a cloisonne vase when she heard Fiona's voice coming from behind her: "I've never really liked that vase, it was a gift from my first husband's mother."

Evangelina's first reaction on turning around was to ask Fiona if she was all right. Though it was half past two in the afternoon, her hair was down and she was still in her dressing gown.

"Yes, yes, of course. I'm fine."

"Are you sure you're all right?" Evangelina persisted, trying not to stare at Fiona's state of undress.

"Yes, yes! I'm glad you came, actually; I want to show you something."

She led Evangelina out into the garden. "What is that?" she asked, pointing at a mound of grass cuttings and kitchen scraps.

"It's a compost heap," Evangelina said. "Are you quite sure you're all right?"

"Take a look at it," Fiona insisted. "What does it consist of?"

"Fiona, I don't need to examine your compost heap to ascertain its contents. I know what's in a compost heap, I have one myself."

"Potato peelings, eggshells, coffee grounds," Fiona began, counting each item off on her fingers. "Apple cores, hedge trimmings –"

"Fiona, what are you getting at?"

"Garbage! It's all garbage! And what is the biggest problem in Baltimore today? The garbage problem."

"So?"

"So we send our garbage to the moon!"

"But that's what I came here to tell you about. Immediately after we left the gun club the other day, Mr Barbicane contacted my husband to tell him about our proposal – which they both found rather amusing – with the end result that Mr Maston has since been reinstated as club secretary and returned to the pursuit of mathematics, while I have this morning hired two men to repair the damage to my garden. So everything has turned out as planned and we can forget about the moon."

"No, no, you don't understand," Fiona insisted. "This isn't about your husband's rift with Barbicane. This is about making the moon a place where human beings can survive, and it can work! What was Barbicane and Nicholl's main objection to the possibility of making the moon habitable? The lack of an atmosphere. But what I am proposing will create that atmosphere."

"How?"

"Of what does our own atmosphere consist?" Fiona asked her.

Evangelina shrugged. "Oxygen, I suppose."

"I think you'll find some seventy-eight per cent of the air we breathe is nitrogen. And what gas does a compost heap produce in abundance?"

"Nitrogen?"

"Exactly! So . . . we send our garbage to the moon where it decays into compost, producing nitrogen to enrich the soil, thus enabling the growth of vegetation. The vegetation produces oxygen. Then we throw in some worms, insects, and small animals to produce carbon dioxide, and voilà! We have an atmosphere."

Evangelina's mouth dropped open. "Where do you get such ideas?"

"Come upstairs and I will show you."

Evangelina followed her back into the house and up the stairs to a large study lined with overflowing bookcases.

Fiona walked over to a desk piled high with open books and several stacks of handwritten notes. "My second husband, though he made his living in textile sales, had a great interest in science, especially chemistry. I've still got all his books, and have been conducting further research of my own at the public library."

Evangelina picked up one of the handwritten sheets and began reading its contents out loud: "Corncobs, cotton, paper, sawdust, wood chips, straw, hops, restaurant scraps, market scraps, hair, feathers, hooves, horns, peanut shells, seashells, seaweed . . . What is this?"

"Just a partial list of things that can be composted, all of which are thrown out every day. When I was at the library yesterday, I found a survey predicting that over the next twenty-five years, the average American city will produce an average of eight hundred and sixty pounds of garbage per

capita. With the current population of Baltimore standing
at approximately five hundred thousand souls, that makes
a total of . . ." She paused to riffle through her notes. "Ah,
here we are: 430 million pounds of garbage. Keep in mind
this figure is for Baltimore alone, and assumes no further
growth in population, which strikes me as unlikely. Now,
consider the population of New York, currently standing at
over three and a quarter millions –"

Evangelina didn't need to hear any more figures to grasp
what Fiona was telling her. "In just twenty-five years, we
could turn the moon into a gigantic compost heap!"

"And that is just the beginning," Fiona said, concluding her
address to an extraordinary meeting of the New Park Ladies'
Gardening Society, called at less than forty-eight hours
notice. "Upon his return to Earth, the third passenger in
Barbicane and Nicholl's projectile, the Frenchman Michel
Ardan . . ."

More than two decades after the Frenchman's only visit
to America, the mere mention of the name "Ardan" was
still enough to prompt a wave of wistful sighs.

" . . . remarked that the greatest disappointment of his
life was to learn there were no Selenites, but I tell you now
that the Frenchman was wrong. Ladies, we are the Selenites!"

The entire membership of the society – all seventeen of
them – rose to their feet to give Fiona a standing ovation.

"Whatever became of Monsieur Ardan?" Hermione whispered to Evangelina.

"He returned to France some years ago," Evangelina whispered back, "and the last I heard, was growing cabbages."

"Cabbages? How perfect! We could invite him to judge
our best vegetable competition!"

Evangelina took a slow, deep breath. "Hermione, he lives
in France."

Chapter Five
A garden on the moon

"Over the same period, Boston, with a population of approximately five hundred and sixty thousand, will produce well over four hundred and eighty-one million pounds of garbage," Fiona informed the trio of gentlemen seated on the opposite side of the table.

"Four hundred eighty-one million and six hundred thousand, to be precise," said J. T. Maston.

Evangelina sat quietly at Fiona's side. The only reason for her presence today was her role in arranging this second meeting. Until the occasion two weeks previously, when she had burst in uninvited with three other women, Evangelina had been the only non-member – and the only female – ever allowed into the Gun Club premises. This special status had only been granted to her on account of her generous financial contribution to the scheme to shift the Earth's axis. Getting Mr Barbicane to agree to a second audience with Fiona had not been easy, but once Evangelina became determined upon something, she usually got her way.

Now there was little for her to do except allow the others to talk while she reflected on her surroundings, and she couldn't help being pleased by what she saw.

The firearms on display had been restored to their shining former glory, the glass cases sparkled, and the air of gloom had lifted. And it was all due to the return of J. T. Maston, once again at his usual place, his good hand scribbling furiously as he recorded every word spoken at the table into his notebook.

"While New York, with a population of approximately three and a quarter million is predicted to produce –"

"Two billion, seven hundred and ninety five million pounds of garbage," said J. T. Maston, entering the numbers in his book with a flourish.

"Correct," said Fiona. "And not only will this raw material cost us nothing, city governments will pay us to take it. The only initial expenses involved would be those of setting up a company and hiring local men to work as our collectors. Once we acquire the garbage, we simply pack it into missiles designed to break open upon impact, and send it crashing into the moon."

J. T. Maston began sketching a design for the garbage missile. "The opening mechanism, here, will require a small explosives charge . . ."

"Or perhaps just a spring?" Fiona suggested tactfully.

"That would work, too," Maston agreed, modifying his drawing.

"And you plan to follow this garbage with seeds," said Barbicane. "What kind of seeds?"

"Whatever is readily to hand, I should imagine," Captain Nicholl interjected before Fiona could answer. "Surely any plant will do as long it produces oxygen."

"Acorns," said J. T. Maston. "If people are going to live on the moon, they will require wood for building houses."

"Yes, trees must be a priority," Barbicane agreed, "because they take the longest to grow."

J. T. Maston drew a large circle to represent the moon. "We could fit an oak forest in here," he said, marking out a section of the northern hemisphere.

"Apple orchards over there," said Barbicane, indicating a section over to one side. "Pear trees over there, orange groves down here."

"We'll need grasslands for cattle," Captain Nicholl enthusiastically joined in, while Fiona insisted there also be room for the purely aesthetic, "The Selenite garden must be a place of beauty, a new Eden if you like."

"Roses, gardenias, et cetera, over there," said J. T. Maston. "Corn and wheatfields here." He looked up from his fevered sketching. "But how do we water all this vegetation?"

"India rubber," said Evangelina, speaking up for the first time.

"What?" said Nicholl.

"Children's toy balloons made from the sap of the India rubber tree," Fiona explained. "Every shipment to the moon will include a number of these balloons filled with water . . .

thanks to a suggestion from one of our members who caught her grandson throwing a water-filled balloon at the neighbours' cat."

"A garden on the moon," Mr Barbicane said wistfully. "If only it were possible."

Fiona's eyebrows shot up in surprise. Even Captain Nicholl seemed a little startled.

"But it is possible," Fiona protested, sifting through her notes. "There's much more I haven't gone into yet. Bees, for example. I didn't mention the bees because they don't come in until a later stage. And there'll be worms. Lots of worms . . ."

"My dear Mrs Wicke, I am sure that your idea is more than possible in theory, it's just impossible in practice."

"But . . ."

"The one thing you have not considered is: how on earth do you expect to send all these missiles to the moon?"

"But you've done it before," Fiona sputtered. "The Columbiad cannon . . ."

"The cannon to which you refer fired one projectile containing three men, two dogs, and a handful of chickens towards the moon on one occasion more than twenty years ago. Firing that one – comparatively lightweight – missile, one time only, required four hundred thousand pounds of fulminating cotton. What you are proposing would seem to involve the firing of an immense number of much heavier projectiles on a daily basis over a period of many years, possibly a century or more. I doubt there is that much explosive in the world, and even if there were, the cost would be prohibitive."

Fiona scoured her pages of notes, searching for an answer.

"But the cannon still exists," said Evangelina.

Barbicane shook his head. "Melted down, years ago."

"And Moon City?" Fiona asked, referring to the Florida base the Gun Club had constructed for that one, long-ago, trip to the moon.

"Long since reclaimed by jungle," said Barbicane. "There was no reason to maintain it."

Fiona turned an imploring gaze to Captain Nicholl.

The Captain responded with a sympathetic shrug.

"What is going on here?" J. T. Maston demanded, slamming his good fist down on the table. "When did Impey Barbicane ever fail to rise to a challenge? When did Captain Nicholl ever withdraw from the prospect of difficulty with a shrug? These are not the men I know! The men I know do not retreat from problems, they thrive on them!"

"Calm down, Maston," said Mr Barbicane. "I merely said it was impossible. I never said we wouldn't find a way to do it."

That evening, Evangelina sat down at her roll-top desk to compose an overseas cablegram.

> Scorbitt House
> New Park, Baltimore
>
> Dear Monsieur Ardan,
>   We have never met, but my husband has always said he considers you the best of men, and I thought you would want to know what is happening here in Baltimore . . .

Chapter Six
The great work begins, and a cablegram arrives

Over the next few weeks, a company was formed, workers were hired, and rubbish collection contracts were signed with cities up and down the eastern coast of America. A team was dispatched to the Florida wilderness to begin the rebuilding of Moon City, the ladies of the gardening society worked on refining their designs for the Selenite garden, Barbicane and Nicholl attacked the problem of the explosives, and J. T. Maston spent his days and nights at the chalkboard, covering it in strange arithmetical symbols that meant nothing to Evangelina, but which he assured her were absolutely vital to the project at hand.

And the following cablegram arrived:

> Le Plessis-Brion
> France

Dear Madame Maston,

Thought my travelling days were over, but your news has rekindled the only passion still burning in this old man's heart. Pull of Selene too strong for this Endymion, cannot stay away. Passage booked on steamer Nereus, arriving Baltimore 7th September. Tell Barbicane: explosives problem solved. Explanation on arrival.

Ardan

P.S. Sorry husband did not notice new hat. Am sure it was very lovely.

Chapter Seven
A Frenchman, a Norwegian, and a cannon

The ladies of the New Park Gardening Society gathered along a railing at the dockside, the new-style S-bend corsets beneath their gaily-coloured outfits contorting their spines into the latest fashionable silhouette: torso thrust forward as if leaning into a wind. Evangelina stood near the front of the group, feeling rather splendid in her ensemble of leg-of-mutton-sleeved dress, white gloves, lace-trimmed parasol, and hat bedecked with silk flowers.

A short distance away from the women, a committee of Gun Club members waited in loose formation, the men almost indistinguishable from one another in their uniform attire of dark frock coats and stovepipe hats.

At long last, the ship's passengers began to disembark.

The ladies twittered in excitement while the men went through a ritual of solemnly clearing their throats, straightening their backs, and tugging at their waistcoats.

A man emerged from the crowd, heading straight for the line of waiting ladies. Tall and broad-shouldered, with weathered skin and a shock of white hair as thick and wild as a lion's mane, he wore no coat or hat, and was dressed more like a farmhand than a gentleman in his open-necked shirt and trousers of the coarsest material. Evangelina asked herself if this could possibly be the person she was here to greet, but her doubts were soon dispelled as the men surged forward to shake the oddly-dressed stranger's hand and slap him on the back. "Is that him?" she asked Prunella Benton.

Prunella nodded, apparently too overcome to speak.

And then before she knew it, the Frenchman was standing before her, taking her gloved hand in his large, callused paw and raising it to his lips. "My dear Madame Maston, it was your siren call that lured this simple man of the soil away from his little cabbage patch. And now I am, and shall ever remain, your devoted admirer," he said, his dark eyes gazing at her with an intensity that made her feel, for that one moment, as if she were the only woman in the world.

"I . . . I . . ." she said.

"Your husband is the most fortunate of men," Monsieur Ardan told her before moving on to give his full attention to the next woman down the line.

A forty-ish bearded man in a brown wool suit approached the group, followed by at least a dozen stevedores wheeling an assortment of trunks and crates.

"Ah, there you are at last!" Ardan exclaimed, striding over to the man. He threw an arm around his shoulders and introduced him to the assembled party. "My travelling companion, Professor Stefan Halstein of the University of Christiania."

The professor bowed to the assemblage before turning to say something to Ardan.

"My friend the professor begs your indulgence as he speaks little English, and asks me to present you with his gift of Norwegian pine cones," Ardan explained, indicating one of the crates, "so there may be a little bit of Norway on the moon. While I . . ." he went on, touching the crate beside it, "have brought you cabbage seeds from France."

The group started to applaud, but Ardan raised a hand for silence. "And herein," he said, denoting the remaining crates and trunks with a sweeping gesture, "lies the solution to the problem of explosives."

"What is it?" everyone demanded to know.

The Frenchman once again signalled silence. "My friend the professor is a pioneer in the field of electromagnetism. Later we will organise a demonstration."

Evangelina sat in a box at the Baltimore Opera House, which Monsieur Ardan and the Norwegian professor had hired for their demonstration. A row of thick wooden planks and metal sheets hung suspended from the ceiling above the central aisle, the seats below them cordoned off. On the stage, Michel Ardan and the professor stood either side of a tiny cannon connected to an array of Leyden jars. Professor Halstein spoke in French; Ardan translated his words into English.

Ardan said something about coils of wire and electro-magnetic forces of attraction and repulsion – none of which she understood – then held up a piece of metal so small she could barely see it. "Please keep in mind, the apparatus we are using today is merely a miniature model expressly designed for this indoor demonstration, to fire a projectile barely one pound in weight. The full-sized version of the professor's electromagnetic cannon will be not be powered by Leyden jars, but by a steam-driven dynamo the size of this room, and will be capable of firing missiles weighing up to two tonnes, with almost no sound, and no recoil." He then went on to talk about the row of targets hanging from the ceiling. There were thirty of them, fifteen metal and fifteen wood, none less than five inches thick.

Ardan handed the piece of metal back to the professor. The professor popped it down the barrel, then threw a switch. Something inside the cannon began to glow bright red; the only sound was a low, deep hum. The professor threw the switch a second time. There was a sudden sound of metal hitting wood, then metal, then wood, then metal, and then everything went silent once more. The targets were lowered from the ceiling. Every single one had a big round hole through the middle.

"But where is the projectile?" someone asked. A search was

instigated, which continued until one of the men noticed a hole in the wall at the back of the upper balcony. Everyone hurried upstairs and into the lobby beyond the balcony, where they found a hole punched through to the outside of the building. One of the men looked through and reported seeing a broken window in the top floor of a building across the street.

"Tell the professor we need to get started immediately," Mr Barbicane instructed Ardan.

Chapter Eight
A new beginning

It was after 11 p.m., but thanks to the array of dynamos thrumming in the night, the crowded streets of Moon City were awash with light. Even the tall cannon looming over the rooftops at the edge of town had been bathed in light for the occasion, and it was to the cannon that everyone was heading. It was the 31st of December, 1899, and the first Earth-to-Moon garbage missile was scheduled for deployment at the stroke of midnight.

Evangelina and J. T. joined the throng making their way past rows of vast warehouses filled with vats of percolating garbage, to the specially-erected stands where the Mastons were to have seats of honour alongside Fiona Wicke, Monsieur Ardan, and the head of the worm department. By 11.30, everyone was seated and glasses of champagne had been distributed to those in the seats of honour.

Monsieur Ardan dabbed at his eyes as the cannon was levered into position. "Oh, to be a piece of rubbish inside that capsule!"

At one minute to midnight, Professor Halstein placed a hand on the switch, and at midnight exactly, he pulled the switch down. There was a brief dimming of the lights combined with a whooshing sound, and then someone shouted, "There it goes, the first of thousands!"

Mr Barbicane raised his glass of champagne. "To the moon, and a new century."

"To the moon, and a new beginning," Fiona said, clinking her glass against his.

Monsieur Ardan and the head of the worm department drank a toast to "the lovely Selene, soon to turn green," then joined in a chorus of Auld Lang Syne. Evangelina turned to face her husband. "Just think about it, J. T., a hundred years from now, people will be living on the moon."

J. T. Maston turned his face up to the blackness into which the projectile had vanished, his mind already racing into the future. "When we get home," he said, "I really must dig out that ornamental pond."

A MATTER OF MATHEMATICS

Tony Ballantyne

"Then, Mr Fuller, you pretend that a woman's personality will never be suitable for the making of mathematical or experimental science progress?"

The American peeled a little yellow square of paper from the pad that he kept in his pocket and folded it carefully down the centre.

"To my extreme regret, I am obliged to Miss Scrobot." He gave the mechanical woman a warm smile, his fingers working busily the while. "There have been some . . . very remarkable women in mathematics, especially in Russia, I fully and willingly agree with you. But with her cerebral conformation, she cannot become an Archimedes, much less a Newton."

"Allow me to protest in the name of my sex!" intoned Miss Scrobot indignantly, the calmness of her metal face contradicting the emotion of her reply. Max gave a little bow.

"A sex, Miss Scrobot, much too charming to give itself up to the higher studies." He straightened and continued the folding of the paper. Miss Scrobot put her metal arms to her hips.

"Well, then, according to your opinion, no female personality seeing an apple fall could have discovered the law of universal gravitation?"

There was a whirring of gears coming from within Miss Scrobot's gunmetal casing. Max Fuller smiled at her, feeling it typical of the weaker sex to become so emotional in an argument.

"I think, Mr Fuller, you criticize me unfairly," continued Miss Scrobot. "You fail to accord me due respect not only because I am female, but also because I am a mechanical intelligence!"

"And a most delightful mechanical device at that, Miss Scrobot!" exclaimed Max Fuller. "Seldom have I seen a casing of such grace and form." Indeed he hadn't. Despite being formed of gunmetal, the upper body of Miss Scrobot superbly resembled a young woman. If you ignored the wheeled cube of her base, concealing the machinery that caused her to move and think, she was quite attractive in her static, statuesque way. "The lines of your body, the engineering of your cogs and gears speaks of nothing but the highest manufacture!" continued Max. "I have the highest regard for your intelligence, but each must take their place in the natural order of things. Look over there . . ."

The Eiffel–Citroën Tower strode across the Paris skyline, daring sightseers crowding the middle deck. The high winds so typical of late no doubt added to their sense of adventure at riding the marvellous device.

"You see the tower," continued Max Fuller. "The intelligence that controls that could be nothing but male."

That pretty face, framed by metal curls, spoke in cool tones. "Ah yes, but you speak of physical strength, Mr Fuller."

" . . . but of course, Miss Scrobot. And there are devices such as yourself made for the gentler occupations. The teaching of children, the keeping of a house . . ."

"But not for any great feats of Intelligence. Two years ago I visited England. Invited there by the Royal Society, no less! Now there is a country where a thinking engine is judged solely on its merits, not its gender."

"And look where that country's thinking is taking us,

Miss Scrobot!" laughed Max Fuller. "Look what it has done to their own land! They have burned so much coal in their ceaseless drive to mechanize the world they have destroyed their climate. Their meteorologists say that in ten years they will have lost the Gulf Stream. Their country grows colder whilst a cloud of smog threatens to smother it!" He quickly lost his good humour as the magnitude of that country's actions settled on him. He took a deep breath and resumed the careful folding of the paper.

"Ah! And look how they respond to such a catastrophe! Do they seek to make good their island home? Do they seek to put right the damage they have caused? No! Such thinking is not within their character! They believe they have the divine right to shape this world and their place upon it, and to hell with the rest of us! Projectiles every day for the past fourteen months. Already the Earth begins to tilt on its axis. Where shall we end up, Miss Scrobot? Where will Paris and Baltimore and Washington end up when the English complete their infernal engineering?"

Miss Scrobot gave a brittle laugh.

"Perhaps you are right. Perhaps the sexes are different. My sex could never own to such a plan!"

"Nonsense! Was not a member of your sex integral to the first attempt to tilt the Earth's axis? I believe it was your name-sake, a Miss Scorbitt, who helped bankroll that first plot!"

"Indeed it was." Miss Scrobot's voice was cool. She knew what was coming next. Max Fuller spoke with a chuckle.

"Ah yes! And was it not also she that scuppered its chances? Had your namesake not walked in on J.T. Maston as he performed the calculations for the firing of the cannon that would effect the reaction to tilt the Earth, had she not disturbed him and caused him to make that mistake in the charge required . . ."

Max Fuller suddenly began to laugh loudly.

"In fact!" he exclaimed. "I must apologise. Your sex has achieved the equivalent in the field of Mathematics to a Newton. You saved the Earth! Albeit by error!"

Miss Scrobot placed her metal hands beneath her chin

and looked up at the American who was now laughing to himself as he finished folding the paper.

"Laugh if you must, Mr Fuller. But who will save the Earth this time?"

Max handed the folded paper across to Miss Scrobot. She accepted it gracefully. A little yellow bird, beautifully made. His face darkened.

"Though it pains me to say it, Miss Scrobot," said Max, gazing at the imposing strength of the Eiffel-Citroën tower as it bent to pick a cargo of wooden crates from some ship anchored in the Seine. "I feel that this is indeed a time where the qualities of my sex are required."

Each time he took the train to England, Max found the journey a little bit more depressing. When it was built, the French end of the Channel Tunnel had had signs written in French first, English second. Now they were all in English only, horrible pressed metal rectangles with blue borders and *sans serif* fonts that drained the joy and adventure of travel from the journey *sous la mer*.

In Fuller's opinion, the French had had the right approach. Travel should hint at the exotic, it was the civilized man's duty. And yet it was the English, with their urge to turn everything to a profit that had won the argument. It was a French train that pulled into the station, but it was a fading confection. A story of past grandeur: aging leather seats, tarnishing brass and scratched wooden tables. What point striving for quality and longevity when the cunning English had devised disposability? When it was cheaper to build five trains that lasted ten years than one that lasted fifty, who cared for quality?

And now the English sought to impose that philosophy on the very planet itself.

Fuller seated himself by the window. A bottle of Macon Villages, its neck wrapped in white linen, waited in an ice bucket. He beamed as the waiter poured him a glass and then sat back to enjoy a first mouthful whilst studying the leather bound menu. The train began to move and Fuller gave a little nod of approval. Forty minutes in the tunnel, another hour or so to get to London. Coffee in the First Class lounge at Waterloo station. His quiet peace was disturbed by the loud tones of an Englishman behind him.

"I can see what it says on the menu, *garçon*. But what I would like is an omelette. An omelette, understand? Do you have that word in French?"

"It is French," said Max Fuller, turning lazily in his seat.

"Max!" called the man, delightedly. "What are you doing on this train?"

"Going to the Proms, Durham. Elgar's seven symphonies over three nights. Where else would a man of culture be heading?"

The other man screwed up his face as if in pain.

"All that orchestral nonsense sounds the same to me," he complained. "Give me some of that American minstrel music any day."

Lord Durham was a tall, thin man with an oversized ginger moustache. He slid out from behind his table with some difficulty, long arms and legs moving in an uncoordinated fashion.

"Hey, *garçon*. I'll be sitting over here at my friend's table. And bring me some rolls. None of that French *pain* nonsense, some good plain English rolls and some yellow butter. And I'll have a beer. Bitter, in a proper glass, with a handle. Don't tell me you haven't got any, go and find some."

He rolled his eyes and pushed his way into the seat before Max, who gave a patient sigh at his friend's appalling manners.

"So, Durham. Your countrymen are still intent on rolling the world to your own selfish ends?" smiled Max. Durham gave a laugh.

"Ah, you Americans are just sore that we're succeeding where you failed all those years ago."

"That was not specifically an American venture, Durham . . ." said Max. Durham gave a laugh that could be heard in the next carriage.

"Forming a cannon out of a mine, seeking to blast a

projectile into space, the reaction of the launch designed to knock the world through 23° and 28 minutes? It was an original idea, I grant you! However, if you'll forgive me, Max, your countrymen's mistake was in adopting such a brute force approach."

Max took another drink of wine. A white jacketed waiter smoothly topped up his glass.

"I believe the Baltimore Gun Club still owns the title to the Arctic region," said Max. "They planned to exploit the coal and oil reserves they believed to be buried there. Maybe they will get the chance now."

"Nothing doing, old chap. Her Majesty's government purchased the title before commencing with project Helios. And at a knock down price, too." Durham wagged a finger at his friend. "Take my word for it. America has lost the way when it comes to business."

The waiter placed a glass of brown beer and a plate of rolls before Durham.

"This is something more like it," said Durham. "Now, fetch me my bag, *chop chop*. The green one over there."

The train rattled over some points, heading for the approach to the tunnel. The carriage was a typical piece of SNCF rolling stock: old-fashioned, over engineered, with an air of grand style slowly coming apart at the seams.

"Ah," said Durham, gulping down the beer. "Best bitter. You should try this, Max, you really should. If only things had gone differently in the trenches, back in 1917, we could all be drinking this and enjoying it."

"I'll stick to my wine, thank you Durham."

"If if if," said Durham, thoughtfully. "If Miss Scorbitt hadn't scuppered your countrymen's original attempt to tilt the Earth the planet might be run by Americans. If the Generals had succeeded in putting down the mutiny the Great War would have gone on with heaven knows what damage to the British economy." Durham took another sip of beer and looked thoughtful. "Might have been for the best," he mused. "That's where the revolution lost its head, you know. Bit more loss of life and suffering by the common soldiers and the proletariat would have seen the true light. The red flag would be flying over Buckingham Palace and the world would be run on good socialist principles. Instead, the British Empire grows ever larger as available land grows smaller. We burn the coal of nations to run our engines, and when the weather changes do we hold up our hands and accept responsibility . . . ?"

Max was getting bored. He pulled a square of yellow paper from his pad and began to fold it into shape.

"Yes, Yes, Durham," he said good-naturedly. "My, you don't half go on."

Durham gave a self-conscious laugh.

"Hah. I suppose I do. Comes of being brought up to lead, I suppose. All those years in public school being trained to run the Empire then one finds that one is no longer required. Job your father had lined up for you is taken by some boy from a comprehensive school. *We're a meritocracy now, old boy, don't you know?* No sense of tradition . . ."

"You're doing it again . . ." said Max, drawing his finger across a yellow crease.

Durham gave a loud laugh and took another drink of beer. His tweed jacket was well made, but old and shabby. Just another of the well-off playing at having a social conscience, thought Max. Still, the man wanted to help, and who was he to argue? Max lowered his voice.

"Do you have the things?"

Durham's reply was so soft that Max could hardly hear it. The change in the man's attitude was really quite sudden. Almost professional.

"In the bag," whispered Durham. "Clothes, papers, money, train tickets. Walk into the public convenience on Waterloo Station as Max Fuller, you'll walk out as Brian Chadwick. Take the tube to Euston and the train to Manchester Piccadilly. Catch the tram from there to Oldham and then on to Bridleworth. You'll probably get there in time to see the June 26th Launch. With luck, that will be the last one that goes according to plan."

Max glanced surreptitiously around the carriage. No one seemed to be listening.

"Your work docket is in there. Electropacker. You've no idea how hard it was to get hold of that. There is some technology the Empire likes to keep an eye on. How do you feel about electrocotton? How was the training?"

"As good as could be expected," said Max and the train plunged into the darkness of the tunnel. A waiter appeared and gave a little bow.

"Are you ready to order, sir?"

Max Fuller selected the Moules Marinières with Dover Sole to follow.

It might be the last decent meal he had for some time.

It was raining in London, but ah, didn't it always rain in London. Not like this, thought Brian Chadwick *née* Max Fuller as he emerged from the gentlemen's public convenience into the Waterloo sunset. This was a tropical rain, great long strips of warm water that swirled over the golden pavements seeking the overfull black mouths of the drains. The newsmen who stood by the street corner electro-presses had put up big black shiny umbrellas. Durham hadn't thought to provide Brian with an umbrella . . . Fortunately, glass tubes had been erected throughout the streets of London for the duration of the realignment. "Brian Chadwick" paid the six pence toll so that he could walk in the dry, out past Empire Hall and on to Waterloo bridge. Through the curved glass of the weather tube he could see the grey water churning by beneath him. "Sweet Thames run softly till I sing my song," he whispered, reciting a borrowed line from The Foundation, that great poem to the promise of the new Empire. Construction Airships floated over the old Houses of Parliament. The head office of ARTEMIS was rising amongst the half disassembled buildings. Miss Scrobot had visited there last year: had been shown the details of project Helios. Brian Chadwick's stride quickened, the glass tube bounced as an electric train, blue sparks arcing in the tropical rain, slid past from Charing

Cross Station. It was so typical of the English! That good old chap syndrome. Playing by the book. They were tilting the world on its axis, and they had invited in representatives of all the foreign powers to discuss the plan. And now as the oceans were rising and falling, as the weather patterns were shifting as a result of their actions, their sleek grey ships were sailing to the corners of the world bringing aid! Accrington brick and Oldham Cotton, Yorkshire Ham and Buxton Water. Clothing the naked, feeding the hungry, housing the homeless. All done with a clear conscience. For when the other civilized countries of the world complained they would rub their chins, adjust their cuffs, look at each other in puzzlement and ask the question:

"When we established colonies in India, did you complain? Or did you join the race to snatch up land to add to your own empires? When we were enslaving the Africans did you tell us to cease? Or did you bargain with us as you sought to buy our black gold with your cotton? Did you listen to us when we opposed the building of the Suez canal? Did you stop us when we purchased the route?

"No! If you had access to supplies of electrocotton, you too would now be doing the same. Your only complaint is that when we do as you do, we do it better!"

And that was it. His own leader, President Ellaby, had had the door to the inner chamber politely closed in his face when he visited Empire Hall to plead the American case, and then was flown back to America with a dozen bottles of good Scotch whisky and a set of Wedgwood plates. And now here walked Brian Chadwick, representative of the opposing powers, seeking to restore the world to balance. Just one man.

But maybe that was all it would take.

The earth shook as Brian climbed the stairs to his lodgings in Oldham.

"Is that a launching?" he asked.

The landlady ignored him. She opened the door to his room and waited sourly as he looked around the tiny space.

A metal bed, a little wooden desk, a new porcelain sink shining palely in the corner by the ancient wardrobe.

"Toilet down the corridor, bathroom next door. Your turn for a bath is from eight to eight thirty Tuesdays, Thursdays and Saturdays. Supplement for other times. Meal times on the back of the door. Don't blame me if the room is too cold. Give it a few months and it'll be as hot as Spain."

She gave a half smile at that, a concession to humour, and then she was gone. Brian dropped his carpetbag on the bed and went to look out of the window. Electric trains slid by outside, the noise muffled by the small anti-vibration unit in the corner of the room. Good old England, he thought. Land of big ideas and small horizons. Every one of Her Majesty's subjects entitled to hot water and a healthy environment. But only three times a week.

He opened his bag and pulled out his papers. Work docket, site pass, a large folded piece of parchment that declared that he was certified to work with electrocotton. He grimaced at the thought of the burns down his left side where he had folded the damp yellow material wrongly and caused an arc back. Four thousand dollars worth of electrocotton ruined that day. Three months later and he still felt the pain.

Further down in the bag were his work clothes and blue goggles. He was turning them thoughtfully over in his hand when there was a sudden tap at the door.

"One moment," he called, hurriedly stuffing things back into the bag. The door had already swung open.

"Alright Steve . . . oh. Sorry, mate. I thought you were someone else." The stranger paused in the door, gazing at the blue goggles laying on the bed.

"Ahah! You're an electropacker," he said.

"I'm going to be," said Brian. "And you are?"

The man came forward into the room, uninvited. He held out his hand; Brian shook it.

"Arthur Salford," said the intruder. He had a firm grip, one that suggested not so much a handshake as a challenge. "I work in blasting." he said, releasing Brian's hand and pulling a little red pad of paper from his pocket. He tore off a square. "I'm interested in electropacking, though. Just got in from Bombay yesterday. I'll stay here for the two-week window before moving on to Ceylon. How about you?"

Brian pulled a yellow square of paper from his pad.

"This will be my first job. I'm hoping to get a call to go on to the next sites."

Arthur nodded. Brian noted the creases he was making in the little square of paper: he guessed Arthur was folding it into the shape of a crane.

"That's an interesting accent," said Arthur, busily folding. "What are you, Canadian?"

"No, I'm actually from Manchester, originally. Denton. I've been working in America for the past fifteen years, helping set up the power grid in the Mid West." Brian began to fold his paper into shape. "That's where I first learned to handle electrocotton."

Arthur had completed his crane. He placed the little red paper bird on the tiny brown table by the bed, then cocked his head and gave Brian an appraising look.

"Denton, eh? I know a few lads from Denton. Which school did you go to?"

"Audenshaw Boys." Brian quickly finished folding his piece of paper. He placed a little yellow cat by the bird. The two men exchanged looks.

"Grammar school lad, eh?" said Arthur. "No wonder you're working electrocotton." He tore off another piece of paper and began folding. "I was in Persia when someone got the order of packing wrong and the stuff just spewed out over the field. We were all sent out to help sort out the mess. They had a little shanty town built just about half a mile from the edge of the bore hole. Wooden shacks, bars, dance halls. You know the sort of thing. All covered in cotton, still holding a charge. We had people like you working out the paths through the tangle, trying to get into the survivors." He stared into the distance. "They kept making mistakes. I stepped into a loop, it discharged right down my right side . . ."

Arthur placed a red paper lion next to Brian's cat.

"I still wonder about the training they give to you packers. It's supposed to be a meritocracy now, this country, but you still see a lot of people who went to the right school getting the best jobs."

"Oh," said Brian. He began to fold another piece of paper.

"I had my application for electrocotton training turned down," said Arthur. "Still, I never made it to grammar school. I was always better with my hands. But isn't that what electropacking is all about?"

He looked keenly at Brian, who stopped folding his square of paper, crumpled it in a ball and dropped it on the bed. Something about Arthur didn't quite seem right. Brian had been warned about spies . . . Could Arthur be one? Play it safe, he thought.

"You're probably right, Arthur," he said. He gave a loud yawn. "Anyway. I'm off to bed," he said. "Early night. I had a long journey up here."

Arthur looked at his watch.

"I'd give it half an hour. Wait until the next launch is over."

Brian Chadwick was up early next morning. He ate breakfast in silence at a tiny table with three other men. Watery scrambled eggs and tinned tomatoes. Heavy rain pounded at the grey windows. Torrential rain. The landlady permitted herself one of her rare smiles as he saw him looking out into the drenched day.

"Cheer up, chuck. Give it a year and we'll be eating our breakfast outside under a parasol."

Brian didn't have a raincoat with him. Lord Durham hadn't thought of that either when packing the green carpetbag.

"There's an ARTEMIS store on the square next to the tram stops," said Arthur, noting Brian standing hesitantly at the front door, turning up the collar of his jacket as he looked out into the pouring rain. Arthur had fixed Brian with another of his keen stares. "Eh, fancy forgetting to pack your mac. You've been in America too long, lad."

"I probably have," said Brian, smiling sheepishly. He pushed his documentation into his pocket and then ran from the house, pell mell through the sheets of rain that bounced from the road, gurgling up around the spaces in the cobbles. Rain plastered his hair to his head, ran down the back of his neck, soaked his trousers so that they clung to his legs. Eventually he reached the square, busy with the blue sparking hum of trams. He saw the store and ran for it, the familiar red and gold sign arched over the plate glass door, the red and gold liveried doorman holding it open for him as he ran squelching in.

"Gentlemen's raincoats and umbrellas, second floor," said the doorman, without needing to be asked.

"Thank you," said Brian.

Napoleon had said that Britain was a nation of shop-keepers. Nothing much had changed, in Brian's opinion, except now their shop was the whole world. Every town in Britain had its ARTEMIS store, and there, in its galleries, was laid out the produce of the world. Even in this rain soaked northern town there could be seen displays of ivory, a pet shop selling apes and peacocks, racks of sandalwood and cedarwood and sweet white wine. The ground floor had its jewellers selling diamonds, emeralds, amethysts and topazes. All taken from the shores of the world. And now that those shores were being swallowed by the changing tides, the signs that Brian passed on the escalator invited customers to visit the estate agents tucked away on the top floor and to speculate on those lands that would benefit from the improved climate.

Brian found a smartly dressed gentleman on the second floor who quickly selected a suitable raincoat for him.

"And an umbrella sir? We have a range made from discharged electrocotton. They actually repel the rain."

Brian chose an umbrella, paid, and then made to leave. Descending the escalator, he was delighted to hear Miss Scrobot's voice.

"Hello there sir. And what do you do? Would you be interested in a Calculating Device?"

It wasn't Miss Scrobot, but it looked like her. Brian felt more disappointed than he would have expected on discovering this. The machine had the same gunmetal hair, the same smooth face. She was dressed, however, in smart grey and lavender tartan. The mechanical woman rolled towards him.

"Would you be interested in purchasing a device to keep your home, sir? I notice from your left hand you are not yet married."

"Ah, but I am betrothed," lied Brian.

"I am not surprised to hear that, from so handsome a gentleman. And have you named the day?"

Brian wiped his forehead of the rain that was dripping from his hair. The sight of the mechanical woman made him feel very lonely and far from home.

"Maybe when the weather improves," he said, sadly.

The tram glided down the hill on which the town was built through wet, cobbled streets. The wide, handsomely proportioned buildings that clustered around the parks at the centre of Oldham gradually gave way to a long, long road lined by red terraced houses that seemed to lead up into the moors. Gradually the houses petered out and Brian found himself travelling over bleak moorland. The tram increased speed, the tracks over which it ran seemed newly laid, no doubt to service the launching area.

Brian looked out of the window at the view, such as it was. There was nothing of interest out there so far as he could see: just endless grey green moor under the drizzling grey sky. They rolled smoothly on for some time across the unchanging landscape, and then, in the distance, he caught a glimpse of movement. He stared hard and realized he was looking at another tram. Then another appeared, and then another. Lots of trams, just like his, all converging on a point. He watched as the closest drew nearer, he could see passengers sitting warm inside the rain slicked varnished yellow wood. Brian noted how the roof pickup had been lowered. Judging by the sparking, the tram now drew its current from the rails.

And now his tram was slowing as they approached the launching site. Looking forward, Brian realized the site was hidden in a valley tucked away in the endless scrubby grass of the moor. They shuddered to a halt by a wooden platform. Other workers were disembarking, pulling out their work dockets. Brian did the same.

He walked down the slippery wooden surface of the platform, one of a mass of people, dispensed by the yellow wooden trams that rolled in over the horizon from all directions. A man stood by a turnstile at the end of the platform checking dockets.

"Electocotton," he said with grudging respect. "First time here, eh? Okay, Staircase 11. Hangar 3." He stamped the docket and Brian found himself on a gravel road that ran along the line of the top of the valley. He walked along until he came to a sign bearing the number eleven and joined the queue that took him on to an enormous moving staircase that ran down the side of the hill to the valley below.

If ever he had doubted the vision and the commitment of the English, he did so no longer. Now he could see down into the wide floor of the valley, and he gasped at the sight of a cleared area through which strode mechanical men the size of the Eiffel-Citroën tower. Huge mechanisms, carrying great wooden crates from the hangars to the launch bore that lay near the centre of the area: a circular hole plunging deep underground. Yellow tractors and land trains ran across the churned earth, corrugated metal buildings rose from the sea of mud. Workmen moved busily back and forth beneath the face of a great white clock erected near the centre of the site on a metal tower. The hands ticked backwards, counting down to the next launching. One hour and twenty minutes.

One hour and twenty minutes to save the Earth.

Brian Chadwick had practised on what electrocotton the American government could afford to buy, but it hadn't been enough. It was inferior stuff, pale yellow, not like this dark green cloth that unspooled from the great reels that hung in the roof space of Hangar 3. This cotton smelled different: richer, heavier. It was a little greasy and wider. There also seemed to be a lot more of it than Brian had been expecting. The reels were almost twice as thick as he had been led to believe they would be. Durham's intelligence was not what it should have been.

At least the packing case was just as he expected: a yellow wooden cuboid the size of a large house. The electropacker just finishing his shift climbed up a wooden ladder from inside the case and shook Brian's hand. His eyes glowed oddly behind the blue lenses of his electrogoggles.

"Hey pal. It's all yours. I've been following an alternate diagonal pattern and I'm having trouble figuring out how to make the eighth perpendicular." He pushed a clipboard into Brian's other hand. "I've marked off where we're up to on the chart there, sign here to show you accept the changeover." A pencil was shoved at him and a lanolin covered finger pointed to a place on the chart ". . . and here," continued the man as Brian signed, ". . . and here. Okay, it's all yours. Good luck!"

With that the electropacker wiped his hands on a yellow duster, pulled off the big white woollen socks that covered his shoes, pulled on his raincoat and marched across the floor of the hangar beneath the great wooden reels of electrocotton brooding above.

Brian took a deep breath and dipped his hands into the nearby tub of lanolin. He rubbed them slowly, taking care to cover the skin. He took a deep breath, and felt the prickly silence of the hangar fall around him and then he descended the wooden steps of the ladder, slippery with more lanolin, and walked out on to the green expanse that filled the bottom quarter of the box. The dark green electrocotton hung down from the wooden reel above, and with a deep breath he took hold of it. He felt a tingling deep within his hands as he walked backwards up the left hand side of the case, laying the electrocotton in a neat stripe as he did so. It was important to be careful because although it did not feel it, such was the force of repulsion from material, the cotton was only one molecule thick. If handled incorrectly, it could slice into flesh without you noticing it. At the end of the case, he turned the cloth through ninety degrees, making a dog-ear shape in the corner of the box and continued along the top. At the next corner he tried the same, but he felt the pressure of the charge in the cotton already laid down beneath his feet fighting his move and so he reversed, going back the way he had come. A yellow length marker came by signalling he had only thirty feet until he reached the perpendicular, where he would have to fold the cloth through a series of shapes so that it unwound correctly when released into space.

Thirty feet. That would be the hard part. He was already sweating as he ran the cotton diagonally from one corner to another and . . . trouble! He gasped as the potential lurking there threw his hands back with a force that wrenched his shoulders. Sweating, he regained his composure. He had been lucky. If the potential there had been negative, it could have pulled the cotton in his hands down causing a flash back.

"You okay there?" asked a passing supervisor looking down from the top of the case

"Fine," said Brian. "Fine."

He took a deep breath and continued packing. The twenty foot marker passed, then the ten foot marker. And then it was time for the knot. This was the tricky part. Brian began the complicated pattern. Gradually he relaxed. It was easier than it seemed. Folding the cotton over itself repeatedly, he formed the pattern that would cause the cloth to unravel at the perpendicular.

Brian continued to fold. Eventually, the knot was finished. He breathed a sigh of relief, and then looked up to see if he was being watched. No one. There were a lot of packing cases in the enormous hangar. Now he did the job that he was here for. Sabotage!

He did the knot again.

No one noticed. He went on packing until the sirens sounded for the launch.

The workers made their way along the paths to the shelters and blast walls that ringed the launch site. There was a crackle of a tannoy.

"Launch in three minutes."

"Bloody good job," said the man on Brian's right. "Sooner they've launched, the sooner we'll be out of this rain. Let it fall on bloody Germany instead."

The other men in the group laughed and Brian joined in.

They took shelter behind a wedge-shaped piece of concrete. Most of the men lit up cigarettes or pulled out one of the day's electrosheets.

"I see that the Americans are protesting about the launches again," said one man.

"One minute," said the tannoy.

"Let them bloody whinge," said another.

Brian accepted a cigarette offered by one of the other men. He took a drag, smelling the sweet lanolin on his hands. The tobacco was good, surprisingly smooth. A lot better than the stuff available in the USA nowadays.

"Ten seconds."

Brian leant out from the side of the shelter. He could see nothing.

"Get back in here, you bloody idiot," said one of the other men, good naturedly.

"Why not watch?" said the man who had offered the cigarette. He was sitting with his back to the wall, enjoying his smoke. "I don't even know why they bring us out here now. They might as well leave us to work. Nothing ever happens at a launching."

Brian peeked around the corner of the wall. He had a good view down a wide road made of concrete squares to the raised lip of the bore hole. A yellow green haze danced in the light drizzle above the launch bore, rain drops sparkling as they fell into the electrocotton lined pit. The launch cylinder would be rifled in electrocotton to set it spinning as it travelled up through the bore hole . . . Brian felt the shock in the ground, a thumping at his feet as the explosive charge was detonated, he saw the yellow green haze brighten tremendously and form a ruled line into the sky piercing the clouds above, and then he heard the noise of the explosion.

It wasn't that loud, but oh! he felt the power. Vibration seemed to fill his entire body, it set his heart and soul resonating . . . but to the rest of the workers it was commonplace. Already men were returning to their work, and after a moment's hesitation Brian followed them, but with a growing sense of awe. Only the English. Only the English could have thought up such a scheme. It was well-known, it had been reported in the electrosheets so often it had become commonplace, but to stand here at the edge of a launching filled one with awe at their sheer daring, their exuberance, their audacity! For the past fourteen months the English had been launching projectiles stuffed with electrocotton into space.

As he trudged back to work through the drizzle the latest cylinder was soaring higher and higher until it reached the discharge point. A current would be activated and the thousands and thousands of miles of invisibly thin electrocotton within the crates would spool out, twisting under its own charge to form a great loop in the heavens. A loop larger than the Earth, one of many arranged in series around the orbit of the Earth, an enormous electromagnetic cannon that stretched out 584 million miles in length. Already the Earth's magnetic field was interacting with electrocotton launched a year ago. As the planet sailed through the great loops its axis of rotation was gently tilted around. It was a bold plan.

Brian couldn't help smiling.

Not any longer. The damage of the last year was done, but the American government had done its calculations, and done them well. With the subtle changes Brian and others like him were making to the folding pattern, the Earth would not be tilting much further in that direction. His smile broadened into a grin that quickly faded as he made it back to the warehouse.

Arthur Salford was waiting there for him. He was dressed in a smart grey suit.

"Good morning Mr Fuller," he said. "I see you took my advice and bought a raincoat."

Max stood despondently on the balcony, looking out over the Paris skyline. The sun shone down from a brilliant blue sky, fresh white clouds scudding across its face.

"Cheer up Mr Fuller," said Miss Scrobot, pouring coffee into a little white cup. "Surely you can enjoy this sunny morning with me?"

She held out the coffee and Mr Fuller accepted it. He took a sip. It was very good, he grudgingly thought.

"Oh Miss Scrobot," he said. "It's just the feeling of frustration. That all our plans should have come to nothing. That they were doomed from the very outset. The English have been on to Durham and his amateurish set-up for years."

Miss Scrobot came close and took his hand in her warm metal grip. Max looked down in surprise. It was not like her to be so forward.

"Never mind, Mr Fuller," she said. "At least you tried. You gave it your best shot. That is what your sex demands, is it not?"

"Ah, Miss Scrobot, but my best was not enough! And the English are so polite about it. That's what galls me! They were such gentlemen, they caught me and treated me so well, as if it were all a game. They treated me to a decent lunch and then had me put on a train with that Mr Salford to travel back here. We talked about cricket and the Proms all the way back. And here I am again and still the world tilts."

Miss Scrobot gave a little giggle.

"I think not," she said.

Mr Fuller looked down at her.

"Miss Scrobot, charming though you are, I think it best that you do not make jokes at a time like this. Serious matters such as these are best attended to by my sex."

Miss Scrobot gave a laugh.

"Oh Mr Fuller, will you ever learn to take my sex seriously? I hesitate to say this for fear of damaging your ego, but you would have found out eventually. Don't you see; your mission was nothing but a diversion? It has always been thus. In this new age, physical force can play its part, but it will always be subordinated by the application of the mind. Long before you set out for England, far more subtle plans were at work. It does not take the mass application of saboteurs such as yourself to set the world aright, but rather the simplest stroke of a pen."

Max looked at Miss Scrobot, his expression one of deepening anger.

"What do you mean, Miss Scrobot? Explain yourself!"

"It was necessary, Mr Fuller! The English must never suspect their scheme has been undone before it was even started. Two years ago, I was invited to visit the Royal Society. There, inspired by the example of my namesake, Miss Scorbitt, I set about atoning for the mistakes of my sex, all those years ago. All it took was an understanding of Mathematics, and the insertion of a simple digit."

"Which digit, Miss Scrobot?"

"The number two, Mr Fuller. The electrocotton the English have placed in space is twice the amount required. The Earth will not just tilt, it will perform a loop! They will end up back where they started!"

Max stared at Miss Scrobot, his expression slowly altering to one of understanding, then admiration, then joy. He squeezed the mechanical woman's hand tighter.

"Ingenious, Miss Scrobot! What can I say?"

"You could ask me to marry you, Mr Fuller,"

She looked down, shocked at her own daring. Max's smile slowly widened.

"I would not dare do otherwise, Miss Scrobot. Or should I say, Janet? When a woman makes her mind up in these matters, what man can stand in her way?"

Janet Scrobot gave a mechanical smile.

"And in matters of Mathematics, Mr Fuller. Will you now admit to female proficiency in that field?"

Max smiled warmly at his metal companion.

"Not proficiency, Janet. Rather I would say, what man could compete with a woman's wiles!"

"Oh, Mr Fuller!"

THE SECRET OF THE SAHARA

Richard A. Lupoff

In the last fifteen years of his life Verne continued to maintain a remarkable output of fiction, unfortunately all too much of it of minimal interest. Who today reads or even remembers César Cascabel *(1890),* Mistress Branican *(1891),* Claudius Bombarnac *(1892),* P'tit-Bonhomme *(1893),* Captain Antifer *(1895),* Clovis Dardentor *(1896) or* The Will of an Eccentric *(1899)? Thankfully there were more exciting novels that captured some of that old adventurous spark, such as* L'Île à hélice *(1895) – also known as* Floating Island *or* Propeller Island *– about the creation of a massive artificial island that unfortunately meets with inevitable destruction because of man's folly. Verne also wrote* Le Sphinx des glaces *(1897), or* An Antarctic Mystery, *his sequel to Poe's* The Narrative of Arthur Gordon Pym. *Other works of interest include* La Grande Forêt *(1901), or* The Village in the Treetops, *and the second Robur novel* Maître du monde *(1904).*

Verne was so prolific that there were sufficient novels stockpiled to appear posthumously, and not all have been translated into English. One of these lesser known works, L'Invasion de la Mer, *was being serialized in* Magasin d'éducation et de récréation *at the time of Verne's death in March 1905. It used an idea Verne had touched upon in* Hector Servadac *and that was the possibility of irrigating the Sahara desert. In* L'Invasion de la Mer, *engineers are constructing a canal from the Gulf of Gabè in Tunisia into the Sahara but an earthquake disrupts the work and causes the Mediterranean to break through and create a huge inland sea. This novel was translated and serialized in America in a much edited version as* Captain Hardizan *in the* American Weekly *during August 1905, a fact long unknown to Verne devotees until discovered recently by researcher Victor Berch. The first full translation appeared as* The Invasion of the Sea *in 2001 and that version inspired the following story.*

Although the Great Hall of the Republic could of course have been commandeered for the meeting, His Excellency the Governor General of the Province of Tunisie Francaise had chosen to entertain his distinguished guests in a smaller, private dining room. Such was a proper decision, for these more intimate surroundings were designed to encourage an open discussion of issues and exchange of views than would the more formal, even ceremonial, atmosphere of the flag-draped and sculpted Hall.

Here in the Governor General's private dining room, a sparkling table had been set and the Personal Representative of the President of the French Republic had entertained his guests in lavish manner. The meal had consisted of a local endive and olive salad, baked Saharan langouste stuffed with salt-water crab, lamb shish kebab, chick-peas and tabouli washed down with Algerian wine, followed by baclava, thick Turkish coffee, and a sweet Hungarian Tokay.

Empty dishes, silver, and other detritus had been cleared away by silent and well-trained servants. Out of respect for their sole female member, the Italian Dottore Speranza Verde, a native of Tuscany, the men of the party had refrained briefly from lighting cheroots. The red-haired and green-eyed Tuscan physician had startled them by requesting a cheroot from her neighbour, the English historian, Mr Black, and drawing upon it with obvious pleasure.

Now as the Governor General, M. Sebastiane LeMonde, rose, the buzz of conversation which had followed the meal ceased and a hush descended upon the room.

"Madame," the Governor General bowed toward the female physician, "and Messieurs, in the name of the President of the Republic I welcome you to French Africa and to our beautiful city of Serkout."

A murmur of approval rippled through the assemblage, following which the Governor General resumed.

"I am authorized by the President of the Republic to offer special felicitations to Colonel Dwight David White."

The Governor General nodded toward a tall, distinguished gentleman clothed in the grey uniform of the Army of the Confederate States of America. This officer's skin was black; his hair, its tight curls cropped close to his skull, shared the colouration of his military garb. The uniform bore the gold frogging and glittering decorations earned in his distinguished career.

The Colonel nodded his acknowledgment of the Governor General's felicitation.

"Sir, this year marks the one hundredth anniversary of a date in the history of your nation, the Declaration of Emancipation issued by your President, Mr Jefferson Davis. As a student of North American history since my first days at the *École de Paris*, I have long felt that President Davis's action was not only a matter of high morality, but a political move of the wisest. By declaring the enslaved persons of his nation free and equal citizens of that Republic and offering them fair compensation for the suffering and deprivation of their lives, he won for the Confederacy a new and most highly motivated Army, which led to the vanquishment of the Union forces and recognition of a new and shining ornament among the family of Nations."

The Confederate rose to his feet and responded, briefly and modestly, to the Governor General's words before resuming his seat.

M. LeMonde spoke once more. "You have assembled here, Madame and Messieurs, in regard to a situation unprecedented in human history. As you are aware, the greatest engineering feat of the past century, greater even than the Grand Canals de Lesseps which connect the Red Sea with the Mediterranean and the Atlantic Ocean with the Pacific at the Isthmus of Panama, was the creation of the Sahara Sea by the engineers of the Republic of France under the leadership of the great M. Roudaire, of happy memory."

A murmur of agreement was heard, accompanied by the nodding of distinguished heads.

"The world has known and applauded this great feat of engineering," LeMonde continued, "but at this moment we face a new puzzle of which only a handful of individuals are aware. The details will be revealed to you shortly. By your own consent, all contact with the general public and the outside world has been interdicted, and will remain so until you return from the mission which you have agreed to assay."

A grumble made its way around the table. The bearded, heavy-set archaeologist, Herr Siegfried Schwartz, ground his Cuban maduro cigar into an ash-tray. "From Berlin I receive my instructions, Monsieur LeMonde."

The Frenchman expressed his concern. "All was agreed to beforehand, Mein Herr, was it not? I hope we are not to dissolve into disagreement at this point."

"Yes, I believe that was the agreement. Otherwise I should have to consult Whitehall at every turn. It just wouldn't do, sir." The blond moustache of the historian, Sir Shepley Sidwell-Blue, twitched as if with a life of its own.

"Very well," Herr Schwartz growled, "continue, Monsieur."

"At this point, if I may be excused," the Governor General stated, "I will turn the proceedings over to the Chairman of your Committee, Monsieur Jemond Jules Rouge." The Governor General bowed and took his leave. He was replaced at the podium by his goateed countryman.

Monsieur Rouge looked around the room, his eyes flashing. "Madame and Messieurs, you represent not merely the great nations of the civilized world but the flower of

your chosen professions. Throughout this day and evening
we have socialized and exchanged credentials. In this room
are assembled the world's most famed archaeologist, the
author of many volumes which I may say cumulatively
comprise nothing less than the history of civilization, the
military officer whose brilliant campaigns have extended his
nation's borders from the Mason-Dixon Line to the de
Lesseps Inter-Oceanic Canal, and, may I offer my compli-
ments to the lovely Dottore Verde, our most accomplished
– pardon my crude pronunciation *s'il vous plait* – hydrologist."

Each participant in the conference – and the meal –
nodded acknowledgment as his or her name was spoken.

The Italian hydrologist, Dottore Verde, had prepared for
this moment. She rose to her feet and strode to the rostrum,
relieving the Frenchman who resumed his place at the now
cleared dinner table.

"Signori, when our colleagues the French opened the
northerly dunes of the Sahara desert and let in the waters
of the Mediterranean to create the Sahara Sea, they created
a new avenue for the ships of commerce and a new home
for the fish of nourishment. We agree – yes? – that the people
of the Africa North are blessed by this new sea. But also
they created, perhaps unthinkingly, the so-they-say Fleuve
Triste, the river which flows between Isola di Crainte and
Isola di Doute. This fleuve, this so-they-say fiume, is not
really a river, but a tidal phenomenon that flows first to the
north, then to the south, again to the north, again to the
south."

A sulphur match flared as Herr Schwartz lighted another
maduro. He sucked loudly at the cigar, then exhaled a cloud
of heavy, odorous smoke.

"I should think, perhaps, that Signor Schwartz most of
all, would take an interest in this phenomenon," the red-
haired Tuscan continued. "For the action of scouring of the
rushing water, back and forth, back and forth, has begun
to carry away the sand accumulated between these two
islands over a many thousands of years span. The French,

by creating this new sea, have changed the – what we call the *idrodinamica* – the hydrodynamics – of the entire Mediterranean region as well."

"So?" Herr Schwartz growled, "to what result, Doktor?"

"Herr Schwartz," the Tuscan smiled, "you of all persons are familiar with the great and ancient civilizations to the east of our present location."

"Ah, of course. The Egyptians, the Mesopotamians, the Hebrews, the Hittites. But here in the Sahara – nothing but sand and palm trees, my dear Doktor. My time I could spend far better in my museum in Berlin. A channel perhaps deeper is made, larger ships it will permit to travel to this city of Serkout. Of interest to me this is not. Only because my government instructed, am I here."

"I see." Dottore Verde gave no indication that she was hurt by the German archaeologist's words. "But your knowledge of the archaeology may yet prove useful. You see, good sir, all is not sand beneath the Sahara seabed."

"Of course not," Schwartz frowned. "Bedrock we will find. Sooner or later, it this inevitable is."

"Not only bedrock, good sir. When the Sahara was a desert, the dunes they rose and fell with the action of mighty winds. But beneath the dunes, the ancient rocks had their own," she smiled, displaying white, even teeth, "their own *topografia*, you understand? The islands between which we cruise, Crainte and Doute, are of the ancient bedrock. But –"

"This lesson in geography, dear Madame – any point at all, has it?"

The Tuscan hydrologist's monologue had turned into a dialogue with the archaeologist, then a debate, very nearly a quarrel.

"What we have found," Dottore Verde went on calmly, "is nothing less than dressed rock of a workmanship most assuredly artificial."

The historian let out a gasp. "Surely, Doktor, surely you do not realize the implications of what you say!"

Dottore Verde shook her head. A strand of her russet hair,

until this moment held in place by an elaborate array of clips and long pins, broke loose from its moorings. With an annoyed gesture she swept it away from her face. She leaned forward, pressing the knuckles of a slim hand against white linen.

"I realize quite well the implications of what I say. We are about to discover the greatest mystery since the discovery of the ancient world. We are about to discover it, yes, but will we solve this mystery? That may be the work of many years and require the efforts of many scholars, but we will be the first to behold these great objects. My friends –"

She looked around.

"*Miei amici, meine Freunde, mes amis,* did the great Egyptians move to the west, did they leave traces of their art in the Sahara land once fertile, only to retreat before the advancing sands? Or did another race, perhaps even a greater race, once call this region their home? Could they have taught their arts and science to the Egyptians, only to disappear, themselves, beneath those sands? This mystery will be solved, and we are the first so honoured to begin its unravelment."

An hour later Colonel Black and Dottore Verde sat in the lounge of the hotel where the members of the party had been inconspicuously housed. Every other customer had departed the room. A pair of Arab musicians played softly upon aoud and tabla, the voice of one rising in tones as soft and as mournful as the long, sad history of his people.

A bottle and two small glasses stood upon the table between the man and woman. A candle flickered beside the bottle, casting shadows on the faces of the two. Only an ornately tooled portfolio stood against one leg of the Tuscan hydrologist's chair to remind a viewer – had there been one – of the session earlier completed with their colleagues from France, Germany, and England.

Colonel White reached to fill both glasses, not for the first time. The two raised their glasses, let them touch rim to rim, then sipped at the delicious beverage. "I didn't like that German," Colonel White whispered. "If he doesn't believe in this mission he shouldn't be here."

Dottore Verde shook her head. "Skepticism is healthy, Colonel. Perhaps it is different for a military man like yourself, but a scientist must treat each claim as a mere possibility, a suggestion perhaps, until it is supported by solid proof."

The Confederate looked into his companion's eyes, his usually serious countenance brightened by what might have been the merest suggestion of a smile. He did not reply, not yet, but instead waited for the Tuscan to resume.

"If we believed every report," Dottore Verde said at last, "we would live in a world of chimerae and of hobgoblins, every wood full of werewolves and ogres, every castle populated by a bevy of ghosts, every tomb the abode of a vampire or a ghoul, the sea filled with mermen and naiads, and the sky at night filled with visitors from the circling planets and the twinkling stars."

Now White did smile. "You don't believe in any of those things?"

"No." Dottore Verde shook her head. The pins and clips had been removed now, and her russet locks fell in graceful waves about her oval face. "I do not say that none of those exist, the world is full of wonders and of mysteries. That is why we must investigate what lies beneath the Fleuve Triste. But until there is evidence, dear friend – I may call you that, I hope? For of all the members of our party, you seem the one to whom I am most attuned . . . ."

"I am honoured, Dottore."

"Until there is evidence, we must reserve judgement. As for me, should I meet a merman or naiad, I should be delighted. But, alas, I do not expect ever to have that pleasure."

She smiled wistfully and lifted her glass. She peered through the smoky liquid it contained, or appeared to Colonel White to be doing so. She tilted her glass to her lips, then lowered it to the table and reached for her portfolio.

"Do you know the work of Herr Schwartz's countryman, Herr Doktor Professor Roentgen, Colonel White?"

"Indeed. We use his wonderful invention in military medicine. Thanks to the good professor I am here tonight, Dottore."

"And how is that?"

The Confederate held a hand to his side. "I don't like to talk about it much."

"As you will, then."

"Very well. It was at the First Battle of Belize. I took a piece of shrapnel between my third and fourth rib. A bomb had exploded and sent our position sky-high. I was just a lieutenant then." He smiled at the recollection.

"They say that I kept fighting, that I led my platoon through the rest of the battle before I collapsed. They say that I killed an entire squad of enemy troops with a bayonet held in one hand while I held myself together with the other. I wouldn't know about that, I don't remember it."

"Yet you received a medal for it, did you not?"

"The Order of Stonewall Jackson, yes."

"Well, then." There was a look of concern on the Tuscan's face. She reached for White's hand and steadied its trembling.

"You have not recovered in fullness, have you, Colonel?"

The Afro-Confederate shook his head. "I'm sorry, Doktor."

She held his hand in both of hers until the trembling subsided. "Please," she smiled at him, "I would appreciate if you might call me Speranza."

He nodded silently, tightening his grip on the hand he held in his own.

"And I may call you Dwight?"

This brought a small smile to the Confederate's features. He relaxed his grip on the Tuscan's hand, and she on his. "I prefer David. My parents must not have been thinking when they named me Dwight White." He managed a hint of a laugh. "It didn't take me long to realize that it was better to use my middle name."

"Sensible indeed." Speranza Verde held her glass between them and the Confederate poured. A waiter appeared, placed a small brass platter of sweetmeats on the table and withdrew without speaking.

"You mentioned Professor Roentgen," the Confederate said.

"Yes. And you said his work had saved you, did you not?"

"At Belize, yes." A faraway look came into White's eyes. He lifted his glass and drained its contents. "When I regained consciousness in the field hospital the doctors told me that I'd actually had a piece of shrapnel in my heart. They couldn't see what they were doing so they used a Roentgen apparatus to guide their instruments when they took it out. If it hadn't been for that, I wouldn't have lived a day."

Speranza Verde nodded. She laid her portfolio on the table between them and took from it a heavy envelope. From this she extracted several heavy celluloid sheets. Lying flat upon the envelope from which they had been removed, the celluloid sheets appeared solidly black. The woman lifted the top sheet from the stack and handed it to Colonel White.

He held it between himself and the flickering candle that stood on the table. After studying it for the better part of a minute he whistled softly and then extended it toward Speranza Verde. She took the sheet from him and handed him another. The procedure was repeated until White had examined all the sheets.

He said, "Do you want to tell me what I've just looked at?"

Before responding she replaced the sheets in their envelope and the envelope in the portfolio. She placed this in her lap. "These are imagistic plates. They were made by combining the technology of Wilhelm Conrad Roentgen with that of my countryman Louis Jacques Mande Daguerre. The Roentgen mechanism can look through solid material. The Daguerre camera records that which the Roentgen machinery sees. What you have seen, David, is that which lies beneath the dressed rocks of the Marée de Fureur, the tidal bed that lies between the Isole de Crainte and Doute."

"Impossible."

"Not impossible."

"But Dottore–"

"*Per piacere,* Speranza."

"Speranza."

She smiled.

"I saw living things. At least, I think they were living things. But things not like any I have ever seen before. Were they alive?"

"No." The russet waves moved as if with a will of their own as she shook her head. "They have not moved. They show no signs of life. But I believe they were once alive, David."

"Creatures like that – mixtures of human and beast. They look like the product of the imagination of a madman."

She shrugged.

"I saw things in the jungle of Belize that I would never have imagined at home in Creston, South Carolina. I spent half my childhood in the water of Lake Marion along with other children. We came to know every creature in that little aquatic world, from the smallest water-bugs to tortoises with the wisdom of eternity in their eyes to eels that could eat a dog in two bites if that dog was foolish enough to swim too close. But in Belize I saw spiders that eat careless birds and plants that eat baby pigs. But still, the eels were eels, the spiders were spiders."

"I did not make these up." Speranza tapped a graceful fingernail on the portfolio containing the Roentgen–Daguerre plates. "The machine has no imagination, even if a madman might."

Colonel White pondered in silence, then shook his head. "Those things," he tapped a powerful finger against the Tuscan's portfolio, "those great star-headed, conical things, and that other, that incredible beast with tentacles like ropes, with legs like a giant beetle and with the mockery of a human face on its carapace – do they really exist?"

A rectangle of light broke the mood. Speranza Verde had reached toward the portfolio, perhaps to open it and remove the envelope of celluloid image plates once again, perhaps to touch Dwight David White's hand with her own, but instead she grabbed the portfolio and placed it protectively on her lap. The Tuscan hydrologist and the Confederate soldier turned to see a trio of silhouettes in the illuminated doorway of the lounge.

As Dottore Verde and Colonel White watched, the three newcomers advanced toward them. The latter trio halted beside the table from which Colonel White rose, his military bearing giving him the appearance of a man taller than his actual stature.

"Herr Schwartz, Monsieur Rouge." The Colonel raised his hand in suggestion of a military salute. The German archaeologist clicked his heels and bowed; the Frenchman bent over the white linen covered table, took the reluctantly offered hand of Speranza Verde in his own and brushed his lips over it.

"We have a pleasant chat been enjoying, Monsieur Rouge and I," Schwartz stated. "We had thought to share a – what I believe you call in your Confederacy a night hat, Colonel White? – before retiring for a few hours sleep."

"A nightcap, Herr Schwartz. Won't you join us?"

Monsieur Rouge bowed once again. "May I present Captain Alexandre, of the *Rosny*."

The third newcomer advanced to the table. She was as tall as a man, like Colonel White she was attired in a uniform, its midnight blue colour contrasting with the Colonel's Confederate grey. Her features were strong but not masculine. Her hair was so dark that it appeared almost to blend with the blue of her jacket, flashes of candlelight seeming to be caught and thrown back from her coiffure. The door through which the trio had entered was closed now, the sole illumination coming from the candle on the table. The Arab musicians had packed their instruments and retired.

Brass buttons on the woman's tunic gave back the flickering light of the candle. The cuffs of the tunic were wrapped in wreaths of gold braid and on her chest the orders and decorations gave testimony of a distinguished naval career. A dark, pleated skirt fell to below her knees.

Herr Schwartz and Monsieur Rouge drew chairs from a nearby, unoccupied table. Rouge held one for Captain Alexandre before seating himself. A waiter brought a bottle of schnapps and placed it before Herr Schwartz and one of cognac which the French explorer and the naval officer would share; glasses were provided for all.

Shortly the quintet were engaged in conversation. Colonel White waited for Speranza Verde to place her portfolio on the table again and share its contents with Schwartz and Rouge, but she gave no indication of doing so. In fact, at one point Jemond Jules Rouge asked if there was something she wished to share, but Speranza Verde brushed aside the obvious suggestion.

"Just a few minor items, Monsieur, nothing of importance."

"We are all together," Colonel White said, "except for our English colleague. Does anyone know where Sir Shepley Sidwell-Blue has disappeared to?"

"I am sure he is preparing for our expedition."

Captain Alexandre drew an ornately engraved watch from a uniform pocket. Holding it close to the candle she announced, "We must be aboard *Rosny* in two hours, so as to depart in three."

"So soon?" Speranza Verde exclaimed.

"It is the tides," Captain Alexandre explained. "The Mareé de Fureur is a most unusual tidal body. It will offer sufficient draft for the *Rosny* today, and she can make faster headway using the electro-atomic power of her Curie engines than creeping along on the Wells track drive. Surely, Mademoiselle Verde, you are familiar with the behaviour of the marée."

"Of course, Captain."

"Have you studied the tide tables for this month, Mademoiselle Docteur?"

"I have. Of course we have only a limited record of tides. The creation of the Sahara sea in 1930 had unexpected results, creating tides in the Mediterranean where none had previously existed, and providing for my profession wondrous new food for thought. The northerly flow will begin at four o'clock in the morning."

"Indeed." Captain Alexandre raised her glass, tested the nose of the cognac, sampled its flavour only with the tip of her tongue, then lowered her glass smiling. "*Bon.*" Her gaze flicked from face to face of her companions. "I trust you have all stowed your scientific equipment and your personal gear – Mademoiselle, Messieurs?"

Speranza Verde said, "I prefer the title of Dottore alone."

"Very well. As you wish, Dottore Verde. My point, however, is that we must sail with the tide or we lose the opportunity. The French Republic has a great fleet but no nation's resources are without limit. We do not wish to waste this time."

"And Sir Sidwell-Blue?" the German asked.

"He will board *Rosny* on schedule or he will find only a sealed bulkhead or a vacant quay. We sail with the tide."

The party dispersed, some to gather such brief moments of slumber as they could, others to remain awake pending the time to board the submersible.

Rosny was an example of the newest and smallest *Nautilus IV* class of submersibles. Barely sixty metres in length, the submersible carried a small crew. Propelled by her Curie engines, she could outspeed and outmanoeuvre any other known submersible craft on the planet. She was also capable of crawling over dry or muddy terrain on extended tracks based on the designs of the Englishman Wells.

Her interior fittings, in the tradition of her kind stretching back to the original *Nautilus*, were of mahogany and polished brass. Her floors were carpeted. Her galley was filled with fresh viands and fine vintages produced by the enological artists of Metropolitan France and her North African provinces.

Only in the department of weaponry might *Rosny* be deemed deficient. Outfitted as the submersible was for purposes of reconnaissance and exploration, she carried neither cannon nor torpedo nor submarine bomb. Her crew had been trained in riflery and such arms were stowed in

the submersible's armoury; her officers, also, were furnished
with sidearms.

Colonel Dwight David White stood at the foot of *Rosny's*
gangplank. He held a single item of luggage, containing
changes of clothing, necessary toiletries, and certain equipment with which he had been furnished by the technicians
and planners of his nation's embassy and military legation
in Serkout.

The Colonel was of course thoroughly familiar with the
courtesies and ceremonies of both the military and diplo-
matic communities of the world. When he boarded the
submersible he saluted the colours of the French Republic,
offered his sidearm, a Harrington and Richardson .32 automatic, to Captain Alexandre and received permission to
retain possession of the weapon.

The quay, of course, had been illuminated with spotlights
to facilitate boarding *Rosny* in the hours of the night. A crescent moon had been visible from Colonel White's hotel room;
from the quay its pale radiance was utterly obliterated by
the brilliance of artificial illumination.

Once on board, Colonel White declined the assistance
of a crew member in carrying his single item of luggage to
his tiny but richly furnished cabin. Here he distributed his
personal items, retaining only his firearm and technical gear
in a smaller case which he removed from his principal
luggage and locked to his wrist with a specially designed
handcuff.

Thus prepared he brushed his hair, straightened his
uniform, and made to join his fellow inquirers.

As had been prearranged, the investigative team assembled in the Captain's cabin as they arrived and settled into
their respective quarters. The cabin was furnished with a
polished conference table and plush chairs. An ornate instrument panel comprising a great clock-face, compass, baro-
meter, and navigational tools filled most of one wall. An
electrical lighting system furnished illumination and the soft
susurrus of fresh air, processed and piped throughout *Rosny*
by the most up-to-date means, gave evidence that the

submersible was a self-sufficient and self-contained world of its own.

The cabin was located above the main body of the submersible and was fitted with large glass panels on both starboard and larboard sides. Upon arriving in the cabin, Colonel White observed the activity of sailors and dockmen on the quay. Not a word was spoken before *Rosny* began to move, so smoothly and gradually as to create the illusion that the submersible remained stationary while the quay with its brilliant lights and scurrying workers was retreating.

But within fleeting moments, to *Rosny*'s forward motion was added a horizontal movement. The black sky with its crescent moon and glittering Saharan stars appeared overhead only briefly, then *Rosny* opened her buoyancy tanks to the Saharan brine.

Soon the world outside *Rosny*'s heavy glass panels became one of utter blackness. Eventually brightly luminescent denizens of the Saharan deep would reveal themselves, Colonel White and his companions knew, but for the moment they might as well have been in the depths of interplanetary space, for all the commerce they held with the sea that surrounded them.

They sat around the polished wooden table, Jemond Jules Rouge at its head, Colonel White, Speranza Verde, Siegfried Schwartz and Sidwell-Blue. The submersible's Captain, Melisande Alexandre, had taken her place inconspicuously away from the table, clearly indicating a desire to observe but not to dominate the proceedings to follow.

Yes, Sir Shepley Sidwell-Blue had arrived at the quay in time, barely in time, to make the sailing of *Rosny*. He was disheveled. He was followed to the boarding ramp by a driver and footman carrying valises from which loose shirt-ends and stocking garters hung, his shirt was rumpled and his blond hair fell across his forehead, but he did not miss the sailing.

After messmen had served coffee and biscuits M. Rouge made welcoming remarks to the assembled group. "We are proceeding beneath the surface, my friends. The tide is with us, flowing in a northerly direction. We should reach our destination within a half-day's cruise. Until then, I hope that we may discuss our plan of investigation."

Gazing around the table, he continued. "Each of you has been selected as the outstanding representative of your chosen profession. Dottore Verde was of course our first chosen expert. Her study of the tidal flow through the Marée de Fureur has been vital, for the hydrological patterns and alterations of the sea bed encountered in this new body of water is a challenge unique."

He bowed to Speranza Verde.

"Herr Schwartz and Sir Shepley are representatives of converging disciplines. Our preliminary findings indicate that the relics we are about to examine are of an Egyptian or pre-Egyptian origin. Their significance and value to the modern world, beyond that of the purely scholarly, are, one surmises, incalculable."

The German nodded acknowledgement of Rouge's words. Schwartz had lighted a black cigar and gestured with it. The Englishman, clad in soft tweeds that complemented his light hair and moustache, fumbled in his pockets for a pipe and tobacco. Finding them, he packed the pipe and held a match to its bowl. The smoke that rose was drawn away by the submersible's ventilation system. Sidwell-Blue muttered his acknowledgment.

"And Colonel White," the Frenchman concluded, "is our military man. A grand concession by France to nominate a representative of the Confederacy to this position, but of course the friendship of our two great Republics is of historic nature, known to all around the world."

Before David White could reply, the room was startled by the clatter of Sir Shepley Sidwell-Blue's pipe on the polished mahogany table. "I say," the Englishman exclaimed, "I fear we're under attack. Just look at that!"

He pointed to the oblong window on the starboard side of the cabin.

A vast creature was charging at *Rosny*. Its eyes were huge, its open mouth contained rows of gigantic, murderous teeth.

Its fins were clawed like those of certain tropical frogs that David White had encountered in his service in the jungles of Belize, and it used them in a manner suggestive of an amphibian crawling toward its hopeless prey.

Strangest of all, the creature appeared to be carrying a lighted lantern in its single hand. Upon more considered observation the seeming lantern proved to be a naturally luminescent organ mounted on a flexible stalk that rose from the creature's forehead.

David White's hand moved instinctively to his sidearm. But he realized almost at once that the Harrington and Richardson would do little to help the voyagers if their aquatic attacker succeeded in bursting through *Rosny*'s glass plate. To his astonishment, the creature swam to within seeming inches of the glass, then hovered, its clawlike fins moving slowly to and fro. At the submersible's rate of speed the creature was obviously a mighty swimmer to maintain pace at all, no less with such seeming ease.

Even as the voyagers, recovering from their initial startlement, left their seats to cluster at the glass, the creature held pace, returning their curious stares with an expression of its own that seemed to duplicate their surprise.

The laughter of Monsieur Rouge drew their attention back from the sea. "A common sight nowadays, my friends. Since the creation of the Sahara Sea, creatures have invaded this new body of water, making their way from the Mediterranean and even in some cases from the cold waters of the Atlantic. The Sahara Sea offers the appeal of a warm and mostly gentle body, and in less than a century that the Sahara Sea has existed, numerous species have come to visit and stayed to raise their progeny."

"By Jove," the Englishman inquired, "are there no native species in this lovely little pond?"

At this moment the ferocious-appearing lantern bearer, its curiosity as to *Rosny* and her occupants satisfied, flashed away from the submersible and disappeared into the darkness.

"Perhaps, if you will return to your places, *Mademoiselle*

et Messieurs, Dottore Verde will enlighten us as to the plan of action once we reach our destination."

Speranza Verde rose to her feet.

"With permission of Captain Alexandre, I have plotted our course to bring us to our destination as the tidal flow ceases. Of course it will in due time reverse its direction and flow back from the Bay of Sidra toward the City of Serkout from which we departed. Such tidal reversals are of course entirely normal."

She paused in her presentation to draw from a cylindrical case which had previously been placed in the cabin a nautical chart of the Sahara Sea, centring up the Iles de Crainte and Doute. This she spread on the table so that all the travellers might see it.

"The lunar and solar attractions that control earthly tides are at this time in unique conjunction. The result will be a period of several hours during which the channel between the two *isole* becomes a dry bed. This phenomenon is not unknown, of course."

She paused to smile, and David White was struck by the brightness and gentleness of her expression.

"Students of the Bible," Speranza Verde went on, "will recall the parting of the Red Sea upon the command of Moses. It is my belief that this event was in fact a tidal anomaly similar to that which is about to occur. When we reach our destination, Captain Alexandre informs me, *Rosny* will rest upon her Wells tracks and use them for any needed short-distance travel. You may rest assured that we will be safe from the waters during this period, but we must all complete our work before the Marée rushes back upon us, however. Our period of safety, according to my calculations, will be approximately four hours, thirty-two minutes, and sixteen seconds."

"I say, I say," Sidwell-Blue put in. He had long since recovered his pipe and was puffing furiously away at it, challenging the ability of the air-circulator to keep up with his production of bluish smoke. "I say, are you *sure* this won't be dangerous? Perhaps we should try this another time, don't you know."

From her position in a corner of the cabin, Captain Alexandre put in, "Quite sure, Sir Shepley. There is nothing to fear."

"And as for another time," Speranza Verde put in, "do you know how long it is since Moses parted the Red Sea? That is how often this peculiar phenomenon occurs. If we do not take advantage of our opportunity, we will all be several thousand years old before another such presents itself."

"Well," Sidwell-Blue stammered, "well, if you're really certain, C-Captain. And, ah, D-Doktor. But, but, it strikes me that this is a dashedly dangerous undertaking. You know, I've always worked in the museum, don't you know. This is all quite new to me, this racing about like a pack of Alan Quatermains and Captain Nemos."

Out of the corner of his eye Colonel White saw what appeared to be a grey-cloaked and death-white-masked figure streak across the room and launch itself through the air. It bounced off the paunch of the unsuspecting Herr Schwartz, eliciting a startled grunt and a violent exclamation, then landed with a skid in the centre of the nautical chart that had been spread on the conference table.

"The apologies of *Rosny*, Mein Herr," Captain Alexandre laughed. "*Madame et Messieurs*, may I present My Lady Bast, our ship's mascot and mouser *par excellence*."

The large cat studied each of the conferees in turn, directing a piercing glance from golden eyes that punctuated a snowy white face while she twitched her powder-grey tail thoughtfully. She made her opinion obvious, redirecting her attention from the conferees to the task of washing her paws.

"You should not barnyard animals on a ship carry," Herr Schwartz growled, "unless they are cargo to market being transported."

Captain Alexandre ignored the German's complaint. She stroked the luxurious fur; My Lady Bast twitched her ears in response. Captain Alexandre compared the time according to her watch, with that indicated by the ship's clock. She nodded to the hydrologist, Speranza Verde, then to the others. "I think it is time to begin your explorations. I will remain aboard *Rosny*. You understand the constraints of time under which you operate."

At Captain Alexandre's command the submersible rose to the surface of the Fleuve Triste. Colonel White found himself standing between Dottore Verde and Monsieur Rouge. A polished metal railing surrounded *Rosny*'s deck. Sea water dripped from it and ran from the submersible's deck into the fleuve.

The sky above was still black. The tropic stars blazed like the flames that astronomers stated that they were.

Each of the explorers carried an electro-atomic powered portable lantern. Further, Colonel White noted to his amusement that the costume of each showed a mysterious bulge which he took to reveal the presence of a clandestinely carried firearm. Even Dottore Verde was so armed. Her weapon, he inferred, was most likely a small but efficient Gilsenti automatic pistol.

Now the sun's first rays illumined the western sky, and within moments the edge of the solar disk appeared over the waters of the Sahara Sea. Bright points of light danced across the brine.

At this moment a buzzing sound was heard, and Colonel White along with his companions turned his eyes skyward. The daily flight from Rome to Serkout appeared, the sun's early rays reflecting off its polished metal exterior. The Bleriot trimotor's propellers were powered by Curie electro-atomic engines similar to those that furnished *Rosny*'s propulsion. The aeroplane's passengers, business travellers, tourists, diplomats, might well be gazing downward at *Rosny* even as *Rosny*'s explorers were gazing upward at the Bleriot.

Now there came a great rushing, roaring sound; the submersible rocked, bounced once, and settled on to the rocky sand at the bottom of the Fleuve Triste. The Curie engine hummed and the submersible's Wells tracks found their footing on the sand and steadied the submersible.

"*Alors*," Captain Alexandre announced with a smile,

"*Madame et Messieurs*, we are here. You have my permission to depart my ship. I wish you well, and shall expect your safe return in four hours, thirty-two minutes, sixteen seconds."

She exchanged handshakes with Jemond Jules Rouge and Shepley Sidwell-Blue. Herr Schwartz instead offered a bow and click of his heels. With Speranza Verde she exchanged a brief embrace, and with Colonel Dwight David White a crisp military salute.

The explorers clambered down the ship's ladder. Standing on the still moist sand of the Fleuve Triste they found it drying rapidly. The tropical sun seemed to have sprung into a brilliant and cloudless sky. Here and there specks of crystal in the Sahara sand reflected as points of brilliance.

Speranza Verde had brought with her the Roentgen-Daguerre plates that she had shown David White the night before, and Herr Schwartz carried a smaller version of the nautical chart that had been left on the conference table aboard *Rosny*.

A grey and white streak whizzed past the exploration party, raced up a sandy hillock and disappeared.

"That, was M-My Lady Bast, My Lady Bast!" Sir Shepley Sidwell-Blue exclaimed. "The creature will be lost. The w-water will rush back in f-our hours and she will be l-lost."

"Too bad for her," Herr Schwartz growled. "But a good thing she did, the way showing us to the finds." He held the map before him and pointed in the direction My Lady Bast had taken. "March!" he commanded.

My Lady Bast had left behind a track of feline footprints in the drying sand. The explorers followed the cat's trail. The sun's rays had already dispersed the chill of night air, and this small stretch of seabed was assuming the torrid glare it had known before the creation of the world's newest sea.

Upon reaching the crest of a hillock the explorers were able to look back and see the submersible *Rosny* resting upon her Wells treads. Sailors moved on her decks polishing metalwork and cleaning hardwood, looking for all the world like miniatures performing in a puppet theatre. And in the other direction appeared a vision denied to human eyes by the dark waters of the Sahara Sea for three decades, and before that by the white sands of the erstwhile Sahara Desert for ten times as many millennia.

These were the rocks, dressed and polished, rising but a short distance from their position, that hid the secret of the Sahara.

Herr Siegfried Schwartz and Sir Shipley Sidwell-Blue raced ahead and dropped to their knees. Bending to examine the carven rocks on which they knelt, the ill-matched pair resembled nothing more than two worshippers come to make obeisance at an ancient shrine.

The uppermost rocks of the formation reflected the sun's rays with a white brilliance; those lower in the ancient structure were still protected from direct illumination by the intervening crest. Schwartz and Sidwell-Blue were running their hands over the carven rocks, studying the figures placed there untold ages before by hands long since turned to dust.

As the sun's illumination spread and the shadows crept away solar brightness struck a glittering point so cleverly concealed within the intricacies of a carving as to be for all practical purposes invisible. As it did so the rock in which it had rested for thousands of years in utter darkness fell away from the kneeling explorers. There was exposed before them a dark opening, its walls as smooth and as carefully crafted as those of the Great Pyramid of Cheops.

There was a flash of grey as My Lady Bast, returning from some place of concealment, streaked past the explorers and disappeared into the blackness.

Herr Schwartz switched on his electro-atomic lantern and sent its rays into the blackness, flashing them this way and that. Still on his knees, the German started down the passageway. As he did so – Colonel White took note – he reached inside his jacket and drew a weapon which White immediately identified as a Bergmann Model Five automatic pistol.

As Schwartz disappeared into the darkness he was

followed by Jumond Jules Rouge and Speranza Verde, each brandishing a lantern and a firearm; Rouge's weapon was a Lebel revolver and Verde the Gilsenti that White had expected.

Sir Shepley Sidwell-Blue alone stepped aside as Colonel White moved toward the opening. "I th-think it would be b-best if one of us s-stood guard out here, C-Colonel, don't you know? Just in case, w-well, don't you know, in case of need."

David White nodded and followed Speranza Verde into the darkness.

The tunnel slanted downward into bedrock. To David White's surprise the air tasted fresh. He could see only a short distance ahead, thanks to the procession of bodies, but at length he heard a grunt and a guttural exclamation, followed by a series of increasingly excited vocalizations as first Schwartz, then Rouge, than Speranza Verde emerged from the slanting passage.

White paused momentarily, pointing his lantern this way and that, then dropped the few feet from the mouth of the passageway into the chamber. Two men and a woman had separated in the chamber; flashing beams from their lanterns criss-crossed in a virtual museum of unknowable antiquity. Statues cast great monolithic shadows in the flashing lantern-beams. Some were tiny and were exhibited on plinths as high as his own waist; others were of human size. At the far end of the chamber a figure rose to herculean heights, its details concealed by distance and darkness.

The walls were covered with paintings that appeared as fresh as though they had been created this very day. The scenes portrayed were those of nature, of forests and rivers, of hippopotami and crocodiles and okapi, the beasts that must have roamed the once-fertile plains of the Sahara before it had dried to form the desert now covered by the waters of the sea.

Colonel White paced slowly past paintings executed with impressive craftsmanship and skill. Yet there was something disquieting and unpleasant about the images.

The paintings, he inferred, represented a chronology, for after a time there appeared among the beasts of the forest primitive human figures, and even more disquietingly, other figures that were those of neither humans nor beasts, but of something . . . other. He thought briefly of the fierce-looking lantern fish that had studied the explorers through the cabin glass of *Rosny* even as they had studied it.

The lantern fish, of course, was fitted by nature with fins for propulsion and with a form adapted to life beneath the surface of the sea. But the creatures in the paintings appeared as if they were distant evolutionary relatives of the lantern fish, great, pop-eyed, piscine beings. White remembered a lecture in a long-ago classroom, where he had heard a savant expound upon the theory that whales, dolphins, sea lions and seals had all evolved from marine creatures on to the land, and had then returned at some time to their ancestral home to become once again creatures of the deep.

Could the unpleasant beings pictured on the carven walls have followed a parallel but opposite evolutionary path, emerging from the sea to live on the surface of the earth even as mammals were returning from the land to live beneath the sea?

More panels of ancient art revealed an ongoing march of progress, if progress it might be called, as both humans and piscines advanced. Cities appeared, and great sky-going machines. The two civilizations developed side by side but there was little commerce and no friendship between them, until in a series of paintings portraying a terrible war the human civilization was destroyed and that of the fish-men emerged triumphant.

There was a yowl from the end of the gallery and White whirled to see My Lady Bast rising on her hind legs, her coat standing on end to give her the appearance of a beast three times her actual size. Her paws were raised and her sabre-like claws were extended. Her needle-sharp teeth seemed to have grown into the fangs of a feline many times her size but no less outraged than was My Lady Bast.

She stood poised before the great statue that ended the

gallery, and as Colonel White and his companions stood in stupefaction she dropped to all fours, ran forward, launched herself into the air and caught at the convolutions of the lowermost part of the statue.

The brilliant beams of four Curie lanterns followed the cat as she clawed and fought her way upward on the statue. The thing was monstrous, a variant of the horrible image that Speranza Verde had shown Colonel White the night before.

The thing was fitted with tentacle-like stalks, uncounted numbers of them, some terminating in sucker-like mouths, others in shining eyes. It had a head, or what must serve as a head, shaped like a five-pointed star, each extremity of this bearing a great, dark eye.

Most horrifying of all, David White stood paralyzed with shock and fear. And know well, even the noblest of men know fear; it is the overcoming of this experience that comprises true courage. That which had paralyzed White was the sight of the five points of the statue's face writhing and turning, turning horribly, until the eyes focused upon My Lady Bast the cat.

From all directions, tentacles tipped with horrid mouths and rows of teeth resembling those of giant, extinct sharks, wove toward My Lady Bast. From the cat there came a blood-freezing scream of raging ferocity as the pleasantly disposed ship's mascot was transformed into a whirlwind of fury and violence.

My Lady Bast flew from the grasping, mouth-tipped tentacles, the points of her claws leaving a trail of punctures from which there spurted a steaming green ichor. Blobs of the foul liquid splashed on the great paving stones with which the room was floored. Each point of contact was transformed into a miniature cauldron that seethed and bubbled and from which a noxious greenish vapour arose.

The cat by now had reached the star-shaped head of the monstrous living statue. Using the claws of two paws while she clung to the monstrous visage with the others, she shredded one baleful eye, then moved to the next and the next. The monstrous living statue yielded to a series of spasms.

David White, watching the incredible battle of a feline analog of his Biblical namesake against this titanic alien Goliath, realized to his astonishment that the star-headed monster was actually terrified. He was aware that Siegfried Schwartz had drawn his Bergmann automatic and was firing at the monstrosity. Other members of the exploring party, Rouge, Speranza Verde, had drawn their own weapons and were pointing them upward.

Bounding forward to place himself between his comrades and the monster, David White waved his arms and cried out, "Careful! Careful! Don't hit the cat!"

Even as the sound of two revolvers and an automatic pistol echoed off the walls and ceiling of the chamber, the great monstrosity, blinded now and bleeding green ichor from its wounds, gave forth a mighty roar that echoed and re-echoed through the hall. It gave a mighty spasm and My Lady Bast, the grey and white warrior, her grasp on the star-shaped head broken by the jolt, was flung from the monster. As if fully accustomed to flight she soared through the darkened reaches of the tomb, falling at last into the welcoming arms of Colonel David White.

But this was no gentle pussy. My Lady Bast had been transformed into a warrior-goddess and she was not so quick to resume her domestic mien. Raking claws shredded White's military tunic and suddenly terrifying fangs snapped within millimetres of his eye, removing a gobbet of flesh just at his cheekbone. Then My Lady Bast flexed powerful legs, launched herself from his torso and disappeared into the darkness of the tomb.

Rouge, Schwartz and Verde had advanced cautiously toward the monster. In its great spasm it had flung itself from its plinth and lay thrashing on the stone floor. Its mouths seemed to possess the power of speech independent of one another, and they uttered sounds that resembled human speech as a horrid parody of the human form might resemble a beautiful woman.

Siegfried Schwartz, surely crude and perhaps cruel as well, was by no means lacking in courage. He had advanced to within an arm's reach of the monster and was speaking to it in a language which David White did not understand, but which he inferred to be that of ancient Egypt. Astonishingly, the monster seemed to hear and understand the German archaeologist, and to reply in a strange and terrible variant of the same language.

Without warning the monster managed to raise itself halfway to a vertical position. It turned its eye-tipped tentacles toward the roof of the chamber.

There, its rays focused through a lens of tinted mica, the sun casting a single, bright beam into the chamber. The beam had obviously been aimed, how many millennia before there was no way of calculating. In its light one of the painted panels on the tomblike wall seemed almost to come to life.

A row of half-human figures knelt in postures of worship. There was a man with the head of a falcon, a woman with the features of a lioness, a hawk-man, a woman in the grotesque form of a hippopotamus, a being with a human body and the head of a crocodile. David White did not know their names, but he recognized them as Egyptian deities. And they were kneeling in submission.

Before them stood a party of star-headed, tentacled monsters like the one whose statue had seemingly come to life only to be slain by the ferocity of a ship's grey and white mascot. And behind the alien beings could be seen a sleek machine, obviously a vehicle that had brought its occupants from some home unimaginable to mere humanity.

From the shadowed passageway through which the explorers had entered the tomb there came an echoing voice. "It's time," came the voice of Sir Shepley Sidwell-Blue. "We'd b-best get back to *Rosny*. Our t-time is r-running out."

The explorers turned toward the passageway. Jemond Jules Rouge leading the way, followed by Speranza Verde and Siegfried Schwartz, preceded Colonel Dwight David White into the passage. White realized that they had all been so busy in dealing with the wonders and terrors of the tomb that they had forgotten the time. It was a good thing that the Englishman had stayed outside the tomb, keeping track of the passing hours.

Once outside the tomb the party formed up and moved off in the direction of the temporarily dry bed of the Fleuve Triste.

They had gone only a score of paces when Sidwell-Blue cried out, "Halt!" The decisive and authoritarian utterance from the hitherto timid and uncertain Englishman startled the others into obedience. To their disbelieving eyes Sidwell-Blue ran back toward the dark opening in the rock. He disappeared into the shadowed passageway. Minutes passed. David White studied his own pocket watch, performed a rapid mental calculation and said, "If we don't move quickly we'll be trapped by the returning Marée."

"But we cannot leave poor Sir Shepley in that tomb!" Speranza Verde cried. She started back toward the rock sepulchre, followed by the others, but before she could reach the opening Sir Shepley Sidwell-Blue emerged into the Saharan sunlight, My Lady Bast nestled comfortably in his arms.

As they approached the submersible *Rosny* a mighty aqueous roar was heard and two walls of water became visible, speeding toward them from both directions. The explorers ran at top speed to the submersible and scrambled up *Rosny*'s boarding ladder. Captain Alexandre herself had awaited them, and followed them into the submersible, counting off as they descended:

"Rouge.

"Schwartz.

"Blue.

"Verde.

"White.

"My Lady Bast.

Even as the first spray of the onrushing waters spattered her midnight-tinted uniform sleeve, the Captain slammed the hatch shut and turned its dogs to seal the submersible against the waters of the Saharan Sea.

Soon all had refreshed themselves and reassembled in the

Captain's conference room. Hot coffee spiked with strong brandy was served, along with nourishing sandwiches. Outside *Rosny's* oblong panels of glass, marine creatures swam up to this strange invader of their realm and studied its occupants with as much curiosity as the men and women of *Rosny* exhibited toward them.

In a corner of the room, My Lady Bast, her coat now restored to its proper state, enjoyed a treat of fresh fish and rich cream.

At the table, the explorers gave their complementary reports on their experiences in the ancient tomb. Speranza Verde took special note of Sidwell-Blue's unexpected heroism. "Beneath this *senza pretese*, how you say, unassuming exterior, eh, there beats the heart of a lion. I salute you, Sir Shepley."

The Englishman turned away shyly. "One c-couldn't abandon that splendid c-cat, you know." Even in the artificial light of *Rosny's* cabin, his furious blush was obvious.

At the end, it was Colonel White who asked Herr Siegfried Schwartz, "What was it that the monster said before it died?"

The German stroked his beard as if in deep thought. "To understand what said the creature, Mein Herr White, it was for me not easy. Its language that of ancient Egypt was almost, but certain differences there were."

He paused and drained his cup. When it was refilled he instructed the crew member to omit the coffee.

"I think it said, 'My parents for me will come. Someday my father and mother for me will come.' You see, Herr Colonel, to us a great monster it was, but in truth that sleeping creature that we awakened, that we killed, of its own kind was a baby."

THE GOLDEN QUEST

Sharan Newman

Few of Verne's posthumously published novels are of much interest, but two do have science-fictional content. La Chasse au mètèore, *was serialized in 1908 and published in England the next year as* The Chase of the Golden Meteor. *Though not very well written (some believe it may have been a collaboration with Verne's son, Michel, who helped his father on several of the last novels) it does contain a fascinating idea. The inventor Zéphyrin Xirdal has created a machine that emits a ray which can capture and control any object, rather like the tractor beam of later science fiction (and of which a prototype was invented in 2001). Xirdal uses this machine to capture a meteorite of solid gold. When Xirdal realizes the financial consequences of this he ensures that the meteorite falls into the sea. Once again Verne did not believe that mankind could cope with scientific progress. But was Xirdal right? Sharan Newman plays back the events of the story to see what might have really happened.*

The young man clutched his felt fedora with sweaty hands. He gazed at the thick oak-paneled door before him as if it were the gateway to Hell. He reflected that for him it might be. And that was only if his request were granted. It's no wonder that Jean Lecoeur needed to screw up all his courage before knocking.

Therefore his heart nearly stopped when he raised his fist to knock and, before he tapped the wood, the door was opened with a jerk and he found himself face to face with a portly man in his late sixties.

"Hello!" the man said in surprise, as he bent down to pick up the afternoon paper.

"Mr W . . . Wells?" Jean could barely get the words out, he was so nervous.

"That depends," the man answered. "Are you a reporter?"

"Oh, no, sir! I am Jean Lecoeur, of Lecoeur Bank, Paris, London, New York, Berlin, Cairo and Buenos Aires." Jean handed the man his letters of introduction.

The man glanced at the letters with disdain and sighed.

"I suppose you'd better come in," he said. "Yes, I'm Herbert Wells. Now what does the owner of the richest bank in the world want with me? You do know I'm a Socialist, don't you? I don't invest in capitalist schemes."

"I am aware of that, sir," Jean said. "I'm counting on it."

Wells gave him a suspicious glance but ushered him in.

When they had settled in comfortable chairs before the fire, Jean's nervousness ebbed a bit. However, he couldn't stop himself from giving a jerk when Wells said firmly, "So, tell me your business, young man.."

Jean Lecoeur squirmed like a schoolboy sent to the headmaster. The fact that he was one of the wealthiest and most powerful men in the world didn't seem to help in this situation. He took a deep breath and started.

"You are assuredly aware, Mr Wells, that the fortunes of my family were greatly expanded at the beginning of the century with the landing and subsequent loss of the Golden Meteor."

"I remember it," Wells said coldly. "Although I doubt you were even alive then. The world believed that the meteor would make gold as common as iron. Your father bought mining stock at bargain prices and, when the meteor fell into the North Sea, his holdings increased tenfold."

Jean winced. "That is correct, Sir, to my deep shame. And it is in the hope of undoing that great wrong that I have come to you."

Wells gave him a sharp look. Lecoeur was very young, not more than twenty-five. He radiated earnest naiveté. In this world such innocence was almost a crime.

"And how do you propose to rectify this social injustice?" he asked.

Lecoeur took a deep breath. "I intend to see to it that the Golden Meteor never falls into the sea," he announced.

Wells raised his bushy eyebrows. "Don't you think it would be more practical simply to donate your fortune to those in need?"

"No," Lecoeur said firmly. "Although that is certainly a laudable endeavour. It's not just a matter of redistributing wealth now. The damage was done nearly thirty years ago."

He leaned forward, his hands clasped in entreaty.

"My father thought he was getting rich, doing his duty as a banker to increase the wealth of his clients," he continued. "But you know what happened. With the cornering of the gold market, social unrest increased. Anarchy became rampant. Eventually the powder keg was lit. You know the results: assassination, revolution, the Great War. Mr Wells, what do you think the world would be like if the War had been avoided? We are now in the midst of an economic depression. Communists run Russia and Germany is starting to rearm. What would England and France be like if the best of our young men had lived to fulfill their potential? Sir, my own two older brothers died at the Somme. I would do anything to prevent that."

He gazed at Wells with great brown puppy-like eyes. Despite himself, Wells was touched. But he knew what was coming.

"M. Lecoeur," he began. "I know what you are going to ask me and it is literally impossible. The time machine is highly imperfect. The one time it was used, the operator was nearly lost."

"I understand you have been working on the machine since then," Jean answered. "My informants tell me that it now might be able to manage short trips through time with an astonishing degree of accuracy."

Wells leapt to his feet, knocking over a vase full of chrysanthemums. "Just who have you been talking to, Sir?" he asked in astonishment. "And what right have you to invade my privacy in this manner?"

Lecoeur remained calm. "An unlimited amount of money will buy almost any information," he said sadly. "I am prepared to commit such gross insults to social custom in order to achieve my goal."

"Are you also prepared to die?" Wells glared down at him.

"Of course," Jean blinked away his tears. "I would give my life if my brothers could be spared as well as the millions of others who died because of my father's greed."

Wells collapsed back into his chair like a punctured zeppelin.

"You realize that, even if you succeed, the War may come all the same," he asked.

"I must try," Jean answered. "My studies indicate that it was this one event that led to all the human disasters of this century."

From the experience of a lifetime, Wells was fairly sure this wasn't true. It took more than one avaricious banker to destroy the world. It needed at least two. But Lecoeur's argument was persuasive. Wells thought back on the horrors of the past years and the fear that the worst was yet to come. Perhaps the man should be given the chance. The recent tests of the machine did indicate that short jumps through time might be completed with some accuracy. It was possible that Jean Lecoeur could go and come back alive.

Two weeks later Jean Lecoeur sat in the cellar of Wells' house, staring in awe at the fabled time machine. Jean was dressed in the clothes of 1904. He had also procured a large amount of pre-war money from various countries.

"I imagine life has not changed that much," he explained.

"Money seems to make everything much easier. In the event of success, I shall be sorry to lose my fortune, but it is for the greater good."

Wells grunted as he twiddled with various controls.

"You'll arrive in London," he said. "In the basement of this house. After that it's up to you to get to Greenland where the meteor landed. If you succeed, you'll need to get back here and into the machine without anyone, especially my younger self, seeing you. Otherwise, you may change history even more, perhaps undoing the good you intended."

"I understand," Jean tried to swallow but his mouth was too dry. "You are certain that you can get me there two weeks before the event?"

"Approximately," Wells answered. "Remember, this machine is still experimental."

"I'm trying *not* to remember," Jean said. "Are you ready?"

Without answering, Wells threw a switch and the world around Jean Lecoeur turned inside out.

He woke up in the blackness of the cellar, retching and cold. It took him a few moments to remember where he was and that Wells had cautioned him to make no noise.

There was another moment of complete terror as Jean groped his way to the door near the coal chute. What if he had gone too far back? His money would be worthless if he arrived before it was printed.

The cool rain of a London summer evening greeted his exit into the alleyway. The clop of hooves and the creak of coach wheels came from the street. There were no auto brakes squealing, nor the blare of radios. He hurried out into the street. There was a newsstand on the corner. Jean ran to it and gave a cry of joy. It was 1904 and July 19th! He had a month before the fateful day.

Jean inhaled the moist air. He had done it. Now to arrange passage to Greenland. He still had to arrive before the meteor fell and then stop his father from sending it to the bottom of the sea.

Even with the large supply of antique cash he had brought,

Jean found it difficult to book passage to Greenland. Treasure seekers, government officials, and the curious were all eager to see the landing of a meteor made of gold. At last he managed to get a berth on a fishing boat for a price that would normally have bought him a suite on an ocean liner.

The port of Upernevik, in Greenland was equally chaotic. Jean had never heard so many languages spoken at the same time or with such urgency. It seemed that everyone in the world had come to see the meteor.

But, while the others were all fixated on reaching the predicted landing site of the meteor, Jean went at cross purposes to the crowd. He was desperate to find his father, Robert Lecoeur, and the instigator of the event, Zéphyrin Xirdal.

Jean had never met M. Xirdal. His father had explained that the man was very rich, very brilliant and completely mad. Xirdal was also a recluse, not from any particular misanthropy, but because, if he were invited to join a party, he would forget about it immediately upon returning home. Consequently, he received few invitations.

It was Zéphyrin Xirdal who had first noticed the meteor, although others claimed that honour. It was also Zéphyrin who had invented a machine to attract the golden orb toward the earth, not for any particular desire for gain, but to see if he could. Jean's father, Robert, was possibly Zéphyrin's best friend, as well as his banker and godfather. So it was to Robert Lecoeur that Xirdal applied when he decided to set the meteor down in Greenland. Robert had purchased the landing site for Zéphyrin.

It was this advance knowledge of the landing that allowed Robert Lecoeur to speculate in gold mines. Somehow, Robert had convinced Zéphyrin to use his machine to send the meteor into the ocean, thus causing mining stock, at an all time low, to increase to a hundred times the price Robert had paid. Jean had heard the story many times as a child.

It was this artificial tampering with the world economy that, Jean believed, led to the social unrest that resulted in

the horrors of the Great War. It was for this that Jean set
out on this dangerous quest. Zéphyrin Xirdal must be
prevented from sinking the meteor!

Jean knew that his father and Xirdal had arrived on the
yacht *Atlantic*. He managed to find a member of the crew
who told him that M. Lecoeur and his odd friend had arrived
several weeks earlier and were already on the property that
M. Xirdal had bought near Upernevik.

With growing uneasiness, Jean joined the flock of treasure
hunters. He was frantic to get to the front of the pack. What
if he arrived too late? Of course his efforts were entirely
misunderstood by everyone else.

"Who do you think you are?" a badly-dressed man shouted
at him in English when Jean tried to pass him. "It'll do you
no good, young man. That meteor is mine!"

"Of course, Sir, if you wish it," Jean replied soothingly.
"I have no interest in the gold. I'm only concerned for my
father, who left earlier. I really must find him before he
comes to harm."

At that statement, the young woman standing next to the
man smiled in commiseration.

"Then we must let you go," she said. "My name is Jenny
Hudelson, and this is *my* father, Dr Sidney Hudelson, the
co-discoverer of the meteor."

Jean bowed. He remembered something about two
Americans who had happened to be the first to spot the
golden meteor and exactly at the same time. It had been an
amusing paragraph in the history of the event.

Another man pushed his way into the group. "'Co-
discoverer' indeed!" he snorted, over the attempts of a young
man to quiet him. "I, Dean Forsyth, was the first to gaze
upon the meteor. This man is a charlatan!"

The two young people looked at each other and sighed.
Jenny explained the situation to Jean, who would have
preferred to take his leave at once.

"Francis is Mr Forsyth's nephew," she nodded toward
the young man. "We were to be married until this horrid

meteor caused a rift between our families. How I hope it sinks into the ocean! That would make everything the same as it was before."

"Oh, no, Mademoiselle!" Jean said in horror. "You do not know what you are saying. That would be a catastrophe!"

He tipped his hat and hurried on. It was already the eighteenth of August. The meteor was due to land the following morning.

A storm blew in that night, driving all the visitors to seek shelter. It would be impossible to reach his father in such conditions. Jean was able to find a few square metres of floor space in one of the wooden buildings of the town. He tried to remain awake in order to set off as soon as the wind died down but weariness from travel and anxiety caused him to fall into a deep slumber.

The arctic summer dawn shone directly into his eyes, waking him. Was it his imagination or did the light seem brighter than usual?

Cursing himself for giving in to sleep, Jean dressed quickly and set off to find the hut where his father and Zéphyrin had set up the machine to attract the meteor.

At once he realized that the light of the sun, low on the horizon, was nothing to the glowing splendour of the meteor, now descending rapidly toward the earth. The heat of the approaching ball of gold was intense. It was so bright that Jean couldn't see the path in the glare. He was forced to crawl the final distance to the hut.

He had almost reached it when there was a crash that shook the entire island and caused Jean to be thrown flat against the ground, clutching at it as if he feared he might slide off the earth.

He didn't see the door of the hut open and two men rush out toward the fallen meteor, only to be driven back by the piercing temperature of the glowing gold.

Zéphyrin Xirdal and Robert Lecoeur stared in rapture at the giant golden nugget.

"It's not solid, of course," Zéphyrin explained. "You can

see the fissures. But it's still more gold than any one country has ever possessed."

"And now it's yours," Robert breathed.

"Yes." Zéphyrin seemed less enthralled than the banker. "I wonder what I can do with it."

"Don't worry, my boy," Robert smiled. "I'll help you think of something."

Zéphyrin nodded. "Those people from the town will be here soon. Why don't you go back to the hut while I let them know that I have claimed the meteor."

Robert protested this, but Zéphyrin was firm that the machine should be guarded and that only he could convince the crowd that the meteor was only on this earth as a result of his invention.

The crowd rushed to the place where the meteor now gleamed, brighter than the sun and, seemingly, almost as hot. Jean had just ascertained that he was neither blind nor deaf as a result of being so close to the crash. He had just commenced his trek to the hut when the masses overtook him. Once there, they were astonished to find the way to the meteor blocked by a ring of fences and the person of Zephryin Xirdal.

"This is my property," he announced. "As is the meteor."

In the uproar that followed, Jean was able to sneak past and make his way up to the crude hut where he knew his father had waited. Eagerly, he knocked on the door.

"You are trespassing, Sir," Robert Lecoeur greeted him.

For a moment, Jean stood transfixed, his jaw hanging. His father could never have been that young! He looked just like the family portrait, taken when his older brothers were little and he not even thought of. The anger, however, was familiar.

"Please, Sir!" he begged. "I must speak with you. I know that you plan to send the meteor into the ocean. You cannot do this!"

"What are you talking about?" Robert stared at him. "Why should I wish to lose all that gold?"

"I . . . I don't understand," Jean stammered. "Aren't you planning to buy mining stock and resell it at exorbitant rates when the meteor is lost?"

Robert drew himself up proudly. "I have no such intention," he said stiffly. "My godson, Zéphyrin, is the owner of the meteor. I have a responsibility to protect his property."

"And you aren't worried that it will be taken from you by some government?" Jean asked.

"I have spent my life learning how to keep money out of the hands of the government," his father responded. "I shall do the same for M. Xirdal, the owner of this land and the meteor."

Jean gave a great sigh of relief. "Yes, yes!" he grabbed his father's hand and shook it with enthusiasm. "You must do that! Don't forget."

He spun about and nearly danced his way back to the town. He had always heard that it was his father who had agreed to let the meteor sink. But now he would refuse to do so. War would be averted and the family would still retain their wealth.

As he drew closer to Upernevik, his steps began to drag.

It shouldn't have been that easy. This was the nineteenth of August. The meteor hadn't been pushed over the cliff into the ocean until the third of September. What if something happened between now and then to change his father's mind?

The thought of spending several more days in Greenland, in the past depressed Jean considerably. However, he must be certain that the meteor remained on land so that it could be divided fairly among the nations. Otherwise all his efforts would be in vain.

The next few days made him increasingly alarmed. As the world waited for the meteor to cool enough to plant a flag on it, gunboats began arriving from every country. Marines from America, France, Argentina, Japan, Italy, Chile and other nations marched into the town of Upernevik, all under orders to protect the meteor from thieves and to preserve the peace.

Jean began to fear that, instead of stopping the Great War, he had caused it to begin ten years early. What was he to do? Mr Wells had warned him that tampering with time was dangerous. But there was no turning back now.

His training in international banking meant that Jean spoke several languages and was accustomed to the use of diplomacy. He offered his services as a translator to the French and American delegations. Although he could produce no references, he had an air of confidence and authority that impressed the admirals. His talents were soon apparent to them, as well. For the next twelve days he talked his throat sore in an attempt to convince the representatives of the various countries that the meteor should be put in a trust and administered by an international council, such as the one already meeting in Washington.

"Think how much goodwill you would earn," he pleaded, "if each nation used a share of the gold to set up an institute for the eradication of disease or to promote scientific research?"

His conviction impressed the various representatives enough that telegraph messages began flying back to capital cities with his proposal. The conference in Washington was disposed to agree to it. Jean had some hope that his efforts were succeeding. Then, on the second of September, came a shocking announcement.

"The meteor is moving! It is heading for the cliff!"

"No!" Jean cried. "It can't be!"

Unlike the rest of the observers, he knew what was causing the sudden movement. Zéphyrin Xirdal had activated his machine again and was pushing the meteor to its doom. But why? He had always assumed that the plan had been totally his father's. What could have changed his mind?

Arriving at the hut, Jean heard the whir and clatter of Xirdal's machine. He pounded on the door.

"Let me in!" he shouted. "You must stop! You don't know what you're doing!"

The door remained shut. Jean looked about for a way in.

On one side of the hut was a crude window. It only took a moment to shatter it and carefully climb in.

"You again!" Robert Lecoeur exclaimed. "Zéphyrin, it's that madman I told you of. The one who thought we were going to destroy the meteor. The one who gave me the idea to buy up the mining stock first."

The inventor looked at Jean calmly. "If he knew that before we did, he's not mad but gifted with amazing foresight. Tell me, Monsieur, how did you know I would decide to get rid of it? I only made up my mind when I saw how unhappy those two Americans were. They couldn't be married as long as the meteor was a source of dispute between their families."

Jean had no time to fabricate a lie.

"I know because I have seen the result of your action," he said. "You and my . . . M. Lecoeur become tremendously wealthy since you alone controlled, that is, will control the gold market. You upset the economic balance of the planet. Monsieur Lecoeur, if you allow this to happen there will be a war the like of which the earth has never seen. Philippe and Marc will both be killed in it."

"What?" Robert Lecoeur went pale at the mention of his sons. "How do you know about my boys? What madness is this?"

"I know it sounds insane," Jean was weeping. "But you must believe me; I've seen it."

Zéphyrin stared at Jean for a long time. He hadn't much experience of emotions but he recognized the passion in the man before him. He looked at Robert Lecoeur.

Robert patted Jean gingerly on the shoulder.

"There, there," he said. "Perhaps you have had some sort of vision, but there's no reason to think it will come true."

Jean raised his head and gazed into his father's eyes.

"Yes," he said. "It will. I am your third son, Jean, named after your grandfather. I have come back in time to save the lives of my brothers and millions more. Only leave the meteor as it is. You can still make money from it. Your lives won't change. I beg you. Please!"

Zéphyrin Xirdal considered a moment, then turned around and twiddled knobs on his machine. The whirring slowed and then stopped.

"Zéphyrin!" Robert cried. "You can't do that now. It will ruin us! My gold mine stocks will be worthless! This man is clearly a saboteur, sent to thwart us."

He rounded on Jean.

"Speak up, young man! Who sent you?"

One by one the lights went out on the machine. Jean felt a surge of joy.

"Father," he said. "I'm . . ."

He vanished.

Jean had neglected to learn the first rule of time travel: never do anything that might prevent your own birth.

Herbert Wells thought he heard someone at the door. When he opened it, no one was there. The paper was on the stoop. He bent and picked it up, glancing at the headlines. Crown Prince Edward had just become engaged to a princess of Greenland. The writer seemed delighted that the matter was settled. There had been talk of marrying him to the Grand Duchess Anastasia but the relationship was too close, especially with the spectre of haemophilia in the family. She had made do with a duke from Austria-Hungary.

Wells sniffed in disgust. Royalty! They seemed to be taking over the earth. It was all because of that damned meteor. With all the fancy talk about doing good with the gold, it had only made the rich, richer and the powerful, more powerful. Countries that had once freed themselves from oppression were now colonies again. There was even talk in the United States of rejoining the Empire for the trade advantages.

He sighed. It would have been better for everyone if the thing had fallen to the bottom of the ocean.

THE TRUE STORY
OF WILHELM STORITZ

Michel Pagel

Verne's other late novel of interest is Le Secret de Wilhelm
Storitz, *serialized in 1910, but not translated (unless later research
proves otherwise) until 1963. The novel had been completed in
1904 but Michel Verne thought it paled in comparison to H.G.
Wells's* The Invisible Man *(1897) and so delayed its publication. Once again Verne considered man's misuse of science, in this
case a somewhat archaic creation of an elixir of invisibility. Here
Michel Pagel explores the links between Verne's and Wells's stories.*

1

Spremberg, 18 May 1754

My dearest son,

I take advantage of a respite in my fever to write you
these lines. By the time you read them, I will have succumbed
to the illness which is eating me away. I cannot tell you how
much it pains me to leave this world when, far from being
an old man, I could still have served Germany through my

work. But it is God's will, and since I have enjoyed a full and pleasant life, I suppose that I should not complain. My last months in particular have counted among the happiest and most eventful of my whole life, and this thanks to a marvellous discovery which I wish to bequeath to you today. Indeed, who else but you, my beloved Wilhelm, whose character is so akin to mine, who else would know how to make the most profitable use of it?

As much as my pride suffers to admit it, I cannot claim this discovery for myself, although it does owe certain of its refinements to me. The manner in which I came into possession of the original formula is so extraordinary that I must recount it to you in a few short words.

This all came about a little more than a year ago, when you had just settled in Hungary. One winter's evening I was returning to the château after having dined with Dr Hebäcker, when I surprised a burglar in the dining room. At least, I believed him to be a burglar. This strangely-dressed man entreated me, first in English, then in a stumbling German, not to be afraid of him. Although he did not appear menacing, I was unwilling to take any risk: the poker from the fireplace was within my reach and I dealt him a vigorous blow to the head. Luckily, he was only stunned.

I was on the brink of ringing for Hermann so that he could go and fetch the police when I discovered the incredible sight which my initial surprise had concealed from me: there, in a corner of the dining room, sat an enormous machine whose function I could not guess at. It had evidently been conceived to carry a man, for a padded seat occupied its centre. Apart from that, it posed a complete mystery – and no less mysterious was the means by which the stranger could have brought it here, for it possessed no wheels and was far too heavy for a single man to lift. I'll spare you the preposterous story he later told me in order to justify his presence here: this man was either a liar or a madman, maybe even both.

Nonetheless he was a scholar; I was convinced of this by my search of the baggage strapped to his machine. Aside from several changes of clothing, just as excessive as those he was wearing, there were predominantly books on science and philosophy – some were known to me, others were not – and three large manuscript notebooks full of diagrams and mathematical or chemical equations. These latter above all caught my attention, for, although myself a chemist – plague upon modesty! – a brilliant chemist, I failed to surmise what kind of experiment they concerned.

My curiosity aroused, I set about returning my visitor to consciousness, if not to reason, with the aim of questioning him. He never revealed his true name to me. "Call me Ishmael", was all I could gain from him, and the tone he used suggested that this was a quip beyond my understanding, something which contributed to the annoyance he quickly provoked in me.

Initially, he refused point blank to answer my questions. Courtesy having produced nothing, I confined him in one of the château's dungeons, which had not been used for more than a century, and there I left him to meditate on the wisdom of his conduct, while I devoted myself to a close study of his notebooks. Without penetrating all their secrets, I quickly realized that they referred to one of the oldest fantasies of man: becoming invisible – but through science, not through sorcery. You may imagine into what state of excitement this discovery plunged me. From then onward, I could have no rest until Ishmael (let us call him such, for want of anything better) agreed to assist me in producing this wonder, of which several essential elements escaped me. In order to attain this result, I found it necessary to keep him chained up for several weeks in his dungeon, on dry bread and water, and still he did not falter in his resolve, save after a visit to the torture chamber where our ancestor, Gottfried, Commander of the Teutonic Order, was accustomed to entertain his captives. (He claimed that invisibility could bring nothing good to humanity, particularly if it fell into the wrong hands, but it is my conviction that he desired to be its only beneficiary.) I was thus not obliged to bring the rack or the irons back into service, but believe you me, if it had proved necessary, I would have brought myself to do it.

Ishmael himself was not the author of the notebooks: they had come into his possession by good fortune, he assured me – I deduced from this that he had stolen them – and thus he was obliged to spend long hours studying them in order to gain their secrets. Gifted with a brilliant intelligence, despite his duplicity, he was also able to use his powers of deduction and his experience to reinvent certain crucial details which the original author had omitted to put to paper, doubtless preferring to consign them to memory so that no one could reproduce them.

Once he had provided me with a detailed formula, I could easily concoct the potion in my laboratory, and could even work out alone the antidote which the potion's inventor had neglected to provide. If it is at times highly useful to be invisible, you may imagine how awkward it would be to be so permanently. My coffer will provide you with a substantial reserve of the potion itself and its antidote, in the bottles labelled respectively no. 1 and no. 2. When this is exhausted, well, you will have the choice of interesting yourself in science (I will leave you all the necessary notes) or engaging the services of a discreet chemist – to whom, if you mark my words, you will not reveal the final outcome of his work; my secret should therefore remain yours: the secret of Wilhelm Storitz.

Thanks to Ishmael, this was the work of four months, but I am convinced that at the price of several years' travail, I would have achieved it alone. On the other hand, what I could never have achieved is the other part of the experiment. Because you see, invisibility is not produced by chemistry alone, but also by that force brought to light by the ancient Greeks or, more recently, by Otto de Guericke: the force called electricity, which our German science still masters so badly, despite its achievements and the brilliant work of Von Kleist.

Although English, Ishmael appeared to know its principles, and was even able to manufacture in an easily portable form the apparatus which provides the particular exposure necessary to achieve the perfect result. If you were to dispense with this, you would not become invisible, but simply white as a sheet, in both skin and hair. The electrical radiance alone, on the other hand, would leave visible your hair, your irises, and the blood that pulses in your veins, so much so that you would resemble a fairground freak, ripe for stoning by the ignorant populace.

On the device you will notice a kind of moveable lever: in its higher position it will produce the effect which I have described; in its lower position, it will cancel it. I cannot recommend too strongly that you guard this apparatus as though it were the most precious of treasures, for if there exists anywhere another savant capable of reproducing it, I know him not. Moreover, it is on this point alone that I sometimes come to doubt my reason and to believe in the possibility of Ishmael's fable. The subject is in any case without interest, for a little while after our success I relaxed my vigilance and my prisoner escaped, taking with him the colossal machine whose true function he had always refused to reveal. Doubtless, I should have subjected him to questioning in order to compel him to disclose it. But, too much obsessed by the secret of invisibility, I postponed that task until it was too late. Whatever the case, I will never see him again, and because he served me admirably, I will cut short my regrets.

For me then began a period of great felicity. Can you imagine what can be accomplished by an invisible man?

Spying without the slightest risk on one's enemies, on one's rivals, to discover their secrets, their projects; spying likewise on one's friends, to discover whether they are well and truly such; spying for ever and a day – even on women in their privacy. I know your temperament: no more so than myself, you will not suffer that a female resists you. Henceforth, if one should reject you, you can take her by force without fearing the vengeance of a father or an outraged husband. I know I will not shock you by telling you that as for myself, whose age and scarred face frighten away young women, I have hardly been the measure of restraint.

All of that you will be able to carry out with impunity. However, if you should take to theft you must exercise the greatest prudence. I do not refer here to the villainous thefts of the common people, from which our wealth distances us; there do arise, however, circumstances in which the most honest man is constrained to steal the belongings of others in order to avert the darkest plots. In my own case, this has proved particularly so in regard to the notes of envious colleagues, for ever on the look out for that which could harm me. If you should find yourself pushed to such extremes, you should be aware that all the objects which you seize upon will not disappear. Slipping them under your clothes will solve the problem, you tell me? No, my son. If it were so, your own silhouette would mask everything behind it, which would outline it clearly, making its invisibility useless. And since we are speaking of clothing, be certain to wear nothing but an immaculate white, for your clothing cannot drink the potion, and the radiance will not work in the slightest on coloured fabric. The least mark will be likely to betray you; thus, you will not be truly safe save in the simplest apparel, but I grant you that this can prove impractical, especially in cold weather.

There, it seems to me, you have all I have to say to you. I hope from the bottom of my heart that my messenger will reach you in time for you to return to Spremberg before my death and allow me the joy of seeing you for one last time. If this is the case, I will myself give you all the preceding explanations. If not, my notary will pass on this letter.

I remain, no matter what should come to pass, your affectionate father,

Otto Storitz.

2

One would judge M. Jules Verne too harshly by reproaching him for having lied in the matter of Wilhelm Storitz. The inexactitudes of his tale after all only concern points of detail, and the truth, if he ever knew it, was too unlikely, too horrible and too shocking to be revealed to an audience primarily composed of adolescents, at the dawn of the twentieth century. As for myself, I only learned of it later, when the letter from Otto Storitz to his son, discovered in the depths of the old family château which I had innocently acquired, provoked my researches.

Before progressing any further, it is appropriate that I should introduce myself: I am he who that monstrous individual which was Storitz called "Ishmael". I was therefore, albeit unwillingly, one of the principal causes of this lamentable tale, and I am compiling this account in part to relieve my conscience, although I do not know whether it will ever be read.

The events which occurred at Ragz, in Hungary, between April and July 1757, are, thanks to Verne's novel, too well known to make it necessary for me to give more than a brief summary of them here. A French portrait painter, Marc Vidal, asked for the hand in marriage of a young Hungarian woman of a good family, Myra Roderich, and was accepted by her as well as by her relatives. Wilhelm Storitz, another of Myra's suitors – this one rejected, which does not surprise me in the least if, in addition to belonging to a nationality for which the Magyars had only contempt, he possessed a quarter of his father's personality – did everything possible to prevent this union, aided, of course, by his famous "secret": invisibility. Not the least of his revolting machinations was to render Myra herself invisible, causing her relatives to believe that he had carried her off. Verne records that Storitz's miserable existence found its end under the sabre of the young woman's brother, and that he thus became visible due to a massive loss of blood. As for Myra, while still invisible she married her fiancé and, ten months later, gave him a child. The loss of blood which she then underwent returned her too to her normal state, so much so that the Vidal family lived happily from then on.

Even if they are inspired by authentic happenings, novelists, those professional liars, seldom hesitate to enhance these. I am well-placed to know, my own biographer having passably well retouched the tale which I told him before passing it off as a work of fiction. In the case which concerns us, however, Verne perhaps acted in all innocence: without a doubt his inspiration came from the memoirs of Henri Vidal, Marc's brother, who was a witness to the events – memoirs to which he remains completely faithful. This autobiographical work, of which only fifty copies were published by the author in 1782, and which must already have been quite elusive by Verne's time, contained enough details for our author to judge any further research pointless – except from a purely geographic point of view, for he liked to sow his novels (a bit too liberally for my taste) with precise descriptions of the countries traversed by his protagonists.

That Henri Vidal himself may have misrepresented the facts to a certain extent is quite conceivable. One should remember that these took place in the mid-eighteenth century: the only dynamos existing at that time were those I had manufactured under duress for Otto Storitz. Perhaps Vidal did not know of them. Perhaps he knew of them, but was unable to guess at their function – which the uneducated servant Hermann would have been incapable of explaining, although he was sure to have seen them in action. Whatever the case may be, the engineer nowhere makes mention of them and attributes the quality of invisibility entirely to an improbable potion. Not too improbable, however, that it couldn't satisfy several generations of readers.

Since only the chemical aspect of the 'secret' was cancelled, it goes without saying that after their haemorrhages, Storitz and Myra did not regain their normal appearance: they became a kind of monster with transparent skin, through which arteries and veins could be seen, as well as a good number of their organs, not to mention the foodstuffs which circulated in their digestive system. A horrific vision, to be sure. The archives which I have been able to consult reveal that Myra Vidal died three months after her confinement; my conviction is that she ended her life after having passed once too often in front of a mirror. All these details, it must be admitted, could not feature either in the memoirs of a respectable engineer in 1782, nor in a novel for the young in 1910.

However, there is worse. The same archives prove without refutation that Vidal's child was born not ten, but eight and a half months after their marriage. Certainly, one can imagine a slightly premature birth, even conclude that passion had brought the two lovebirds to anticipate the consent of society and the Church to their union – this second hypothesis amply justifies the discretion of those that recounted their lives. Nonetheless, a much more sinister possibility springs to mind, one supported by the fact that following the death of his wife, Marc Vidal placed his child with a tutor and never again wished to hear tell of him. In my opinion, the following occurred:

The secret of invisibility, one should remember, only acted on a perfectly white material. That Wilhelm Storitz himself made use of clothing in white fabric or leather is probable. That Myra Roderich was likewise wearing an immaculate costume the day he entered her home with the purpose of making her invisible is on the other hand more than doubtful. What then did he do? He compelled her to drink the potion, and without doubt a soporific, then to undress completely. And thus, this man who is described to us as completely amoral, ready to perpetrate anything to satisfy his vices, found himself in the company of the woman he had desired for months, naked and at his mercy. Should we believe that he reclothed her in a chaste white gown and respected her virtue? I believe instead that he abused her and that this detestable union brought forth fruit. The dates concur.

And it is this image, that of the monster leaning over his innocent victim, that haunts me by night when sleep eludes me, for without me, this ignoble act would never have taken place.

I now arrive at the manner in which I came into possession of the three famous notebooks with the aid of which I perfected the technique that allowed Otto, then Wilhelm, Storitz to give free rein to their baser instincts. Contrary to the chemist's insinuations in his letter – he easily lends his own vices to others – this was not by theft: I quite simply purchased them.

This came about some time before the events which my biographer recounts in fictionalised form in the book consecrated to myself. Upon returning from a study trip, I stayed one evening in a small hostelry that I knew near to Port-Stowe, whose landlord, a jovial individual named Mr Marvel, never failed to amuse me with his colourful conversation. Exceptionally, that evening I found him morose. Since I was more or less his only client, he sat at my table without hesitation and, while we dined, he explained the reason for his sombre mood. His establishment was in jeopardy: two other inns had opened in the vicinity. One, which was more respectable than his own, was favoured by the bourgeoisie and their wives; the other, which was much less so, attracted heavy drinkers and light women en masse. A few old faithfuls hardly sufficed to keep things going, and because they were old in all senses of the term, the day would not be long before this small clientele disappeared in its turn. Marvel had therefore decided to pack his bags and, weary of England, to seek his fortune in the Americas. Alas, having found no buyer for his doomed inn, he had not managed to put together the necessary sum to pay his passage.

Over after-dinner drinks, when he had brought a bottle of his best whisky to the table, *on the house*, he declared that I could help him to realize his project, assuring me straight away that he was not asking for charity, but that he possessed an item which would without a doubt be to my benefit to acquire. Did I recall that invisible man that had sown terror in the region several years earlier, before being beaten down by a furious crowd? How could I not remember it? I had followed the affair in the newspapers and since then Mr Marvel himself had regaled me with it each time I had stayed at his inn, which was, moreover, named The Invisible Man. He liked to boast that he had played a part in it which, although minor, gained in importance each time he related the story.

I realized much later that my biographer, always in search of out-of-the-ordinary events, had by a curious coincidence produced another novel drawn from this occurrence, a novel as yet unpublished at the time of my stay in Port-Stowe – luckily for Marvel, as the indiscreet author revealed within it that Marvel had in his possession the notes made by Griffin, the invisible man, which had never been found by the authorities.

When the inn-keeper suggested selling them to me, intrigued, I asked to examine them. Having refilled my glass and his own, he rose with an expression on his face which was the most solemn he could adopt, and went to open the locked drawer of a sideboard, which held a small coffer from which he drew three volumes bound in brown leather and, it must be said, somewhat worn in appearance. He set them in front of me as though they were sacred relics, swearing by all that is holy that he had never before shown them to anyone, which I could well believe. I later learned that there had been at least one exception, but my biographer had always known how to get what he wanted.

Although I leafed through them without close attention, this brief glance convinced me that they came from the pen of a scholar: the equations I discovered there seemed well-balanced and not in the slightest fantastical. Perhaps they would at least give me material for reflection. Led astray by the whisky, and desiring to be of service to my host, I enquired as to the price he wanted, bargained a little on principle, and quickly concluded the deal.

The next day I returned home. Too preoccupied by my current work, I put the books away in my library, where they remained for some long months.

As for Mr Marvel, I learned later that he well and truly left for the New World. There, the ex-vagabond and ex-landlord of the inn made a name for himself in the state of Kansas, where he became a travelling fortune-teller under the name of Professor Marvel.

There remains to explain how, to my great unhappiness and that of so many others, I came to encounter Otto Storitz.

If the events related by my biographer make me appear a greater hero than I ever was, they do remain at least generally accurate. Upon my return I was devastated, depressed by the loss of Weena, universally disgusted by the world and by humanity. I decided to occupy myself from then on with myself alone, and wished to change my environment as a symbol of this new existence. However, when I left, this was not intended to be a new voyage into a distant future, but a simple journey of several weeks, designed to exhaust the patience of my friends and to ensure that there would be no further risk of their presenting themselves at my door. This done, I organised my departure discreetly. I took only what was strictly necessary; a few personal effects, my machine, and the contents of my library. Trusting my new place of residence to chance, I put on a blindfold and threw a dart at a planisphere. It landed in the very heart of Germany, and it was thus for Germany that I departed.

Once there, I realized that I was hardly content, no more so than I had been in England, and doubtless no more so than I would have been in any other European country, where a strained political situation produced the incessant threat of war. I had known enough violence; I only hoped for peace.

Then an idea came to me. I suspected that nowhere in the world would have brought me what I desired during my time, but, of all men, I was the sole one not constrained by the immutable course of time.

Suppressing my scruples, thanks to my machine I had no difficulty in gaining fabulous riches on the horse tracks. After having changed my winnings for gold, the only currency I presumed eternal, I began the long process which would end in the discovery of the peaceful era in which I live at the present time of writing, an era which I have no intention of identifying here, except to say that it can be found in a future not too far distant from that which I had left.

While I was hesitating between remaining in Germany, where fate had led me, and returning to England (two nations that however no longer existed as such), my attention was caught by the auction sale of a superb medieval château in old Spremberg. I had, I admit, always dreamed of owning one, and the temptation was too strong. Money being no problem, I carried off the auction with a high hand and went to install myself in my new domain, after having had part of it restored in order to make it habitable. I left the rest as it was for the pleasure of the sight.

This new existence brought me all the happiness of which I had dreamed. Several months later I fell in love with a young woman of the region, married her, and undertook the task of begetting children. We now have three, two boys and a girl, who are our pride and joy.

My unhappiness was brought about by a mixture of curiosity and idleness. One evening, when my wife and our then only child had gone to visit her parents for a week, I was bored to death and, after several glasses, the idea came to me to make use of my machine again. I had never, after all, explored the past. What harm could be done by a rapid foray into the memories held by these old stones which surrounded me? Perhaps I could even visit my own château at different periods, from the time of its construction, and on my return write a dissertation on its history using first-hand information . . .

Decisions taken quickly, after one has drunk a little, are often foolish, and this was no exception to the rule: my machine held pride of place in the large room which was formerly a dining-room, but which now served as my laboratory, so I was able to depart that very evening. I had no fear that my absence would be noticed, having the firm intention of returning the instant following my departure. Since I had, however, no idea how long I might be spending in the past, I decided to take some reading matter. It was upon exploring my library that I came upon the three notebooks bought from Mr Marvel, the existence of which I had almost forgotten. I stowed them into my bag thinking they would provide a welcome source of intellectual stimulation.

The rest can be imagined. Following two or three visits to past times where I wisely avoided being noticed, I arrived in 1753. Finding the château deserted, I was preparing to explore when Otto Storitz surprised me. I then committed the error of desiring to speak with him, rather than throwing myself on to my machine and departing. It is well-known what this cost me.

Upon my return, older by more than a year and still having no idea of the wrongs caused to innocent people by my thoughtlessness, I did not dismantle my machine: I purely and simply destroyed it.

Since I discovered the misfortunes of the Vidal family, I have come to regret this gesture, and to believe that on returning to the time just before these events took place I could influence their course. The desire to construct another machine, however, leaves me as quickly as it arrives: it is too dangerous to wish to change history, and I have already brought about too many catastrophes. Who knows if the remedy would not be worse than the disease? For as much as this weighs upon me, I must continue to live with my guilt, hoping that on Judgment Day God will see fit to pardon he whose incomplete and inexact, but unique biography names only –

– The Time Traveller.

Translated from the French by Finn Sinclair

THE SHOAL

Liz Williams

In 1978 the City of Nantes, where Verne was born, opened a Jules Verne Museum in celebration of Verne's achievements. There is no doubt that Verne was a major influence in popularising science and causing men of science to look to the future. The following story was inspired by a visit to the Museum and, in its vision and outlook, is a fitting conclusion to our own celebration of the works of Jules Verne.

He knew that something was wrong as soon as he looked into the mirror. His own face, dark and secret-filled, seemed curiously transparent, as though the light of the meagre room was shining through it. He knew what it meant and a great elation, coupled with fear, raced through him, filling his veins with ice and fire. The past snapped at his heels, ready to tear him back, and he was ready to go. But leaving meant that he would have to make it back to the rift, and he did not know yet how he was going to accomplish this without the vessel.

He wandered out into the warm Sri Lankan night, heavy with rainfall and the song of crickets. *No matter*, he thought, with a patience accrued over many, many years. An answer would present itself. The universe had started to align itself for him, as it always had, as if in compensation for all that had been taken away, and would now be returned.

A day after that, he read the newspaper article in the little bar along the street, and realized with dismay that his answer was waiting for him. And he could not let it happen.

The museum fascinated me as a child. It stood perched on its hill above the curve of the Loire, high over the silvery gleam of the river. In winter, my mother used to take me there after school, shaking her head, saying, "Jacques, wouldn't you like to go to the cinema instead?" She was a practical woman, but science bored her, and I think she thought that the museum was little more than a folly, a legacy of the last century. Perhaps she was right. But I was enchanted with the diagrams and pictures, the dioramas, the mock-up of the submarine's steering room with its plush red-velvet seats. I used to imagine that I was its captain, battling sea monsters from the deep and when we came out of the museum, I would stare down the estuary to the chilly line of the Atlantic and think: *one day, I will sail out there.*

When I was eleven, however, my father was transferred to a plant on the outskirts of Paris and we went with him. I could no longer see the sea, and over the years I forgot about the museum. I followed in his footsteps, first intending to become an engineer, but rapidly becoming diverted into information technology. I found myself working for a dotcom in Germany, and then running one. It seemed as though nothing could go wrong, for a while, but I could see the crash coming, like a great wave towering above the horizon, and I sold out just in time. I made a fortune by the time I was twenty-five, and my luck held. By the time I was thirty-six, I was quite unspeakably wealthy, living partly in France but mainly in California.

I saw what a lot of people did with their money, and it didn't disgust me, exactly, but I did wonder why they bothered. They seemed to be scrambling through the here and now, without any thought to the future beyond their kids' inheritances. Perhaps it was the fact that I didn't have children that led me toward developing the Shoal.

I don't think I consciously had Verne's little museum in mind when I first started idly sketching the blueprints. My Breton past had receded to a kind of hazy childhood vista: rainy school-days, sunny summers on the beach. It had been happy enough and so I rarely thought about it: I'm not much of a one for introspection. But what I did know was that I wanted to leave something for the future, something tangible, and something big. As soon as I thought of it, I knew that it was going to happen: it was like a crackling in the air before a storm hits. Next morning, I called an architect friend of mine and got him to put me in touch with some of his contacts.

A year later, the Shoal was beginning to become a reality. I'd got the financial backing, and we'd been in talks with the Pakistani government for some months. Dealing with them proved to be a steep learning curve for me, but we made it. In early autumn, I took a boat out to the patch of sea that would one day become the building site of the Shoal.

It was located just off the mouth of the Indus, a calm stretch of rippling waves with the red bluffs visible in the distance. There wasn't much there, obviously: only a few sand-spits rising above the shimmering water, but in my mind's eye I could see the Shoal rising above the waves, its great shell gleaming. I envied those who would be its first guests, who would see it for the first time as they raced across the sea, who would not have been privy to the long, laborious planning process. Fascinating though I found it, I should have liked to have seen the Shoal in its entirety, feel its impact without prior knowledge.

Within months, construction had begun. I wanted to start in winter, as the climate was milder then, the heat less fierce. It went too smoothly: the rigging arching up from the dry-dock like a curling ammonite, growing day by day. The under-structure, as I termed it, grew more slowly. This section, the service part of the hotel – the malls and golf courses and restaurants and gardens – would be towed out first, and then the shell would be attached. I supervised the operation, and watched the Shoal grow day by day, until to my slightly incredulous wonder, it was almost complete.

And then, one night, I had a dream. I rose from the couch in my office in the Shoal, in which I had fallen asleep, and walked through the silent, half-finished corridors to the platform where my speedboat was docked. I knew that it had been night when I fell asleep, but this looked like noon: a high, burnished blue sky and blazing sun, glittering from the metallic hulls of the craft that surrounded the Shoal. I gazed in wonder at all kinds of ships: huge clippers with crimson sails, gleaming with bronze and gold; a spined iron vessel that churned the waves into a froth of milk, and on the horizon, something huge and hulking, a ship that must, from this distance, be close to a mile in length. I thought, with a burst of joy: *I am seeing the future.*

I wanted to see more, but it was not to be: the dream ended, and I woke to find myself in the quiet office, with the dawn coming up over the waves. But the exhilaration at seeing that display of naval invention stayed with me throughout the day, and with it the knowledge that perhaps I was contributing to that future, with the building of the Shoal.

When the man first came to see me, I was not unduly surprised. Initially I thought he was a local – yet another of the clerics or politicians who had caused me no few difficulties to date. He wore a turban, like a Sikh, and he was dark, with a close-cropped beard and black eyes. To my surprise, however, he spoke excellent French. He gave his name as Rashid, said that he was a local businessman, but did not specify in what.

I had matters to see to, and so I was reluctant to make time for him, but I did not want to antagonise the community. We sat over coffee while he made small talk about the weather and France, with which he seemed familiar. Impatiently, I waited for him to get to the point of his visit, but then he asked me where I was from.

"Nantes," I replied. "It's a small town, in Brittany. It –"

"But I know it well, Monsieur Hoenec," he replied in some surprise. "I used to visit it, often. I had a close friend there."

"Extraordinary," I said, still being polite. "Whereabouts?"

"In the district of Mebec. A very elegant part of town."

I frowned. "It must have been some time ago, then. Mebec hasn't been elegant for many years."

"Oh, it was a long time ago," Rashid said, smiling, although I would not have placed him much above fifty. "But I can see that you are busy, Monsieur, and pleasant though it is to reminisce about old haunts, there is something I must say."

"Please do," I said, eager to terminate the interview and return to work. Through the window, I could see the shell of the Shoal rising above me like a promise.

"You cannot build here. I am sorry to have to tell you this, but these waters are too unstable to support such a structure as you have in mind. You will have to tow your hotel to a safer location. I would have come before, but I was detained."

I sighed. I'd had to take a great deal of advice from various local authorities: some of it good, of course, but much of it simply irrelevant to the facts.

"Look," I said. "I appreciate your concern, but we've done a full marine survey. My architects have taken immense care to test the seabed – obviously, this whole region is prone to fault-lines. But you have to understand that the Shoal is, essentially, afloat. It has in-built seismic testers which will give due warning if there's any shift in the earth's crust, and can be moved out of harm's way."

"That is not what I am talking about," Rashid said. He leaned forward, clearly in deadly earnest. "It is not a question of location as such, but of time."

"Time? I don't understand."

"This is a very old place, Monsieur Hoenec. One of the oldest locations of civilization on the planet. It may not look so to you, but under these placid waters lies a great rift."

"The survey showed nothing," I said, with a slight shake of my head. "What evidence do you have for such a thing?"

He conceded my point with a smile of his own. "Let us just say that the knowledge has always been in my family."

A mystic, I thought, or perhaps even mad. "Even if what you say is true," I said, "I cannot simply cancel the project without evidence. As I say, we've had exhaustive surveys carried out."

"I see that I cannot persuade you," Rashid said. "Only show you. May I come again to your hotel, tomorrow evening, and do so?"

I sighed. "Very well." I wanted to keep on the right side of the local community: animosity could go a long way in affecting good relations – not to mention prices. I already knew that we had been cheated on some of the local goods, but I had factored it into the profit margins. "Shall we say seven?"

Rashid paused for a moment, then nodded. "Thank you, M. Hoenec. I appreciate your courtesy in humouring me." There was a flash in the dark eyes that told me that he was quite well aware of my unease. Embarrassed, I coughed to hide it.

"I shall see you at seven, then," I said.

But next day, the storm came.

It began just after noon, a darkening of the distant horizon: a grey line between the blue. I noticed it out of the window of my office and for a moment, the shadow of the Shoal's shell seemed to fall across me. I blinked and it was once more back to its glittering arc. I thought to myself that it was probably nothing more than a tropical monsoon and would hurl itself out over the waters before it reached the coast, with only a swift lashing of raindrops across the bay. I devoted myself to some legal documents and when I next glanced up, some two hours later, I realized that it had become quite dark.

The phone rang. When I answered it, the foreman's voice echoed through my office. "Looks like a typhoon. You want me to evacuate?"

I was confident of the Shoal's ability to ride out any storm, once complete – but it was as yet unfinished. It was best to be on the safe side. Cursing under my breath, I told him to get the men to shore.

"What about you?"

"I'll sit it out for a while," I said. "Don't worry about me."

It was perhaps foolish, but I could not bear to leave the Shoal to the mercy of the storm. We would confront it together. I reassured the foreman and a few minutes later, I saw the boats speeding toward the bluffs. Then I sat staring out of the window at the oncoming storm. It did not look like a typhoon to me. It looked like a wall of mist, at once barely substantial and completely solid.

There was a knock on the door of my office. Frowning, I rose and opened it. Rashid was standing on the other side. I gaped at him.

"I am sorry," he said, and I could see horror in his dark eyes. "My calculations have not been correct. We have no more time," – and at that moment the whole Shoal lurched violently to one side as if it had been struck a blow by a giant hand. Rashid and I fell against the wall. I think I cried out. The Shoal righted itself with as much violence as it had shifted and then we were plummeting downward, as though the whole structure had been placed within some gigantic elevator. The breath was ripped from my lungs. I tried to scream, but could not. Staring in horror through the window of my office, I saw at first only water, but then I realized that I could see other things through the straining glass: startled faces lining the decks of a great-sailed ship, the configuration of the red bluffs along the shore shifting and changing, becoming wooded, then bare of trees, then wooded once more. The images became dream-like. My fear ebbed like a tide.

"I am sorry," I heard Rashid say softly into my ear. "I was too late. I thought I knew when it would be, but I was wrong."

"What's happening?" I said.

"This was a journey that was meant for me, and me alone. I hoped to show you just the beginning of it but it started more swiftly than I ever imagined."

"I don't understand," I said again, but suddenly I remembered my dream, that shining future of glorious ships and a strange hope leaped in me.

He sighed. "Soon you will."

The shifting, changing landscape was slowing now. I felt a bump, as when the landing wheels of an aircraft are released. The Shoal sighed as it settled. We were on dry land.

"Come," Rashid said, sadly. "I will show you."

He led me through the tilting corridors to the outer doors of the Shoal, which in its natural environment led to one of the docks. Numbly, still unable to take in what had happened to me, I followed him out on to the platform.

The bluffs, the storm, and even the sea itself had disappeared. The arc of the Shoal listed above me as it perched on a rolling plain. Before us, stretched the city: massive walls made of ochre earth, sloping up to high ramparts with gilded domes of temples visible above them. A flock of immense birds flapped slowly overhead, with the glitter of metal collars clearly visible. Far in the distance, I saw a waterfall cascading down a crag, contained within the city limits themselves.

"This is Indec-Herat," Rashid said. "This is my home."

"*When are we?*" I heard myself say. "Is this the future?"

"Alas, no. It is the far past. Many thousands of years before your own time, when the cities of the coastal plains of Earth held sway and the great maritime civilization of the Indus ruled the world. A far more civilized time than your own, full of science and learning and peace."

"Atlantis?" I murmured, shocked, and he gave a bitter laugh.

"Atlantis is the memory of a myth. There was no great

island in the midst of that ocean, but all around the shores of the continents were cities. We were –" he looked briefly exultant, fleetingly sad, "– the greatest seafaring nation that this world has ever known. And then the waters rose, and swallowed it. Everything – gone in a span of years. We saved those we could, sending the ordinary folk into the mountains, and for those of us of the elite – time-bending, sent into the future to preserve what knowledge we could. But time wears thin, Monsieur Hoenec. It frays, like elastic. It snatches us back again. I knew my time was coming. I have been in your world for several centuries. I felt myself growing faint."

"You spoke with him, didn't you?" I said. "With the writer, with Verne?"

"Of course. He wove a few of my stories into a dream, but he did not really believe what I had to say. In that regard, I failed."

"And your *Nautilus*?"

"Is real. It was my ship, of course. It's gone now, long gone. I searched for a while for another vessel, but I did not have the resources to rebuild it, and anyway, what was the point? I knew I would be coming back, if I lived."

"And what about me?" I asked, but I thought I already knew the answer to that.

"Monsieur Hoenec . . . I am truly sorry."

The shock hit me then, punching a hole through my heart. I barely registered it when a barge glided in from the city, filled with men in red robes who greeted Rashid as a brother and took us both into Indec-Herat. I remember little of its magnificence.

They treated me well, that first day: bringing me fruit that I had never seen before, and dishes of grains. They did not, Rashid informed me, eat meat. He told me a little about the cities of the coasts: their maritime goddesses, their marvels, and I listened like a child, with as much wonder and the same suspension of belief. Dimly, I saw that Rashid's face sharpened into concern and when he held out a fizzing glass and said, "Here, drink this. It is a sedative," I did not hesitate. I think I hoped to wake and find it a dream, but when I opened my eyes the next morning the sun was already high above the gold-and-crimson domes. I went with Rashid compliantly, letting him lead me down through the city. I observed with a remote, detached interest the lines of priest-esses in their blood-coloured robes, the huge leathery birds wheeling about their heads, and the sellers of gold and jade and strange vegetables. There were all manner of people here: some immensely tall, others squat and barely human with slate-blue skin. The human species, in this pre-catastrophe world, seemed much more varied. It was starting to dawn on me what we had lost.

"I will show you something," Rashid said. "You'll find it of interest, I think." He was smiling and I returned it with, I am sure, a wan grimace of my own. We took a barge down through a series of canals and I watched the city glide by into unreality.

And then we came to the harbour. Ships bigger than any I had ever seen, with vast gleaming sails, span out across the Indus sea. I could see the spined back of a submarine, cresting the water briefly before it dived. Smaller boats, clearly equipped with some form of engine, darted like dragonflies between the hulls of the larger craft. It was a level of technology that put my own Shoal into the shade. And I knew then, with a lift of the heart at all I was to witness, and a sinking of the spirits at the thought of all that would be lost, that there was no point in looking either forward or back.

CONTRIBUTORS

Kevin J. Anderson (b. 1962) has written several *X-Files* and *Star Wars* novels, as well as collaborations with such writers as Kristine Kathryn Rusch, John G. Betancourt, and Brian Herbert, with whom he has written the continuing Dune saga: *House Atreides* (1999), *House Harkonnen* (2000), and *House Corrino* (2001). With Doug Beason he wrote the SF novels *Lifeline* (1990), *Assemblers of Infinity* (1993), and *Ignition* (1996), a techno-thriller. His solo work includes *Resurrection Inc.* (1988), *Blindfold* (1995) and *Hopscotch* (1997). His 2002 novel, *Captain Nemo*, was subtitled "The Fantastic History of a Dark Genius".

Tony Ballantyne, author of the impressive stories "Teaching the War Robot to Dance" and "Indecisive Weapons", has had over twenty short stories published in *Interzone, The Third Alternative*, the anthology *Constellations*, and elsewhere. His work is regularly translated and published in European SF magazines and selected for anthologies such as *The Year's Best SF 9*. His first novel, *Recursion*, was published in July 2004, followed by *Capacity* (2005).

Stephen Baxter was born in Liverpool, England, in 1957. He worked in engineering, teaching and information technology, but is now a full-time writer with over twenty published novels to his credit. He has earned a considerable reputation in recent years for his high-tech science fiction novels such as *Raft* (1992), *Flux* (1993) and *Titan* (1997), but he also has a fascination for the history of science fiction. He has already paid homage to H.G. Wells in his sequel to *The Time Machine*, entitled *The Time Ships* (1995). His next books will be *Sunstorm*, a collaboration with Arthur C. Clarke, and *Transcendent*, the latest of his "Destiny's Children" series.

Keith Brooke spent a long time as a promising young SF writer, with three novels published in the early 1990s (*Keepers of the Peace*, *Expatria* and *Expatria Incorporated*) and over fifty short stories published around the world since 1989. Now he's a promising mature writer and online publisher, launching the web-based SF, fantasy and horror showcase *Infinity Plus* (www.infinityplus.co.uk) in 1997, featuring the work of around 100 top genre authors. He is co-editor with Nick Gevers of *infinity plus one* and *infinity plus two*, anthologies based on the website. His latest books are the novel, *Lord of Stone* (1997; revised edition 2001); a collection of short stories, *Head Shots* (2001); and *Parallax View* (2000), a collection of stories written with Eric Brown. His new novel, *Genetopia*, is due in the US in autumn 2005. Hiding his identity behind the pen-name Nick Gifford, he likes to scare children, with several novels published by Puffin. Keith lives with his young family in the English town of Brightlingsea. You can find out more about Keith and his work at www.keithbrooke.co.uk

Apart from co-editing this anthology, and when not growing prize marrows or reviewing curry-houses, **Eric Brown** (b. 1960) has written over twenty books and eighty short stories. He has twice won the BSFA short story award, in 2000 and 2002. His first collection was *The Time-Lapsed Man* (1990), and he has recently sold his sixth, *Threshold Shift*, due out from Golden Gryphon in the US. His first novel was *Meridian Days* (1992). The third book of the Virex trilogy, *New York Dreams*, appeared in 2004, as did his novel *Bengal Station*. Recent works include *The Fall of Tartarus* (2005) and *The*

Extraordinary Voyage of Jules Verne (2005). His website can be found at: http://ericbrownsf.port5.com/

Molly Brown has been at times an armed guard and a stand-up comic. She writes in a number of genres. Her publications include *Virus* (1994), a science-fiction thriller for teenagers, *Cracker: To Say I Love You* (1994) a novelisation based on the television series, a humorous historical whodunit *Invitation to a Funeral* (1995), and a short story collection, *Bad Timing* (2001). Several of her stories have been optioned for film and/or television. Her website is at: www.mollybrown.co.uk.

Peter Crowther (b. 1949) is the indefatigable editor and publisher at the helm of PS Publishing, a small – but rapidly growing – specialist press devoted to novellas, novels and collections in the SF, fantasy and horror genres. Somehow he finds time to write long, complex, and moving stories, as well as edit the magazine *Postscripts*. He recently moved from Harrogate, and now lives in a sprawling house close to the sea, surrounded by many thousands of books, magazines and CDs. His first SF collection, *Songs of Leaving*, appeared in 2003 and *Dark Times*, a third collection of his dark fantasy stories, appeared in 2004.

Paul Di Filippo (b. 1954) is the author of countless bizarre and wonderful short stories and novellas. His industry, like his imagination, knows no bounds. He has published seventeen books since his first, *The Steampunk Trilogy*, appeared in 1995. If you count from his first professional appearance in 1985, this does not quite average one book per year but he hopes by 2010 (the 25th anniversary of that debut) to have twenty-five books to his credit. Meanwhile, he continues to live in Providence, Rhode Island, with his mate, Deborah Newton, two cats named Penny Century and Mab, and a cocker spaniel named Ginger. Among his recent books are *A Year in the Linear City* (2002) and *Fuzzy Dice* (2003). His website is at: www.pauldifilippo.com

Laurent Genefort was born in 1968, in Montreuil s/bois. He studied literature at the Sorbonne in Paris and the title of his doctorate (University of Nice Sophia Antipolis, 1997) was "Architecture du livre-univers dans la science-fiction, a travers cinq oeuvres." He has been writing SF since 1988, with around thirty novels and ten short stories to his credit, including the "Omale" cycle, *La Mecanique du Talion*. "Arago" won the Prix de l'imaginaire in 1995. "The True Story of Barbicane's Voyage" is his first story to be published in English.

Johan Heliot was born in 1970 at Besançon, France, and now lives in Remiremont, near the Vosges mountains. His many books include *La Lune n'est Pas Pour Nous* (2004) in which Albert Londres strikes against the Nazis' attempt to destroy the moon, *Faerie Hackers* (2003), *Obsidio* (2003) two short horror novels and a novella, *Pandemonium* (2002) about vampires from outer space which terrorise Paris in 1832, *Reconquerants* (2001), and *La Lune Seule le Sait* (2000) in which Jules Verne flies to the moon in an extraterrestrial ship.

Sarah A. Hoyt (b. 1962) has published three Shakespearean fantasy novels with Ace. The first one, *Ill Met By Moonlight* (2001) was short-listed for the Mythopoeic Award. Her short stories have been published in *Asimov's*, *Analog* and *Weird Tales* and as a collection – *Crawling Between Heaven and Earth* (2002).

Tim Lebbon (b. 1969) wins awards like they are going out of fashion. They include two British Fantasy Awards, a Bram Stoker Award, plus the Tombstone Award for the collection *Exorcising Angels* (with Simon Clark). His latest books include *White and Other Tales of Ruin* (2002), *Changing of Faces* (2003) and *Fears Unnamed* (2004). Forthcoming books include *Desolation*, the dark fantasy novel *Dusk;* and *Into the Wild Green Yonder* (with Peter Crowther). His work has been optioned for the screen on both sides of the Atlantic. His website is at www.timlebbon.net

---

James Lovegrove was born in 1965 and is not averse to giant leaps of the imagination. His novel *The Hope* (1990) is set on board a vast ocean liner which has been cruising the seas for decades and contains all manner of horrors. Likewise *Days* (1997) takes place in a massive department store which welcomes you in but may not let you go. Verne would have loved them. He has also written *Escardy Gap* (with Peter Crowther), *The Foreigners*, *Untied Kingdom* and *Worldstorm*. He has published a short-story collection, *Imagined Slights*, a novella, *How The Other Half Lives*, and a double-novella, *Gig*. His works for younger readers include *Wings* and *The House of Lazarus*. A new novel is *Provender Gleed*, and a third children's book, *Ant God*. He has recently moved to a small village in Devon with his wife Lou and son Monty. It is very quiet there, and he thinks he likes that.

Richard A. Lupoff (b. 1935) was introduced to the works of Jules Verne when he was eight by a sympathetic elementary school librarian. His interest in matters Vernian has never faltered, although it has broadened to include a wide range of literature and other media. He holds the distinction of having his stories selected for *Best of the Year* anthologies in three allied fields: science fiction, horror, and mysteries. He is also the winner of a Hugo Award, and has been nominated for both the Nebula and the Oscar. His recently-issued and in-production books include *Claremont Tales I* and *II*, *One Murder at a Time*, and *Quintet: The Cases of Chase and Delacroix*, as well as a new edition of his classic study *Edgar Rice Burroughs: Master of Adventure* from the University of Nebraska.

F. Gwynplaine MacIntyre (b.1948), Froggy to his friends, is a Scottish-born, Australian-raised, American-resident author. His stories have appeared in *Analog*, *Isaac Asimov's Science Fiction Magazine*, *Amazing Stories*, *Weird Tales*, *Absolute Magnitude*, *Albedo* and numerous anthologies, including Terry Carr's *Best Science Fiction of the Year #10*. His non-fiction has been published in the *New York Daily News*, *Literary Review*,

Games Magazine and many British and U.S. publications. In 2003, he was short-listed for the Montblanc/Spectator Award for his arts journalism. He is the author or co-author of several books, including the science-fiction novels *The DNA Disaster* (1991), *The Woman Between the Worlds* (1994), and his collection *MacIntyre's Improbable Bestiary* (2001).

Michael Mallory is the author of some eighty short stories, many featuring Amelia Watson (some of which are collected as *The Adventures of the Second Mrs Watson*, 2000) and whose exploits are also chronicled in the novel *Murder in the Bath* (2004). He also created and co-edited the anthology *Murder on Sunset Boulevard* (2002). Outside of fiction, Mike has written two books on pop-culture, *Hanna-Barbera Cartoons* (1998) and *Marvel: The Characters and Their Universe* (2002), and his articles – more than 350 to date – have appeared everywhere from the *Los Angeles Times* to *Fox Kids Magazine*. He lives in Southern California.

Sharan Newman (b. 1949) is a medievalist specializing in France. She is the author of the Guinevere fantasy trilogy, *Guinevere* (1981), *The Chessboard Queen* (1983) and *Guinevere Evermore* (1985) and the Catherine Levendeur mystery series, set in twelfth century France, which began with *Death Comes as Epiphany* (1993). The tenth of that series is *The Witch in the Well* (2004). She is also the author of the non-fiction work, *The Real History Behind the Da Vinci Code* (2005).

Michel Pagel was born in 1961. His first novel was published in 1984, since when he has published about twenty-five novels or collections in the SF, horror and fantasy genres. He considers his most important work to be a series of modern supernatural novels/short stories entitled *La Comédie Inhumaine* (*The Inhuman Comedy*). His SF novel *L'Equilibre des Paradoxes* (*The Balance of Paradoxes*) and his historical fantasy about King Philippe Auguste *Le Roi d'Août* (*The King of August*) were critically well-received, both winning awards in France. He is working on a new series of historical fantasy novels entitled *Les Compagnons d'Ishtar* (*The Brotherhood of Ishtar*). He has translated the works of Peter Straub, Joe Haldeman and Neil Gaiman. His SF novel *Cinéterre* (*Filmworld*), set mostly in London in an alternative world based on the Hammer horror films, is looking for a British publisher.

Adam Roberts is thirty-nine and is Reader in Nineteenth-Century Literature at Royal Holloway, University of London. His first novel, *Salt*, was nominated for the Arthur C. Clarke Award in 2000. He had published several academic works on nineteenth century poetry and science fiction. His novels *On* (2001), *Stone* (2002), and *Polystom* (2003), have been praised both for their striking ideative content and originality. His latest novel is *The Snow* (2004). His website can be found at www.adamroberts.com

Justina Robson was born and brought up in Leeds. She studied Philosophy and Linguistics at university and began writing in 1992. Her first novel *Silver Screen,* appeared in 1999 and her second novel, *Mappa Mundi*, was published to acclaim in 2001. Both of them were short-listed for the Arthur C. Clarke award and won the amazon.co.uk Writers' Bursary for 2000. Her latest books are *Natural History* (2004) and *Living Next Door To The God Of Love* (2005). She also reviews science fiction for the *Guardian*.

Brian Stableford (b. 1948) is a renowned and prolific writer of science fiction and fantasy. He has been selling professionally for forty years but his work has always explored the cutting edge of technology, from the days of his Star-Pilot Grainger series, which began with *The Halcyon Drift* (1972) and are now all available in the omnibus *Swan Songs* (2003) to such collections as *Sexual Chemistry* (1991), dealing with genetic engineering and *Designer Genes* (2004), exploring biotechnology. He has published more than fifty novels and two hundred short stories, as well as several non-fiction books, thousands of articles for periodicals and reference books, several volumes of translations from the French and a number of anthologies. He is a part-time Lecturer in Creative Writing at University College, Winchester. His recent publications include two story collections, *Complications and Other Stories* (2003) and *Salome and Other Decadent Fantasies* (2004), and a *Historical Dictionary of Science Fiction Literature* (2004).

A former lecturer in Future Studies, **Ian Watson** (b. 1943) is the award-winning author of nearly fifty novels and short-story collections from *The Embedding* (1973) to the recent *Mockymen* (2003), and including the Vernian *Japan Tomorrow* (1977) for young adults. He wrote the Screen Story for *A.I. Artificial Intelligence*, the Steven Spielberg movie based on the "robot Pinocchio" project of Stanley Kubrick with whom Ian worked for a year. PS Publishing are issuing his tenth story collection, *Butterflies of Memory*, at the end of 2005. In 2001 DNA Publications produced his first poetry collection, *The Lexicographer's Love Song*. He lives in a little village in South Northamptonshire. His website is at www.ianwatson.info

Liz Williams (b. 1965) is the daughter of a conjuror and a Gothic novelist, and currently lives in Brighton, England. She has a PhD in philosophy of science from Cambridge and her anti-career ranges from reading tarot cards on Brighton pier to teaching in Central Asia. She currently writes full time. Her novel *The Ghost Sister* was published in July 2001. Further novels include *Empire of Bones* (2002), *The Poison Master* (2003), *Nine Layers of Sky* (2003), and *Banner of Souls*, (2004). She has had over forty short stories published in *Asimov's*, *Interzone*, *Realms of Fantasy* and *The Third Alternative*.